They saw it, standing on a gilded easel, swathed in purple drape, the Waldegrave portrait.

Vincent walked over to it with mechanical steps and stood staring at it. He was incapable of saying what he had immediately seen. At the very edge of the picture, pale and staring, stood Thomas; his own son Thomas, in a black velvet Victorian suit with knickerbockers and a white lace collar, staring and submissive, painted in the immaculate style of Walter Waldegrave.

The Grays had stolen his son.

=GRAHAM= MASTERTON

PICTURE OF EVIL

TOR

A TOM DOHERTY ASSOCIATES BOOK

PICTURE OF EVIL

Copyright © 1985 by Graham Masterton

Reprinted by arrangement with Wiescka Masterton

First printing: September 1985

A TOR Book

Published by Tom Doherty Associates
8–10 West 36 Street
New York, N.Y. 10018

ISBN: 0-812-52199-4
CAN. ED.: 0-812-52200-1

Printed in the United States of America

One

Bouillon, November 12

As soon as he saw her standing under the lime trees, her thumb lifted, her red nylon rucksack propped against the railings beside her, he knew she was a suitable victim. He drove ten or twenty yards farther on and then drew the huge black Vanden Plas limousine over to the curb.

He sat there without moving, the engine still warbling, watching her fixedly in the rearview mirror. He saw her pick up her rucksack, take two or three steps toward him, then hesitate, obviously uncertain if he had stopped for her or not. She's pretty, he thought. She's perfect.

It was a foggy, spectral morning. Silent and steamy beyond the railings, the Semois River slid by. On both banks of the river, the crumbling old buildings of Bouillon crowded the hillsides like the abandoned nests of house martins and winter wrens. It was November in the Ardennes, close to the French border. A time of wet leaves, dripping trees and penetrating silences. A time when the clouds were so low you could easily begin to believe the rest of the world had disappeared altogether.

Now the girl was jogging up to him, her rucksack slung over one shoulder. He took a cigarette from a gold case but didn't light it. As she came up to the car, he wound down the window and waited for her. There was a sharp smell in the morning air of smoked meats and tobacco and river water.

"*Merci, monsieur*," the girl panted. "*Je suis en voyage à Liège.*"

"*À Liège?*" he smiled. Although he was sitting in the car, she could tell that he was tall, over six feet. He had a bony,

5

aristocratic-looking face. Gray brushed-back hair, hollow
cheeks, heavy-lidded eyes. A thin, refined mouth. He wore
one of those gray, hand-tailored suits that seem to be specially
designed for the owners of lavish Italian hotels. His pale cream
shirt was of a quality categorized as "gentlemen's linen." On
his knobby left wrist he wore a Piaget wristwatch, so thin and
understated it must have been impossibly expensive.

"*Allez-vous vers Liège?*" the girl asked. Her accent was
strongly American, and now that she was close to him, he
could see how American she was. Dark blonde hair plaited into
long pigtails; wide China-blue eyes; a full-lipped, innocent-
provocative mouth crammed with healthy white teeth. She was
younger and smaller than he had first thought, although under
her yellow quilted windbreaker, he saw the kind of rounded
figure he always preferred.

"You're American?" he asked.

"Yes," she replied, regarding him curiously because his
accent was American, too. The clipped, careful consonants of
the better parts of New England. Cape Cod perhaps, or rural
Connecticut. "And you? You're an American? If you don't
mind my asking you."

"Please," he said, "get in. I can't take you all the way to
Liège, but I can certainly get you to Rochefort, and you should
easily be able to hitch another ride from there."

"I think you saved my life," the girl told him. "I thought I
was going to be standing there forever."

He leaned across and opened the door for her. She tossed her
rucksack into the backseat and climbed in. "At least I managed
to have a bath and wash my hair this morning," she said.

"Ah," he replied. He was fragrant himself with Christian
Dior cologne.

"This is a beautiful old car," she commented as she closed
the door. "Just look at that paneling. Real wood."

"It's a Vanden Plan Princess limousine," he told her. "It
was built in England in the nineteen sixties for Count Louis de
Rochelle. He lets me use it from time to time, when I feel the
need to get out and about."

"You're friends with a count?"

He smiled again, rather vaguely this time. "My family and I
have been living in part of his château for the best part of the
postwar years. He spends most of his time in the south of

France, so we don't see very much of him. He gambles, you know. He inherited more money than was good for him and he feels the need to throw it away."

He pulled away from the curb without making a signal. The car's transmission whined noisily as he drove up to the intersection on the west side of the Bouillon bridge. "I ought to introduce myself," he said, holding out his hand. "I am Maurice Gray."

"Should I know you?" the girl asked. He had announced his name as if she ought to.

"No, of course not," he replied. "I may be a native son but I have been living on foreign soil for too long now for anyone to remember me. I read only last week in *Time* magazine that my very last acquaintance from the old days had passed away."

The girl was about to remark that he didn't *look* so very old. Fifty-five, maybe. Sixty at the most. But then she decided it was probably more polite not to, and so she simply smiled, nodded and said, "Well, *tempus fugit*," which, she thought, was a terrible cliché but better than saying anything embarrassing. Her mother always said embarrassing things, like asking doctors of philosophy to look at her bunions, and she had promised herself she would never be like her mother.

"I'm Alison Shrader. Ball State University, Muncie, Indiana."

"Well, well," Maurice Gray said. "Muncie. I once knew an optician from Muncie. He committed suicide shortly after the war."

Alison didn't know what to say to that. They drove over the old stone bridge, while beneath them the river mist swirled like a regretful memory.

"You've eaten?" he asked.

Alison pointed back toward the far bank of the river where there were two or three seedy-looking cafés. "I had breakfast in the *Café de la Citadelle*," she said, pronouncing the name as if it were the grandest restaurant in Belgium. "Black pudding and a glass of Stella. It was great. Well, not bad. Edible."

Maurice Gray smiled. "I hope you know what black pudding is made of."

"You don't have to remind me. But it's nutritious, isn't it? And I couldn't afford anything else. I'm trying to keep my budget down to a hundred fifty francs a day."

"Very commendable. You can live like royalty on a hundred fifty francs a day if you know where to eat and your friends are rich." He steered with one hand through the back streets of the town, reached inside his jacket with his other for his cigarette case. "Would you care for a cigarette?"

"I don't smoke, but please don't let that stop you."

"No, no," Maurice Gray said. He tucked the unlit cigarette back in the case. "I respect the rights of those who don't smoke."

"That's a beautiful case."

"Yes," he replied. "It was given to me by my father, to take to the Sudan with me. One side is highly polished, you see, so it could be used as a heliograph."

He tilted the case from side to side, pretending to send Morse messages across the desert. "Camels . . . dying . . . send . . . champagne . . ."

They slowed down while a noisy moped, carrying an old man and his heavy-legged wife, wavered around in front of them. The wife was perched on the luggage rack, her arms filled with loaves of French bread, celery and sausages.

"You really live in a château?" Alison asked.

"Not a very elegant one, I'm sorry to say. Well, not many of them are. Most have been pillaged over the years by successive invaders, and most have been knocked about a bit. Ours is no exception."

They drove out of Bouillon and up the winding hill toward the main highway to Liège. On either side, the fields were pale with fog, and the white Friesian cattle lay in the silvery grass like a landscape painting by Brueghel. At the top of the hill there was a huge memorial to the casualties of World War II, a rusting, welded collection of abstract swords and plowshares. It looked jagged and primitive in the fog, the symbol of a pagan battle.

Alison said, "I guess I'm on a pilgrimage, sort of."

"A pilgrimage?" Maurice Gray asked. He glanced down at her faded jeans, at her mud-stained Care Bears. She had a perky, classically American profile. Marilyn Monroe, Candice Bergen and Bo Derek all shaken together into a cocktail of freckles and freshness. "What sort of a pilgrimage?" he wanted to know. "Spiritual, or temporal?"

"My father fought here during the war," Alison said. "He was in the Battle of the Bulge."

"Ah," Maurice Gray said. His eyes were curiously dead, as if her statement meant little to him.

"He was wounded at Liège," Alison explained. "A German mortar bomb, that's what he said. The fragments went into his head." She touched her left temple with her fingertips as if she could feel the shrapnel herself.

"I never knew what he was like when my mother first met him, of course, but she always said that he was lively, and funny. I can only remember that he was very distant, very remote. You could look at him, and talk to him, and you could tell that he was thinking about something else. He never said what. Mom used to say that when he came back from the war, she felt that she had lost him, just as much as if he had been killed. She had lost the man she married. Instead, she had a person who *looked* like her husband and *talked* like her husband but just wasn't anybody at all. I think the only reason she got pregnant with me was to see if she could bring him back; you know, mentally, from whatever kind of psychological plane he was living on."

Maurice Gray was silent for a while. Then he said, lifting his hand in a slight gesture of regret, "There were many tragedies during the war. It is quite right that you should come here to remember and honor them."

Alison wiped her breath from the window with the end of her scarf. "My father's dead now. He died last year. I felt I had to come see the place where he was wounded, the place where he was actually *himself*. I thought maybe the surroundings would help me understand him. I don't know. I thought in a peculiar way that perhaps he would still be here. Does that sound strange?"

Maurice Gray shook his head. "Who are we to question what parts of the human presence might survive long after they are supposed to have expired?"

Alison said, "A friend was going to come with me, then she changed her mind. Well, her parents made her change her mind. They said they didn't approve of ghost-hunting."

Maurice Gray smiled. "They are not exactly the height of sophistication, are they, the people of Muncie, Indiana?"

"*I'm* from Muncie, thanks very much."

"Of course. But there are always shining exceptions—of which you are a fine example—to every prejudice."

They had turned off the main highway and were driving along the straight, narrow road leading to Rochefort. Away from the river, the fog had begun to clear and a liquid sunshine illuminated the fields, the gray-painted barns and the yellow and amber trees.

"Is your château far from here?"

"Not far," he replied. "It is just outside a small village called Vêves. I don't suppose you have heard of it."

Alison shook her head. Sunlight suddenly filled the interior of the car and sparkled on the highly polished walnut dashboard.

Maurice Gray said, "You are in a hurry, I assume, to get to Liège?"

"Not especially. I have another week in Europe."

"Well, it was just a thought."

"What was?"

He smiled at her ruefully. "I was wondering if perhaps you would care to visit my château and have lunch with me. I very much dislike being on my own; that is why I stopped and asked you if you wanted a ride. I love company and bright conversation. But you mustn't feel obligated. If you prefer, I will drive you straight to Rochefort, without feeling at all upset."

Alison couldn't help smiling back at him. "You're so old-fashioned. I mean, I'm not saying that rudely. I love it. But your manners are so—I don't know—they're just like a movie. *Gone With the Wind.* Something like that."

"Well, I have been living here in Europe for quite a long time," Maurice Gray explained. "I suppose the charm of European manners does rub off on one. The Europeans are very charming people."

Alison unzippered her windbreaker. With a surreptitious look sideways, Maurice Gray caught the swell of a breast beneath a soft white sweater, the sharp glint of a silver crucifix.

"It's real warm in this car, if you don't mind my saying so."

"The heater has only two settings. Antarctica and Hades."

Alison laughed. "Do you really want me to come to lunch? I won't be upsetting anybody?"

"Who could you possibly upset?"

"I don't know. Don't you have servants or something?"

Maurice Gray inclined his head. "Yes," he said, "we have servants. But our servants are there to *serve* us. We don't have quite the same domestic problem as people do in the States. Our domestics are helpful and obedient, just as they used to be in the old days, the days of grace."

"Well, as long as it's okay."

Maurice Gray raised a hand as if he were about to lay it on Alison's thigh, but then he refrained and returned it to the steering wheel. "I promise you," he said in the quietest of voices, "it's very much okay."

It took them an hour to reach the high massif overlooking the valley of the Meuse River. The clouds had gathered again and the sky was steel-dark. All the same, they could see for miles around, as if they were on the roof of the world. Forests and fields and distant mountains, and the wind whipping chaff across the road.

Maurice Gray turned right, down a narrow road signposted "Vêves." Because he could sense for the first time that Alison was beginning to feel uncertain about having accepted his invitation for a ride, he smiled reassuringly and hummed a few bars of a silly song, *Le Pingre de Paris.*

The road wound down between sloping fields. The sky grew so threatening that Maurice Gray had to switch on his headlights. It began to rain, transparent droplets that quivered on the windshield.

"My father always said he wanted to come back here," Alison said. "The country's really wild, isn't it? I feel like I'm right inside some kind of fairy tale. You know, 'The Sleeping Beauty,' with the thorns growing up around the castle."

"You shouldn't read too much," Maurice Gray remarked. "Reading is bad for the spirit. You remember what someone once said: 'Those who read the symbol do so at their peril.'"

"I'm not sure of what that means."

"It means there is always a risk in exploring beneath the surface."

They passed the Château de Vêves, a high, round-turreted castle supposed to have been Walt Disney's inspiration for the fairy castle in *Snow White.* Maurice Gray remarked that he couldn't picture Walt Disney in his shiny, wide-trousered suit standing here in the depths of the Ardennes admiring the Château de Vêves. "Those who live in Hollywood never admire anything, especially anything that promises to be immortal. When they capture a beautiful place—a castle or a palace—on their accursed film, they destroy it as surely as if they had arrived with a wrecking crew. It is the same with people. Whomever they film, they kill, just as effectively as if they had pointed a loaded gun instead of a camera at their heads."

"I'm really not sure I understand what you're trying to say," Alison said.

Maurice Gray lifted a finger. "It's very simple. Your image is what you are. Can you understand that? The image you present to the world is what you actually are. Why do you think African tribesmen used to be so frightened of being photographed? They knew that—these days—our vanity has allowed us to hide from ourselves. They knew that every time someone paints your portrait or takes your picture, he does just that— literally *takes* something from you, something of your image, something of yourself. Your face grows old not from within, not from age, but from without, from use and abuse by other people. Your face grows old from being looked at, from being photographed. You still don't understand me? Well, you will. Your face is the same as a car tire, if you will forgive me for making such an uncomplimentary metaphor. It is scuffed and worn by everything with which it comes into contact. Not from inside, but from external friction. Why do you think Arabian women wear the *yashmaq*? Not from modesty, but to protect them from the gaze of others, to keep them young."

Alison said, "I really don't know. I mean, I really don't. You're saying that people's faces grow old just because other people look at them and take their photograph?"

Maurice Gray slowed down and then turned right, over loose grit, up a steep and shadowed lane. Beneath the low-hanging trees on her left, Alison could see an unnaturally green field where sheep were grazing. Ahead there was darkness, a tunnel of trees. Maurice Gray drove into the darkness with a lack of concern born of long experience. Then they emerged onto a wide, white-gravel forecourt, and before them stood a huge Gothic château with a high central tower. Among the spires, the turrets and the blue-slated dormers, there must have been at least a hundred windows; on the lower floors there were tall French doors, rows and rows of them, shining like quicksilver in the dark of the morning, signifying ballrooms, reception rooms and hallways.

It looked as if a massive London railway station had been magically transported to the forests of Belgium and set down on the crest of a high hill overlooking a romantic garden with a circular pool, a gushing fountain and groves of ash trees. The effect was both dramatic and overbearing: man attempting with wealth and arrogance to impose his will on nature, and for some reason she couldn't define, Alison began to feel isolated and depressed. When Maurice Gray stopped the car in front of the gray stone steps, she wished she had the courage to ask him to take her back to the highway so she could continue on her way to Liège.

"This is incredible," she said, looking around.

Maurice Gray stood a little way off, his hands tucked neatly into the pockets of his jacket, like pink letters waiting to be posted. He smiled and said, "You like it? It's pretty vulgar, really. But come and have some lunch. I can show you around afterward. Do you like hare? The game here is quite good."

They mounted the steps and walked into a huge, echoing lobby lined with white veined marble. There were palms in pots and a dusty red Chesterfield, but the whole place had the dismal feeling of having been abandoned.

Alison's sneakers squeaked on the marble as she turned and said, "Maybe we'd better forget lunch. Why don't you just drive me back to the highway? I'm sure I can easily hitch a ride to Liège. I mean, you don't have to bother anymore."

"It's no bother at all," Maurice Gray said. "Please don't be put off because it's all so overbearing. Come upstairs, let me show you the tower. It's really very unusual."

"Listen, I'm embarrassed," Alison said.

Maurice Gray's voice echoed. "You don't have anything to be embarrassed about. Why should you. be embarrassed? Please." He spread his hands wide and smiled at her encouragingly. "I'm only asking you for lunch."

Alison nervously rubbed the back of her thumbnail against her teeth and said nothing.

"Please," he repeated.

Alison looked around the hallway. Dust fell silently in the premature twilight, dust that must have been falling for scores of years.

She said, "I'm sorry, this is all wrong. I feel like I'm intruding."

"Of course you're not," Maurice Gray reassured her. He held out a beautifully manicured hand. "It was I, remember, who invited you. That can hardly be called an intrusion." He smiled. "Come on. While we're waiting, I can show you the tower."

"I don't think I want to. I mean, I know it sounds stupid, but something about this place has got me really spooked. I guess I never knew anyone who lived in a house quite so *old*."

"Old?" asked Maurice Gray. "This place isn't old. It was only completed in nineteen eleven. Now you could hardly call that *old*. Don't be put off. I know it's rather cavernous. None of my family like it either, except for my sister, and she has always had delusions of grandeur. But it's home, you know, and in the summertime it can be quite charming."

"I think I made a mistake," Alison said, a little panicky now. "I think I'd better leave. Please. It's just me, being hysterical. But the whole thing has kind of overwhelmed me, if you know what I mean, and I really would prefer it if you could take me back to the highway."

"Without lunch?" he asked.

"Please. I'm not very hungry."

Maurice Gray smiled. "Well, for goodness' sake, the last thing I want to do is to hold you here against your will. If you don't want lunch, all right, I understand. I realize I've been rather too forceful. Please forgive me. I was lonely and bored, and I didn't stop to think of the effect I might be having on you, talking strange talk and bringing you all the way out here to a grim-visaged château. I'm sorry. Please forgive me. Say you do."

"Well, I forgive you," Alison murmured uncertainly.

"That's marvelous. You needn't be afraid of this place. Let me show you the tower; it's really quite splendid."

"Well, okay," she said. "But where are your servants?"

"In the kitchen, I expect," Maurice Gray explained, off-handedly. He led the way through two enormous oak doors into a long, high, marble-floored hallway. To their right, a grand staircase descended from the upper floors. On every wall there were oil portraits of displeased-looking men in period costumes.

"The family de Rochelle," Maurice Gray remarked. "Nothing to do with *our* family, I hasten to tell you. Look at their piggy little eyes. It takes centuries of avarice to produce eyes like that. The greediest dynasty in Europe, I would say."

He mounted the echoing staircase, and Alison had no choice but to follow him. She noticed that the backs of his black Italian shoes were perfectly polished. He stopped on the first landing and showed her a cabinet of Sèvres porcelain. "You see this dinner service? It was originally made for Louis Sixteenth. It has four hundred and eighty-five pieces, every one of them painted by hand."

They had reached the second landing when a side door opened and a young Belgian appeared. He was thin and slight, with a pointed nose and hair that stood up on the crown of his head like a cockatoo's crest.

"Ah, Paul," Maurice Gray said. "I was wondering where you were. I have invited this young lady for lunch."

The young man stared at Alison with watery gray eyes. Then he nodded and said in a strong Flemish accent, "Of course, Mr. Gray. I shall call you when we are ready."

Alison felt more at ease now that she knew she was not alone with Maurice Gray. Being brought out to a strange Gothic château in the middle of the Belgian forests was a little too much like the prelude to a horror movie. Even though she tried to persuade herself that Maurice Gray was a perfectly respectable man and that there were plenty of other people around, she still felt oddly unreal as she climbed up yet another flight of stairs. Looking out the windows of the tower, she could see the gravel courtyard outside, the bright-green gardens and the inky-colored sky. Maurice Gray's car, parked by the steps, looked as tiny as a toy.

"I have a room of my own up here," he told her. "It is the only place I can find any solitude."

"You sure have a fantastic view," Alison said.

They reached Maurice Gray's room. It was comparatively small, no longer than twenty feet and no wider than fifteen. Its leaded Gothic windows faced west toward the hills bordering the Meuse. The waxed oak floor was covered with a blue and gray Persian rug. There was no pictures on the walls and the furnishings were sparse: an oak bed covered with a white bedspread of Brussels lace, and a desk with a chair.

"Kind of monastic, if you don't mind my saying so," Alison remarked.

Maurice Gray nodded in amused agreement. "I suppose you're right. But after one has tasted every kind of food, drunk every kind of wine and experienced every kind of romantic interlude—well, what can be left but monasticism?"

"Can we go down now?" Alison asked.

"Of course. But first let me show you the view from the clock room."

They climbed the last flight of stairs—a tightly winding spiral of decorative iron treads. The clanging of their feet echoed all the way down to the hallway at the foot of the tower. At the top there was a small, dark room in which the mechanism of the tower's four clock faces slowly ticked. Cogs and springs and spindles, all softly gleaming with oil. Only one shaft of light penetrated the room, entering from a tiny observation port beside the east clock face.

"Have a look out through there," Maurice Gray suggested. "You'll be quite amazed at what you can see."

Alison bent forward and peered through the slit. A sudden ray of sunlight illuminated her right eye, as if she were being examined by an optometrist. An eye as blue as a cornflower. Maurice Gray stood behind her, his hands by his sides, his chin slightly lifted, a man practicing his haughtiness in the privacy of his very own clock room.

"I can see the fountain," Alison said.

"And what else?"

"The stables. Well, they look like stables."

Maurice Gray drew from his inside pocket, where it had been sheathed, a short, broad-bladed knife. As he held it up, it glinted brightly.

"What do you see just beyond the stables?"

"An orchard, I guess. A pear orchard?"

"Yes. The finest Williamses."

The clock mechanism ticked and whirred. Maurice Gray stepped forward silently, the knife held lightly in the open palm of his hand.

He said, "It's almost noon. We ought to go down now, before the clock starts chiming. We don't want to have ringing ears for the rest of the day."

Alison asked, "Is that an herb garden there, past the wall?"

Maurice Gray leaned forward as if he were going to peer through the tiny window. Instead, he pushed the knife straight into Alison Shrader's back, where it entered with an audible crunch.

"Ah-h-h," she said in a choking voice, then collapsed to the dusty wooden floor.

Maurice Gray stood over her for a moment. He left the knife where it was, embedded in her back. He had stabbed her with the intention of paralyzing her, not of killing her. To withdraw the knife now would start her bleeding. Fastidiously he wiped his fingers and then bent over to examine her face.

She was white. Her gasps for breath came thick and short and uneven, like the gasps of someone deep in a nightmare. Her eyes were wide open, but she was unable to move.

"Well, now," said Maurice Gray. "The perfect stroke."

The door of the clock room opened behind him. It was Paul; he had taken off his jacket and rolled up his sleeves. Together they lifted Alison, Maurice Gray taking her feet and Paul holding her under her arms, and carried her carefully down the spiral staircase. She whimpered once, but neither of them took any notice. Outside, it began to rain again, and drops pattered noisily against the windows as if clamoring for attention.

"I found her in Bouillon," Maurice Gray explained. "She has been hitchhiking alone in Europe. No one will miss her for months; by then, anybody who might have seen her will have forgotten."

"Mademoiselle will be pleased," Paul said, not altogether respectfully.

They carried Alison into Maurice Gray's room, where they laid her on the Persian rug. Paul stripped off the white-lace bedspread, revealing a starched surgical sheet. Then they lifted her onto the bed, face down, the handle of the knife still protruding from the back of her yellow windbreaker.

Maurice Gray bent down and looked closely into Alison's face. Her eyes stared back at him in helpless terror. *What have you done to me? What has happened? Please—I can't move. Please—I can't feel anything.* Maurice Gray smiled and said to Paul, "Can you imagine how frightening it must be to be totally helpless?" Then to Alison he said, "But don't worry, my dear, this will soon be over. Soon you will be at peace."

Paul unlaced Alison's Care Bears and set them neatly side by side on the floor. Then he reached around her, unbuckled her belt, tugged down her zipper and wrestled off her jeans and panties. They were dark-stained and damp; when Maurice Gray had stabbed her, she had lost control.

With scissors they cut up the back of her windbreaker and sweater so they could remove them without having to extricate the blade. Since Alison wore no bra, she was naked now, except for her silver crucifix.

"The dressing," Maurice Gray said.

Paul opened the top drawer of the desk and took out a sterile dressing pack. Maurice Gray snipped it open and laid it on the bed. Then he grasped the handle of the knife and slowly drew it out. Dark crimson blood welled up out of the cut instantly and poured down on either side of Alison's waist, but Maurice Gray quickly pressed the dressing against the wound and taped it down.

"Good," he said, more to himself than to Paul. "Now may I have the instruments, please?"

Paul had already taken out of the second drawer a small mahogany instrument case lined with dark-blue velvet. He laid it down beside the blood-streaked knife, and Maurice Gray opened it. There were rows of surgical scalpels as well as clamps and suture needles. Without hesitation, he picked out one of the scalpels and held it up between index finger and thumb.

"They were all sharpened this morning," Paul said quickly as if he were afraid of being criticized. Maurice Gray gave him a testy, equivocal smile and then bent over Alison's bare back.

"You could bring me a brandy," he suggested. "This is going to take an hour or two, at the very least."

"Do you want anything to eat?" Paul asked.

Maurice Gray glanced at him, scowling. "Of course not, fool."

Paul merely nodded. It was obvious that at a time like this, he felt he could show his contempt for Maurice Gray. At a time like this, Maurice Gray was at his weakest, as is every man when he is indulging his most compulsive desires.

Maurice Gray worked with the flowing capability of long experience. Out of his instrument case he took a flat, triangular blade rather like a surgical pie slicer. He inserted it sideways into an incision he made in Alison's back and gradually began to lift her outer skin away from her body, systematically, and with some elegance.

Paul returned an hour later and switched on the bedside lamps as Maurice Gray stood back, pausing for a moment. "Quite beautiful, don't you think?" he asked the servant. Alison was full-breasted, narrow-waisted, her stomach still flat with youthfulness. Maurice Gray rubbed a few of her fine blonde pubic hairs between his fingers as if he were rubbing tobacco leaves. "Quite beautiful. And scarcely a blemish."

Then he bent and continued cutting and lifting, until at last he had a ghost of skin—an extraordinary translucent cloak— that had once belonged to Alison Shrader.

Outside, it was growing dark. Rain was pattering hard against the windows. Maurice Gray was sweating and had to take out his handkerchief to dab at his face.

"The best you've ever done, monsieur," Paul remarked with mock obsequity. He always said that, every time.

"Just take it to mademoiselle," Maurice instructed sharply. "Tell her that the face will not be long."

"*Monsieur*," Paul nodded. "Whatever you say, monsieur."

When Paul had departed, Maurice Gray leaned over Alison and looked down into her face. She stared back at him blindly, and he knew she was suffering beyond all human understanding. If only he could tell her just how much *he* had suffered, he and every member of his family. It was a life for a life, a skin for a skin. He felt genuinely sorry for her. Genuine remorse. But if she could ever know how agonizing *his* life had been, how fearful, how threatened, how *damned*, she would at least have some comprehension of why she had to die so painfully . . . even if she could not find it in her heart and soul to forgive him. Sighing, he set to work on her face.

She opened her eyes only one more time. He understood the message that was there. He nodded and smiled. Then, taking the scalpel in one hand, blowing her a kiss with the other, he drew the knife quickly and deeply across her throat.

He stood back, his right hand covered with blood. A good way for anybody to die, he thought. A short hour or so of terrible suffering, followed by quick release. The suffering she had endured would ensure her access to heaven, would make certain she wouldn't linger in purgatory.

Paul came back carrying a white napkin in which to enfold

the facial skin; then he disappeared again. Maurice Gray went downstairs to the second landing and into the bathroom to wash his hands. Blood streaked the white ceramic of the basin. In the mirror, he thought he looked rather tired. It would not be long before somebody else would have to be found. Cordelia, late in the fall, always needed to look for new people; he, in the depths of winter. It wearied him. It hurt him too. But what else could they do?

He clasped his hands over his face as if in meditation. The years weighed on him so heavily now.

He walked along the landing until he reached the library. It was a small library considering the size of the château, densely packed with books, a few of them in old and cracked leather bindings but most of them modern. Almost all of them dealt with beauty, cosmetics and surgery. But Maurice Gray looked at none of them. Instead, he went straight across to the carved oak cabinet in the corner, unlocked it and took out a decanter of brandy. He filled a glass with shaking hands.

" 'Those who go beneath the surface do so at their peril,' " he quoted to himself. " 'Those who read the symbol do so at their peril.' "

He went to the window and looked out over the grounds of the château. He had told Alison lies, of course. The château had once belonged to the Count de Rochelle, certainly, but the Gray family had bought it from him years ago, when it was decrepit and deserted and half of the roof had collapsed. Who knew what the Count de Rochelle was doing now? He was probably dead, or drunk, or half-dead, or half-drunk. Maurice Gray crossed himself and prayed without any hope that the Lord would forgive him for what he had been forced to do.

He sat in the library for nearly two hours while Alison Shrader lay dead upstairs and the sacrifice she had made was put to use. He drank three large glasses of brandy before his ears began to buzz and he was no longer sure he could keep himself steady.

At last, when it was dark outside and the windowpanes were poured full of ink, he heard gramophone music echoing along the corridors. "L'Arlesienne," by Bizet, one of Cordelia's favorites. He heaved himself up out of his chair, but even as he did so, Paul arrived at the library door with a tinkling glass of Perrier water and a supercilious smile.

"Miss Gray is ready to see you now, monsieur," he said.

"You'll, er . . . ?" asked Maurice Gray, nodding upward toward the room where Alison Shrader lay.

"Of course, monsieur. What do they say in *Snow White*? The deepest and darkest part of the forest? Game for the game."

Maurice Gray took the Perrier off the tray and ravenously drank three-quarters of it. Then he gently but firmly pushed Paul aside and walked along the corridor to Cordelia's room. He knocked at the oak door.

"*Entrez!*" Cordelia called.

He opened the door and stepped inside. The room was large, three times the size of the library, but the drapes were tightly drawn so that it was impenetrably dark.

"Can't we have a light?" he asked patiently. He kept his hand on the doorknob.

"Tomorrow you can see me, when everything's settled," Cordelia said.

"You're—all right, though?"

There was a long silence. He knew he had said the wrong thing; Cordelia was upset.

"It was beautiful skin," he said.

"It was adequate," she retorted.

"You're not unhappy, though? You're pleased with it?"

"It was adequate."

Maurice Gray knew there was little point in arguing with Cordelia when she was in one of these moods. He opened the door wider and said, "I shall see you at breakfast?"

She was silent for a long while. Then she said, "Maurice, I can't stand very much more of this."

"Very much more of what?"

"You know what I mean. This exile. This isolation. This way of life."

Maurice said nothing. He had heard this complaint from Cordelia many times before. And many times before he had argued that the risks of going home were far too great; that in Belgium, at least, they could continue to survive without being discovered; that their victims could be dragged into the forests to be buried in shallow graves, to be devoured eventually by the wild pigs. Unknown, undetected, forgotten, as they themselves were.

Cordelia said, "Tomorrow I shall talk to Father again."

"That's your privilege, of course."

"For God's sake, Maurice, don't be so unctuous. You're my brother, not my priest."

"I'm trying to be your protector."

Another silence. Then, "I know," she said. "I'm sorry. But I really do want to go home."

"It would take only one person to recognize us for the same to happen as happened before."

"Not if we have the portrait."

Maurice Gray lowered his head and said with the quietness of monumental impatience, "You know as well as I do there is no chance whatsoever we shall ever find it. We were routed, Cordelia; that is the only word for it. Routed and exiled."

"I shall go to Luxembourg again. I shall talk to Eustachio Rossi."

"I cannot prevent you."

"No, you can't," she replied. "And, yes, I shall."

Two

New York, December 12

He told Edward he would probably be back by five, six at the very latest.

"But supposing somebody wants to buy something?" Edward asked.

"If somebody wants to buy something, sell it to him," said Vincent, shrugging on his dark-blue Bijan overcoat. "This is a business, you know. Not a museum."

Edward looked around the gallery with distinct unhappiness. "Perhaps I should wait until you get back. Pre-Raphaelites aren't exactly my strong suit."

Vincent tugged on his black-leather gloves. "They're only pictures, for Christ's sake."

"Well, I guess," Edward agreed. It was typically irreverent of Vincent to refer to seventeen million dollars' worth of mid-Victorian masterpieces as "only pictures." There were three Rossettis, two Holman Hunts and a recently discovered portrait by Millais. But then, Vincent came from a family that had been buying and selling works of art long before Rossetti, Millais or Holman Hunt had ever picked up a paint brush. Vincent's grandfather used to get drunk with Monet, and his great-grandfather had been a friend of Sisley's. Vincent himself had been one of Mark Rothko's closest supporters, and he regularly had lunch with Richard Anuskiewicz.

When Edward opened the door for him, a sharp blast of December cold penetrated the warmth of the gallery. The door was kept locked: anyone who wanted to come inside and look at the pictures had to press the doorbell first and peer hopefully through the security glass. Outside, a siren whooped; a tractor trailer blared its horn. There was a smell of winter and traffic and burning bagels. Vincent said, "Just one thing: don't let anybody take the Millais yet. Dick hasn't had a chance to photograph it. Oh—and if Aaron Halperin calls, tell him I shall be coming up to the country this weekend. I've got two Johnsons I want him to clean."

"Okay, Commander." Edward lifted a hand in salute and then closed the door. He stood there for a moment watching Vincent walk away before he turned and looked around at the paintings on the gallery walls as if they were disobedient children who had been left in his care.

"God damn it," he said. He disliked being left in charge of the gallery. Whenever he was left on his own, someone difficult came in. Like the last time, when an elderly Iranian exile had wanted to buy four John Kanes all at once, for cash, and have them delivered to the Pierre Hotel by taxi. By *taxi*, for God's sake. And then there had been the time before that, when a well-dressed, silver-haired man, apparently wealthy and apparently sane, had suddenly and furiously struck out with his umbrella at an original Paul Fairley bronze. Art, for some reason, seemed an irresistible magnet to eccentrics, and Edward always seemed to be there alone when those eccentrics made an entrance.

For the first half hour, nobody rang the bell; it was mid-morning, freezing and threatening to sleet, a slack time for the selling of great art. After lunch was always far more profitable, when wealthy men were returning to their hotels from the Four Seasons or "21," full of rich food and richer wine, anxious to impress those pretty young ladies with whom they shouldn't have been having lunch at all.

Edward walked up to the gallery's second-floor landing. He drummed his fingers on the balcony railing. A slight, athletic, curly-headed young man of twenty-five, he wore a charcoal-gray suit with a contrasting vest and the sort of Ivy League necktie of which *Playboy*'s fashion editor would have approved. But although he was stylish and reasonably smart, somehow he always managed to look as if he would have been more comfortable in a jogging suit.

Edward was the middle son of three. His older brother had gone straight into the family brokerage. His younger brother had dropped out altogether and gone to sell catamarans in San

Diego. But Edward—mainly because he hadn't been able to think of what else to do, and also because he had wanted to impress his father that he was independent—had somehow found himself here, at the Pearson Fine Arts Gallery on East 61st Street, with the questionable title of "Executive Curator." In truth, he was Vincent Pearson's telephone-answerer, letter-typer, excuse-maker, diary-keeper and general factotum.

Edward liked art, especially the Impressionists, but had no artistic talent of his own. If he could have portrayed this winter on canvas, however, he would have rendered it pure lamp-black. In October, he had crashed his beloved Dodge Charger on the New Jersey Turnpike, wrecking it beyond repair. In November, he had lost his fiancée Laura to a broad-shouldered, tight-suited hotshot lawyer who had looked to him more like an Armenian meat-packer than an attorney; and two days after that, he had been mugged outside his apartment house and robbed of all his credit cards.

As he paced around the gallery this morning, he felt more than a little ill-starred.

It was while he was looking down from the second-floor balcony that he first caught sight of the woman. She was looking in through the gallery's left-hand window, where a small Holman Hunt, "Amos and the Basket of Summer Fruit," was displayed on an artistically arranged rumple of emerald-green silk.

She was pale, but even from this distance—even through the reflections of the security-glass window—she was beautiful. She wore a dark fur hat and coat. One hand, as white and perfect as a sketch by Leonardo, clasped her collar.

Edward watched her for a while. She seemed strangely agitated; she kept turning away from the window and then turning back. Every now and then she raised her hand as if she were trying to shield her eyes from the glare of the gallery's spotlights.

Not another brick-thrower, Edward prayed. Even if she didn't manage to crack the window, he would have to call the police and then there would be crowds, and questions, and the usual wrangling. One woman had smeared a pecan pie all over the window simply because she objected to the "indecency" of two pink-painted metal cubes entitled "Uncertain Nudes."

But this woman kept her distance from the window and

didn't produce any bricks from her pocketbook. She didn't go
away, though, in spite of the cold and the jostling lunch-time
crowds.

After five minutes or so, Edward came down into the main
body of the gallery and approached the window for a better
look at her. She was tall—much taller than he had at first
imagined—and exceptionally striking. She had the lean, well-
bred face of an upper-class European woman, possibly English, more likely French. Her eyes were large, feline and
heavy-lidded; her lips were somewhat parted, and Edward
could detect the glint of slightly overbiting teeth. For some
reason, teeth like that had always appealed to him; a woman
with a slight overbite looked as if she might be on the verge of
experiencing some faintly erotic pleasure.

He continued to watch her, and every so often she stared
directly back at him, but there was no indication in her
expression that she had seen him or that she was concerned that
he was observing her so intently.

At length, however, just when he began to think she was
going to leave, she approached the gallery door and pressed the
bell.

Oh, well, he thought. *Here we go. Eccentric of the month.*
He came forward with his warm, executive curator's smile and
unlocked the door. Cold mink brushed his hand as she stepped
inside. Edward conscientiously locked the door behind her and
then turned. She was white-faced, her head held high and
proud.

"Are you the owner?" she demanded. Clear, cut-crystal
English.

"I'm the executive curator. The owner's out right now."

"Will he be long?"

"Well, he told me not expect him before five, and with him,
that usually means six."

"So," said the woman. Then, more quietly, "so." She
stalked slowly toward the nearest hanging, "The Wedding
Feast," immaculately painted, immaculately varnished, sheen
upon sheen until it was almost impossible for the eye to
penetrate.

"Rossetti," she said.

Edward nodded. "I can tell you the price if you're
interested."

She raised her head and looked around at the other paintings. "Excellent. An excellent collection."

"Thank you," Edward acknowledged.

The woman frowned. "I wasn't complimenting you. I was complimenting the artists. It is the artists who create. Collectors only collect. And galleries—galleries are the money-changers in the temple."

Edward tried to look unperturbed. "I'm afraid that pre-Raphaelites aren't exactly my forté," he said. The woman, as he spoke, turned her back on him. He added, "I'm more of an Impressionist man, myself."

Her face hidden, she said, "I have always associated the Impressionists with weakness. They seek to interpret light rather than form. Light is nothing; light has no substance. Only skin and bone have true meaning. Flesh and muscle."

"That's an interesting point of view," Edward replied, trying to be polite. After all, the woman was obviously wealthy. Who knew? She might make an offer for one of the Holman Hunts. He followed her, his hands clasped tightly behind his back, as she walked around the gallery's semicircular floor, glancing at each of the paintings in turn.

"Upstairs," he said helpfully, "we have a previously unattributed Millais. A portrait of Wilkie Collins, painted just before he married Effie Ruskin."

"Yes," said the woman, and Edward had the peculiar feeling she knew the painting.

"It's, ah—" he said, raising his hand toward the balcony. "Would you care to take a look at it?"

"No."

"Oh," Edward murmured. There was an uneasy pause. Then he said, "Is there anything else you're interested in?"

"Yes." She inspected the paintings one more time before turning back and staring at Edward. "Waldegrave. Do you have any paintings by Walter Waldegrave?"

Edward leaned forward as if he hadn't quite heard her. "Waldegrave? I'm sorry."

"He was English, born in London. He painted landscapes, mostly. Very few portraits. But there is one portrait in particular I am quite keen to acquire."

"Can you . . . describe it?"

"It measures five feet wide by three feet high. It is a very dark portrait, showing a family of twelve in a red-lined drawing room."

Edward flushed for a moment and then slowly shook his head. "I'm sorry. You'll have to talk to the owner." He felt embarrassed, and for some reason, peculiarly fearful. On his second day at the Pearson gallery, Vincent had taken him back to the stockroom where there were two or three hundred mid-Victorian paintings stored in slide-out racks, all kept at a constant temperature and humidity. Vincent had shown him some of the finest, some that were merely entertaining daubs, some he was anxious to sell to anybody at almost any price and some he could hardly bear to part with.

When Edward had rolled out one large canvas, however, Vincent had stepped straight across the aisle and rolled it back out of sight. "Not to be sold, that one," he had said briskly. "That belongs to the Pearsons' private collection."

Edward had rolled it out a few inches again. "I can see why," he had said. "It's a marvelous piece of work. But aren't they all hideous? I wouldn't like to meet *them* on a dark night, especially not *en masse*."

"It was my grandfather's," Vincent had explained, insistently pushing it back out of sight. "For some reason, he was very superstitious about it. He used to say it was like a family charm—that as long as we kept it, it would keep us safe."

"In that case, I can see why you do," Edward had remarked. "But why do you keep it here? It would look terrific in your apartment."

"It used to hang over the living-room fireplace when I was a boy," Vincent had told him. "But lately it's begun to deteriorate. I'm sending it up to Aaron Halperin next week to have it restored."

"It's kind of spooky, isn't it?" Edward had asked. "I mean, all these ugly old people. Do you think Waldegrave painted them from life?"

Vincent had shrugged. "They were probably nothing more than a fantasy. A figment of the artist's imagination. Waldegrave was pretty odd toward the latter part of his life, mixed up in witchcraft and demonology and all that kind of hocus-pocus. Mind you, Stuart Heathcliff thinks this painting was nothing more than a satire on Waldegrave's critics: every art commentator who had ever given him a bad notice, all of them collected together and made to look as ugly as their reviews."

"Must be worth something just as a piece of history," Edward had commented.

"Yes, but it's not for sale," Vincent had replied with an emphasis that ended the discussion. Edward had hesitated for a moment, then made a face and followed Vincent out of the stockroom.

But here only two months later was this white-faced woman in furs asking him about the very same painting. Twelve people in a red-lined room; although according to what *she* had said, the twelve people were not critics, not art commentators, but a family. Perhaps Waldegrave hadn't liked them, either. Perhaps they were his in-laws.

The woman said, "I was given to understand on good authority that Mr. Pearson is the present keeper of the Waldegrave portrait. I have in fact been trying to locate it for a long time."

Edward found himself smiling rather inanely, although he didn't really mean to; it seemed the only response his face was able to make. "The name Waldegrave does ring a bell," he remarked.

"Walter Waldegrave," she enunciated clearly without taking her eyes from his face. Such extraordinary eyes; they looked at him and yet didn't seem to see him at all. They were more like mirrors than eyes. "Born March seventh, eighteen forty-three. Died April thirteenth, eighteen eighty-six. That was a Tuesday, you know, and in Connecticut, it was raining."

Edward thought: *here we go. The first cracks in the apparently sane exterior. The next thing, she's going to be stripping off her clothes, or attacking the paintings with a bottle of India ink.*

He said, "I really don't know anything about such a picture. I've seen all of Mr. Pearson's collection, even his watercolor portfolios, and I'm afraid that. . . ." He lifted his hands to show he was no longer able to help.

"You've seen it, haven't you?" she asked. "I can tell by the look on your face. You've seen it. What kind of condition is it in? Is it undamaged? Is it still unmarked?"

"I'm sorry," Edward said, "we're really talking at cross-

purposes here. It would be much better if you came back later
and talked to Mr. Pearson."

The woman paused and then said, "I am prepared to pay you
a very great deal of money for it, if necessary."

"Well, I'll tell Mr. Pearson that. I'm sure he'll give you the
promptest attention possible."

"You're very loyal, aren't you? A very loyal executive
curator. Well, I suppose I can't blame you. There was a time
when men were dashing. These days they're too concerned
about losing their jobs."

Edward said, "Shall I tell Mr. Pearson you'll be calling
again?"

"If you wish."

"Shall I tell him your name?"

"You may, if you want to."

Edward went across to the little desk where customers
perched on a rococo chair to write out their checks. He picked
out a pen from the ivory holder and said, "Yes?"

"Tell him that Miss Vane called. Miss Sybil Vane. I won't
leave my number. I'm staying with friends at the moment; I
don't think they would appreciate being disturbed by calls from
trade."

"And when do you expect to return?"

"Tomorrow. I'm not sure of whether it will be morning or
afternoon. But certainly tomorrow."

"Thank you," Edward said courteously and led her to the
door.

"You're very security-conscious," she remarked as he made
a point of glancing into the street before he unlocked the door.

"Well, we have to be. This isn't exactly Woolworth's."

She smiled at him. "You've been charming. I shall look
forward to seeing you again tomorrow."

"Good-bye, madam," Edward said dutifully.

He locked the door after she left and watched her cross 61st
Street against the traffic. In a moment she disappeared. He
turned back into the gallery and walked over to the desk where
the card lay, the name "Sybil Vane" scrawled across it. He
picked it up, fanning it between index finger and thumb.

There had been something remarkable about that woman.
Something not quite real. She had been cold and testy, not
particularly polite, and yet there had been a quality about her, a

chilly charisma that had left him feeling he would like to see
her again, if only to look at her. She had left a strange perfume
in the air, too. It was nothing he had ever smelled before. It
smelled like closed rooms crowded with flowers; it smelled
like spices kept in sealed ceramic jars; it smelled like the scent
of a woman inhaled from a small, embroidered handkerchief
long after she has departed.

He could almost fantasize that under her long black mink
coat, she had been naked. Pale shining thighs, black silky
stockings.

He suddenly felt very young and immature, the same way he
had felt in high school when he had tried to ask Sally
Vanderhogh for a date; yet elated, too, and slightly frightened.

When he put the card down and turned around, it was with a
slight shock that he noticed a man outside in the street
watching him through the glass door. Their eyes met for a
moment; then the man was gone. For some reason, Edward
thought of the woman's saying, "That was a Tuesday, you
know, and in Connecticut, it was raining." And it was his
memory of that remark, the strangely matter-of-fact way in
which she had said it, that disturbed him more than anything
else.

Three

Nepaug, December 12

Sleet was slanting across the reservoir so furiously they could scarcely see the shore. Gordon had retreated under his army-surplus raincape; all Wesley could see of him was the glowing butt of his cigarette and the twin reflections it sparked off in the lenses of his round rain goggles. Wesley remained where he was, well forward in the prow of the boat, casting and reeling in and recasting in spite of the sleet, his waterproof hat hanging down over his ears like a sodden cabbage, determined not to row back to shore until he had caught himself at least one more perch. The fish had been laughing at him today, and Wesley was not the kind of man who cared to be laughed at, either by fish or by women. Gordon couldn't have cared less who laughed at him, but then, Gordon hadn't been through two divorces, and Gordon hadn't lost a ten-year-old son in a boating accident, either, like Wesley had.

Although the police had dragged that part of Candlewood Lake three times, they had never found the boy's body. That was six long years ago now, and Wesley was still taking out his anger on the fish. Nobody ever mentioned it, not out loud, but the terrible implication of Wesley's anger was that the fish had actually eaten his son.

Gordon lit a fresh cigarette from the butt of the last and noisily cleared his throat. "Weather forecast didn't say nothing about no sleet," he remarked, as if that would cheer Wesley up.

"Weather forecasters don't know shit," Wesley said, tugging at the line. "Anybody with half an eye could have seen there was sleet coming. You can tell it by the clouds."

Gordon asked, "You want a sandwich? Marjorie packed me some pepperoni."

"I'll have a beer, if there's any left."

"Sure."

Gordon shuffled around inside the makeshift tent of his khaki raincape, and at last produced a can of Miller. He was wet and bone-cold and uncomfortable, but he knew better than to suggest to Wesley that they row back to shore yet. When you went fishing with Wesley, you stayed out on the reservoir until Wesley was satisfied he had massacred enough fish. Only then did you head for home. The compensation was that when you went fishing with Wesley, you always caught yourself three times as many fish as when you went fishing with anybody else; and Wesley would give you the whole of his catch, too. Wesley never ate fish. Nobody ever asked him why.

The sleet rattled across the surface of the lake in gray, chilly salvos. It was almost impossible to make out the shore line now, except for a dark, serrated line of pine trees. Wesley sniffed and wiped his ginger mustache with the back of a hand. Then he tugged open the ring pull on the can of beer and drank. "Crazy, isn't it?" he said to nobody in particular. "I'm sitting out here on three hundred million gallons of water, having another half million gallons dumped on me from heaven above, and I'm thirsty."

Gordon blew smoke and said nothing.

For a long time there were no sounds but the sleet, the persistent slapping of wavelets against the side of the boat and the sharp whirring of Wesley's reel. "Fucking fish," he muttered.

Gordon tossed his cigarette butt into the reservoir. "You still seeing Marlene Adams?" he inquired. He never got into discussions about fish.

"Sure I am. I took her down to Bridgeport last week, to the Johnny Cash concert."

"She like Johnny Cash?"

"All country music. Dolly Parton, Waylon Jennings, Smoky River Boys, you name it."

"Never would have thought it, not to look at her."

Wesley finished his beer and crumpled the can in his left fist. "All women like country music. It's sentimental, that's why.

Give them something sentimental and that's all they need. Something with tears in it. You know what her favorite is? That one about the little girl who turns up on the doorstep with her little puppy and then dies in the night."

Gordon sniffed philosophically. "Well, never would have thought it. Not to look at her." He paused and then said, "The little girl, you mean?"

"What?"

"The little girl dies in the night?"

"And the puppy, both."

Gordon nodded, then checked his watch. It would be turning really dark soon. He wondered if he ought to eat his last pepperoni sandwich or leave it until later. From where Gordon sat, Wesley looked in the sleety twilight like Captain Ahab searching for his nemesis. Hunched and determined and unforgiving. *Moby Dick* was the only classic book Gordon had ever read, apart from *No Orchids for Miss Blandish,* and he had scarcely understood a word of it. He liked to tell people he had read it, though, and to quote from it from time to time. "Better to sleep with a sober cannibal than a drunk Christian." That was his favorite line.

He was still debating with himself about the sandwich when Wesley suddenly jerked his line. "Shit!" he shouted. "I've got something, something real big!"

Gordon started to scramble forward, but Wesley shouted, "Stay where you are! Don't rock the fucking boat so much!"

There was a short zizz of line going out; then Wesley began to reel in. "It's big!" he said excitedly. "Biggest one today, easy."

Gordon crouched in the middle of the boat, straining his eyes against the darkness. "Can't see nothing," he said.

"There! Look, there! You can just see the splash!"

"Still can't see nothing."

"Well, come here and give me a hand, pinhead. This thing weighs a fucking ton."

Clumsily, Gordon made his way forward and helped Wesley with the fishing pole. Whatever Wesley was reeling in, it was tugging against them with enormous sluggish resistance; but to Gordon, it felt more like a deadweight. It wasn't struggling, it wasn't fighting against them; it was just dragging in the water

like a half-submerged log. If it was alive, anything that size
would have whipped both of them straight out of the boat.
Gordon had gone fishing for blue marlin off the Florida Keys
once, and he knew just how powerful and lively those suckers
could be.

"It's a log," he told Wesley.

"Don't talk crap, this isn't no log. This is the big one. This
is the fucking big one."

Nepaug, like all lakes and reservoirs, had a legendary,
monster-sized fish. The local fishing enthusiasts called it "Old
Whiskers," but Wesley never referred to it as anything other
than "the big one." Half the fishermen in Litchfield claimed to
have hooked Old Whiskers on their line at one time or another.
All of them, of course, had been forced to cut him free.

Gordon said, "Still can't see nothing. If this was a fish, it
would be struggling. This isn't struggling none. This is a log."

Wesley turned and stared at him, white-faced. "You're
trying to tell me I don't know no fucking log when I catch one?
This isn't no fucking log! This is it! This is the big one!"

Almost hysterical, Wesley wound and wound at his reel.
Gordon tried to help him, but Wesley angrily pushed him
aside. Through the sleet, Gordon could make out herringbone
ripples in the water where Wesley was reeling his catch toward
them. Whatever it was, it was dark and it was big, and it sure
looked like a log. Gordon took off his goggles and wiped them
with his damp, crumpled handkerchief.

Now the dark shape in the water floated toward them under
its own momentum. Gordon thought Wesley must know it
wasn't a fish, that it was only a piece of wood or a tangle of
weeds and trash, but still Wesley kept on winding until the line
was taut and the object bumped against the hull of the boat.

"Now, you bastard!" Wesley cried, almost sobbing, and
whipped back his fishing pole so the object reared out of the
water.

Gordon screamed like a woman. The object, as it jumped up
almost as if it were alive, was a human body—hairless, raw red
all over, the grisly scarlet of fish bait. Its eyes were lidless, its
teeth were bared, and it stared at them in mute agony before it
splashed and wallowed back into the water.

"Jesus Christ!" Wesley shrieked. "Jesus Christ!" He

scrabbled for his knife to cut the body loose from his line; he
was shaking and whining and cursing. The body spun around
and knocked against the boat again, and Wesley yelled out,
"Get away! Get away! For Christ's sake, get away!"

In the end, unable to cut the line, he tossed his fishing pole
overboard and sat rigid with horror, watching the body
gradually float around and around and away.

Gordon stumbled to the stern of the boat and yanked at the
starter of the old Evinrude motor. For once, with a deafening
burp, it burst into life the first time. Without a word, he turned
the boat around and piloted it toward shore. Wesley didn't say a
word either but knelt in the waist of the boat, his hands
clutching the gunwales, his knuckles white, his head bowed,
only his shoulders betraying the spasms of fear and disgust that
rippled through him.

And, worst of all, the unspoken words: *My son must have
looked like that after the fish had been at him. Oh, God above,
my son must have looked like that!*

They reached the wooden jetty on the northwest bank.
Gordon tied up the boat with freezing, banana-fingered hands,
his face contorted against the sleet. Wesley remained kneeling,
staring at Gordon's lunchbox as if it somehow contained the
terrible secret to the dreadful thing they had just witnessed.

Gordon took his arm. "Wes, Wesley. Come on now."

Wesley glanced up. His face looked as if it had been
disassembled and put back together not quite in kilter.

"Come on, Wesley, we've got to call the police. That was a
body out there."

Wesley said, "It wasn't—?"

"No," Gordon reassured him. "It wasn't Donnie. Donnie's
long gone, remember. And Donnie was a boy. That was a man,
or maybe a woman. Somebody full-grown."

Wesley stood up unsteadily and allowed Gordon to half-lift
him up to the jetty. Gordon's Chevrolet wagon was parked a
little way off, its windshield heaped with frozen slush. Gordon
helped Wesley to cross the sloping bank of the reservoir and
eased him into the passenger seat.

"The way that thing came jumping up out of the water,"
Wesley said. "By God, Gordon, that scared the living shit out
of me!"

"Well, me too. But let's go call the police."

There was a gas station at Warren. Even though it took them over half an hour to reach it across the rough wooded tracks, they hardly spoke. The windshield wipers squeaked monotonously, clearing triangles through the sleet. Gordon smoked as he drove, his eyes squinted against the gathering darkness. Wesley sat sideways in his seat as though he were an invalid, as though every nerve in his body had been rubbed raw.

Wesley stayed crouched in the wagon while Gordon called Sheriff Jack Smith at Torrington. He watched with glazed eyes as Gordon stood in the sleet-swept telephone booth, gesturing with his cigarette. When Gordon came hurrying back and opened the door, Wesley said, "Well?"

"They're coming. We have to get back to the reservoir."

Wesley shook his head. "I don't want to go, Gordon."

"You have to. You can stay in the wagon if you want to. You don't have to—you know, look at it or anything. They won't make you do that."

Slowly, pathetically, Wesley began to cry. He clamped his hands over his face, but the tears ran down his wrists. Gordon watched him, biting his lip, feeling helpless; but then he tugged the wagon into gear and headed back toward the Nepaug Reservoir.

The sheriff's wagon arrived within an hour, its blue lights flashing in the darkness. The sleet had eased off and was replaced by a thin, wet, penetrating drizzle. Gordon and Wesley stayed in the wagon as the sheriff walked toward them, his flashlight bobbing and ducking with every step. He opened Gordon's door and said, "How are you doing, gents? This isn't the day for it."

Gordon climbed out and nodded back toward Wesley. "Wesley's taken it kind of hard, Sheriff. It's shook him up. I guess, you know, it kind of reminds him of what happened before. To his boy. He didn't take that easy, either."

Sheriff Jack Smith was stocky and short, with a big, good-looking face that had always reminded his wife Nancy of Richard Burton's. He wore a dark-blue waterproof hunting cap and a dark-blue raincoat. He was thirty-eight, the most outspoken and pragmatic sheriff Litchfield County had elected for years. He believed in drug programs, and constructive welfare work, and community service for young offenders; and he had never shot at anyone in his life. He knew he was the legal custodian of a countryside in which the native farming population was falling fast, in which the old values and the old customs were disappearing. After all, this part of Connecticut, in the 1980s, had a lower population than it had boasted in the 1780s.

Jack Smith also knew that his obligations included looking after the mainly empty properties of wealthy New Yorkers who came up to Connecticut only on weekends, as well as, when they *did* come up, keeping an eye on their big-city tastes for cocaine, for women who weren't their wives, and for domestic disturbances.

Ten to one, he thought as he stood in the shifting rain, ten to one this floater doesn't come from Litchfield, nor died here neither.

"Dan Maskell's coming over," Jack told Gordon. "He's bringing the inflatable boat and a searchlight. He should be here in just a while."

"Wesley thought he'd hooked a fish," Gordon said.

"Whereabouts was it?" Jack asked, flicking the beam of his flashlight into the darkness.

"Just floating around in the middle there someplace. But you should have seen it. It was kind of red all over, like it was painted or something, or burned. Did you ever see anybody burned?"

"Frequently," Jack told him. His brown eyes gave nothing away.

"Well, I don't never want to see nothing like that, not again," Gordon said, shaking his head. "That damned thing's going to give me nightmares the rest of my life."

In twenty minutes Dan Maskell arrived in a police pickup with an inflatable dinghy and a collection of generators, searchlights, nets and boat hooks in the back. While the dinghy was being filled with air, a Datsun arrived from the county coroner's office and Wallace Greenstreet stepped out, as haughty and tall as a stork, wearing a London Fog raincoat that looked as if it had been used as a Little League football.

"Sorry to drag you out, Wallace," Jack said, unwrapping a stick of gum and folding it into his mouth.

Wallace briskly rubbed his hands. "This time I have to admit it was quite a relief," he said affably. "My sister had just arrived with that half-witted husband of hers. When you called, he was striking up a conversation on the relative merits of rented rug steamers."

"Gum?" Jack asked.

Wallace fastidiously shook his head. "What do we have here? Have you located it yet?"

"Give us an hour or so. It shouldn't be hard to find."

For the next twenty minutes, Jack and Dan rowed around the reservoir in systematic circles, carefully searching the surface. Their flashlights crisscrossed through the rain; their voices echoed.

Quite suddenly they bumped something. Jack shone his flashlight at it . . . and there it was. Scarlet, as Gordon had said, tangled up in fishing line. On first sight, it reminded him of a dead seal he had once seen on a beach in Newfoundland, skinned for its pelt. It was lying face down, which usually indicated a male. In spite of the cold, the smell of decomposing flesh was strong.

"Let's just take it in tow," he told Dan. "Get a hook around that fishing line, then we can bring it in behind us."

Dan Maskell's face gloomed in the flashlight like a wrinkled Halloween pumpkin. He was fifty-three years old, a policeman with thirty-two years of service. He had dragged so many dead bodies out of automobiles, out of lakes, out of bedrooms, out of rivers, out of woods, that one more dead body didn't make much difference as far as he was concerned. He caught hold of Wesley's fishing pole, made it fast and then headed the dinghy back to shore.

"We're not looking for anybody special, are we?" Dan asked. Usually, when a gangster disappeared in New York, Jack's office would be sent a message to be on the lookout for his corpse. They had once found Vittorio Seccone in a burned-out car deep in the woods near Ivy Mountain.

Jack glanced back at the red body they were towing. "Nobody I know of. Besides, this doesn't look like mobsters had anything to do with it. Too grisly. Only amateurs ever get this grisly."

They brought the body into shore and carefully carried it to the end of the jetty. Jack and Dan wore gloves, but even so, Jack could feel the slipperiness of the flesh. When they laid the body on Wallace Greenstreet's gurney, they drew close to inspect it.

"Is this the body you saw?" Jack asked Gordon.

Gordon could scarcely look at it. The masklike face without eyelids or lips, the red, slimy chest. He nodded and said, "Unless there's another one floating around out there exactly the same."

"Don't bet that there isn't," put in Dan Maskell, lighting up a wine-flavored cheroot and then obviously wishing he had taken his gloves off first.

"Will Wesley make an identification?" Jack asked.

Gordon shook his head. "Wesley's got this idea . . . well, you know. It's all to do with Donnie. He saw this thing come rearing up and all he could think about was Donnie."

Jack steadily chewed his gum. "All right, then," he said. "I'll talk to Wesley later. Why don't you take him home, give him a couple of drinks? I'll call by later and see how he's shaping up."

"Okay," Gordon said, clasping Jack's shoulder. "Thanks for everything."

As Gordon drove away, the others gathered around the gurney. Dan had brought the floodlight out of the dinghy and set it on its tripod a few feet away so they could examine the corpse more closely.

"Well, a male, all right," Wallace said, lifting the slippery mass of genitals with his index finger. "Caucasian, judging by his blue eyes, although you can't tell by his skin. The entire epidermis is gone."

Jack said, "The fish hadn't gotten to his eyes yet."

"Indeed," Wallace said, "and that would indicate to me, as it obviously has to you, that this body hasn't been floating around in the water for very long. Possibly for only a few hours."

"Then how the hell did his skin get like this?" Dan asked. "He isn't burned, is he? And he hasn't been nibbled by fish."

Wallace looked at the body more closely. "What you see here is the corium, or true skin. The outer skin, the epidermis, is completely gone. Not just in patches as you might expect from a burn or an accident, but completely and perfectly. Look here, and here. Those are marks from a knife. A surgical scalpel probably, or something similar."

"I don't follow this," Jack said. "What are you trying to say?"

"I can't be conclusive, of course," Wallace replied. "Not by the side of a lake in the middle of a downpour. But I'd say that this poor fellow was almost certainly literally skinned."

Jack's chewing slowed down. He looked at Wallace intently. "*Skinned*? You mean deliberately?"

Wallace nodded.

Jack stood with his hands on his hips and studied the body head to toe. "*Skinned*?" he said again. "Holy Moses!"

"Do you think he was still alive when they did it?" Dan asked. "Is there any way of telling?"

"Well, no, not really," Wallace answered. "But I would certainly *guess* he was still alive, and probably conscious, too. Otherwise, what on earth would have been the point of doing it! This is torture, in my view. Deliberate, calculating torture, carried out most efficiently. Whoever took this man's skin off was a real expert."

Jack looked down at the ghastly face. "What the hell would anybody want to do something like this for? I mean—you can hurt somebody just as much without peeling him like an apple."

"Well, you're the one who has to look for the motive," Wallace told him. He unfolded a plastic sheet and spread it over the corpse. "Maybe it was part of some Mafia ritual; maybe they wanted to make an example of him."

"But if they wanted to do that, why did they throw him in the reservoir? We found him only by accident. What's the point of going to such lengths to make an example out of someone and then dumping his body where the chances are nobody's ever going to see what you've done?"

Wallace buckled the straps around the corpse and then looked at Jack with one of his bland don't-ask-me expressions. "I'm only the medical examiner, remember? All I can give you is fact, not conjecture. The fact is, this man was flayed, probably while he was still alive, and probably by somebody whose skills were as good as a top-flight plastic surgeon's.

Anyway, they might have disposed of the body but you remember that old Jewish joke about 'When they circumcised you, my friend, they threw away the wrong bit.' "

"What the hell are you talking about?" Jack demanded.

Wallace raised a hand to calm him. "I'm simply saying that while they have disposed of the body, they still have the skin."

Jack stared at him. He stopped chewing. "And you think they might have used his skin . . . as an example? Kind of exhibited it? Here's the skin of Don Whatever-his-name-was; if you don't watch out, the same thing could happen to you?"

Wallace shrugged. "As I say, Jack, all the conjecture on motivation is up to you."

As they talked, another car drew up, an elderly Volkswagen, and a young man in a duffel coat climbed out and hurried toward them, swinging a camera.

"Hi, Dennis," Jack greeted him.

Dennis was a young reporter for the Litchfield *Sentinel*. He was lanky and tall, with an incipient black mustache and a crowd of angry pimples on his chin. "Somebody dead?" he wanted to know.

"No, no, that's Deputy Cohen under there, rehearsing his part in *Frankenstein*."

"A floater?" Dennis asked, unabashed.

"Found floating," Jack corrected him.

"Not drowned, then?"

Jack shook his head. "Killed first, floated later. So far, I'm treating it as homicide."

"Can I take a picture?"

"Not this time."

"Aw, come on, Sheriff. The public's got a right to know."

Jack said, "Knowing doesn't include prying. Nor does it include the taking of obscene pictures."

"What's obscene? That's a body, not the gatefold of *Hustler*."

Jack said, "Give me your camera."

"What?"

"Give me your camera," Jack repeated and held out his hand. Reluctantly, uncertainly, Dennis passed it over. Jack said, "Now you can look. Go on. Make up your own mind whether it's obscene or not."

Wallace, with thinly concealed amusement, noisily folded back the black-plastic sheet to expose the corpse's head. Dennis stood staring at it for almost half a minute. Then he looked away, nodded and went back to Jack to retrieve his camera.

"What did they do to him?" he asked in a hoarse voice. "What the hell did they *do* to him—to make him look like that?"

"The way it appears to us now, they hurt him a very great deal to do that," Jack said. "If you want more details, come to my office tomorrow morning."

"You've got it," the reporter said and left. They watched his taillights flicker away across the fields and into the woods.

"Poor kid," Dan remarked. He scratched his stomach as if he had nervous hives.

But Jack said, "All right. That's it. We've got work to do. Wallace—get that body over to the morgue. Dan, you can start taping off this whole area, all around the landing stage. I'll call the forensic guys, get them out here straightaway. We need to look for footprints, clothing, splashes of blood, anything."

"Supposing we find his skin?" Dan asked.

Jack looked at him, his face showing baleful in the floodlight, the crags of his cheeks overemphasized by shadow.

"Don't ask questions you don't want to hear the answer to," he replied. "Now, come on, let's get going."

He went back to his car, a three-year-old Caprice with a dent in the door. He called back to Torrington and asked for Frank Davis and Marshall Pryor of the forensic department. Then he had himself patched through to his home, in Harwinton.

"Nancy? It's Jack."

"Oh, darling. Are you going to be late?"

"Very, by the look of it. We just brought in a body from the Nepaug Reservoir."

"Oh, no. Was it a drowning?"

"I can't talk about it now. I'll see you later. But give my love to Benny, won't you? And lots of love to you, too."

Dan came up, holding Wesley's fishing pole.

"Do you want me to stash this stuff in your car?" he asked. "You can take it around later."

Jack hung up the intercom. He unwrapped another stick of chewing gum. "I'm not sure poor old Wesley is going to want to see any of that fishing tackle ever again."

Dan stood and waited, the cold rain falling all around, and neither of them knew what the hell they were going to do.

Four

New York, December 13

By three o'clock that afternoon, there was still no sign of the woman who called herself Sybil Vane. Vincent came out of the stockroom, where he had been wrapping up the two Johnsons he wanted to have restored, and said, "It looks like your lady is a no-show."

Edward had been sitting with one buttock perched on the edge of the desk watching the doorway. It was impossible for him to explain to Vincent how disappointed he was by Sybil Vane's failure to appear. He felt almost as if he might have invented her, the frustrated fantasy of a young man who had just lost his fiancée to an Armenian meat-packer. Correction, attorney.

"She was quite clear that it was the Waldegrave she was after?" asked Vincent. He had taken off his coat; in his seven-button vest and his starchy white shirt, he looked as relaxed as Edward had ever seen him. He was handsome in a rather too clear-cut way, with curly gray hair, a squarish, Italianate face and a short, straight nose. He could have posed for Michelangelo's "David," except that he didn't look as effete as that. His girlfriend from the Metropolitan Museum of Modern Art, Charlotte Clarke, called him "God in a three-piece suit." They didn't sleep together; she might have called him something else if they had.

Edward said, "She described it exactly. Twelve people in a red-lined room. She knew Waldegrave's dates, the date of his birth, the date of his death. She said she'd been looking for the portrait for a very long time."

Vincent checked his watch. "Well, I can't stay much longer.

47

Not if I want to get up to New Milford in time to collect
Thomas."

"I could always tell her to come back next week," Edward
suggested.

Vincent fastened his cuff links. "I don't think there's very
much point. I'm not going to sell her the painting, whatever
she offers."

"She said she'd pay a good price for it."

Vincent straightened his tie, lifted his coat off the back of the
rococo chair and shrugged it on. "I'm sorry," he said. "It's
simply not for sale, and that's that. Apart from which, it's
beginning to fall to pieces. You know what those mid-Victorian
amateurs were like. They never mixed their paints properly.
Too much turpentine, too little pigment. And Waldegrave was
one of the worst."

"What shall I tell her, then, if she comes?"

"Tell her precisely that. Tell her the picture is not for sale.
Tell her it's in terrible condition and that even if she were to
buy it, she'd be wasting her money. Quite seriously, I give that
picture two years, if that. It's always happening, even to the
best of paintings. Just before you came here, I had to take a
John Frederick Lewis off display. A beautiful picture, Saturday
morning in the *hhareem*, one of those Oriental studies. But the
paint was falling off it like dandruff."

Edward challenged him, a little impertinently, "You're not
going to tell me you're superstitious about it? The Waldegrave,
I mean?"

Vincent smiled benignly. "Of course I'm superstitious about
it. Why shouldn't I be? My grandfather said that if we held on
to it, it would keep the family safe. And if that's what my
grandfather thought about it, it's good enough for me."

"But you don't *really* believe it, do you?"

"Stop psychoanalyzing me. Do you want a Christmas bonus
or not? And make sure to set the alarm properly before you
leave. I'll be back in the city very early Monday morning and
I'll probably come by your apartment to collect the keys."

"All right," Edward said. Neither of them commented on
the fact that this was the first time Vincent had trusted Edward
to lock up the gallery himself. Edward felt the beginnings of a
pleasant familiarity between them, the budding of an amicable
working relationship that might well develop into a close

friendship. Vincent was formal in his manners, traditional in his dress, but Edward sensed his genuine appreciation of the people who worked for him and the people he loved.

Vincent left and walked down to 61st and Third, where he collected his dark-green Bentley Eight. He drove back to the gallery and parked it outside so Edward could carry out the two Johnsons for him.

"If Milo Kasabian calls, tell him he can reach me in the country," he said. "And if Charlotte calls, tell her I'll be with her in five minutes flat, traffic permitting." He looked up and down the street. "Still no sign of your mysterious Miss Vane?"

Edward shook his head.

"Think it'll snow?" Vincent asked.

"It's my birthday next week," Edward said. "It never snows before my birthday."

Vincent drove off and Edward returned to the gallery. He checked his watch. Only another hour before he would go home. But Vincent made a point of keeping the gallery open at all advertised hours, citing the story of the evening Nubar Gulbenkian walked in at one minute to five and asked if it was too late for him to purchase a Thomas Hart Benton, "Susanna and the Elders."

Edward went through to the office and plugged in the electric kettle; Vincent didn't approve of coffee percolators. On a tray on top of the filing cabinet there sat a copper Belgian coffeepot and a copper container of Douwe Egberts dessert coffee.

Edward was sitting at his desk reading Charles Holmes' biography of James Thurber when the doorbell rang. The ringing startled him, so much so that it left a salty taste in his mouth. He put down his book and went to the door, taking his keys out of his vest pocket. It was she, white-faced as before and wrapped in her furs.

He unlocked the door. She came into the gallery as fluidly as an animal. She looked around and asked, "He's here?"

"Mr. Pearson? I'm afraid you've just missed him. He had to go up to the country for the weekend. I thought you might have been able to stop by earlier. He left, what, only ten minutes ago."

"Well, what a pity," the woman said, although she sounded distinctly unconcerned. "I was looking forward to meeting him."

"I'm sorry," Edward said. "Can you return on Monday? He'll be here then."

"Did you talk to him about the Waldegrave?"

"Yes, I did."

She came up close to him, inspecting his face as intently as if she were reading the pages of a book. Again Edward could smell that extraordinary perfume, and potpourri, and closed rooms, and oil of musk, and sex. Her even breathing ruffled the fur on her wide collar.

"Did he admit that he *does* have it? The Waldegrave?"

"Well, yes, he does have it. It's been in his family for seventy years."

"Seventy years, yes," she nodded. "Seventy-three, to be exact."

"But . . . I'm afraid, well, he won't sell it."

The woman pressed her fingertips against her lips as if she were afraid of what she might say. Then she turned away.

"I did ask him," Edward told her.

"And?" she queried without turning back.

"He said it was something of a family heirloom, not for sale. Apart from which, it's not wearing too well. Mr. Waldegrave wasn't too handy at mixing his paints, apparently. They're all flaking off. Mr. Pearson said he wouldn't give the painting longer than two years, even with restoration. He said you'd be wasting your money, if you want the honest truth."

The woman stared at him, her eyes like mirrors seen at night. "Two years? Is that what he said?"

Edward made an apologetic face. "I'm sorry. But he was quite adamant. It's not for sale."

"You told him I would pay whatever he asked? You told him how important it was?"

"I'm sorry," Edward repeated.

Sybil Vane tapped her fingertips together, worriedly. Then she became conscious that Edward was watching her and she smiled. "Ah, well. If Mr. Pearson cannot be persuaded to sell, then Mr. Pearson cannot be persuaded to sell."

"If there's anything else I can interest you in," Edward suggested. He felt strangely upset that he had been obliged to disappoint her; he felt almost as if he needed her approval. He didn't want her to leave the gallery disappointed and, above all, disappointed in *him*. He couldn't understand the feeling, but it was strong enough to make him unusually anxious.

"I have been searching for this particular portrait for so long," she explained, more to herself than to Edward. "I have been trying to reassemble a collection, you see, that used to belong to my family. Only a few paintings remain to be located; no more than eleven or twelve. The Waldegrave, however, is by far the most important. I must tell you, Mr.—?" she paused and raised a questioning eyebrow.

"Merriam," Edward told her. "Edward Merriam."

"Not the Norfolk Merriams?"

"No, I'm afraid not. The Rochester Merriams."

"I'm sorry?"

"You wouldn't have heard of them," Edward smiled. "They weren't in society."

"Ah," she said. Then she lifted her hand toward him. He took it, wondering if he were supposed to kiss it. Her fingers were cold and there were enough diamond rings on them to lacerate a man's face to ribbons, like a marmoset's claw. When he looked at her, she was waiting for him, and so he pressed his lips lightly against the smooth skin. The hand of a very young woman: no wrinkles, no liver spots, no protuberant veins.

"My name, of course, is not really Sybil Vane," she said. "That was just my little joke."

Edward said nothing but watched her and waited for her to explain. He didn't understand what kind of joke it could possibly be for a woman to call herself Sybil Vane, but he found that he was prepared to listen. Perhaps it was a joke against herself, a gibe against her own vanity.

"My name is Cordelia Gray. If you were thirty years older, you would have heard of the Grays. In those days, everybody had. But we have all been in Europe for a while. Well, for some years. It is quite remarkable how quickly one is forgotten. You have no need to be ashamed that your family was not in society. Society is nothing but a basket of snakes, with memories no longer than their own tails."

Edward said cautiously, "I'm pleased to know you."

"Well, Edward," she said, "the pleasure is quite mutual."

"How long have you been back from Europe?"

"Less than a month. We have been staying in Newport for a while. But we hope to be moving back into the family home in

Connecticut before long. That is why I have been trying to track down our former paintings and furnishings. So much of it was dispersed when we had to go away."

"That's quite a project, putting an art collection back together again."

"Yes. So far, however, it has been very successful."

"Until now, with the Waldegrave," Edward put in.

Cordelia nodded, brushed fur away from her face. "Until now, with the Waldegrave," she agreed.

There was a short silence, crowded with unspoken approaches. When they spoke again, they spoke together and then laughed. Edward said, "Please, after you."

"I suppose it sounds forward of me," she said, "but I was wondering if you yourself might be interested in helping me."

"You mean, to put your collection back together?"

Cordelia nodded. "It wouldn't take up much of your time. It certainly wouldn't affect your work here. But I would pay you well for it, and perhaps you would come up to Connecticut and help me hang it and catalog it."

"It's a very tempting offer. I mean, it sounds like fun. But I have to say that I couldn't get hold of the Waldegrave for you. I mean, that couldn't be part of our arrangement."

"Of course not," Cordelia said. "I understand what Mr. Pearson has said to you, and if the painting is not in a fit condition in any case . . . well, perhaps we had better forget about it. But I would certainly appreciate your assistance. Do you think you could be interested in doing that for me?"

Edward hesitated for a moment, then gave her a cheerful, assertive nod. "Okay. I think I'd like that. If you will give me a list of your collection, we can talk it over."

Cordelia looked at her watch. "I must go now; I have an appointment. But are you staying in the city this weekend?"

"I usually do."

"Are you free for lunch on Sunday? At twelve perhaps? There is a small restaurant on East Sixtieth Street called *Les Images*. I will meet you there."

"All right, then. As long as you let me be your host."

Cordelia came close to him and touched the lapel of his suit as if she could convey extra meaning through her fingertips. "I wouldn't dream of it. The invitation is mine."

Edward stood staring at the door for a long time after she had gone. He felt as if he had drunk too much dry white wine: a sourish taste in his mouth, a tight sensation around his scalp. He took a sip of coffee but it was cold now, and he grimaced with disgust.

There was no doubt that the presence of Cordelia Gray had an unusual effect on him, like nothing he had ever experienced before. It was almost like free-basing, although Edward had done that only twice. He could imagine that miners sometimes felt like this when they were being gradually overcome by firedamp. It was only when they breathed fresh air again that they realized how close they had been to asphyxiation.

He set the alarm and locked up the gallery, then stood for a while in the doorway. The night was cold and noisy, the streets were crowded, and the red taillights of passing cars were drowned in a wet asphalt lake. He walked over to Fifth Avenue with his coat collar turned up, his hands in his pockets. For a moment, across the street, he thought he saw the face of the man who had peered in through the gallery door yesterday afternoon after Cordelia Gray had left. A truck passed between them, and the face was gone.

Edward whistled for a taxi. Three splashed past his toes ignoring him, until a fourth pulled up, driven by a saintly looking Puerto Rican who looked as if he were three parts high. Santana vibrated on his stereo, "Samba Pa Ti."

"Wentworth Apartments," Edward said. "West Sixty-third and Tenth."

"Faster than a speedin' bullet," the taxi driver told him.

Edward jostled in the back of the taxi as it headed west across Central Park South; he tried not to think about lunch tomorrow. She was only a middle-aged woman, after all. A middle-aged woman from a cobwebby Connecticut family, and all she was interested in was her art collection. So why get so disturbed? Why think about her eyes, and her soft, smooth hands, and that faint zizz of one silk-stockinged thigh rubbing against the other?

"West Sixty-third and what was it?" the taxi driver yelled over his shoulder.

Five

New Milford, December 13

They drove north out of New York into an evening of overwhelming darkness. Vincent had to use his headlights on the Major Deegan Expressway; they illuminated a cold and hostile future-world of concrete underpasses, distant apartment blocks, scrubby trees and abandoned Thunderbirds robbed of their wheels.

Charlotte Clarke sat beside him, the hem of her Oleg Cassini skirt drawn up higher than it ought to have been, revealing slim legs in shiny dove-gray pantyhose. She hummed along with Vivaldi. Vincent always played the "Four Seasons" when he drove back to Connecticut from New York. He said it prepared his mind for the country: for real trees, for people who didn't snarl at you, for quiet roadside restaurants and red and yellow cornfields.

Charlotte said he was being pretentious, but Vincent didn't particularly mind about that.

Charlotte was the youngest woman board member at the Metropolitan Museum of Modern Art. Also, by far the most beautiful. Vincent would have taken almost anything from a woman with her qualifications. He liked his women companions to be intelligent rather than beautiful. When they were both, as Charlotte was, it was what he described as a "heavenly bonus."

Charlotte said he was arrogant and stuffy. But Charlotte also knew that he was unusually kind and that no matter how assertive he was, he would never hurt her.

Her taste in art was too advanced as far as he was concerned. She liked splotches of color on huge canvases, and stacks of bricks, and old bathtubs with inexplicable messes of enamel down one side. But physically she was just his type. She was tall, with a figure like one of Eric Lagerfeld's fashion models and a shaggy mane of straw-blonde hair. Her eyes were a startling violet; her face was a perfect heart shape, with the slightly weak chin and the full, pale mouth of a true High Renaissance virgin. The very first time he met her, Vincent had called her "Venus," which had annoyed but also flattered her. Who did he think he was, the Hugh Hefner of art? Yet they had been friends from the moment they first clasped hands, and they frequently lunched together and spent weekends together at Vincent's country house in New Milford, Connecticut.

They had never become lovers, though. Somehow their close and intimate friendship had never crystallized into an affair.

Vincent sensed this was probably because they were too much alike; and they had each sensed that if their relationship became physically entangled, it would never survive, like a horse caught up in a thorn thicket. They valued each other's continuing company more than they valued the prospect of a short and incandescent moment of sex. They kissed often. At New Milford they shared the sauna and the jacuzzi together. But there were always separate beds. Charlotte was between lovers, in what she described as "a breathing space," and at the moment, she was far more interested in her work for MOMA than she was in men.

Vincent was occasionally dating a twenty-one-year-old girl named Meggsy, an editorial assistant at a small midtown publishing house that specialized in art books. Meggsy liked Meat Loaf, wore tinted designer glasses and DD-cup bras, and was far too young for him. She had been brought up in Akron, Ohio. Vincent took her along to prestigious dinners and openings just to tantalize the older members of the New York art establishment and to infuriate the gays.

As they drove through the Lake Taconic valley, the sky as dark as a dragged-over blanket, Charlotte suddenly asked, "Did that woman come to see you?"

"What woman?"

"You know. The woman who wanted the Waldegrave."

Vincent glanced at her, taking in her nylon-shiny knees, and said, "No. It was one of those dead-end inquiries, that's all.

Just like those out-of-towners who spend twenty minutes standing in front of a Monet, ask you how much it is and promise to return the following morning with a certified check to pick it up."

"Seems odd, though," Charlotte said.

"What does?"

"Well, if you want to impress a gallery, you don't ask for a Waldegrave, do you? That's like walking into Sardi's and asking for tuna on toast."

"Well, I don't know," Vincent said. The lights on the instrument panel shone on his face with an eerie tinge of green. "Maybe it was a severe case of reverse snobbery."

Charlotte smiled. "It just strikes me as peculiar that she should want it so much."

"There's a man in Houston who collects used tires. Waldegrave did have his fans. Queen Victoria once asked him to paint the view from her library at Osborne."

"And did he?"

Vincent shook his head. "He died about three months later. He drowned himself, as far as I recall."

"Poor old Walter Waldegrave."

"It was probably the Lord's punishment for painting so poorly."

Charlotte was silent for a while. They passed a yellow traffic sign reading "Danbury, pop. 54,900." They passed the Danbury fairground on their right-hand side, followed by warehouses, suburban rooftops and rows of parked school buses. Charlotte asked, "Why won't you sell it?"

"The Waldegrave? I just don't want to."

"You don't *really* believe it keeps your family safe. How could it?"

Vincent made a face. "I don't know. But if you had something from your grandmother—a ring maybe, or a necklace—and your grandmother had made you promise to keep it safe because it would be bad luck to you and your children if you sold it, well, what would you do?"

Charlotte shrugged. "I'd keep it, I guess. But not out of superstition. I'd keep it out of love and respect, and in memory of my grandmother. Not that she *did* give me anything."

"Well, that's what I'm doing," Vincent told her. "I'm

keeping the Waldegrave out of love and respect, and also
because I don't like to sell anything that's bad art. Which the
Waldegrave is. It's terrible. Badly composed, badly painted
and falling to pieces in front of your very eyes. I wouldn't sell
it to anyone, not for anything."

"Why did your grandfather want to keep it if it was so bad?"

"Search me."

"But he was a very good art dealer, wasn't he, your
grandfather? I mean, he was the one who really built up the
family business?"

"That's right."

"So why should he want to keep a painting as bad as the
Waldegrave, unless he had a special reason for it?"

"Charlotte," Vincent said a little testily, "I really don't
know."

"But didn't your *father* ever tell you? He must have
known."

"My father was too busy traveling to Europe and amusing
himself with well-known and occasionally notorious ac-
tresses."

"Is that what Thomas is going to say about you?"

"Of course not," Vincent rounded on her. "You're not an
actress, and you're not notorious. And you don't come from
Europe."

"I still think it's strange, this woman wanting the Waldegrave so badly. And I still think it's strange that you didn't sell
it to her."

"I'm a man of integrity," he said half-jokingly.

Charlotte reached across and touched his cheek, then his
lips. "Is that why you never take me to bed?"

They turned north on Route 7, through Brookfield, until they
reached New Milford: a small, neat, colonial town built on the
side of a low hill overlooking the northern end of Lake
Lillinonah. There was a town green, a town tavern, a
gingerbread-fronted newspaper office, the New Milford Savings Bank and a white-painted church with a weather vane. In
the middle of the green stood a cannon from 1775 and a
bandstand, and on the perimeter were rows of benches where
the older residents liked to sit on fall days, watching the
crimson leaves drift down around their feet.

Charlotte called it "Stepford Wife Country" and swore that

every man who lived there was either a geriatric or a chauvinist
pig and every woman a domesticated robot.

Vincent, whatever he thought about it, called it home.
Because five miles farther on, up a winding road, stood the
huge country house known as Candlemas, the Pearsons' rural
seat; and however much time he spent in New York and
London and Los Angeles, Vincent always had to come back to
Candlemas, if not to rest and refresh himself, to at least pay
homage to his roots. His great-grandfather had lived and died
here; his grandfather had lived and died here; his father had
lived here and died on Omaha Beach. He himself had been
born here, on the day Britain declared war against Germany.

They drove between the tall wrought-iron gates, which this
evening had been chained back in preparation for Vincent's
arrival. The house stood at the end of a long brick drive, lit by
glass-globed carriage lamps. Lights shone from the downstairs
windows, and fragrant woodsmoke rose from the chimneys.
Vincent had called Mrs. Miller two hours before he left New
York and asked her to open up the house and light the fires.
Mrs. Miller and her crippled son Ben lived a half-mile back
toward New Milford, in what had once been an old 1920's
roadside restaurant. Ben always grumbled that his mother had
enough work to do cleaning up at the New Milford supermarket without "drudging" for the Pearsons. But Mrs. Miller
had been "doing" for the Pearsons for nearly thirty-five years,
and she felt that Candlemas and the Pearson family belonged to
her by right and by duty. She couldn't have countenanced the
thought of Harriet Whitney cleaning up for Mr. Pearson, or
Betty Elsmore poking around in "her" linen cupboard.

Mrs. Miller appeared at the front door as soon as Vincent
drew the Bentley to a crunching halt on the driveway. She was
a small woman—serious, bespectacled, martyred—with fray-
ing white hair and a mannerism of patting her left shoulder
when she spoke, as if to reassure herself that she was still
there.

"Well, well now, right on time," she said as Vincent carried
suitcases into the hallway. "But it's a dreary day, isn't it? I've
made a sirloin for you. It should be ready in half an hour."

"Mrs. Miller, you will get your reward in heaven," Vincent
said, setting down his load next to the huge colonial side table.
"I'll have a word with Archangel Gabriel in person."

Mrs. Miller gave him a flattered but flustered smile. She didn't approve of blasphemy. Hadn't she prayed enough that Ben would find the strength to walk? Hadn't she sprinkled his wasted knees with water from Lourdes? Hadn't she suffered enough of his anger and frustration? And now to be told as a joke that she would find her place in heaven. Well, young Mr. Pearson wasn't half of what his father had been.

Charlotte said, "The house looks lovely," and Mrs. Miller sniffed, trying to pretend she wasn't pleased. "There's sirloin steak and *champignons de bois*," she said. There wasn't the slightest hint of a French accent in the way she said *Cham Pig Nons De Boys*. That was the way it was written on the card in the supermarket and that was the way she was going to say it.

Mrs. Miller preferred Charlotte to any of Vincent's other "lady visitors," as she referred to them. Charlotte was the only one who actually used the guest bedroom that was prepared for her—with soap, linens, lotions, everything. The others only pretended to use it, and Mrs. Miller knew perfectly well they were sharing Vincent's four-poster colonial bed in the big master bedroom overlooking the garden. As far as she was concerned, the master bedroom was the "marriage bedroom," and always had been. Mrs. Pearson had slept there alone for twenty years after her husband's death. Mrs. Pearson had died there. It seemed like sacrilege to fornicate on that bed, which had known such gladness and such sorrow.

"How's Ben?" Vincent asked as he walked through to the long, low-ceilinged living room. A log fire was crackling in the cast-iron grate, and the green-velvet drapes had been drawn. "Charlotte, would you like a drink?"

"Ben's not a happy boy," Mrs. Miller said. She untied her apron. "He says the space shuttles are affecting his legs, not to mention his alfalfa rhythms."

"Alpha rhythms," Charlotte said carefully.

"That's just what I said," Mrs. Miller agreed. "He says everybody in the world has different alfalfa rhythms; some get disturbed and some don't."

Vincent laid a hand on Mrs. Miller's shoulder. "Just tell him that if there's anything I can do—"

"The doctor gave him pills for it," Mrs. Miller said. Vincent knew she disapproved of medication, especially of placebos. If the doctor was giving Ben placebos, that meant the invalid was deranged; and Mrs. Miller absolutely refused to accept that her son was deranged. He was injured; he was suffering from stress. But he certainly was not deranged. Those times when he swore and cursed, those times when he sat in his wheelchair screaming at his fate—Mrs. Miller could accept those, just as long as he wasn't deranged.

"It's the space shuttles," she insisted. "The way they affect the atmosphere . . . it gets him down."

"Can you come up here and clean on Monday?" Vincent asked her, laying a gentle hand on her back.

"Well, surely," Mrs. Miller replied. "I can fix you breakfast, too, if you want."

Vincent shook his head. "We have to get back to New York very early. You know what it is. Another day, another ten thousand dollars."

"I remember your father," Mrs. Miller said. She didn't have to say anything else. Vincent remembered him, too, although mostly through photographs, and black and white home movies, and stories his mother had told him. Six years ago, Vincent had gone to Omaha Beach, stood knee-deep in the water and known for sure that his father had gone. He would go through the rest of his life missing his father. So would Mrs. Miller, who had somehow expected the world to be different after World War II. More like *When A Girl Marries* than *Peyton Place*.

After Mrs. Miller had driven off in her old beige Rambler, Vincent went back into the living room and poured himself and Charlotte large glasses of Jameson's whiskey. He sat down by the fire and raised his glass in a toast. "Here's to us. And may the space shuttles leave poor Ben Miller in peace. Especially his alfalfa rhythms."

"Poor woman," Charlotte remarked.

"She's not as much of a poor woman as she likes you to think. She just enjoys the sympathy, that's all."

"It was good of her to make us a meal," Charlotte said, curling up her legs on the tapestry-covered sofa.

Vincent swallowed whiskey and shrugged. "She does it only because she wants to feel that she's in charge. I don't think she ever forgave my mother for dying and allowing me to inherit the house."

"Oh, don't be so hard on her. How can you say that?"

"I can say it because it's true. But she's an excellent housekeeper, so who's complaining?"

They went upstairs to shower and change. They shared the same bathroom without embarrassment, although when they were naked, they were more conscious of the understanding at which they had silently arrived. Vincent stood shaving in front of the mirror, wrapped in nothing but a large bath towel. Charlotte undressed, folding her clothes on the black *papier-mâché* chair. She was small-breasted, "thin as a wire," as Vincent put it, but elegant in her leanness. Her nipples were as darkly red as damsons; her skin was still lightly tanned from her September holiday in Colorado; her pubic hair rose up like a downy powder puff.

Vincent changed into a cream silk Pierre Cardin shirt and a pair of gray Italian trousers. That was his idea of dressing casually. Charlotte wore a long, loose paisley dress by Geoffrey Beene, tied with a thin leather belt. Vincent kissed her on the cheek and said, "Well, the picture of chic."

Charlotte kissed him back. "I couldn't possibly disgrace your sacred ancestral home in my green jeans and my Fruit-of-the-Loom T-shirt."

They went downstairs again to play some music and finish their drinks. They were about to go to the kitchen to see about supper when the telephone rang. Charlotte picked it up and then handed it to Vincent. "It's for you. It's Mrs. Miller."

"Mrs. Miller?" Vincent asked, standing up to disentangle the telephone cord.

"Oh, Mr. Pearson, I didn't mean to trouble you, but it's Ben."

"What's the matter, Mrs. Miller?"

"He was all right when I first got home. He was real quiet. He was having his TV dinner and watching the *Dean Martin Comedy Hour*. But then he spilled his dinner all over himself and all over the floor, and he's acting so *strange*, Mr. Pearson, he's acting so *strange*. I don't know what to do."

"Did you call the doctor?"

"I left a message on his recording machine. I told him it was urgent."

"Well, listen, Mrs. Miller," Vincent said reassuringly, "I'll come right over. He's not having any difficulty breathing, is he? He doesn't look like he's choking or anything like that?"

"He's acting strange, that's all. I can't even begin to tell you."

"You hold on, Mrs. Miller. I'll be right there."

He put down the phone. Charlotte asked, "What's wrong? She sounded really distraught."

"She says Ben is acting strange. I'd better get over there and see what's wrong."

"Do you want me to come with you?"

Vincent went to the hall chest, opened the deep middle drawer and took out one of the thick Arran sweaters that were always stored there in case a weekend guest felt like a walk. He tugged it over his head and said, "I won't be long. Why don't you start supper? There's a case of Beaune in the cupboard next to the larder; open a bottle and help yourself."

"The Stepford Wives strike again," Charlotte complained. "What is it about Connecticut that turns perfectly sane and sensitive men into boorish tyrants over women?"

Vincent kissed her, then walked across the driveway and climbed into his Bentley. His hair was still slightly wet from his shower and his scalp tingled in the cold. He drove back through the gates and down to the main road.

He switched on the radio, catching the end of the news: ". . . said a second body discovered late this afternoon in a storm drain at Oyster River Point had been mutilated in exactly the same way and there was every reason to believe the perpetrator in both cases was one and the same. . . ."

He switched the radio off. On his left, next to a small, run-down trailer park and a gas station, fenced off from the road with a low, peeling picket fence, was the one-time restaurant Mrs. Miller had lived in for the past eleven years, following Ben's accident. Vincent's headlights swung across the shabby boarded front, the overgrown yard, the rusting tables and chairs that had been sitting at the side of the restaurant ever since it closed. There was still a faded sign on the door reading "The Copper Kettle" in fancy Gothic lettering.

Vincent parked the car and climbed out. A dog was barking over by the trailer park. In the nearest trailer, someone was watching television with the volume turned up to Cataclysmic. Mr. Dunfey probably; Vincent had met him once. Deaf as a wall but wouldn't admit it.

He went up the uneven wooden steps and knocked at Mrs.

Miller's door. She answered almost immediately, wearing a long flowered apron and looking white and worried.

"I'm so thankful you came," she told him. "I had a call from the doctor not more than a minute ago. He was over at Washington; he's going to get here as soon as he can."

Vincent stepped into the house. It was crowded with cheap furniture, the walls papered with red and white Regency stripes. There was a musty brown smell common to all really old houses, mingled with the sourer undertones of food, cigarette smoke and bedsore liniment. There were wheelchair ramps built over the steps that led down to the kitchen and up to the living room. The downstairs toilet door was half ajar, and Vincent could see the chromium handrails installed for Ben Miller's use.

"He's in here," Mrs. Miller said. "He's no better. He was sick a minute ago. I'm worried he's going to choke himself."

Ben Miller was sitting in a wheelchair in the middle of the living room, his head arched back, his neck swollen. The room was suffocating with the smell of vomit, and there was a plastic washbasin on the floor, full of bleachy water.

Ben was nearly twenty-seven, but eleven years in a wheelchair had given him the appearance of a large, malformed child. His hair was spiky and scruffy, he was badly shaved, and most of his front teeth were missing from eating endless candy bars. His eyes were closed now, and he was gargling in the back of his throat.

"Has he been like this all the time?" Vincent asked.

Mrs. Miller twisted her apron with worried hands. "He doesn't open his eyes, but he keeps on talking, saying things. I don't know what they mean. Every now and then he hits out. Mr. Pearson, I don't know what to do for him. I don't know what's wrong."

Vincent stepped forward cautiously and looked at Ben more closely. The invalid was muttering to himself, occasionally twitching his head. His eyes were fluttering under his eyelids as though he were having a nightmare.

"Ben?" Vincent said. He touched Ben's shoulder. "Ben? Can you hear me? This is Vincent Pearson."

Ben suddenly thrashed wildly at the air with both arms, lurching forward so violently he almost toppled out of the wheelchair. Vincent caught his shoulders, but Ben twisted away from him and then hunched himself forward, his head buried under his hands.

"They gah!" he babbled. "They gah! They gah!"

"Ben! Please! It's Momma!" begged Mrs. Miller. She knelt down beside him, trying to pry his intertwined fingers apart and lift his head. "Ben, listen to me; nothing's going to hurt you. Nothing's going to get you."

"They gah! They gah-gah!" he repeated, his voice muffled.

"Help me get his head up," Vincent said. He took hold of Ben's wrists, and gradually, using almost all his strength, he managed to tug Ben's hands apart. Then he braced his thigh against the back of the wheelchair and levered Ben into a sitting position.

Ben's face was purple and contorted; his tongue was hanging out, his eyes rolling madly.

"Ben," wept his mother. "Ben."

"They gah, they gah," he spluttered, twisting around in his chair and clutching at his mother's dress.

"Ben, Ben, Ben," crooned Mrs. Miller, tears running down her cheeks. She looked up at Vincent, her distress so intense she couldn't speak. Vincent held on to Ben's contorted torso as firmly as he could, although Ben was shuddering and writhing so violently it was almost impossible to prevent him from sliding progressively downward in his chair. His thin, helpless legs were folded under his bulky body like broken coat hangers.

For nearly five minutes Vincent and Mrs. Miller hung on to him, wordless, while he battled against demons no one else could see.

"They're guh—they're bah—they're *bah*!"

"Ben," wept his mother.

He twisted his neck around and stared at her in catatonic fury. "They're back!" he foamed. "They're back! They're *baaaaack*!" He sounded as if he were tearing shreds of flesh from the back of his throat.

"What's he *saying*?" Mrs. Miller pleaded to Vincent. "For pity's sake, what's he saying?"

"They're back, they're back, they're back!" Ben garbled. His hands beat a furious tattoo on the arms of the wheelchair. "Oh, God, save me, they're back! Don't let them get me! Please, Momma, don't let them get me!"

Suddenly he flung his head back, and his spine locked in a rigid curve, so rigid that Vincent was unable to straighten him. Ben clenched his teeth until blood ran down on either side of his mouth; his body began to shudder as if he were on the point of spontaneous combustion. There was a moment of utter convulsion; then he began to shake his head frantically from side to side, faster and faster, flinging blood and sputum about like a mad dog.

"Oh, Momma, I'm so frightened! Oh, Momma, oh, God, *I'm so frightened!*" Then, wretchedly, he wet himself, a subdued fountain that poured through his gray track-suit trousers and down his thighs.

At last his tremors began to subside. After a while he dropped into a shallow, restless coma, his eyelids twitching, his muscles jerking, his breathing rough, labored and intermittent.

Cautiously Vincent released him and stood back. Mrs. Miller got to her feet, too, and stood there watching her son in perplexity and anguish. Every now and then he flailed one of his arms and growled unintelligibly. Whatever phantoms were pursuing him through the dark corridors of his unconscious mind, they were terrifying and relentless, and they wouldn't let him escape.

"They bah . . ." he muttered.

Vincent helped Mrs. Miller carry the limp figure through to the bedroom on the opposite side of the hallway. There was a narrow bed with a yellow candlewick spread, a painted bureau and a bedside locker with a fringed lamp on it. Beside the bed was a neat stack of recent *Playboy* magazines. Mrs. Miller might have been modest and religious, but she could hardly deny her paralyzed son a look, at least, at what his accident had taken away from him.

He had been up on the roof of the Parker house, nailing shingles. The ladder had slipped, and he had fallen like a swimmer, headfirst, arms outstretched, straight onto the concrete sidewalk. The surgeons had been sure he was going to die. He had told his mother often enough that he should have died. He had also told her he would have preferred to have been more seriously brain-damaged so he could have spent the rest of his life contentedly smiling at the ceiling, oblivious to how much he was missing.

They laid him on the bed. Although Mrs. Miller was shaking, she unbuttoned the cuffs of her blouse, rolled up her sleeves and set about tugging off Ben's track-suit pants so she could bathe him. Vincent helped her. He knew she needed to do something practical and matter of fact to help herself calm down. She brought a bowl of soapy water and a washcloth and wiped Ben's bony, wasted legs with the deftness of one who has done it many times before.

"He's had a lot of bad turns since the accident," she said. "He never had them before; only childish ones, like the boogeyman and wolves in the cupboard. But since the accident, he's always having them."

"Not as bad as this, though?"

"Never as bad as this."

Vincent helped her push Ben's legs into a fresh pair of pajama trousers. She drew the blanket over him and laid a trembling hand on his forehead to see if he were running a fever.

"He don't seem too bad now. He seems to have settled."

Vincent watched Ben dozing. "What kind of bad turns?" he asked.

"Like nightmares almost, except that he's awake. Some to do with trying to walk, of course. But others, too. Real strange things that he can't explain. So scary, some of them, that he has to sit up in his wheelchair all night because he's afraid to go to sleep just in case the nightmare gets him when he can't protect himself."

"What did the doctor say about them?"

Mrs. Miller picked up the bowl of water. "I guess we could leave him now," she said. "He must be exhausted with all that shouting and twisting about."

Vincent followed her through to the kitchen. She emptied the bowl into the sink and then rinsed the sink with scalding water.

She said, as she turned off the faucet, "The doctor told me that people who nearly die—the way Ben did when he fell off that roof—well, sometimes they get this kind of second sight. Do you know what I mean? Because they've actually died, because they've actually gone beyond the end of their life, they've seen what it's really like when you pass away."

Vincent looked at her for a moment. "And that's what gives them these waking nightmares?"

"Seems like. They can't tell for sure. You have to die yourself to tell for sure."

"Well, that doesn't sound like a very encouraging commercial for the afterlife, does it?"

"No, no," Mrs. Miller said. "It's not the afterlife itself that gives them the turns. Dr. Serling said that most patients who come out of a coma start weeping because they didn't make it to the other side, and that they spend the rest of their lives yearning for death because they've seen for themselves how beautiful it is."

"What does give them turns, then?"

Mrs. Miller busily wiped the pine-topped kitchen table. "What gives them turns is what they've learned about the world and what's in it. That's what gives them turns."

"I don't understand."

"Well, I don't suppose anyone does," Mrs. Miller sighed. "Has Ben ever described them to you, these turns?"

She shook her head. "He says he can't. He says he doesn't want to. But I remember one night about two years ago when things were really bad and he couldn't sleep, *wouldn't* sleep rather, and he begged the doctor for Benzedrine to keep him awake. I asked him then what was wrong and he said it was nightmares and daydreams both, except that they never seemed like dreams at all; they seemed like they was real. Only somehow they wasn't real, either."

She paused, slowly wiping her hands on her apron, and then said, "It was like seeing the world for the first time, he told me. He said, 'Momma, there's so much evil in the world, and everybody walks past it like it was invisible or something.' He said his accident had given him special spectacles, if you know what I'm trying to say. Before the accident, he could sit in a room and it seemed like it was full of his friends. But afterwards he could see there were devils in the room, too, and evil people, and spirits so lewd he wouldn't describe them, not to anybody. And yet all his friends were still sitting there unconcerned, like they couldn't see nothing."

They heard a car outside, then a door slammed.

"That should be Dr. Serling now," Vincent said.

Mrs. Miller held his arm. "You know that sometimes I can be sharp, Mr. Pearson. Sharper than I mean to be."

Vincent patted her hand. "You don't have to worry about that, Mrs. Miller. You're the best housekeeper in Litchfield County. Probably in the whole state."

"Thank you anyway for coming down to help me so prompt," she told him. "And listen, all that stuff about the special spectacles and the devils and such, please don't repeat it. Ben finds it difficult enough as it is to make any friends around here. If they thought he was deranged as well as crippled . . . well, he'd no doubt lose the two or three friends he does have."

There was a brisk knock at the front door.

"I won't repeat it," Vincent promised. He kissed her cheek. "Now I'd better get out of Dr. Serling's way, and yours, too. And there's a sirloin waiting for me back at the house. If there's anything you need, though, during the night, don't you be worried about calling."

Mrs. Miller said, "God bless you."

They were simple enough words of thanks, and yet there was an unusual inflection in her voice, which, as he drove home afterward, made him frown at himself in the rearview mirror.

"*God* bless you," she had said. As if she were trying to make certain he wasn't blessed by anyone or anything else.

Six

West Haven, December 13

Captain Hoskins led the way to the morgue, his large bottom moving busily, one side of his crumpled shirttail hanging out. "My first thought was a surgeon," he said. "One of your high-class tit-reshapers gone crazy. That does happen, you know. They work under a lot of strain, these people, and they get to think of the human body with contempt, do you know what I mean? Like when you and I look at a car, we see the shiny outside of it, but what does an auto mechanic see? He sees rust and dirt and wires and junk, and that's the way these surgeons look at the human body."

Jack Smith silently followed Captain Hoskins down the long, waxy-floored corridor, his head bowed in frustration. One skinned corpse per working week was quite sufficient, so far as he was concerned. Now the West Haven police had found another, on the beach, and from Captain Hoskins' preliminary descriptions, it sounded even worse than the body they had fished out of the Nepaug Reservoir. What was worse, he couldn't even offer Captain Hoskins any educated guesses as to who might have killed and skinned these people.

He had been unable to find any clues at the Nepaug Reservoir; no footprints, no tire tracks, no clothing fibers, no drops of blood. No one had come forward to say he had witnessed anything suspicious; no hunchbacks dragging sacks through the night; no screams; no dark, mysterious limousines.

But somebody had picked up a twenty-three-year-old from the University of Connecticut at Storrs, a graduate student named Karl Madsen, while he was hitchhiking from Canaan, where his parents lived, to Storrs. And that somebody, or somebodies, had taken Karl Madsen to someplace unknown and stripped him completely of his outer skin and left him floating in the Nepaug Reservoir. The medical examiner had said he had never seen anything like it, ever. Only the epidermis had been removed, with consummate skill, and that was like peeling the rice paper off the back of an almond cookie without tearing the paper and without disturbing a single crumb of the cookie.

And now here was another.

Captain Hoskins said, "The seagulls were at him when he was found, so it's kind of hard to tell what he was like when he was dumped. But there isn't any question, somebody skinned him, and skinned him alive."

"What makes you think that?"

Captain Hoskins pushed open a swinging door marked, "Police Mortuary." "I don't know. It was something to do with the way the blood was clotted. Like, wherever the seagulls hadn't been able to get at him, he was one huge scab. I don't know. You'll have to ask the doctor."

They entered the wide, tiled, echoing mortuary. There was a strong smell of industrial disinfectant, and another smell, sweetish and sickly, that no amount of scrubbing and disinfecting could conceal. It was instantly recognizable to anyone who ever fought in a war, or worked in a hospital, or opened up the trunk of an abandoned car and discovered a week-dead body.

A young morgue assistant with spiky hair and outsized rubbers came out of the office to meet them. He wore glasses taped with bandage, and there was a red spot on the end of his nose.

"You want to see the guy with no skin on?" he asked.

"If you'd be so kind," Captain Hoskins replied with exaggerated Oliver Hardy courtesy.

The assistant walked across to the storage wall, where the remains of those who had recently died in West Haven in violent or suspicious circumstances were evenly chilled at two degrees C. He rolled out one of the middle drawers and said, "Help yourself. Hope you didn't eat breakfast."

Jack needed only one quick look. The body was a raw, garish scarlet, just like the corpse of young Karl Madsen. There were no eyes; the gulls had taken those. The mouth was stretched back in a hideous, toothy smile.

"Okay, roll him away," Captain Hoskins ordered.

They left the mortuary and walked out across the parking lot toward Captain Hoskins' car. It was a windy, damp morning, the leaves clinging in the puddles and the clouds moving past quickly and silently. Captain Hoskins, buttoning his sheepskin jacket, said to Jack. "This is going to be a weird one, believe me, and if you and I can't come up with something, the shit's going to fly. If there's one thing Commissioner Neuman doesn't want, it's 'The Connecticut Cutter.'"

"You didn't pick up any clues at all?" Jack asked.

Captain Hoskins replied, "No blood, no footprints, no fingerprints, no hair samples, no fabric fibers, no nothing. Just the same as yours."

Jack lit a cigarette, and blew smoke into the wind. "The question I keep asking myself is, why now?"

"What do you mean, 'why now'?"

"Well, suddenly somebody starts abducting young men and peeling their skin off. I mean, why now?"

"Search me. Everybody has to start sometime. You could ask that selfsame question about anything you like. Why did you join the police department on the day you did? Why did everybody suddenly decide to vote for Ronald Reagan last year? Why did Columbus decide to sail to America in fourteen ninety-two?"

"But that's exactly the point I'm making," Jack said. "I joined the department on the day I did because of specific reasons: because of my age, because of the length of the course at the police academy, because I wanted to take Nancy on vacation to Key West before I actually started duty. The same goes for the people who voted for Ronald Reagan, and for Christopher Columbus' decision to set sail. There were reasons why these things happened when they did, and there's a reason why these young men were murdered when they were."

Captain Hoskins thrust his hands into his jacket pockets and looked away. Jack knew the captain from way back. Hoskins didn't put any faith in theorizing or lateral analysis. He preferred clues that could be seen, and touched and held up in a court of law, a label dangling from them marked "Exhibit A."

"If we can answer 'why now,' we should be able to answer 'why,' Jack went on. "And if we can answer 'why,' we should be able to answer 'who.'"

" '*Who*' is a total fruitcake, that's who," Captain Hoskins said. "A genuine, certified product of the *Allen Street Bakery*."

"Well, you're probably right. But he has incredible skill, no matter how crazy he is. Do you know what the coroner at Hartford told me? He said the killer even took the skin off Madsen's balls, like tomatoes. Can you imagine that?"

"I wish to hell I couldn't."

They agreed to keep in touch with each other. Captain Hoskins drove off to his headquarters; Jack climbed into his Volkswagen Passat and drove toward Litchfield County and the small town of Harwinton, which was home. The sight of the body in the West Haven morgue had depressed and unsettled him, but it had also given him a lot more to think about. He realized now that the homicide at Nepaug Reservoir wasn't a single, isolated killing. It wasn't a case of gruesome curiosity, a sadistic experiment to see what a human body looked like stripped of its skin or to find out how much a man would scream when flayed alive. No, it had been done for a purpose, and the purpose had a pattern, even though so far the murderer had struck only twice. Once meant random; twice meant a reason. And no matter how much he prayed it wouldn't happen again, Jack had a feeling, born of dull professional certainty, that it would.

Something must have changed in the murderer's life to trigger him off like this. It wasn't just a change in locality. Jack had checked with the FBI computers in Washington, going clear back to 1908, when records were first kept, and learned that not one person in the whole country had been found dead by having been skinned alive. The only historical parallels he had been able to discover were the use of human skin during the Middle Ages for the binding of books on necromancy, and the flaying of Jewish prisoners in concentration camps during the war so their skin could be used for lampshades, cigarette cases and other ornaments. Perhaps the only pertinent clue to be found in history was that those who had skinned other people seemed to have done so not for the cruelty of it, but because they actually *wanted the skin*. They displayed another characteristic too: an attitude of complete superiority over their fellow human beings. They had taken the skins because they regarded their victims as nothing more than animals, their hides as trophies.

Jack reached home shortly after lunch. The wind was calmer now, the puddles nothing more than dark stains on the sidewalk. He turned into Torrington Park, a small development of six new houses in a landscaped dead end, a kind of unglamorous *Knot's Landing* with tricycles in the roadway, washing flapping in the backyards and the next-door kids slowly and greasily dismantling a jacked-up Imperial Le Baron in the front driveway. Jack parked in front of his house, the second from the end. He could see Nancy in the living room, talking to her friend Pat Lerner. He hadn't seen Pat in a while; and he thought it darkly appropriate that she should have turned up in a week so crowded with malignant happenings. Apart from being a grade-school teacher, and an obsessive macramé-maker, Pat was a "sensitive." She could read fortunes (tea leaves or Tarot); she could contact dead relatives (although they rarely seemed to say anything sensible), and she could predict the weather by listening to the chirruping of crickets. Jack and Nancy had known her for so long, however, that it never occurred to them that Pat's spiritual sensitivity was anything else but a rather clever knack, like being able to play the accordion, or juggle with oranges.

Jack smiled and waved; Nancy came to open the door for him. She was small and pretty and brightly blonde, and Jack absolutely adored her voice because she always sounded as if she were about to burst into tears, even when she was at her happiest. She worked mornings at the Harwinton Grade School, teaching kindergarten. He loved her very straightforwardly; he had never had to lie to her about anything except once, three years ago, when he had disarmed a man in Washington Depot who was threatening his wife and children with a shotgun. If Nancy had ever found out what he had done that day, she would never have let him go back to work again.

"You're early," she said, kissing him. She was wearing jeans and a blue-checkered shirt—what he called her "hayseed" look. "Pat came over to read my fortune."

Jack hung up his coat in the hall. The house wasn't large, but Nancy kept it neat. There was a natural-stone fireplace with glass ornaments on the mantel and a reproduction of William

Ranney's "Pioneers" hanging above. There were horse brasses and an aquarium and a walnut antique-style dining suite.

"Foretelling the future again, hey?" Jack asked Pat, rubbing his hands to warm them. "Do I get new squad cars this fiscal year?"

Pat shook her head. "So far all I've turned up for Nancy is a long sea voyage, an unexpected letter and a new husband."

"Well, that's an encouraging start," Jack smiled, sitting down in his favorite armchair. "When do I leave?"

Pat was kneeling in front of the coffee table, dealing out cards. She was a thin woman with long, dark, braided hair and a sharp, almost Red Indian profile, although she was Jewish. Her husband sold Pontiacs. She busied herself with every neighborhood charity she could lay her hands on, as well as the business of everyone in Harwinton under seventy and still capable of adultery, or at least of being suspected of adultery.

"I'm using new cards today," she said. "Usually I use the Tarot, but today I decided to try out Mademoiselle Lenormand's pack."

Jack leaned over. "Could I see those?" He picked up two or three cards and examined them. One showed a painting of stars shining in a deep night sky and a rhyme promising that "A chance of luck befalls tonight." Another showed a golden crucifix with the warning that "A cross weaves pain, historically sad."

"I've never seen these before," he said.

"Do you want me to tell your fortune?" Pat asked.

Nancy came back into the living room and said, "Would you like some coffee? Pat and I were just about to have some."

"Sure. I might as well have a last cup before your new husband moves in."

"The cards didn't really say that," Nancy told him, sitting next to him on the arm of the chair and putting an arm around his shoulders. "Pat's only trying to stir up marital discord. It's her favorite hobby. That and the Heart Foundation, of course."

Quickly Pat laid the thirty-six cards out on the coffee table, four rows of eight and one row of four. "This is you, the Cavalier, card number twenty-eight. Your immediate fortune is represented by the cards closest to you; the other cards have a lesser influence on you, depending on how far away they are."

Jack inspected his cards carefully. "What's this? A wheat field? I'm going to give up being a cop and take up farming?"

"Well, that doesn't mean anything much," Pat said. She looked the cards over and frowned; then suddenly she gathered them all up.

"What's the matter?" Jack asked. "I don't have any fortune?"

"I set it out wrong, that's all."

"Well, come on, try it again. I want to see whether I get those cars or not."

Nancy said, "Sounds like the coffee's ready," and went off to the kitchen. After a moment she called, "Would you like some cookies? We have pecan chip, chocolate chip or coconut."

"I'm watching my figure," Pat called back as she shuffled the cards and then dealt them out again. "It's not getting any thinner, but I'm watching it."

Jack shifted forward in his chair. "Well now, what do the mystic cards have to say this time? Hey, look, I'm still going to be a farmer. You didn't shuffle them well enough."

"I shuffled them," Pat protested. "Jack, I swear I shuffled them."

"They're all the same. They're all exactly the same."

Nancy came in with a tray. "Maybe that's what your fortune is no matter which way you shuffle them. There are more things in heaven and earth, Horatio."

"Horatio?" asked Pat, looking up in surprise. "Is that what you call him?"

"It's a quotation," Nancy told her.

"Well, lookit, I'm going to be a farmer. That's what the cards predict, and that's all there is to it," Jack said. "And I'd better hurry this cup of coffee because they want me back over at Bristol by two."

Pat said, "Jack, this card doesn't mean you're going to be a farmer."

Jack looked at her. Her voice had been unexpectedly stark.

"It's not bad news, is it?" he asked, smiling.

"There's a scythe on this card. There, look, resting against the wheat. And the interpretation is, *'Where the scythe is bare, that's where danger stalks. Beware of strangers, because they can hurt you.'*"

Jack set his cup of coffee on the table. "Pat," he said. "I'm a policeman, not a mail carrier, or an insurance salesman. I spend fifteen hours of every day dealing with strangers who can hurt me. That's not news. That's not even a prediction."

Pat was relentlessly solemn. "You must be careful of knives and sharp objects. Unless you watch out, somebody is going to cut you, quite seriously."

Jack said nothing for a time; then he picked up the card with the picture of wheat on it and examined it closely. Putting it back on the table, he asked, "What do the rest of the cards say?"

"They're not good cards," she told him. "Maybe the vibes are wrong. Maybe they're not *your* vibes at all. You haven't been close to any really bad criminals recently, have you?"

"Only my accountant."

"Please, Jack, don't make a joke of it."

He picked up his coffee again and swallowed two hot mouthfuls. Nancy was always nagging him for gulping his coffee too quickly. "I went to see a cadaver this morning," he said.

"A cadaver? You mean a murder victim?"

"That's right."

"And did this . . . cadaver's death have anything to do with knives? Or something sharp?"

"I can't tell you that, not at the moment. It's still confidential. I haven't even talked to the commissioner yet, although I expect to soon."

Pat let her finger wander to the next card, the card that was positioned directly above the Cavalier's head. Number VII, the Serpent. A poisonous green snake, coiled on a rock. The card warned: "Vile is the serpent who lulls with a bite . . . flee every moment she turns on the charm. . . ."

"What does that mean?" Jack asked.

"It means that you have to be wary of a very cunning and alluring woman," Pat replied. "She will seem to be seductive but in fact she will be out to do you great harm, even to kill you."

Jack glanced at Nancy and then said, "Go on. What about this one on my left? The owls sitting in a tree."

"Grief," Pat said.

Nancy interrupted, "I had that card and you said it meant a long sea voyage."

"From you, the card was far away. That means a voyage. But from Jack, look, it's very close. That means grief."

"Anything else?" Jack asked. "I mean, just in case I start to feel cheerful?"

"Below you, here, the Mountain," Pat pointed out. "That signifies that somebody is lying in wait for you, that you will have a very difficult time in the next few weeks, and that just when you believe you have achieved what you set out to achieve, just when you think you have won, this 'Beast in His Lair' will strike out at you."

Jack finished his coffee and rubbed his hands slowly and thoughtfully. "Did you ever know any of this stuff to come true?" he asked Pat.

"This is only the sixth or seventh time I've used this particular deck," she said, "but all I can say is, it's alarmingly strong. It gives off a truly remarkable power."

"And you believe in it?"

"I don't see any reason not to. It's been used for well over a hundred years now, with a lot of success."

"Tried, proven, empirically evaluated success?"

Pat gathered up the cards. "There isn't any such thing, Jack. Not for the testing of cards or for the catching of criminals, not even for the baking of chocolate fudge cake."

"Wash your mouth out with soap and water," Jack teased her. "You're supposed to be watching your figure."

Pat was tucking the cards back into their box when one of them dropped to the floor. Jack reached down to pick it up. When he handed it back to her, he suddenly realized that his hand was full of blood. Blood was running freely down his sleeve, pumping out over his suit, the lemon-yellow carpet and the coffee table, all in the space of a few silent, shocked, horrified seconds. It took Jack a moment or two to realize what had happened. The edge of the fortune-telling card had sliced painlessly into the palm of his hand, just where the radius and ulnar arteries join, and his heart was busily pumping blood out of him at seventy jets a minute.

Nancy stared at the blood splattering across the coffee table; she couldn't understand where it was coming from. It seemed almost as if the ceiling had opened up and blood was raining from the sky. But then Jack yanked the tea cloth out from under the coffee cups, tipping cups and spilling coffee, and pressed it firmly against the palm of his hand. Instantly the cloth was soaked bright red, but the pressure of his thumb began to suppress the flow.

"Jack!" Nancy cried out. Pat dropped her cards and stared at him in horror.

"It's okay," he reassured them. "The edge of the card cut my hand, right into an artery. It's deep, but it's not long. All you have to do is fetch me a bandage from the first-aid kit, a large handkerchief and something like a pen or a pencil."

Pat watched in silence as Nancy bound Jack's hand with a bandage, then knotted a handkerchief over the wound and pushed a pencil through it so she could turn it around and around, tightening it as a tourniquet.

"That should hold it," Jack said. Although he was calm, he was beginning to feel faint now, and unsteady from shock. "If you could drive me down to Emergency, I'm sure they can fix me up."

Both Nancy and Pat helped him into his Volkswagen and got in themselves. When Nancy reached across to buckle him into the passenger seat, he tried to smile bravely at her. "You look like death," she told him, kissing his cheek.

"I just cannot *believe* that a playing card did that," Pat said as they drove out of Torrington Park. "It seems unreal."

"It happens all the time," Jack told her. "You know the Silver Lake paper mill? About two years ago one of the workers lost half an arm, cut clean through by the edge of a large sheet of kraft paper. I mean by comparison, this is nothing."

"I'm so sorry," Pat said. "If I hadn't been doing those stupid cards. If I hadn't been so clumsy—"

"It's not your fault," Jack reassured her. "I should have watched what I was doing."

His hand was stitched and bound up at Harwinton Emergency. A young nurse with a wide smile, huge breasts and winsome freckles brought him a cup of coffee. The doctor gave him an antitetanus shot, sneezing uproariously as he did so and then taking out his handkerchief to worry at his nose. "The things you can catch, Sheriff, when you work in a hospital. You wouldn't believe it. And the classier the hospital, the classier the disease."

The doctor let him go after two hours. Nancy and Jack

dropped Pat off at her house and then turned into their own
driveway. Nancy had already called Deputy Norman Goldberg
at the Harwinton police headquarters and told him Jack would
be late.

"I think I could use a drink," Jack said as they opened the
front door and stepped into the hallway. The wall clock was
just chiming three.

"You know what the doctor said, no alcohol. It dilates the
arteries and starts up the bleeding again. How about some
coffee?"

"I'm awash with coffee."

They went into the living room. It looked as if someone had
been murdered there. Blood was sprayed all over the carpet,
the table, the chair. There were several bloody footprints as
well as squiggles of blood on the wall and tear-shaped drops on
the pale gold drapes.

"I don't know," Nancy sighed. "You've never been tidy,
have you? You can't even *bleed* tidily."

Jack put his arm around her and kissed her. "I'll call the
carpet cleaners right away. You know those people over at
Bristol? They cleaned all the blood out of Gilbert's carpet."
Gilbert Wagner, who lived about a mile away, had accidentally
taken off his left thumb with an electric knife while carving the
Thanksgiving turkey the year before.

Nancy picked up the bloody tea cloth and Pat's cards.

"Here's the card that cut you," she said and handed it across
to him.

Jack took it, holding it carefully between index finger and
thumb. On the back of the card there was a red pattern with a
drawing of a wide-eyed owl in the center. He turned it over. On
the front there was a picture of a wheat stalk, a scythe resting
against it. The bottom third of the card, which included the
blade of the scythe, was blotched with Jack's blood.

"*The scythe looms bare, danger stalks too. Of strangers
beware, they can harm you.*"

Jack turned the card around a couple of times, then shrugged
and handed it back to Nancy.

She said, "You don't think—uh—"

Jack shook his head. "It was an accident, that's all."

"Well, Pat's been right before."

"Right about what? Mrs. Piatkowski's dog catching distemper? A rainstorm on the day of the PTA Bring-and-Buy?"

"Yes, I know they were small things, but—"

"But what?" Jack demanded with a smile.

Nancy laid the card down on the sticky coffee table. "I don't know. But *something*. Something's going on. Something's going wrong. I can feel it. Can't you?"

Seven

New York, December 15

Cordelia Gray was waiting for him at a small table at the back of the restaurant. Her lipstick was assertively scarlet, and she wore a striking gray hat with a gray ostrich plume on it. The restaurant was pretty, with mirrored walls, pink tablecloths and glass vases full of freesias.

"I hope I'm not late," Edward said. When Cordelia offered him her hand, he was slightly surprised that she obviously expected him to kiss it. Closing his eyes, he did so.

"I have asked for champagne. I hope that wasn't too forward of me," she told him. Her perfume was slightly different today, but there was still something about it that made him feel heady and disturbed, as if he were sitting in a closed room while a snake slid sensuously up his trouser leg.

"Champagne's perfect," he said.

Cordelia smiled, tight-lipped. "Krug, nineteen seventy-three. For the price of one bottle, you could feed an entire Ethiopian family for a month."

Edward ran his hand through his hair. It had been windy outside on 60th Street. "Is that supposed to make me feel guilty?" he asked.

"Guilt is a complicated affair," Cordelia replied. "There are those who ought to feel guilty but don't, and there are those who feel guilty when they have no need to. Then, of course, there are those for whom the concept of guilt has no meaning whatsoever."

They ordered *potage du Père Tranquille*, a creamy lettuce soup, on Cordelia's recommendation. "It is named after a mysterious capuchin monk," she said. "But it is also named for the drowsiness-lettuce is said to create in those who eat it."

They followed this with grilled sea bass. "Very plain, excellent for the strength and perfect for the complexion." She wanted no dessert, only cheese and fruit, but Edward asked for crystallized chestnuts.

At the next table a party of executives from Cleveland was drinking heavily and laughing loudly. One of them was extolling the virtues of his new Mercedes-Benz. "So it's German. What's wrong with German? That doesn't mean they used your grandfather's hide to make the seat covers."

Cordelia smiled and sipped her champagne. "I am pleased that you came, Edward. If it hadn't been for you, I would have had to eat alone today, and I cannot bear to eat alone. It is almost like a punishment, don't you think? Each mouthful is a reminder that you have nobody with whom to share your meal."

"I'm growing used to it," he said.

"You live alone?"

"My girlfriend used to live with me. Then she upped and married someone else. Danny Monblat. Now she's Mrs. Laura Monblat, if you can imagine that."

"Laura Merriam would have sounded far more mellifluous."

"Yes, well," Edward muttered in resignation. "I think I've gotten over it now."

"Did you really love her?"

He looked up from his dessert. "Yes," he nodded, "I loved her."

"But you don't love her anymore?"

"I don't know. Even if I did, what difference would it make?"

"You think she's beautiful, though?"

"Yes, as a matter of fact, I do." He spooned up more chestnuts, wondering where all these questions were leading.

Cordelia ate her food in an extraordinary way. Edward had first noticed it when she had started to eat her sea bass, but of course he had been too courteous to remark on it. First she picked out a piece; then, as she lifted it to her mouth on the end of her fork, she cupped her other hand over it so that the food disappeared like a conjuring trick. After glancing at her several times during the course of the meal, he realized he never once saw her open her mouth and put a piece of food directly in it.

She chewed oddly, too. Somehow, even though she didn't appear to be moving her jaws, her cheeks rippled. That was the only way Edward could describe it. He thought it would be rude of him to stare at her too closely, however. Perhaps she had false teeth, for all of her elegance and beauty, and found chewing difficult. After all, she must be at least—well, how old? Thirty-eight, forty? Maybe older. It wasn't easy to tell. Her skin was still as smooth as a young girl's; there were no wrinkles around her eyes. And yet there was an air about her that made him think he was sharing this table with a very much older woman. He looked at her again and realized with perplexity that he couldn't actually make up his mind as to what her age might be.

"So, Mrs. Danny Monblat," Cordelia said, fastidiously cutting herself a tiny slice of Brie.

"That's right," Edward said. He didn't really want to discuss it. It still hurt.

"And now you live quite alone?"

"The hermit of Wentworth Apartments."

Cordelia passed her hand over her mouth, swallowing the fragment of cheese she had just cut. As she did so, a small white morsel dropped from behind her hand onto her plate. Instantly she pinched it up between finger and thumb and conjured it back into her mouth.

She did it so quickly that Edward wasn't able to tell what had happened. Yet he had been left with an uncomfortable feeling that he had seen the morsel *twitch*, as if it were alive. He stared at her in hope of a gratuitous explanation, but she stared back at him as remotely and as blankly as ever with those eyes that were simply mirrors.

He cleared his throat. "Would it be impertinent of me to ask you the real reason you invited me to lunch?" he asked. "I mean, I know you're interested in having me help you rebuild your family's art collection. But it isn't a little bit to do with that Waldegrave picture, too, is it?"

"You are beautifully naive," she said, smiling. "Tell me, shall we go for a walk in the park and talk about the family collection?"

Edward finished his glass of sambuca. "Yes, I'd like that. As long as you don't mind the wind."

"The wind?" Cordelia laughed. "Why, I remember once I was out on a boat off Long Neck Point, and the wind—"

She stopped in mid-sentence. She stared at him with an expression he couldn't fathom. Caution? Fear? There was something curiously anxious about it. She lowered her eyes and said quietly, "The wind was very strong, you know. Almost gale force."

She paid the check in cash, he noticed, freshly printed fifties. Then they walked west to the park, against the wind, while grit and newspapers whirled through the air and smoke from hot-chestnut stands and bagel carts fled through the crosstown streets like cindery ghosts.

Cordelia held his hand as they strolled through the park. Joggers passed them with monotonous sneaker-slapping; children squealed and called for their mothers to watch them, sounding to Edward like distant sea birds. Three blacks passed with a ghetto blaster thumping out "Chaka Khan."

Cordelia said, "I hope you've decided to say yes."

Edward smiled. "I've thought about it very favorably. It sounds like an interesting job. I'm not sure I can spare the time away from the gallery, that's all."

"You could be hired out to me for a while. I'm sure Mr. Pearson wouldn't object to that. I would pay him for the temporary loss of your services."

"Well, as long as he doesn't mind . . . then yes, I'm interested."

"And the Waldegrave?" she asked.

Edward squeezed her hand. He felt oddly lightheaded, as if he had been breathing laughing gas. It was probably nothing more than the two bottles of Krug champagne they had managed to drink between them, followed by the wind and fresh air. "I'm sure I can persuade Vincent to sell you the Waldegrave. He's stuffy and traditional, that's all. He should have been alive in the eighteen eighties, not the nineteen eighties."

"You don't live far from here, do you?" Cordelia asked. Her voice sounded as if it was reaching him from the other end of a tunnel. "Wentworth Apartments, wasn't that it?"

"That's right. You know the building where they shot *Rosemary's Baby*? Well, it's right next door to that."

"I would love a cup of hot tea," she told him, pressing close to his arm. "Do you have tea?"

"China, if you like China. *Lapsang-Souchong.*"

"That's my favorite."

They left the park and caught a cab outside the Plaza. The driver thought he was Enrico Caruso, or at the very least, Mario Lanza, and sang "Vesti la Giubba" in a wavering baritone all the way to the Wentworth Apartments on West 65th. Cordelia sat close to Edward, her black-gloved hand holding his left arm with possessive tightness. He smiled at her from time to time and wondered why he felt so detached and woozy.

When he paid the fare, the taxi driver peered at the twenty-cent tip as if an overflying pigeon had dirtied the palm of his hand. "Don't you like opera?" he demanded.

"I love it," Edward told him. "That's why you get only twenty cents."

Cordelia, waiting on the sidewalk in her long back overcoat, the lapels lifted up to enclose her face like the petals of a black tulip, smiled at Edward and reached out her hand. He thought he had been rather witty. The taxi driver grumbled, "Asshole," and screeched away from the curb.

They pushed their way together through the heavy glass and mahogany doors of the Wentworth Apartments, into the hushed and dusty lobby. Above them, a huge glass chandelier hung like the transparent skeleton of a giant spider that had died in its own web. The thin winter-afternoon sunshine barely penetrated the windows, which were leaded to resemble the windows of a Gothic castle. There were even shields on the wall, bearing coats of arms.

Edward said, "It's incredibly pretentious, I'm afraid. But my grandfather bought an apartment here in the thirties and we kept it on."

Cordelia stood still for a moment and looked around, breathing in the musty air. "I like it," she said. "It reminds me of . . . I don't know. I can't remember what it reminds me of. But I know I have been somewhere like this before. Somewhere almost exactly like this."

"Perhaps you've been *here* before," Edward suggested, a

little uncertainly. "It's not the most memorable block of apartments ever constructed."

"Perhaps," she agreed.

They walked across the long lobby to the elevators, which were embellished with bronze doors bearing heraldic devices, lions rampant and crowned helms. Edward drew back the gate so she could step inside.

She hesitated for a moment. "I haven't been too pushy with you, have I?" she asked, but it was plain by her intonation that she didn't expect any answer except "No."

"No," Edward said.

She held his left wrist, encircling it with black-leather fingers. "There are always times in life when we must allow destiny to carry us forward, wherever it wants to take us. We must never try to swim against the current."

Edward closed the doors and the elevator rose upward with a deep, subdued humming. Unlike most women, Cordelia didn't look once at the mirror in the back of the elevator car. She kept her eyes steadily on Edward.

"Do you wonder what kind of woman I am?" she asked. "A woman who insists on buying a young man lunch and then asks to be taken to his apartment for tea?"

"You want me to rebuild your art collection for you," Edward reminded her.

Cordelia said nothing for a moment, then laughed, baring her teeth. He noticed they were neither crooked nor false. In fact, they were original and perfect.

The elevator reached the seventh floor and quietly stopped. Edward opened the gates and they stepped out into the corridor. He walked a little way ahead, turning back now and again to make sure she was following. Each time, she gave him that strange smile. She was quite right, of course: he was wondering what kind of a woman she was. But he was far too flattered by her offer to bring the Gray collection together again and far too intrigued by her extraordinary claustrophobic eroticism to end this strange afternoon.

He reached his apartment, No. 797. He unlocked the door and then courteously stood back so she might enter first. Inside, it was warm and gloomy; Edward reached around the door and flicked the switch for the table lamps. One of the radiators on the far side of the living room was knocking loudly; it always did. Edward's grandfather had complained that it sounded as if the Count of Monte Cristo were imprisoned in the next apartment and was tapping on the pipes. The living room was steeped in brown. There were dark-brown velvet drapes, dark-brown mock-Stuart chairs and tables with twisty legs, a rug the color of dried tobacco leaves. Above the carved-oak fireplace hung a portrait of a man in a brown coat with a misshapen brown beret to match. The fireplace itself was home to a small collection of houseplants: two brown ferns, two knobby little cacti and a leprous yucca.

On the coffee table, the latest issues of art and design magazines were heaped in untidy stacks. A banjo leaned against one arm of the old-fashioned tapestry sofa. There were no flowers anywhere. Only ashtrays and empty wine glasses.

"Well, this is rather fine, but I can tell that a man lives here, on his own," Cordelia smiled.

Edward looked around, his hands self-consciously propped on his hips. "Yes, I suppose you're right. I rather miss having Laura here. All those little touches, like fresh-pressed table-cloths and bowls of potpourri. The last party I had, one of my friends *smoked* all my potpourri. He said it was better than Colombian gold."

Edward walked through to the kitchen and noisily opened up the pass-through to the living room. He filled the kettle and then scrabbled through the cupboard to find his small tin of *Lapsang Souchong*.

"If I were to rebuild your collection," he said, "when do you think you would want me to start?"

He looked out the pass-through, and when he saw Cordelia Gray, he slowly lowered his hands to his sides and stared at her.

She had taken off her long black overcoat. Now she had turned her back on him and was slowly and deliberately unbuttoning her tailored gray dress. She kept her hat on, her gray, plumed hat. Her dark hair was sharply and beautifully cut on the nape of her neck. With an easy movement, she let the dress slide from her hips, gathered it up and folded it over the arm of the sofa.

No words were spoken. She stood in the center of the room, her skin as white as an unprinted page; and just as he had fantasized, she wore black underwear. A black-lace bra, a black garter-belt, and sheer black stockings, with seams, sleekly encasing each long, slim leg. A tiny black *cache-sex*

barely covered her between her legs and was drawn tight with
black-braided silk between the cheeks of her white bottom.

She turned now and faced him. He could see the dark-red
smudges of her nipples through the lace of her bra. The
feathers of her hat nodded like funeral feathers in the dimness
of the afternoon.

"This is no time to talk about art," she said in a whispery
but clear voice.

Edward said nothing but momentarily ducked his head aside
and let out a short "Hah!" of surprise and pleasure; and then he
smiled at her, bashful and gratified and more than amazed at
what was happening to him.

She reached behind and unhooked her bra; it dropped from
her shoulders, baring small, rounded breasts. Then she
unfastened her garter-belt and peeled off her stockings. She
was naked now, except for the small black triangle that
concealed her sex.

"Bring me a knife," she said.

"A knife?"

"Just bring me a knife. The longest and sharpest knife you
have."

Edward frowned. Then he obediently opened the cutlery
drawer and took out his Sabatier carving knife, ten inches of
carbon steel, sharpened and resharpened until it could cut
through bone. The kettle started to boil; he switched it off.

Cordelia turned to greet him as he entered the living room.
Her eyes were challenging, but she stood with her arms by her
sides, making no attempt to conceal herself. Her breasts were
high and tight, almost like the breasts of a girl of sixteen,
although the nipples were wide and crimson-tinted, as if she
had taken a handful of strawberries and crushed them against
each one. Her stomach was slightly rounded, which attested to
at least one childbirth, but there were no blemishes on her body
whatever. She was strangely flawless, as if she had been
molded from bisque porcelain.

"Bring the knife here," she whispered. Edward approached
her, hesitantly holding up the knife in his right hand. Her
perfume seemed to be stronger than ever, and he found he
could hardly focus his eyes. Cordelia reached out and stroked
his cheek, running her fingertips lightly across his lips, around

his eyes, touching his forehead, his hair and the lobes of his ears. He could see her nipples rise.

"Now," she murmured, "you must cut the string that ties the prize."

She lowered her hands and held out the thin braided-silk tie that kept her *cache-sex* in place. Edward at last understood; without further hesitation, he slid the cold blade between a bare white thigh and the thin string of silk.

Cordelia half-closed her eyes. "Cut," she instructed him, so softly he wasn't sure he had heard her. There was the merest sizzle of steel on silk, and then her *cache-sex* dropped away. She had only the faintest fan-shaped covering of dark hair on her vulva, as if she were an adolescent girl who had only just started to grow it. Edward felt himself hardening, and he knew now that there was nothing he could do to resist her. It was like an extraordinary dream: a blurred and grainy vision of a scene he had once played out when he was sleeping but had long ago forgotten. He felt her fingers loosening the knot of his necktie; then the buttons of his shirt, slowly, one by one; and when his shirt fell to the floor, it seemed to float and whirl and crumple as if it were falling in slow motion.

Naked, time forgotten, the tea forgotten, he carried Cordelia to his bedroom. She was so light that she was as easy to carry as a child. He laid her down on the dark-blue satin bedspread and kissed her, tasting her perfume, her skin, exploratively at first but then with increasing urgency. She returned his kisses with a tongue so long it almost seemed she was licking the back of his throat, and as she did so, she gently scratched her long fingernails all the way down his stomach, stroking it tenderly.

Making love to Cordelia Gray was unlike anything Edward had ever experienced. She was yielding but cruel, continually biting at his neck and his nipples, continually scratching him, but then parting her thighs widely and wantonly, or twisting around so she could take him into her mouth, so deeply he couldn't imagine why she didn't choke.

She led him farther and farther away from safety and reality, out into a black, erotic sea, where she herself seemed to be able to swim with extraordinary skill but where Edward began to feel he was drowning.

It seemed to him as if whole hours went by. All he could hear were murmurs, kisses, the accompaniments of sliding satin and slippery skin. The room grew darker. He shuddered—lying on his back, Cordelia astride him—in the last possible climax he could manage. She leaned forward, her nipples softly touching his chest, and whispered, "Perhaps it's time for tea now." Then she left him.

"Mmm," he nodded. He rested his head on the pillow. He closed his eyes. He could hear the radiator clanking in the living room, and Cordelia walking around. He had never felt so content in his life. An excellent lunch, an afternoon in bed with the most demanding woman he had ever met, and now peace, and darkness, and a chance to sleep.

He thought briefly of Cordelia, of their lovemaking. His body was satisfactorily sore. The sensations she had given him had been stunning. There had been one moment, at the height of her first orgasm, when the inside of her vagina had literally *seethed*. Edward had never imagined anything like it.

He heard her come back into the bedroom. She sat down on the edge of the bed next to him and lightly touched his shoulder.

"Darling," she whispered, "are you asleep?"

"Mmmph," he replied without opening his eyes. "Not yet, but nearly."

"You must sleep," she murmured, touching his eyelids with her fingertips.

Edward slept, deeply and dreamlessly, sinking so far into unconsciousness that his breathing became shallow and his pulse rate slowed. Cordelia called "Edward?" once or twice, but after five minutes, she stood up and walked naked back into the living room.

She dressed quickly, not forgetting to pick up her discarded *cache-sex* and tuck it into her pocketbook. Before she left, she also picked up Edward's jacket, brushed it down and then systematically searched all his pockets. In the right-hand pocket she found his keys. In the left-hand pocket she found his maroon-leather address book. She leafed through it until she came across "Laura Kelly," with what must have been her family address, 2206 Maple Avenue, New Rochelle. Underneath, Edward had written, in far smaller letters, "Mrs. D. Monblat, 65 West 10th." Cordelia tore out the page, folded it once and put it in her pocketbook along with the keys.

She looked around to make sure she had left nothing behind. Then she left, closing the door softly.

Edward half-opened his eyes, raised from sleep by the strange impression that he was alone now, that something had gone wrong. He knew he should get up and entertain Cordelia, but somehow he felt paralyzed with tiredness; he simply couldn't summon up the energy to stir. He closed his eyes again and slept. It was six o'clock now, on a dark December evening, and outside his window, New York echoed and roared and bustled, two weeks to go before Christmas, nine shopping days left, and over on the opposite side of the park, children were clustered around the brightly lit windows of F.A.O. Schwarz, looking at the glittering fairy castle, and the toy railroad, and the smiling bear who flew around and around in his bright-yellow helicopter.

Cordelia Gray had taken Edward's keys and a page from his address book. But she had left him with four or five souvenirs in return.

As Edward slept, a small off-white maggot emerged from the warm, sweaty crevices around his testicles and slowly made its way up his hairy thigh, its brown-tinged, sightless head weaving from side to side. Soon it reached the crest of his flaccid penis where it rested against his leg. The maggot crawled over the top of it, and then underneath, until it found the crevice of his urethra. It waggled its way gradually inside and disappeared.

The maggot was soon followed by another, and another. A fourth maggot began the long, wriggling journey up his stomach to his chest, toward his slightly open mouth.

Still Edward didn't awaken. The carriage clock on his bedside table chimed seven. The last maggot finally reared itself up on Edward's lower lip and dropped silently into his mouth.

Eight

Bantam, December 14

It was dusk by the time Vincent reached Aaron Halperin's house, which sat on a dark and wooded hillside just outside Bantam, on the Litchfield road. Aaron lived in a rambling building that had once been part of an eighteenth-century coaching inn. It was dominated by a huge oak; as Vincent drove up to the house through the unkempt bushes, he saw the oak standing high above the rooftop, raising its branches to the sky like a soundlessly shrieking giant.

Vincent parked outside Aaron's studio, which was a long, low shed at the back of the house, lifted the two Johnsons out of the trunk and walked across to the lighted porch. There a blue pottery sign said "Halperin," and a notice underneath announced "*Ars Longa, Vita Brevis.*" Aaron translated that as "He who has protruding buttocks should avoid wearing small briefs." Vincent rang the old-fashioned doorbell and heard it jangle at the far end of the studio, where Aaron usually worked.

After a few moments, the door juddered open and Aaron appeared, his arms outstretched. "My wandering boy!" he cried. He was big and gingerbearded, with gold-rimmed glasses and a nose that looked as if it had been marinated in cherry brandy. He wore a white, floor-length apron streaked with scores of different colors: ultramarine and Alizarin crimson, Naples yellow and brilliant green, Terra Verte and lemon chrome. Aaron used his aprons rather than paint-rags, Vincent always used to say that instead of washing them, he ought to sell them as works of art.

"You're late," Aaron said. "But don't worry, I've still got

some wine left. Home-brewed. You can drink it or clean your
paintbrushes in it; it's just as effective for either purpose."

"I had a little trouble back at the house," Vincent said,
leaning the two Johnsons against Aaron's paint-spattered
worktable. "My housekeeper's son decided to throw a fit."

"Mrs. Miller? Her son? Isn't he crippled or something?"

"That's right. Mrs. Miller says he's never been the same
since he fell on his head. He keeps having nightmares; or
*day*mares, rather. He sees devils, and demons, and all kinds of
things."

"Phew," Aaron said. "That doesn't sound too happy."

He brought over a magnum-sized bottle of dark-red wine,
labeled *Bantam Beaujolais*, and poured out a generous glassful
for Vincent. Vincent sniffed it and remarked, "Well, an
interesting bouquet anyway."

Aaron finished his own glass of wine and splashed himself
another. "We don't call it bouquet around here; we call it
odor."

Vincent set down his glass, reached into his coat pocket for
his gold penknife and slit open the wrapping paper around the
Johnson paintings.

"These are really beautiful. You'll enjoy working on them.
They need a general cleaning more than anything else, but I
think the seascape could do with a little restoration around the
top left here. You can see that the paint's beginning to flake
quite badly."

Aaron held them up, one after the other. "They're good.
Two of the best Johnsons I've seen."

Vincent walked along the length of the studio while Aaron
examined the paintings more closely. Aaron's worktable ran
almost the whole length of the building and was crowded with
palettes, brushes, bottles of linseed oil and turpentine, gesso,
rolled-up canvases, glue, fixative and literally thousands of
tubes of oil paint in every color imaginable, mostly French and
British, all crumpled, squeezed-up and heaped together.

Beside the end window, which faced north, there were
fifteen or sixteen easels, each bearing a canvas Aaron was in
the process of restoring. Although he was recognized as one of
the finest restorers of nineteenth-century oil paintings in the
country, Aaron found it impossible to work on any one picture
for longer than seven or eight days at a stretch; for this reason,

he always kept at least a dozen jobs going at once so he could refresh himself by changing from a landscape to a nude, from a portrait to a still life, whenever he began to feel jaded.

Vincent picked up a small landscape by John Frederick Kensett and angled it so he could see it better. "Is this the one you're doing for Milòs?"

Aaron glanced up. "That's right; it's almost finished. It's a beauty, isn't it?"

"You said you were having trouble with the Waldegrave."

"Yes. You really should take a look at it. The dang-blang thing's driving me crazy. I'm beginning to wonder if it's worth restoring at all. You're going to spend five hundred dollars and wind up with a painting worth about five cents.. Maximum."

Aaron put down the Johnsons and walked around the end of the table toward one of the larger easels standing in the corner. Although the painting had been removed from its frame, it was enormous, five feet wide and three feet high. It was draped with an old green-velour bedspread, with fringes.

"First of all," Aaron said, beckoning Vincent over, "smell it."

Vincent moved nearer and cautiously sniffed. The air in the studio was so aromatic with paint and turpentine that he couldn't distinguish the smell at first, but eventually his nostrils sought it out. A thick, sweetish smell, like chicken skin that has decayed and gone green, only somehow more pervasive, more cloying.

"Jesus," he said. "That's terrible."

Aaron said, "You ain't seen nothing yet," and dragged the bedspread off the canvas. There it was: twelve white-faced people posing stiff, straight-backed and formal in a crimson room; black-suited and black-dressed; the men clasping their lapels with all the severe dignity of morticians; the women with their hands tucked together in their laps, two of them holding black-lace fans; the other caressing a small, dark creature that could have been a cat. Vincent had never been able to make out exactly what the creature was, and his grandfather had consistently refused to tell him, although he had always asserted that he knew. It might have been a rat, Vincent supposed, but it could have been nothing more than a black tangle of fur. A muff maybe, or a fox fur wrap.

The pose was the same, the room was the same, but the

faces had altered beyond recognition. The white paint was
crumbling away, making them appear decayed and leprous.
Some of them were so badly disfigured that it was impossible
to make out their facial features; noses had flaked off, eyes had
deteriorated into murky gray sockets. They had the appearance
of a family fatally and irrevocably diseased, a twelve-strong
company of death.

Vincent frowned and stared at the painting.

"It really does smell bad, doesn't it?" he commented.
Carefully he picked at one of the faces with a painter's spatula
and examined the paint under the light. "What causes this? Do
you have any idea at all?"

"I've never seen anything like it before in my whole
career," Aaron said. "Usually this kind of appearance is
associated with disintegrating canvas at the back, which
destroys the paint film on the front. But in this case, the canvas
is totally sound. I've examined the paint under the microscope,
and I've taken about twenty ultraviolet pictures of each face.
Sometimes you might get decomposition of the surface paint if
someone has painted over the original picture. As you know,
that happens pretty often with portraits. Someone puts a new
face on an old one, or changes the clothes, or the background
scenery. But all of this particular painting is completely
original."

"Did Waldegrave use some kind of unusual additive maybe?
Was there something he might have mixed into the paint that
has started to go bad?"

Aaron swilled the wine around his mouth, swallowed and
shrugged. "Occasionally that happens. I've come across
vegetable dyes, and ox blood. Gauguin used to mix some of his
yellows with turmeric. But this paint seems just like ordinary,
well-mixed, turpentine-based oil paint."

Vincent stared at the Waldegrave for a long time. There was
something about its rotting facelessness that depressed him,
made him feel uncomfortable. He lowered the bedspread over
it and turned around. "Is there anything else you can try?" he
asked.

"I've sent a small sample over to the laboratory at Hartford
for a complete analysis. But I don't think they're going to come
up with anything new. This painting of yours is falling to

pieces, and nothing I or anyone else can do is going to prevent it."

"Well, wait until you get the results from the lab."

"It's the goddam *smell*," Aaron complained. "Van Gogh won't even come in here. He thinks it's a skunk. And if I've been working on it, he won't let me stroke him until I've washed my hands." Van Gogh was Aaron's marmalade tom cat.

"Can't say that I blame him," Vincent remarked, sniffing at his own fingers.

"It's strange that it should have started to disintegrate so suddenly," Aaron said. "I mean, why *now*, all of a sudden? You've had that picture in the family for donkey's years, haven't you?"

"As far as I'm concerned, it's a relic. But my grandfather always insisted that we keep it, and keep it safe. He said it was like a talisman; it protected the family from evil."

"That doesn't sound like your grandfather. He wasn't a superstitious man, was he?"

Vincent shook his head. "I guess everybody has his one good-luck charm, though. A rabbit's foot or a four-leaf clover."

"Or a clove of garlic," Aaron added.

"You're right," Vincent said. "Damn, but that picture does look like an annual convention of vampires."

Aaron poured Vincent more wine, even though Vincent protested. "Aaron—it's very good. Plenty of body. Plenty of fruit. But I'm driving. And apart from that, I have to be back in New York tomorrow, early."

"It's too late. You've already drunk one glass. That means you're irrevocably condemned to a crushing hangover, and probably a drunk-driving charge thrown in."

Vincent lifted his hands in resignation. "In that case, Aaron, *prost*! And may your mother soon be happily married."

Aaron took the wine bottle by the neck and led the way through to the house. It was untidy, the house, but warm, with crackling log fires in the hearths. Scores of mellow old pictures hung on the walls, most of them Early American watercolors and framed Puritan samplers. Aaron's three daughters were playing checkers in the small side sitting room; his wife Marcia was baking cookies in the low-ceilinged kitchen; and his only son Michael was playing "Hunchback" on his computer. Aaron adored chaos, lots of people, and laughter.

"Come sit by the fire," he told Vincent. "Marcia's going to be bringing in those cookies pretty soon; it seems a shame to drive all the way up here and miss them. Did you ever taste hot Kinkawoodles?"

"I never did," Vincent smiled.

"Well, it's very interesting. Back in the eighteenth century, all those fussy New England ladies used to make up silly names for their cookies, just for the fun of saying them. There're Kinkawoodles, and Snicker Doodles, and Jolly Boys, and Rhyming Jacks."

"How did a nice Jewish boy from Newark, New Jersey, ever get so interested in the gastronomic history of the goyim?"

Aaron laughed. "Maybe if I eat enough goyish cookies, I'll get to turn into one. You know. Dr. Jekyllstein and Mr. Hyde."

Then Aaron turned serious. "About that painting again. I looked it up in the records of the Royal Academy in London; that's where it was first put on public display."

"That's right," Vincent nodded. He had seen for himself the discolored Royal Academy label that still adhered to the back of the canvas. In brownish ink, it certified inclusion of Waldegrave's "Family Portrait" in the summer exhibition of 1881, twelve years after the Academy had moved from the National Gallery in Trafalgar Square to its present location at Burlington House.

Aaron crossed the living room and brought over three old leather-bound volumes, which he spread out on the hearthrug. Vincent noticed that the toes of Aaron's shoes were speckled with thousands of tiny droplets of multicolored paints. "Here it is," Aaron said. "'Family Portrait,' by Walter John Waldegrave. Dimensions, sixty-two and a quarter inches by thirty-seven and a half inches. Oil. Painted February, eighteen eighty-three, at Northwood House, near Harrow."

"Anything else?"

"Nothing much. Waldegrave is listed in Duxford's *Biographies of the Notable Painters*, published in nineteen two by Blackie. Here we are: 'Walter Waldegrave, born March seventh, eighteen forty-three at Bourne, in Lincolnshire. First made his mark as a painter at the age of eighteen, when he was employed by Peter Robert, Lord Willoughby de Eresby, to restore frescoes and ceiling paintings at Grimsthorpe Castle. At this point, he became interested in occult and religious subjects and painted a notable series of six allegorical pictures depicting the voyage of the spirit after death. These pictures were shown at the Underwood Gallery in London in eighteen sixty-five but were taken down after only one week because of complaints about their pernicious and blasphemous content. They were returned to Grimsthorpe Castle to be sequestered in the vaults, where they remain today. Waldegrave returned to London in eighteen sixty-seven and made his living for several years as a minor portrait painter. Very few of his portraits from this period of his life survive, although his portrait of Mrs. Adrian Hope is a notable exception. In early eighteen eighty, Waldegrave became friendly with Oscar Wilde and Frank Miles, who at that time were sharing quarters in Salisbury Street, close to the Strand. Frank Miles introduced Waldegrave into society, and in eighteen eighty-two, Waldegrave traveled to America with Lily Langtry. In eighteen eighty-three, Waldegrave painted what were probably his three best works: "Family Portrait," "Lady Archibald Campbell" and "Ellen Terry." In eighteen eighty-five, at the age of forty-two, Walter Waldegrave inexplicably gave up painting and returned to Lincolnshire. His drowned body was found on the beach at Skegness in April, eighteen eighty-six.' "

"Is that all it says?" Vincent asked. "It doesn't give any more details about the family portrait?"

"There's a footnote," Aaron said. " ' "Family Portrait" was exhibited at the Royal Academy of Arts Summer Exhibition of eighteen eighty-one and appears in the lower right-hand corner of William Powell Frith's celebrated painting "Private View at the Royal Academy 1881"—à picture in which the central figure is Oscar Wilde. "Family Portrait" was removed from the exhibition at the painter's request only three days after the public opening, for no specified reason. There has been considerable conjecture over the years as to the identity of the family shown in the portrait, and to the location, since the room in the picture is *not* Northwood House, where it was painted. Waldegrave himself would only say that his subjects were a family of quality and that the room was painted from memory.' "

Vincent sipped his wine and then set the glass aside. *Bantam*

Beaujolais was every bit as potent as Aaron had promised, and he couldn't drink any more. "You know something?" he said. "There's a story here, a real story. A young country painter gets his first professional experience in restoring oil paintings at someone's private castle; then he becomes interested in the occult; then he paints a series of pictures that scandalize everybody; after that, he makes friends with Oscar Wilde and Frank Miles, paints three well-known pictures and winds up five years later drowned."

Aaron said, "I was trying to find out if Waldegrave used some special kind of paint. But all I could learn about his technique was this: look here, a passing reference in Andrews and Milner's *Nineteenth Century Realism*. 'Some portrait painters were renowned for their photographic likenesses: perhaps the most accomplished of these was Henry DeVere, whose portrait of Richard D'Oyley Carte was considered by some critics "too realistic to be good." Then there was Walter J. Waldegrave, whose most distinctive painting "Family Portrait" was considered by Whistler to be "so animated that it was almost frightening."' "

"Well, it's certainly taken on a life of its own," Vincent agreed.

Aaron closed the books, one by one, and sat back. "Every painting's different. Every painter has his own way of applying his paint. Sometimes when I'm making a restoration, I can feel the personality of the original painter, like it's flowing right through me. I know he would approve of what I'm trying to do; I know he would appreciate my care. But this painting, this Waldegrave, it's like a swamp; the more I work on it, the more it falls apart. I feel like a medical examiner trying to dissect a decomposing body. The faces in that picture, they don't even *feel* like paint. They feel like rotting flesh."

"If you feel that bad about it, don't work on it anymore. Throw it in the trunk of the car and I'll take it away."

"No, no, it's a challenge. It's something new. Let me wait until I hear from Hartford."

"If that's what you want."

Marcia came in with the Kinkawoodles: hot, crumbly cookies tasting of almond. Marcia was slim and funny and very New York, although she always swore she had renounced the city forever. She sat cross-legged in front of the fire, stroking Van Gogh, and wanted to know the latest from the city.

"It's Christmas," Vincent told her.

"I know. Santa Clauses ringing bells and smelling of sherry. Bagels. Lights. Christmas trees. Skating at Rockefeller Center. Taking the kids to Macy's to be scared to death by Father Christmas."

"Bantam, Connecticut, is okay," Vincent smiled.

"Sure," Marcia said, resting against Aaron's paint-bespattered knee. "The things you do for the man you love."

Van Gogh struggled away from her lap and padded off to the kitchen. Vincent and Aaron ate more Kinkawoodles, and Vincent managed to drink more wine. Marcia began to explain her plans to redesign the upper floors of the house, which had fallen into disrepair, and describe how she was going to make the living room more flowery and comfortable, when Aaron suddenly lifted his head and said, "Was that a scream?"

"A scream?" Vincent asked.

"I don't know. I thought I heard someone calling out."

Vincent put down his glass. "I didn't hear anything."

"I'm sure of it," Aaron said.

He stood up and walked through to the kitchen. "Where's Van Gogh?" he asked Michael.

Michael was eating a peanut-butter sandwich he had made for himself. The peanut-butter jar was open, the knife sticky on the counter, crumbs scattered everywhere.

"I don't know," Michael replied, his mouth full.

Aaron walked quickly through the kitchen to the studio. Unsure of what was going through Aaron's mind, Vincent rose and followed him. The door of the studio was still open, as they had left it, and the lights were still on. It was unnaturally bright in there after the cozy firelight of the sitting room; it was as if they were standing under one of the spaceships from *Close Encounters*.

"What's the matter?" Vincent asked. "What's wrong?"

"I don't know. I heard someone screaming, that's all."

"Are you sure? It wasn't Michael's video game, was it, or one of the girls?"

"I heard someone screaming," Aaron insisted.

They looked around: at the easels, at the crumpled tubes of paint, at the stacks of frames and canvases. They could see their own reflections in the dark glass of the studio windows, pale and hesitant.

"There's no one here," Vincent said. "You must have imagined it."

Aaron stood still and silent for a long time. "Well, maybe I did," he acknowledged at last.

Marcia came through, still munching a cookie. "What's the matter, honey?" she asked Aaron, linking her arm through his.

"Nothing. I thought I heard a scream, that's all. Maybe it was just my overworked imagination."

"Aaron," crooned Marcia, sharing her cookie with him. "You don't need any imagination." She smiled at Vincent. "Believe me, Vincent, he doesn't need any imagination."

"Sure, sure he doesn't," Vincent said, standing aimlessly with his hands in his pockets. He took a last look around the studio. He had a feeling that he ought to go over to the Waldegrave and take off the drapery, but he didn't particularly want to.

"Imagination is the thief of sanity," he misquoted, and switched off the lights as they left.

Nine

New York, December 16

"He's not here," Vincent said, climbing back into the car and irritably slamming the door.

"What do you mean, he's not here?" Charlotte asked. "It's only seven-thirty in the morning. Where else could he be?"

"Maybe he went to the gallery."

"At seven-thirty in the morning? Anyway, you told him you were going to stop at his apartment to collect the keys. Are you sure he wasn't in?"

"I rang the doorbell about two hundred times; then I went down to the lobby and had the concierge call him on the telephone. Nothing."

"Maybe he went to an all-night party," Charlotte suggested. "People do still have them, you know, even if old fogies like us can't stay awake until eleven o'clock."

Vincent moved out into the early morning traffic, his windshield wipers shuddering and squeaking. "Believe me, Charlotte, I don't care what the boy does, just so long as it doesn't inconvenience me. And right now, I've been inconvenienced."

"Oh, don't be so pompous," Charlotte prodded him.

"All right, I'm being pompous. Now and again a man has a right to be pompous. Especially at seven-thirty in the morning when he's pushed for time and he's trying to get hold of the keys to his own goddamn art gallery."

He U-turned, incurring at once the one-fingered annoyance of a cab driver who had been following close behind him and a mooselike blast of the horn from a truck plowing northward on 8th Avenue.

"Get us killed," Charlotte remarked airily. "Just because you have a right to be pompous."

"I'm sorry, all right?" Vincent said moodily.

He drove back across Central Park South; with every minute, the rain grew heavier until it thundered on the Bentley's leather-lined roof and the windshield wipers tossed frantically.

"This is all I need," he said.

"You don't want the trees and flowers to grow?" Charlotte teased him.

"Trees and flowers, for God's sake."

They arrived outside the gallery twenty minutes later. Vincent said, "Wait here," and climbed out of the car. His head bowed against the rain, his collar turned up, he dashed across the sidewalk to the gallery doorway and peered inside. Only the display lights in the window were on, and they were controlled by a timer. There was no sign of Edward. Vincent shaded his eyes so he could see right to the back of the gallery, but there was no one there.

He ran back to the car.

"No luck?" Charlotte asked.

Vincent shook his head, brushing rain from the shoulders of his Jupiter raincoat. "That boy is going to get scalped when I find him. I'm going to really hang him out to dry."

"He's not usually unreliable, is he?"

"Once is enough," Vincent fumed.

"Maybe he's on his way and got held up in traffic. Maybe he couldn't get a taxi and had to walk."

"He couldn't have taken any longer to get from Eighth Avenue than we did. Even if he *was* walking."

"Does he have family?" Charlotte asked.

"What does that have to do with it?"

"Well, maybe something went wrong at home and he had to leave urgently."

"Without calling me? He knows my number at Candlemas. And he knows damned well I don't have any keys to this place."

"What are you going to do?"

Vincent splayed his fingers on the steering wheel. "To be totally honest with you, I haven't the faintest idea. I have four-dozen paintings to catalog; I have a representative from Sotheby Parke Bernet calling at nine-thirty; I have three meetings with dealers and two with artists, as well as about twenty pages of accounts to check. And I can't even open the door."

"Are you sure he's not there?"

"Go look for yourself."

Charlotte hesitated for a moment and then opened the door. The rain had eased off a little now, and the sidewalk was bright and wet. She crossed over to the gallery and looked inside. Vincent let down the passenger window and heard her knocking with the flat of her green-gloved hand.

Vincent called, " ' "Is there anybody there?" said the traveler, knocking at the moonlit door.' "

Charlotte, undeterred, knocked again, and then she turned the door handle.

"It's open," she said.

"What!" Vincent exclaimed. He had just turned on the Bentley's motor, ready to leave; now he switched off the ignition.

"It's open," Charlotte told him. And with a flourish, she pushed the gallery door wide.

Vincent, under his breath, said, "My God. There are thirteen million dollars' worth of other people's paintings in there." He hurried to join her at the gallery entrance. She was right. The door was unalarmed, unlocked, and anyone who had accidentally or out of curiosity tried the handle, as Charlotte had, would have had unrestricted and undisturbed access to one of the finest private collections of pre-Raphaelite paintings New York had ever seen.

"Edward!" Vincent shouted, stalking across the floor. "Edward!"

There was no answer. Vincent opened the office door, looked around, and then came back to the middle of the gallery and stood with his hands on his hips, baffled disbelief on his face.

"There's nobody here," he said.

"Is anything missing?"

He shook his head. "Not from this collection. Not unless somebody's taken one of the pictures and substituted a perfect fake."

"What about the storeroom?"

"The storeroom has a combination lock. Edward doesn't know the code."

"Still," Charlotte suggested, "perhaps you ought to look."

He walked along the corridor to the storeroom, switching on lights as he went. Charlotte looked away while he unlocked the door: she respected his security. But she came up close behind him as he stepped into the storeroom and switched on the fluorescent lights.

"I can't imagine Edward leaving the gallery unlocked," she said. "He's so conscientious; it just isn't like him."

It was cool and dry in the storeroom compared with the stuffy, sinus-drying heat of the gallery itself. The fluorescent lights flickered for a moment and then sternly illuminated the long rows of gray steel shelving, each row labeled with its school and its year. Vincent listened, his head raised, and then called out, "Edward! Are you in here?"

Charlotte reached across, caught hold of Vincent's wrist and said, "*Ssshh!*" But there was no reply, no muffled cry from a gagged Edward tied up by art thieves, nothing. Only the dull whirring of the air-conditioning plant and the occasional click of the thermostat.

"Maybe he's already been here this morning," Charlotte said. "Maybe he just stepped out for a sandwich or something."

Vincent shook his head. "He knew that I would meet him at his apartment; I made that clear. And even if he was only stepping out for a couple of minutes, he would never leave the gallery unlocked. At least, I sincerely hope not."

He paced down one of the aisles, running his hand along the edges of the stored pictures. "I suppose it's conceivable that somebody mugged him and took his keys. But what for? They didn't take anything. Not from the main gallery, at least. Obviously I'll have to check through the inventory in here, but I can't see how anyone could have cracked that combination. That's a Heustadt lock, the best there is."

"Perhaps the thief didn't like pre-Raphaelites."

"Well, that's a possibility. A video-recorder is usually a darned sight easier to get rid of than a Holman Hunt."

They were about to leave the storeroom when the telephone

rang. Vincent lifted it off the hook by the door and said, "Pearson Fine Arts. Can I help you?"

He listened for a while and then said, "Okay, thank you," and hung up.

"What was that?" Charlotte asked. She couldn't help but notice his frown.

"The daytime concierge at Wentworth Apartments. He just arrived on duty. I left him a message to call me."

"And?"

"He said Edward arrived home yesterday afternoon with a woman, and the woman left about six o'clock, on her own."

"So what does that mean?"

"It means that neither the daytime nor the nighttime concierge has seen Edward leave his apartment. As far as they're concerned, he's still there."

"But he didn't answer his doorbell."

"That's what worries me."

Vincent went into the office and quickly checked through his diary. "The first dealer won't get here until ten-thirty, so that's okay; and I'll have the message service take my calls."

"How can you lock the door without the keys?"

"I can lock it on the latch. I'll just have to pray that nobody tries breaking a window and that I can find those keys before I get back."

They went out into the rain again. Vincent slammed the gallery door, silently cursing his luck at the same time. He climbed into the Bentley and pulled away from the curb with a squittering of tires.

Traffic had eased off a little; it didn't take them long to get back to the Wentworth Apartments. They crossed the echoing lobby to the small, glassed-in office where the concierge sat reading the *New York Post* through a large, smeared magnifying glass and smoking a King Edward cigar.

"I'm Mr. Pearson," Vincent said. "You called me just a short while ago about Mr. Merriam."

"That's right," the concierge nodded. He coughed and took the cigar out of his mouth. "Mr. Merriam ain't been out since yesterday afternoon, and I can swear an oath to that."

"Is there any other way out of the building apart from this entrance?"

"A fellow could jump, I guess."

"Well, I hope not," Vincent said. "Is it okay if I go on up and try knocking on his door again?"

"Be my guest," the concierge said.

Vincent and Charlotte took the elevator up to the seventh floor. Charlotte said, "I didn't realize Edward lived anywhere so grand."

"It belongs to his family. His father's a broker, something like that. They filmed *Rosemary's Baby* in the apartments across the street."

Charlotte made a face. "I thought there was something redolent about it."

They reached Edward's door and rang the bell. There was no answer, although they could clearly hear the bell ringing inside.

"Could be asleep," Charlotte said.

Vincent hammered on the door with his fist and called, "Edward! Edward? It's Vincent!"

Still no answer.

Then he said, "Do me a favor, would you, Venus, and ask the concierge to bring his passkey up here. I'll keep on knocking."

Vincent knocked and knocked until the apartment door opposite opened and a silver-haired woman in a pink-silk bathrobe snapped, "Quiet that noise, will you? My husband's not well, and he can't stand so much banging."

"I'm sorry," Vincent apologized. He wiped his forehead with the back of his hand. "It's just that I can't seem to rouse my colleague here."

"Sleeping the sleep of the unjust, shouldn't be surprised," remarked the woman.

"I beg your pardon?"

"Well, it isn't like me to pry or to listen to business that isn't mine, but Mr. Merriam had a lady in his apartment yesterday afternoon, and from the sounds they were making, I would say it was hanky-panky."

"Oh, you would?" Vincent asked sharply.

The woman folded her arms, not the least abashed. "She came out of there quickly enough, quickly and quietly like somebody guilty. She was down that corridor and into that elevator before you could say knife."

"What was she like?"

The woman sniffed. "Good class, I'd say; although you can't tell these days, can you? Even the hookers dress finely. Thirty maybe, going on forty. Pale face, high cheekbones; an attractive woman. More to *your* taste and age, if you don't mind my saying so, than young Mr. Merriam's. That Laura of his, now she was *such* a pleasant girl."

"I'm surprised you saw his visitor so clearly," Vincent said.

"Oh, for sure. I was just going out the door to get Howard his prescription, and she came out of Mr. Merriam's apartment at the same time."

Just then Charlotte returned with the concierge, who was jangling his keys vigorously in irritation at being disturbed.

"Good morning, Mrs. Turzynski," he snapped tautly from one corner of his mouth.

"Mr. Maggs," the old woman acknowledged, then retreated into her apartment like a turtle withdrawing into its shell.

"Now what?" the concierge demanded, looking up at Vincent, one eye squinched closed against the smoke of his cigar.

"My friend isn't answering," Vincent told him. "And that lady, as well as you, is convinced he must still be inside."

"Well . . ." said the concierge, "there's no ordinance says he has to answer. No law."

"All the same," Vincent said as encouragingly as he could, "it does strike us as rather unusual that he doesn't. We would appreciate it if you would use your passkey, simply to make sure that Mr. Merriam is all right."

"The agents will have my ears if they find me doing this," the concierge protested. "This is supposed to be a security building, you know? The residents pay for security." This was concierge code language for "How much will you pay me to make it worth my while?"

Vincent said, "We must be able to come to some kind of understanding." He took out his wallet and counted out five five-dollar bills.

"I learned about Abraham Lincoln at school," the concierge said, briefly noting the face on the bills before tucking them into his cardigan pocket. "The Gettysburg Address, I used to know that by heart."

"How nice," Vincent replied tartly.

The concierge unlocked the door of Edward's apartment, and Vincent pushed the door wide and cautiously stepped inside. "Edward?" he called, but there was silence, and darkness, too. Vincent groped around for the light switch, eventually found it and lit up the room. The drapes were drawn tight, and there was an odd smell in the air, like perfume, only ashier. It reminded Vincent of his grandmother's apartment in the Beresford; a smell of long ago. In the far corner of the living room, the radiator clanked intermittently. Outside on Central Park West, a police siren wailed mournfully.

"Edward?" Vincent repeated, more softly this time, as if he knew he wouldn't be answered.

Charlotte held Vincent's arm. "He's not here," she said in a whisper. "He'd answer if he were."

"Let me try the bedroom."

"I'll, ah, wait here," Charlotte told him. "Just in case he's—well, you know, not decent. Or something."

Vincent walked through to the bedroom. The door was slightly ajar. He didn't know why, but he hesitated. He wasn't afraid. At least he didn't think he was afraid. But what if Edward were sick, or asleep? He wouldn't particularly want Vincent and Charlotte marching into his bedroom, would he?

You're making excuses, he told himself. *Get on in there.*

He slowly pushed open the door. The room was utterly silent. He was about to call Edward again, but somehow the words dried on the back of his tongue.

Edward was there. He was lying on the bed, the satin bedcover drawn up to his neck. His eyes were closed, one hand resting on the pillow next to his face.

Vincent turned and whispered to Charlotte, "He's asleep."

"Asleep? Are you sure he isn't dead?"

"No, he can't be dead. Look. The bedcovers are moving."

Charlotte edged a little closer. "He looks dreadfully pale."

"Maybe he's been sick."

"Do you think we'd better wake him?"

"Well, I guess so. If he *has* been sick, we ought to call a doctor."

Vincent went across to the window and drew back the drapes. Gray, rainy daylight illuminated the room. Then he crossed back to the bed and leaned over Edward. "Edward. Edward, it's Vincent. It's time to wake up."

Edward remained silent, his eyes closed.

"*Edward*!" Vincent called more forcefully, and he shook Edward's shoulder.

Charlotte stood back a little and frowned. "He hasn't gone into a coma, has he, or something like that?"

"I don't think so. Look—you can see his eyes moving under his eyelids, the way they do when you dream."

"Reactive eye movement," Charlotte said. "Known as REM."

"Edward!" Vincent repeated.

"Take a look at his eyes. Maybe he *is* in a coma."

Vincent reached down and lifted Edward's right eyelid with his thumb. Instantly, with a horrified shout, he snatched his hand away and almost stumbled over himself as he jumped back from the bed.

Charlotte shrieked.

For out of Edward's right eye socket, a wriggling knot of off-white maggots dropped and fell to the pillow, where they separated and writhed as they tried to seek shelter. One or two more wriggled their way out from under Edward's eyelid.

Shaking with disgust and terror, deaf to everything except Charlotte's screaming, Vincent reached forward and took hold of the top of Edward's bedcover, the bedcover that had been moving as if Edward were still breathing beneath it. He hesitated for a moment, and then he whipped it back.

"Oh, my God," he gasped, and felt a wash of bitter bile rise to his mouth.

It was the writhing that disgusted Vincent more than anything else, a scene he would never be able to erase from his mind. The mindless twisting and turning of thousands of semitransparent bodies, and the way they glistened in the daylight.

Vincent's arm jerked upward in shock, as if he had been unexpectedly struck by a doctor's reflex hammer. "God!" was all he could manage. Then he took Charlotte by the arm—she seemed too dazed to know what to do next—and dragged her from the room. He closed the door behind him and then stood there, staring at her in disbelief and horror.

Charlotte said in a high, off-key voice, "Vincent, what happened to him? How could that have happened?"

Vincent shook his head. There was a gray, greasy taste in his mouth; he found it impossible to speak.

Charlotte covered her face with her hands for a moment, and then she retched.

"Quick, the kitchen," Vincent said, leading her through to the sink. She bent over, holding up her hair, and vomited up her breakfast. Vincent felt his own stomach tighten into knots, but he managed to swallow two or three times and control himself.

"Are you okay?" he asked her after a while. "I'd better call the police. And an ambulance, too, although I don't know what they can do except carry him away."

Charlotte nodded. Her face was bleached with disgust.

At that moment, the concierge came in, still jingling his keys. "Are you people through yet? I have to get back downstairs."

Vincent said, "I have to call the police. Mr. Merriam is dead."

"Dead? What do you mean, dead?"

"He's dead, that's all, in the bedroom."

The concierge took the cigar out of his mouth and peered hard at the bedroom door as if attempting to see through it. "What, he kill himself or something?"

"I don't know. I don't think so. Now, if you'll excuse me."

Vincent picked up the phone and dialed 911. The concierge kept hovering around him, sucking noisily at his cigar.

"What is it, messy or something? He shoot himself, or what?"

"I don't know. It's impossible to tell. Now, please. We've both had a severe shock and all I want to do is call the police."

Charlotte, trembling, came through to the living room. She took out a pack of cigarettes and lit one for Vincent, then one for herself. He very rarely smoked, but he took the cigarette gratefully and drew on it deeply. Anything to fumigate the diseased air he had breathed in that roomful of maggots.

The concierge sucked at his cigar and realized it had gone out. "You know something?" he said. "I get nothing but tragedy in these apartments. The things I seen, you know? The tragedy. You wouldn't believe it. All the lonesome lives that get lived out here, even the rich people, lonesome as hell. And now this. Only a young guy, wasn't he? Mid-twenties?"

Vincent at last was connected through to the police. "I wish to report a death," he said in a voice that didn't sound the least bit like his own.

Ten

New York, December 16

Laura was slicing zucchini in the Cuisinart when the door chimes rang. She wiped her hands on a towel and called out, "Just a moment!" Then she switched off the processor and walked across the polished floor in her flip-flapping Japanese mules, her scarlet-fingernailed hands held out on each side of her like little cherubs' wings.

She reached the front door and frowned through the peephole, her long eyelashes batting as she tried to focus. Because the two boys who lived downstairs were always "borrowing" the light bulbs in the hallway, it was almost impossible for her to see who was out there. But she could distinguish a pale face, a face that looked like a woman's, and that reassured her. Danny always told her that if the face was male, or black, or both, she wasn't to open the door, no matter *who* the caller said he was.

"Are you Mrs. Laura Monblat?" the woman called. A high-pitched, well-educated voice.

Laura called, "That's me. What do you want?"

"My name is Sybil Vane. I'm an old friend of your mother's. May I come in? I'm afraid there's been an accident."

"Accident? What kind of accident?"

"It's your father. Please. It's very difficult to talk through the door."

"What's happened?" Laura insisted.

"He's had rather a bad fall. He's in the hospital. Please, if you open the door, I can tell you about it properly."

Laura slid back the bolts, top and bottom, then turned the key in the eight-lever deadlock. There had been two rapes and

117

eight burglaries in this building in less than a year, and Danny Monblat wasn't going to go off to the office leaving his young wife unprotected.

The woman stepped into the apartment. She was slightly taller than Laura, although that could have been due to her high-heeled black shoes. She had on a long black winter coat, on which a scattering of melted snowflakes glistened like stars in a suffocating universe. She wore a black turban hat with a nodding gray feather. Her face was as white as milliner's tissue, and although she had obviously once been very beautiful, she looked tired now, and wrinkled.

"When did this happen?" Laura asked. "Why didn't anybody phone?"

The woman tugged off her gloves. "Your mother tried to call you from the hospital, but your line was busy. She called me instead and asked me to come over. I have an apartment on Gracie Square."

"Is it really serious?" Laura asked.

"The doctors seem to think your father might have fractured one or two of his lower vertebrae. They're going to be running more tests on him tomorrow, and taking more X rays. It could be very serious if there's extensive spinal damage. I'm sorry."

Laura was flustered and shocked. "He won't—I mean, he's not in any danger of dying, is he?"

"I don't think so, my dear. But he may partially lose the use of his legs."

"Oh my God, that's awful. Can I call my mother? Do you have the clinic's telephone number? Which clinic is it?"

The woman called Sybil Vane touched Laura's arm and smiled sympathetically. "Your mother was hoping you could come straight up to New Rochelle. That's why she asked me to come over. My car's outside. I can drive you."

"Well, I don't know. I ought to call Danny."

"Please do, by all means. But your mother does very much want you to come just as quickly as possible."

Laura untied her apron and went through to the kitchen. "I was right in the middle of making zucchini bread," she said, almost shamefully, as if somehow she should have been looking after her father instead.

The woman stayed in the living room. The loft was bright, well-lit and warm, with one wall stripped down to its natural red brick. There were palms and ferns in big basketwork planters, and the furniture was glass and chrome and natural beech. The woman's fingers touched the walls as if she wanted to sense the vibrations of the lives being lived here, as if she were tuning herself in to Laura's emotions.

Laura came out of the kitchen and quickly brushed her hair. "Do you know how it happened?"

"I'm not sure," the woman told her. "Your mother said something about going to fetch a glass of water from the bathroom and slipping. She was very upset."

Laura picked the phone off the wall and punched out the number of Danny's office. "He's always been so *healthy*, my father," she said as she waited for the operator to answer. "Well, if you're a friend of Mother's, you probably know that already."

"Your mother and I were at school together," the woman said. And smiled again as if that answered everything.

Eventually, Laura got through to Danny's secretary. The woman watched her as she spoke. A very pretty young girl indeed. Dark auburn hair, greenish eyes, an oval face; almost Irish-looking. Skin as fine and pale as orchid petals. Overly made up, of course, as most American woman were, but nothing a little cold cream couldn't cure. And a trim figure, too. Narrow hips, well-proportioned legs, not too extravagant in the bust. A very slight blemish on the left cheek, probably a childhood accident, but nothing too serious.

"I see," Laura said, talking to Danny's secretary. Then, "All right. But could you tell him what's happened as soon as he returns?"

"Isn't he there?" asked Sybil Vane.

"He was called across town. One of his most important clients is planning a merger. His secretary doesn't think he'll be back for at least an hour."

The woman smiled yet again. She had such a strangely sweet and indulgent smile; despite herself, Laura found it comforting. "I have a telephone in my car," the woman said. "You can try calling Danny again while we drive. Meanwhile, why don't you leave him a note?"

Laura scribbled a message on the blackboard in the kitchen. "Do you know which hospital it is?" she asked.

"The Boardman. I don't have the number with me, but your husband can easily find it through information."

"Okay. Just let me get my coat and lock up."

"Don't be too long. My car is parked in the towaway zone."

Sybil Vane stood patiently studying a framed poster for *It Happened One Night* while Laura put on her coat, switched off the lights and spread out fresh litter in the cat box.

"Have you seen my cat?" she asked the woman, frowning. "She was here a moment ago."

"She's very probably asleep somewhere. You know what cats are like."

Laura knelt down, still buttoning her coat, and looked under the furniture. "She's not here. Phoebe! Phoebe! Puss, puss!"

She went through to the bedroom and looked in the bathroom, but there was no sign of the cat.

"I don't mean to rush you," Sybil Vane said, "but we really ought to be going."

Laura gave Phoebe one last call; still there was no response. She followed Sybil Vane out into the hallway and double-locked the door behind her. Together they walked down the four flights of stairs to the street. The woman's high heels clattered like nails being hammered into oak.

"The doctors couldn't say whether it might affect his walking or not?" Laura asked.

The woman shook her head. "They weren't prepared to commit themselves to a specific prognosis. That's what your mother told me, anyway. We can give her a call, though, once we're in the car, and you can ask her for yourself."

Laura said, "Poor old dad. He's always so active. He won the New Rochelle Amateur Golf Tournament year before last."

"Yes, I know," Sybil Vane said. She took Laura's hand and squeezed it. "Let's look on the bright side," she said with a smile. "He's probably done nothing worse than chip a bone."

"Oh, God, I hope you're right," Laura said.

The car was parked by the curb: a black Fleetwood limousine at least ten years old, its polished hood beaded with rain drops.

"You drive this yourself?" Laura asked.

The woman opened the door for her. There was a strong smell of leather, and ashes of roses. "It's my only self-indulgence," she said. "It belonged to my brother. He used to say that no self-respecting American should ever drive a car less than twenty feet long."

Laura climbed into the limousine and closed the door. Sybil Vane slipped off her five-inch heels. Then she twisted the key in the ignition and the Fleetwood's engine started up with a roar. She pulled out into traffic without signaling and drove to the end of the block, where she turned into Sixth Avenue and headed uptown.

"Are you warm enough?" she asked. She drove with a kind of imperious inaccuracy, tutting and clicking her teeth impatiently whenever another vehicle cut in front of her, slowed down or otherwise irritated her.

Laura said, "It's very warm, thank you." In fact, the inside of the car was stifling and she had already unbuttoned her coat.

"I can't bear the cold, you see," the woman said. Her diamond rings glittered as she handled the wheel. "The cold makes my head ache."

They passed Radio City, its red neon lights garish on the Fleetwood's long, black hood. It was still snowing; the sidewalks were clustered with umbrellas.

Laura asked, "Did you say you met Mother at school?"

"That's right. We were the closest of friends; and after that, we always kept in touch."

"You should have come to my wedding."

"I wanted to. Your mother invited me. But unfortunately I was in Europe at the time. Family business, it couldn't be helped."

"I'm surprised you never visited at the house."

Sybil Vane turned and looked at her. "Of course I did! I used to visit regularly until my poor husband fell so ill. I can remember you when you were just a little girl."

Laura half-expected the woman to elaborate on her reminiscences, but she didn't. They sat in silence until they reached Central Park South, where the woman turned right. The Fleetwood's worn suspension clonked loudly over the potholes and drain covers, and the windshield wipers shuddered and protested with every stroke. Laura found the car so perfumed and stuffy that she let down her window an inch or two. The chilly late-afternoon air eddied in and for a while she felt refreshed, but then Sybil Vane said, "If you don't mind keeping the window closed. The cold does so disturb me, you know."

"Oh, I'm sorry," Laura said, and closed the window again.

They headed north. As they reached 125th Street, it began to snow more furiously, and the woman was almost in collision with the back of a bus. She didn't sound her horn but tutted menacingly and made an elaborate fuss of driving around the side of the bus, causing even more disruption and provoking a volley of horns from nearby cars and taxis. Laura was beginning to regret that she hadn't waited for Danny to come home to drive her up to New Rochelle, and she found herself gripping the handle and the worn-out leather of the seat, praying the woman wouldn't get herself involved in an accident.

"No courtesy these days," the woman remarked. "You should see how they drive in Europe. With *style*, and supreme politeness. Here—these hogs—well, that's the only word for them. Hogs."

"Are you sure this isn't too much trouble?" Laura asked.

"Trouble?" Sybil Vane countered, as if it were a foreign word she had never heard before.

"Well, it's a pretty bad night, and New Rochelle's a long way from Gracie Square. I could always take a taxi instead. I mean, you could let me out and I could go the rest of the way by taxi."

The woman laughed sharply. "Let you out? In Harlem? On a snowy night, with your father lying sick in the hospital? What on earth do you think your mother would say to me if I did a thing like that? Now, just look at this lunatic, slowing down right in front of me."

"Please be careful," Laura urged. "The roads are really slippery."

"My dear," the woman replied, "I've been driving for more years than—*look* at that fool, just look at him!"

Laura could do nothing but sit where she was and swallow her nervousness. Sybil Vane was right: she could hardly get out of the car here in the teeming snow, in the middle of Harlem, in the dark. Her chances of finding a taxi were practically nil; her chances of being mugged or worse were appreciable.

"My brother always used to *adore* driving in the snow," said the woman, airily. "It separates the tigers from the oxen, that's what he used to tell me. In the snow, you have to drive like a tiger!''

Laura said, ''You told me there was a phone in the car.''

''Yes, there is. My brother made sure of that. He used to drive so much! A regular Wolf Barnato.''

''May I use it?'' Laura asked.

''What?''

''The phone. May I use it?''

''Of course. It's in the glove box.''

Laura opened the compartment. There was a cellular phone neatly packed inside, as well as a pack of mint imperials from Taylor's of Bond Street. She picked up the phone and switched it on. The red pilot light flickered but all she could hear in the receiver was a long, slow, fizzling sound.

''I don't think it's working.''

''Probably the snow. It never seems to work in the snow. Nor in the rain, either, for that matter.''

''I have to call Danny,'' Laura insisted. ''He's going to be worried about me.''

''Well, that's all right,'' the woman said quite pleasantly. ''As soon as we reach a gas station, we'll stop and then you can get out and phone him.''

''Oh, please, if you don't mind.''

They were crossing into the Bronx now. Traffic was thinning out and the woman was driving more steadily. Laura watched the melted snow tremble on the windowpane beside her and listened to the ceaseless sizzling of the tires on the concrete roadway; although she still regretted having accepted Sybil Vane's offer of a ride to New Rochelle, she began to feel safer now, and she reassured herself that her parents would be pleased to see her, and that Danny would soon be driving up to join her, and that everything was going to be fine. She hadn't been to see her mother since the wedding and she began to look forward to it.

Sybil Vane, as she drove, began to talk. She started off by telling Laura about what she had been doing in Europe. Then she went on to discuss fashion, and shoes, and how poorly they were cut these days. It was an extraordinary monologue, about everything and nothing, and she recited it in a remarkably repetitive voice, emphasizing the same patterns of syllables again and again so that Laura felt as though she were listening to a long, monotonous piece of music rather than a woman's voice. The Fleetwood swept on through the night, the windshield wipers skidding regularly from side to side, and the woman talked on and on in the same mesmerizing tone, until Laura closed her eyes for a moment, and then for a longer moment, and then she slept.

She dreamed, as she slept, that she was flying through the night on the back of a black, scaly creature, a creature whose huge wings shed fragments of flesh and bone with every downward sweep. She dreamed that she was lost in a maze of black-cindered hedges, burned and shrunken; a maze in which voices could be heard around every corner but no one could be seen. She dreamed that she was alone in a rainswept house, a house about to be demolished around her ears. She wept in her dreams, and talked, and wrung her hands; and when suddenly the Fleetwood swung around in a semicircle, and there was a crunching of tires on gravel, and the engine abruptly stopped, she woke up to find her cheeks wet with tears.

She stared at the woman, who was still sitting next to her. Then she looked out the window. It was dark outside, apart from a single old-fashioned lamp post. The snow had eased off, and now it was raining.

"Are we here?" she asked in bewilderment. "I must have dropped off for a while."

"We're here," the woman replied. She turned and smiled at Laura, and Laura suddenly realized how shrunken and wrinkled the woman appeared. She seemed to have aged ten years since this afternoon. Also, there was a different look in her eyes. No longer kindly, but cold and scrutinizing, as if she were peering at Laura through the torn-open apertures in a mask.

"Is this the hospital?" Laura asked. She rubbed her eyes; her head felt thick and muzzy, as if she were suffering from a hangover. She peered out of the Fleetwood's rain-freckled window. "This isn't the hospital."

"No, of course not. This is my home. Since you fell asleep for so long, I thought you might like to come in and freshen up a bit before we drive down there. Also, I have one or two things I promised to take to your mother."

"What's the time?" Laura asked. Her watch seemed to have stopped.

"Ten after seven."

"Ten after seven? But that means I've been sleeping for two hours! Why didn't you wake me? We were supposed to stop at a gas station and call Danny."

"Don't worry," the woman smiled, although her expression seemed to Laura more like a grimace. She patted Laura's hand. "You can telephone from here if you wish. Look, here's my brother Maurice."

A tall, gray-haired man wearing a-black raincoat appeared out of the rainy darkness. He bent forward and looked into the car, then smiled, and opened Laura's door. "Well, well," he said. "You must be Laura. Cordelia has told me so much about you. Please, step out; I'll show you into the house. I'm sure you could use a cup of tea after your journey."

Laura eased herself out of the Fleetwood and buttoned her coat. It was chilly and damp here, and smelled woodsy. It was impossible to see very much; the woman had switched off the Fleetwood's headlights, and there was no illumination but the old-fashioned lamp post. The man's black raincoat rustled, just as the wings of the black, scaly creature in her dream had rustled. Somewhere, not too far away, a dog was barking.

"The dogs can always scent strangers," Maurice Gray remarked happily. "Come now, follow me. The pathway is rather dark, and you'll find that the bricks are slippery. We haven't had time yet to scour off the moss. Cordelia, my dear, you be careful too."

"Cordelia?" Laura asked. "I thought you said your name was Sybil."

The woman came up and took hold of Laura's arm. There was the clinging, familiar smell of ashes of roses, even through the rain. "Calling myself Sybil Vane is just one of my little eccentricities," she said. "It used to be my stage name, many years ago. I was an actress, you know. A very good one in my way. I was a marvelous *Magda*."

They made their way cautiously along the dark path. At length they reached a high, red-brick wall, heavily overgrown with clematis, bare and brown now, and dripping with rain; Maurice opened a rusted iron gate that squeaked dolefully. Beyond the gate was a brick-laid yard and then the dark outlines of an enormous house. There were no lights at the windows, and as Laura followed Maurice toward the front porch, she could smell freshly turned earth, and drains, and damp.

Maurice opened the peeling, gray-painted front door. "It's all rather decrepit at the moment, I'm afraid. Cordelia probably told you we've been away in Europe for quite a while. We came back only two weeks ago, so we haven't been able to do much."

Laura said nothing as Maurice shuffled around inside the dark porch for the light switch. She couldn't imagine why he hadn't left the light on when he came out to greet them. But at last he found it, and a bulb burned brightly in a cobweb-covered lamp over the steps, and Maurice ushered her in.

"I'd like to use the phone straightaway, please," Laura said.

"Of course. Come with me; I'll show you where it is."

"Are we far from the hospital?" Laura asked. "Falling asleep has made me lose my sense of direction. I mean, this is New Rochelle, isn't it?"

"The telephone is this way," Maurice said. He switched on the main chandelier in the hallway, lighting wainscoted walls, a curving oak staircase and a dull, uncarpeted floor. The house was very cold, which surprised Laura since Sybil—or Cordelia, or whatever her name was—had made such a fuss about the cold. It was so cold, in fact, that their breath appeared as little embryo ghosts.

"This *is* New Rochelle?" Laura repeated, suddenly uncertain. There was something about the way Maurice was standing at the far end of the hallway, his hands clasped like a retired thespian; something about the way Cordelia had turned away from the lights; something unnatural about it, something staged and tense and disturbing.

"This is *close* to New Rochelle," Cordelia assured her.

"Close? How close? Come on, I've come all the way out here on trust. I want to know exactly where I am, where the hospital is and what the hospital's telephone number is so I can call my mother."

There was a lengthy and difficult silence. Maurice looked past her at Cordelia and shrugged as if to say, "what's the use?" Laura said, unevenly, angry and frightened now, "I *have* to know."

Cordelia stepped forward, her heels clicking like a metro-

nome on the bare floor. She held out a hand, although she
obviously didn't expect Laura to take it.

"My dear," she said, "I have to tell you that your father is
perfectly well, at least as far as I know. You are not in New
Rochelle; in fact, you are in Darien, Connecticut."

Laura stared at her. "This is incredible," she said. "This is
absolutely incredible. But why? Why on earth did you bring
me clear up here? I want to phone my husband, *now*."

"I'm sorry," Maurice said gently. "That won't be possible."

"You were going to let me phone him just now."

"No, no, my dear, I wasn't. I was simply going to put you in
the library. In fact, I am going to *lock* you in the library."

Laura felt her breath tighten and her heart beat in deep,
painful thumps. "I'm leaving," she said. "You can't stop me.
I'm leaving."

"You mustn't be frightened," Maurice said.

"I'm going!" Laura shouted at him. "I'm going, and that's
all there is to it!"

She turned around and strode toward the front door. She
tugged it open, and there he was. A tall, handsome young man
with dark curly hair, wearing a well-tailored gray suit and
smoking a cigarette. There was a carnation in his lapel, and
Laura suddenly felt the whole hallway was dense with the
fragrance of carnations. The young man didn't move but drew
in a leisurely way at his cigarette; he was smiling at Laura with
amusement and pleasure. "Well, well," he said in a sharp,
English voice. "Is this the young lady you were speaking of,
Cordelia?"

"Have you been out?" Cordelia asked him; it was plain that
she was displeased.

The young man stepped into the hallway and closed the door
firmly. He nodded his head just a fraction, as if he acknowledged Laura's fear and desperation. "I walked around the rose
garden, that's all. I needed some air. I took my large black
umbrella, the one Frank gave me. It was rather pleasant.
Rather perverse, too, I suppose; but rather pleasant."

Maurice came forward and touched Laura's shoulder with a
gentle, appreciative hand. She recoiled and stared from one to
the other, scarcely able to believe that what was happening to
her was real. She was half-convinced that she was still in the

passenger seat of the Fleetwood, driving toward New Rochelle through the snow, asleep and dreaming.

"This is Henry," Maurice said. "Henry is our *older* nephew, the son of our father's brother John. Henry, this is Laura. Cordelia collected her today."

"Well, she's very pretty," Henry said, walking around her. "Is she for Aunt Isobel, Cordelia, or are you keeping her for yourself?"

Cordelia said stiffly, "Whoever has the greater need."

"She's your mother," Henry said, with feigned offhandedness. "Whether you want her to survive or not, well, that's up to you, naturally. I must say, the roses are in a terrible state."

Laura swallowed dryly and announced, "I'm leaving. Will you please let me pass?"

"Leaving?" Henry asked in surprise, tapping his cigarette ashes on the floor. "My delightful young lady, you can't be serious. Why, you have arrived by luck amongst the most hospitable and amusing people in the whole of Connecticut. Surely you can stay for a drink? Surely you can stay for one of dear Aunt Isobel's tiny cakes, with pink sugarfrosting on top? Why, you must stay for Christmas."

Cordelia grasped Laura's wrist; her grasp was bony, relentless and surprisingly strong.

"Christmas *chez* Gray is always a wonderful occasion," she said in a sing-song tone. "You must stay, if only in spirit."

She kissed Laura's cheek with lips as cold as iced liver, and it was then that Laura felt the first slow drenching of utter dread. She thought she might have screamed, but she wasn't sure.

Eleven

New York, December 17

"You can understand, sir, why your story doesn't altogether add up," said the black detective in the smart new tan raincoat.

"Yes," Vincent said, "but I can't tell you anything more than the truth."

"Your man was in the kind of condition we normally expect to find after ten days of decomposition in summer weather. Yet you insist that you saw him alive on Friday evening, about five o'clock?"

"That's correct," Vincent confirmed. He shuffled the sheets of his latest inventory and methodically blocked them into a straight pile. Then he fastidiously clipped them together with a gold Gucci stapler. "I'm sure that plenty of other people must have seen him, too, if you'd care to make inquiries up and down the street."

"Well, we've done that, sir, and nobody remembers too well."

"Isn't that what's called selective amnesia, brought on by a chronic fear of being subpoenaed as a witness?"

"That's conceivable," the detective admitted. What's *more* conceivable, however, is that Edward Merriam wasn't here at all on Friday but was already lying dead and decomposing in his apartment, a situation known to you, and possibly known to Miss Clarke, too."

"Detective Green," Vincent said as patiently as he could, "Mr. Merriam's concierge remembers him returning to his apartment on Sunday, along with a middle-aged woman. If he was still walking around on Sunday, how could he possibly have been dead and decomposing on Friday?"

Detective Green tugged at his thin Little Richard mustache. "We do have a theory that the man whom the concierge claims to have seen wasn't Mr. Merriam at all, but a look-alike. That concierge couldn't see very well. He wears thick eyeglasses; sitting in that office of his, he could easily have been mistaken."

"I have invoices signed by Mr. Merriam on Thursday and Friday," Vincent insisted, trying not to sound irritable. "Good God, man, he sold two watercolors on Thursday morning. I can contact the buyer and have him confirm it for you!"

Detective Green let out a testy breath. "Any of these invoices could have been altered. All you had to do was change the date. And if you had happened to have somebody here who looked like Mr. Merriam, well, that would be quite sufficient to delude any customer, wouldn't it, into making a positive identification, especially when the remains we have in the morgue don't have much of a face left to make a comparison with?"

Vincent stood up straight and lifted a steady finger. "Let me tell you something, Detective Green. I appreciate your difficulties; believe me, I am just as anxious as you to find out what happened to Edward on Sunday. But Edward was here on Friday; I believe he was still alive on Sunday; and I take grave exception to these unsubstantiated accusations you are attempting to make that either I or Miss Clarke had something to do with killing him."

Detective Green spread his hands. "*Killing*? Did I say *killing*?"

"You didn't have to. The implication was enough."

"Well, all right, then, if it's cards on the table. Whatever you say about Mr. Merriam being here in this store on Friday afternoon—"

"Gallery," Vincent winced. "Gallery, please."

"—here in this gallery on Friday afternoon—the categorical fact remains that the condition of his body was consistent with ten days of decomposition and that is in the *summer*, and this is the *winter*, and there is no possible way according to the medical examiner that Mr. Merriam could have been alive on Sunday, and that's it."

Vincent let out a long, patient breath. "Very well, I see your point. Something appears to have happened here that defies the normal laws of medical science."

"Either that or you and Miss Clarke are not being as accurate in your recollections as you might be."

"Yes," Vincent agreed. "You have to consider, of course, what possible motive either of us could have had for killing Mr. Merriam; or, even if we didn't kill him, what possible motive either of us could have had for failing to report his death at the time your medical examiners seem to believe he died."

"There's always the famous love triangle," suggested Detective Green.

Vincent shook his head in subdued exasperation. "Miss Clarke and I are friends, not lovers; and Mr. Merriam certainly had no interest in either of us. So that rules out any possibility of a love triangle, straight or gay."

"So *you* say."

"Well, yes. So *I* say."

Detective Green looked pugnaciously this way and that, nodding his head as if to make a silent and continuing comment about the gallery, and about Vincent, and about everything he saw around him: paintings, *huhn*, old-time pictures worth millions of dollars, when there were families just about destitute at this Christmas time, and poor old derelicts sleeping in cardboard boxes in the side entrances to Macy's, and it was cold out there, and people were killing each other.

"I'll be back," he told Vincent, a challenge in his eyes.

Vincent said, "I'm sure you will."

After the detective left, Vincent went into the office, took a bottle of Jameson's whiskey from the desk and poured himself a small glassful, which he knocked straight back. He firmly rescrewed the top on the bottle, closed the desk and then went back to his inventory. He was still haunted by those off-white, wriggling maggots. He had thought about them so much that he was beginning to feel they had actually penetrated his skull.

Detective Green was quite right. It was impossible for Edward's body to have been eaten away so dramatically by maggots in such a short space of time. At the very longest— even if Edward had died soon after Vincent had seen him—he could have been lying there in bed for only two days and two nights. Under normal circumstances, his body would scarcely have started to give off any odor by then, and certainly no maggots would have yet appeared.

Vincent returned to his desk and went through his accounts once again. The gallery may have been broken into sometime over the weekend, but nothing had been taken, not even the petty cash. He was convinced that the mysterious woman seen with Edward at his apartment was responsible for taking his keys and letting herself in here. Who else could it have been? She might even be responsible for Edward's death. But Detective Green had not been amused. None of Vincent's pictures had been stolen, and Mrs. Turzynski had not only failed to remember what the woman looked like, but even if she had come out of Edward's apartment at all. The gallery keys had disappeared and Vincent had been obliged to have a new set cut, but what did that prove? Nothing, except that Edward might have been careless.

Vincent was going through the inventory list for the third time when the gallery door opened and a stocky, dark-haired man walked in, wearing a creased blue three-piece suit. His face was sallow, and he didn't look as if he had washed or shaved that morning. There were heavy gold rings on his fingers, though, so he couldn't have been impoverished.

"Can I help you?" Vincent asked. "Or would you just like to look around?"

The man came straight to the point. "I'm looking for a guy named Edward Merriam. He work here?"

Vincent eyed the man with care and thoughtfully drummed his fingertips on the desk. "He *did* work here. May I ask who wants to know?"

"You mean he's gone?"

"In a manner of speaking, yes."

"Where did he go? Did you see him go? Did he have a girl with him? Twenty-three years old, slim, reddish hair? Did you see them?"

Vincent said, "I would like to know who you are, please."

The man said, "All I need to know is where they went. If they took off, where did they go? That's all."

Vincent walked around the desk. "Were you a friend of his? Of Edward's?"

"I know him, why? Not too well. We aren't exactly compatible, if you know what I mean."

"He's dead," Vincent said.

The dark-haired man turned even more sallow. "He's *dead*? He didn't—not Laura—he didn't touch Laura, did he?"

"Laura?" Vincent frowned.

"Laura's my wife. Laura Monblat. My name's Danny Monblat. Laura used to live with Edward Merriam before I met her, before we got married. When I got home yesterday afternoon, Laura wasn't there, and I kind of assumed she might have gone back to Edward. She was always talking about what a decent guy he was, that kind of thing. I just assumed."

"I'm sorry. But Edward was found dead yesterday morning in his apartment on Central Park West. There was nobody with him when he was found."

Danny wiped his hand across his mouth. "That's terrible! Was it natural, or did somebody kill him or something? Jesus."

Vincent nodded toward the doorway. "That was the police, just leaving. They don't yet know what could have happened to him. Apparently there was a woman with him shortly before he died—but no, wait a minute before you get upset—this woman was middle-aged, with a black coat and a black hat with a feather in it."

"Well, that wasn't Laura," Danny said with relief. "Least it doesn't sound like Laura, unless she's taken to wearing disguises. The trouble is, I still don't know where Laura could be."

"You've told the police?"

"Oh, sure, and they just stared at me like I was an idiot for even bothering to tell them about it. Do you know how many people go missing every single day? In New York alone? Thousands, they said. Not hundreds. Thousands. Can you imagine that? And one of those thousands is Laura. But they don't care. They *can't* care. You can't even *expect* them to care."

Vincent looked soberly down at his inventory. Then he said, "You've called her parents, I guess?"

"Sure. They were the first."

"And?"

"They were as upset as I am. They don't have any idea of what could have happened."

Danny Monblat ran his hands through his hair unhappily. "I just can't imagine where she might have gone. The funny thing is, I was supposed to be going home early; she was making a special dinner for me. Then I had this call from Farrar and Bibbie, or at least it was supposed to have come from Farrar and Bibbie—they're special clients of ours—and I had to go all the way across town. When I got there, nobody at Farrar and Bibbie had any idea of what I was talking about. It was then that I went home, and it was then that I found her gone. The dinner was still there, everything. The Cuisinart was full of —sliced zucchini."

Danny Monblat had to take a breath to steady himself. He lifted his hands helplessly, then dropped them. "She didn't leave a note, nothing. It wasn't like there was any kind of explanation. I mean, I could cope with that. I'd know what to do. But when a woman just disappears, how the hell do you go about finding her?"

Vincent asked, "Did you tell the police about that call you had from—what was their name?"

"Farrar and Bibbie."

"That's right, Farrar and Bibbie. Did you tell them about that?"

"I mentioned it in passing, but they didn't seem to be particularly interested."

"You realize that it might have been a diversion of a kind. A way to keep you out of the office while—well, while your wife disappeared."

Danny Monblat stared at Vincent narrowly. "What are you saying? That somebody dragged me halfway across town on purpose? You mean like Laura was kidnapped or something?"

"I don't know, Mr. Monblat, it's only a supposition. I don't want to alarm you. There's probably a very simple explanation, and tomorrow you'll find you're both laughing at how worried you were. Maybe she had to go help someone who was sick, someone who had a crisis on his hands."

"She didn't take the car," Danny Monblat said, slowly shaking his head. "And besides, she still would have found time to write me a note. She's that kind of girl. She knows how much I care about her. Like she always locks the door properly, chains, bolts, everything, and never lets anybody suspicious in."

"That only strengthens my theory. If she wasn't in the habit of opening the door to suspicious strangers, she probably went out of her own accord. You may even find that she's back home now. Do you want to call?"

Danny Monblat said, "I've been calling all day. But—sure, okay. Thanks."

He picked up Vincent's phone and dialed his home number. He waited, but there was no reply. At last he hung up.

"Would you like a drink?" Vincent asked.

He shook his head. "I want to keep a clear head. Listen, I think I'll go on home and wait to see if she comes back. That's probably best."

Vincent laid a hand on his shoulder. "You can call me if there's anything you want."

"Well, it's not really your problem. But thanks anyway."

Danny Monblat left; Vincent sat down behind his desk again and rubbed his eyes wearily. He had the unsettling feeling that as winter was drawing darkly around him, so strange and inexplicable forces were beginning to stir and flicker in the shadows of his life. What puzzled him most was the feeling that somehow he was personally responsible for Edward's death, and even in a tangential way for Laura Monblat's disappearance. Well, maybe not actually responsible, but certainly *involved*. He knew there was no logic behind the feeling, no sensible or reasonable way in which he could have had any connection with Ben Miller's catatonia or Edward's hideously rapid decay, but he seemed to find himself in the eye of such a black and silent hurricane that the feeling was impossible to shake.

Some invisible but insistent hand was tugging at his sleeve; some unheard but persistent voice was speaking in his ear. The world had tilted into a different kind of winter this year, and Vincent felt an apprehension unlike anything he had ever experienced.

"They're back," Ben Miller had insisted. *"They're back."*

When the phone warbled, Vincent jerked in involuntary shock. Then he picked it up and said with reasonable aplomb, "Pearson Gallery. How can I help you?"

It was Margot, his not-so-recent ex-wife. She sounded aloof and harassed, as though she were just about to run out the door to do something more important but recognized her duty to let Vincent know what was going on.

"About Christmas," she said. "I wonder if you'd mind if I

brought Thomas over in the afternoon rather than in the morning"—the implication in her voice telling him he had better *not* mind.

"I think that would be okay," Vincent told her. "Is there any particular reason?"

"Well, it's just that Bruce is coming up from Baltimore that Wednesday, and I do want Thomas to get to know Bruce better."

"Bruce, hm?"

"You don't have to say 'Bruce, hm' like that," Margot protested, her aloofness beginning to crack a little. "Bruce is a fine, dedicated and intelligent man."

"Did I once say he wasn't?"

"At least Bruce doesn't go around expecting everybody to be supernaturally perfect."

It had been Vincent's neatness, tidiness and sense of perfection that had finally brought their marriage to a painful but inevitable finish. Whereas Margot was scattered and erratic, and never minded if anybody else was, Vincent had always wanted his life to be ordered and meticulous. It may have been a hidden fear that if he didn't regulate his personality, he would end up as forgetful and disorganized as his father: well-loved but always tangled up in the messiest of legal, financial and personal problems. Or it may simply have been that as much as he liked Margot, as charming and as witty as she could be, he had mistaken a potential friend for a potential lover, and realized his error only after Thomas had been born and it was far too late.

Vincent said, "All right, don't let's get into an argument. Bring Thomas over after lunch. But not too late, please. We're having a few neighbors in for drinks, and then we're going carol-singing."

Margot said, "You still haven't told me what you want for Christmas."

Vincent smiled. "I don't know. Whatever I ask for, you always buy me something different. Anything, as long as it's not another one of those Mexican ashtrays."

"What Mexican ashtrays?"

"The red and blue and yellow thing, with pictures of chickens on it."

"Vincent, that isn't a Mexican ashtray. That's a Portuguese spatchcock press for cooking chicken in."

"Oh, I'm sorry. But it does make a very good ashtray, too."

"I'll see you on Sunday," Margot said, not altogether warmly.

Vincent put down the phone. It was almost twelve o'clock now; he decided to close up the gallery for lunch and see if Meggsy would be interested in joining him in the Oak Bar at the Plaza for two or three of their excellent martinis. The shock of Edward's death was just beginning to make itself felt: a coldness of the nervous system; an urge to do something spontaneous and irrational to show that Edward's sudden disappearance from the world hadn't gone completely unnoticed.

He was about to put on his coat when a rotund Greek couple came in, wearing curly haired fur coats. They wanted to look at anything with a classical Greek subject to it, preferably with plenty of marble pillars and diaphanously draped nymphs. They were building a villa on the Island of Nisiros and were interested in a painting "one hundred forty-two centimeters by one hundred eighty-seven centimeters" for the downstairs half-bathroom.

It was over an hour before Vincent was able to satisfy them with a painting of the "Gardens of the Cyclades," by Leonard Pym, an eccentric American painter who had lived in Delaware for most of his life. It was too late now for Meggsy's lunch break; he would just have to go and drink on his own. He switched on the security alarm and was halfway to the door when the phone rang.

"Goddamit," he muttered. That would be Margot again, with some sharp retort to his using her Portuguese spatchcock press as an ashtray. Margot, like most people, could never think of a smart reply until it was too late, but unlike most people, she would pursue you when she had thought of a put-down and make sure she told you later. Occasionally three months later.

"*Margot—*" he began. But it wasn't Margot.

"Mr. Pearson? I'm sorry to trouble you again. This is Danny Monblat. You said I could call if I needed anything."

"Of course. How can I help?"

"Would it be too much to ask you to come down to the Village?"

Vincent frowned at his watch. "Well . . . I'm a little pushed for time."

"I know I'm out of line, asking you this. But you're the only person I could think of who might understand."

Vincent thought: I don't really feel like sitting here all afternoon, anyway; and I certainly don't relish the idea of drinking martinis on my own. So what do I have to lose? Besides, he thought, I've made an offer of help and it would be churlish not to honor it only an hour later.

"Give me your address," he told Danny Monblat.

Outside in the streets, it was bright and noisy and wickedly cold. Vincent managed to hail a taxi on the corner of Fifth Avenue, heading south, and in spite of the traffic, he was down on 10th Street within twenty minutes. His driver was Chinese and carried on the front dash a baseball bat signed by the entire South Korean baseball team.

Vincent walked the last half-block to the Monblats' apartment building. When he rang the doorbell, Danny answered almost immediately without asking who it was. He looked gray, and his necktie had been dragged loose, as if he might have been sick.

"Come in," he said. "Thanks for coming."

"What's the problem?" Vincent asked, stepping into the apartment. His expensive shoes were loud on the bare floor.

"Come and take a look in here. I didn't find it the first time I came back; I was looking for Laura, that was all. But when I returned this afternoon, well, I suddenly realized the cat wasn't there either, so I started hunting around: and this is it."

He led Vincent along the hallway, which was lined on one side by white-painted louvred doors. He opened the end door and said tersely, "Look."

The top shelves inside the cupboard were stacked with sheets, blankets and towels. At the bottom there was a cluster of large glass bottles, as well as two or three boxes of winemaking equipment. Vincent didn't understand what he was supposed to be looking at to begin with, but then Danny Monblat repeated, "*Look*," and pointed toward one of the jars at the back of the cupboard.

Vincent leaned forward, straining his eyes into the shadows. What he could see was so extraordinary that it took him a second or two to realize what it was. Then, when he began to make out the shape of it, he took one and then another step back. He stared at Danny Monblat, feeling chilled and frightened, and he didn't know what to say.

"I haven't touched it," Danny Monblat said. "I didn't have the courage."

"But how could it—that's your cat?"

"That's my cat. I haven't looked too close, but I can tell."

Vincent hesitated for a moment and then reached into the cupboard and moved aside three of the large glass bottles standing in the way. Carefully he eased out the bottle at the very back and lifted it into the daylight. He could have retched, but he held his breath, took out his handkerchief and pressed it against his mouth; after a while the feeling of nausea subsided.

Somehow the Monblats' cat had managed to squeeze itself into the empty wine bottle, even though the open neck was no wider than three inches in diameter. Once inside, the cat appeared to have tried to bite and tear itself to pieces. The bottom of the bottle was an inch deep in dark, crimson blood; the walls of the bottle were a smear of blood, congealed fur and strings of feline sinew.

"No one could have done that except the cat itself," Danny Monblat said in an unsteady whisper.

Vincent said, "If I hadn't seen it for myself, I wouldn't have believed it. For Christ's sake. How wide is the neck of that bottle? How could it have gotten its head through there? And *why*? Cats aren't stupid. They may get stuck in trees, but they don't generally get themselves caught in places they can't get out of. *Look* at that thing."

Danny Monblat turned away, his hands in his pockets. "I guess it went crazy, that's all."

"You saw the cat yesterday morning? It was all right then?"

"Sure. It was as sweet as pie."

"Then what made it do anything as terrible as this?"

"It reminds me of something," Danny Monblat said.

"Well, I'm glad it doesn't remind *me* of anything," Vincent told him, shaking his head. "I never saw an animal destroy itself, not like this. I don't know what to say."

"You know what it reminds me of?" Danny Monblat persisted. "It reminds me of a picture I saw in a book from *Life* magazine. It showed a prisoner trying to get away from the Germans, who were going to burn him alive, and this guy somehow had managed to force his head and half of his shoulders through this tiny space underneath the walls of this wooden hut. They killed him all the same, but you should have seen the tiny space he managed to get through."

Vincent looked at him. "What does that mean?" he wanted to know. "I mean, what kind of conclusion are you drawing from that?"

"I don't know. I just think the only thing that could have made that cat force itself into that bottle was the will to live."

"You mean it was trying to get away from something? Trying to hide where it couldn't be reached?"

Danny Monblat nodded.

Vincent turned around and walked back into the living room; his stomach still felt unsettled. He stood by the window for a long time, looking out over 10th Street, at the tarred rooftops and the water barrels and the rusted air-conditioning vents, and then he said, "If that cat was trying so desperately to hide, then somebody it wanted to hide from must have been here."

"That's why I called you," Danny Monblat said, on the edge of tears.

"I only wish I could help you. I only wish I could think of something sensible. Maybe we'd better call the police. At least they can go through the proper investigative procedures. I mean, once they've seen that cat, I don't believe they'll treat Laura's disappearance like just one more missing person."

Danny Monblat stood in the corridor next to the bottled remains of his cat and asked Vincent plaintively, "Do you think she's dead? Do you think somebody killed her?"

"You have to have hope, Danny. For Laura's sake as well as your own."

"Hope?" Danny Monblat echoed. "Hope? That's my wife you're talking about. That's my *life*."

Twelve

Harwinton, December 18

When Jack woke up, it was snowing. The bedroom was full of that unnatural lilac light that snowfields reflect in the early hours of morning; he could hear the softest kissing of snowflakes against the windowpane. He lay there for a while, knowing that he ought to get up but allowing himself just five more minutes of peace. In a week it would be Christmas. He had made a special effort this year and bought his presents for Nancy a month early; a bottle of Cartier perfume, a French cookbook and three pairs of sexy black panties. Nancy was still asleep, her hand raised to her face like a child. It was 7:21. Jack stretched and decided it was probably time to get up.

He was down in the kitchen, his bare feet freezing on the blue-tiled floor, when the telephone rang. He poured himself a freshly perked cup of black coffee with one hand and lifted the receiver with the other.

"Smith," he said harshly.

"Sheriff? This is Norman Goldberg. I'm sorry to trouble you so early, but we may have found ourselves a lead in the Nepaug murder."

"What kind of a lead? When?"

"Early hours of this morning, Sheriff, round about two a.m. Dunkley picked up a twenty-nine year old white Cauc hitchhiker on Goshen Road not far from Dog Pond. The hitchhiker said he was lucky to be alive. Apparently some man had picked him up, then tried to persuade him to stay the night with him. When the hitchhiker refused, the man attempted to inject him with a hypodermic. The hitchhiker twisted the wheel, the car stopped, and after a struggle, he was able to get out of the car and make an escape. According to the hitchhiker, the man kept talking about his skin and what a miraculous thing skin was. Stuff like that.''

"Where is the hitchhiker now?"

"Still here, sir. Sleeping, the last I looked."

"Don't let him leave. I'll be right with you."

"Yes, sir."

Jack hurriedly finished his coffee, dressed and kissed Nancy on the cheek before battling his way out into the snow. He cursed his laziness for not having put the car into the garage the night before; the Volkswagen was almost completely buried. He spent an exasperated ten minutes scraping snow off the windshield and the side windows; when at last the car was reasonably clear, it took six or seven whinnying attempts at the ignition before the engine abruptly clattered into life.

It was a skiddy and frustrating drive up to Torrington. Several times the windshield wipers clogged up and Jack had to stop and clear them with his bare hands. Twice the car slid sideways in the middle of the highway, and once he collided with a fence post. He asked God out loud what the hell he was doing out here in this blinding white wilderness when anybody with any sense at all would be sitting home by the fire and calling his boss to plead that he was snowbound.

At last he reached Torrington. There were no other vehicles around except for a parked snowplow and a couple of four-wheel drives with snow chains. Jack parked the Volkswagen next to a huge, sloping drift and crunched his way across the parking lot, furiously rubbing his hands to warm them. The sky was the color of corroded zinc, and the town was so hushed he could easily have believed its thirty-four thousand inhabitants had died in the night.

The modern, glass-fronted sheriff's headquarters was over-heated and bright, and there was a brisk clattering of typewriters and a shrilling of telephones. Jack went straight through to his office and flung his wet leather gloves into his "out" tray. Norman Goldberg appeared almost immediately, fat and gentle-mannered and beaky-nosed, a Jewish deputy who took considerable pride in the evenhanded way in which he policed a wealthy enclave of Anglo-Saxon Protestants.

"The guy's waiting for you downstairs," Norman said.

"In the cells?"

"We also have him on a vagrancy charge. He says the man who picked him up must have stolen his wallet; but he has several priors for vagrancy, hitchhiking and petty theft."

"I want to see him right away. Have Jenny bring some coffee down, would you? One for the hitchhiker, one for me. And a couple of doughnuts, too. That drive from Harwinton was hell on ice."

"You should have let Bradley come for you with the Cherokee."

"Bradley's dangerous when he's walking down the sidewalk. You don't actually think I'd let him *drive* me?"

The hitchhiker was lying on a bunk in the end cell of three. His eyes were closed but Jack knew he wasn't asleep. There was too much tension in him. He was thin and young, with dark, scraggly hair and the kind of unwashed, unshaven good looks that had characterized the youthful American bum from pioneering days to the Great Depression to the Beat generation. He wore a green-checked workshirt and faded Levis.

Norman unlocked the cell and Jack stepped inside.

"There'll be coffee and doughnuts in a short while," he said without waiting for the hitchhiker to open his eyes.

The boy didn't move for a while but then he looked at Jack and swung his legs around so he was sitting up.

"Are you going to let me out of here?" he asked in a distinct Southern accent. He didn't have to ask who Jack was; the Litchfield County sheriff's badge said it all.

"It's more than likely. It really depends on how much assistance you're prepared to give me."

The boy shrugged. "You name it. I'm no lawbreaker. I was just hitchhiking, that's all."

"Hitchhiking is against the law in the State of Connecticut, and almost every other state, come to that."

"Well, I wasn't doing what you could call any *serious* hitchhiking. It was just to save some money."

Jack looked at him steadily. The boy held his stare for a moment, then dropped his eyes and folded his arms.

Jack said, "I want to know what your name is."

"Elmer John Tweed."

"Where are you from, Elmer?"

"Moultrie, Georgia, originally."

"What are you doing here in Connecticut?"

"I was here to see some friends, that's all. A couple I used to hitchhike around with four or five years ago. You can check up on them if you like. Nathan and Carla Prescott. They live on a farm in Canaan, making pottery and stuff."

"So why were you thumbing a ride in the middle of the night on the Litchfield road?"

Elmer made a face. "I don't know. I spent two nights at Canaan and then I guess I just got claustrophobic. Nathan and Carla were so darn homemade, all the time kissing and cuddling, and putting logs on the fire, and baking this wheatmeal bread. In the end I just had to get out of there, before I died of wholesomeness. Well, I'd been drinking, too. Nathan's home-distilled pear brandy. We had what you might describe as a forceful difference of opinion. That's strong stuff, that pear brandy. It can make you disagree with just about everything."

Jack reached into his shirt pocket and took out a pack of chewing gum. He offered some to Elmer, but the boy declined. "I'll wait for the doughnut, thanks."

"Tell me what happened last night. Right from the start."

"You mean right from when I was picked up?"

Jack nodded.

"Well . . . I'd been walking along the road for quite a while. There isn't too much traffic at that time of night, must have been twenty after one in the morning, and even when a car does come along nobody likes to stop on account of you're probably a criminal or a lunatic. I was getting desperate, as a matter of fact, because the pear brandy had all wore off and I was freezing cold, and then it started to snow, and I was beginning to think somebody was going to find my body lying by the side of the road froze stiff solid in the morning, dead of exposure, and I've seen a few of those."

Jack said nothing but waited for him to continue.

Elmer began to look nervous now, and his narrative became more discursive, as if he were afraid to describe what had happened in any particularity in case he invoked too sharply the terrors of the previous night.

"All of a sudden, a large black Cadillac drew up beside me. Fleetwood, maybe fifteen years old. I hadn't even heard it coming; the snow must have muffled it, I guess. I couldn't believe my luck. Well, would you, on a freezing highway in the middle of the night? I couldn't see the driver's face, but he reached across the car and opened the passenger door for me, and I slung my rucksack in the back and climbed in. He said, 'Where are you headed?' and I told him anywhere at all as long as I could get myself warm and maybe buy some breakfast. So off we went."

"What was he like, this man?"

Elmer shrugged. "Middle-aged, hard to say."

"Well-dressed?"

"Sure. What would you expect from someone driving a Cadillac? I don't know, gray suit, white shirt, neat but kind of old-fashioned. I remember the way he smelled, though, like lavender water."

"Lavender water? What does somebody like you know about lavender water?"

Elmer looked down at his hands. "My grandmother always wore it, back in Moultrie. She was a real old-style Southern lady. *Her* grandmother used to have twenty slaves, or so she said. She said that lavender water—*that* was the mark of a lady of quality."

"So you took this man who picked you up and gave you a lift to be a person of quality?"

"He spoke like it, and dressed like it, too."

"What did he talk about?"

"This and that, not much, not to begin with. He told me he was fresh back from Europe and glad to be home in Connecticut; and then, after maybe ten minutes or so, he said he was driving to his place in Darien and would I like to come along all the way?"

"What was your response to that?"

"I said Darien was fine. Darien was better than no place at all."

"When did you start to get suspicious of him?"

Elmer rubbed his hands and kept on rubbing them, around and around. "Pretty much straight after. He said that if I was going to ride with him all the way to Darien, then perhaps it wouldn't be such a bad idea if I spent the night at his family house. Well, I've got to tell you, the number of faggots who stop on the road these days when you're hitchhiking, and start laying their hands on your knee when they're driving along and asking you to come home with them, or back to some motel or other, you get pretty damned wary whenever some guy starts coming on about spending the night, even if it's perfectly innocent. So I said no, thanks all the same, I'd find myself someplace to sleep, I didn't want to impose on him or nothing. But then *he* said that he insisted and that he could give me a comfortable bed and a good breakfast; and I thought, sure, and a poke up the ass, too, if I wasn't careful.''

"You told my deputy something about skin. He mentioned skin.''

"That's right. That was a little later. By that time, I thought he'd kind of forgotten about inviting me home; he was just driving and listening to the radio, some classical music or other. But then all of a sudden he said, 'It's real hard to find boys of your age with excellent skin, do you know that?' Well, that confirmed it so far as *I* was concerned. The guy was a gay. But then he said something that didn't sound gay at all. He said, 'Do you know something? If you were to remove all your skin from your body and lay it out flat, it would cover an area of four and a half square meters. Just enough to upholster the driving seat of a Rolls-Royce.' With that, he touched my wrist and said, 'If you knew the qualities of the human skin, you would never take yourself for granted again.' I could smell his breath, he was leaning over so close, and it smelled like peppermints or something, as if he had bad breath and wanted to hide it.''

Jack folded another stick of gum into his mouth. "Is that when you told him you wanted out?''

"Not straightaway. But then he started saying how good-looking I was and all kinds of creepy stuff I can't even remember, and I said, 'Listen, this'll do. Just drop me off here.' ''

"What happened then?''

"I tried to open the door but it was locked. I guessed, well, it was snowing outside, so I wouldn't do myself too much harm if I rolled into a snowdrift. I told him to unlock the door. I said, 'Will you please unlock the door? I want to get out.' But he kept on driving and didn't say nothing. So I asked him again. I said, 'Will you please let me out?' But he said, 'You're not going anyplace. Now sit still, keep quiet and behave yourself.' I said, 'You can't take me nowhere, not unless I want to go. That's kidnap.' But he didn't say nothing; I just waited a while, until the road was pretty long and straight, and then I seized hold of the wheel and yanked, and the car slid around on the snow and we ended up facing back the way we'd come, up against the rocks at the side of the road."

Jack had been watching Elmer's face all this while; he couldn't remember any other witness he'd interrogated who had been so consistently agitated, who had wrung his hands so relentlessly as he told what had happened to him, whose eyes had flicked from side to side as if following fragments of frightening memory around the room. Not even assault victims, or rape victims, or witnesses to terrible highway accidents.

"Go on," Jack encouraged him, gently this time. "What happened then?"

"I don't, I don't recall for sure, not exactly for sure. It couldn't have lasted more than a second or two. I get clear pictures, then it seems like I can't remember nothing at all; only dark and fighting and that noise he made."

"Try," Jack said. Flatly, not insistently; no more demanding than a small-town optician coaxing an eye patient to read the smallest letters on the chart.

Elmer took a long time to reply. Jack waited without saying anything, steadily chewing gum. At last Elmer said in an oddly muffled voice, "He took hold of my wrist, and he was much stronger than he looked, strong like a mad person, you know, or somebody having a fit. And all the time he was struggling around in his coat pocket with the other hand, and he managed to take out something that shone. I saw it shining and I thought 'Jesus, he's going to stab me,' but when I wrestled myself around, I saw him biting a plastic cap off the end of it, and I realized it was a hypodermic. I hit him with my right hand, the flat of my right hand, twice, once across the face, although it wasn't much of a blow because the car was too cramped inside. But the second time I hit him, the hypodermic dropped onto the floor."

Elmer was perspiring now, even though the cell was far from warm.

"Go on," Jack said.

"He ducked down, bent forward—I guess to pick up the hypodermic. I managed to pull my wrist free and shove up against him, and he kind of caught his head against the steering wheel. I reached around behind him and released the door locks, and then I was out of that car so fast it wasn't even real. I caught my elbow on the way out, you can see the bruise.''

"There's something else, isn't there? Something you saw?" Elmer nodded.

"You can tell me," Jack encouraged him.

"I was standing in the snow, and the door of the car was open. He lifted his head and turned around and stared at me, and I never saw anybody's eyes look like that, they could've been molten lead; and he stretched open his mouth and he roared at me, and, Jesus, it was like twelve men roaring at once, the sound it made, and my hair stood up like icicles, and something came blasting out of his mouth. I thought it was foam at first, you know, like mad dogs, but it was white and it splattered everywhere, almost as if he was puking with rage. That was when I ran. I ran and I ran and I kept on running until I saw the police car.''

Jack eased a small Sesame Street notebook out of his shirt pocket and made a few notes next to a smiling picture of Ernie and Bert. Then he sniffed and said, "You'd been drinking, hadn't you? You sure you couldn't have imagined any of this? Maybe not all of it, but part of it?"

"No, sir," Elmer said. He was white now, and he couldn't seem to stop wringing and rubbing his hands. "No, sir. Everything I told you happened for real.''

"And the man in the car said he was going to take you to Darien, where he said he lived?"

"Yes, sir, Darien.''

Jack jotted down a few more notes and then he tucked the pad away. "You just get yourself some rest, Elmer. If you need anything, all you have to do is call. We won't be keeping you here long, but it's thick snow outside, and I need you around for a couple of hours while I do myself a little checking up.''

Just then Jenny came down with a tray of hot coffee and doughnuts. Jack took his coffee off the tray and nodded to Jenny that she leave Elmer's on the fold-down table. "See that this gentleman gets everything he needs," he told Jenny with exaggerated courtesy; then he carried his coffee back to his office.

"Well?" asked Norman, who had been waiting for him.

Jack shrugged. "Hard to say. Could be hysteria. Could be drugs. Could be nothing more than too much home-distilled liquor and two or three hours in sub-zero temperatures."

"But you're going to check it out?"

"Sure I'm going to check it out. This mysterious, well-dressed, middle-aged man claimed to live in Darien, after all, and how far is Darien from New Haven? Or even from Nepaug, for that matter. And the way he talked about skin . . . well, that would indicate to me somebody with a slightly unusual turn of mind, to say the least."

Outside the window, the snow continued to fall with felty softness. Jack knew he probably wouldn't get home all night, he called Nancy and told her not to wait up for him this evening, and could she remember to call Freeman the plumber and have that yard faucet fixed before it turned the back of the house into a skating rink.

Nancy said, "I love you," and Jack said, "I love you, too."

While Norman ate half of Jack's doughnut, Jack called his old friend at Darien Police Headquarters, George Kelly. George was the kind of officer who believed in traditional community policing: in getting to know everybody from the most influential members of the Rotarians to the boy who cleaned windshields at the Ocean Street gas station, and everything about them. He was popular in Darien because he fitted *The Saturday Evening Post* image of a small-town policeman who rescued lost dogs and returned small boys who had run away from home, and upheld all those straightforward 1950's values of honor and decency and American fair play. Only a few of his brother officers knew that he had been relocated from Manhattan's 17th Precinct fifteen years ago after a particularly questionable shooting incident, although all of them knew that when the occasion called for it, he could be hard and quick and that his vocabulary could be as harsh as sandpaper.

"George?" Jack said. "I need a little help here."

"You want a shovel to dig yourself out with?" George returned. "I hear you've got it pretty bad up there."

"George, I'm looking for a well-dressed, middle-aged man who drives a black Fleetwood, maybe a seventy or seventy-one model. He says he lives in the Darien locality, although he returned there only recently from Europe. Do you have any ideas?"

George said, "You want to hold him?"

"I want to question him first. We have a hitchhiker who claims this man assaulted him last night after he gave him a ride; there may be some connection with the Nepaug Reservoir homicide."

"Well," George said slowly, "I know your man. One of the Grays."

"You *know* him?" Jack asked. Norman blinked and stopped chewing Jack's doughnut.

George said, "For sure. Everybody in Darien knows about the Grays. They came back from France or Belgium or someplace about a month or so ago. They're a real old Darien family, dating way back before Independence. They've always kept up a house here, called Wilderlings, out on the New Canaan road. They hadn't been living there, though, for fifty or sixty years, maybe longer. The house was looked after by trustees for most of the time, although from what I've seen of it they didn't look after it too good. It's pretty run-down."

"How come they suddenly decided to return?"

"Who knows? Fred Archer, he's the president of the First Darien Bank, he said it was something about European taxes being too high for them. He wasn't too clear. He said they were wealthy, though. Just to keep up a house like Wilderlings for half a century without even living in it, that takes some pretty heavy inherited lettuce."

Jack sipped his coffee. It had come out of the beverage machine in the police station lobby, and the styrofoam cup tasted of chicken soup. "So who's my suspect?" he asked. "And who else is in the family?"

"Your suspect sounds like Maurice Gray. He's just about the only member of the family who's seen around town, although he sometimes has a lady with him. Once or twice I've seen them together at the post office, and they had dinner one time at the Steppan House, but that's about all. You could say they are recluses. Young Bill Farkas, though, he delivers groceries for the Colonial Supermarket, he's been up to Wilderlings twice a week since the Grays came back, and he's seen a young man 'round about twenty or twenty-two years old, and two women walking in the garden, and a wheelchair, although there wasn't anybody in it.''

Jack said, "Tell me more about Maurice Gray. He drives a Fleetwood?"

"Black Fleetwood limousine, that's correct."

"Do you have any idea of what he does for a living?"

"I don't think any of the Gray family do anything for a living. People of leisure, so to speak."

"Do you know where they got their money originally?"

"I guess I could find out."

Jack smiled. "I guess you could."

George said, "What do you want me to do about Maurice Gray? Do you want me to haul him in for you?"

Jack sipped more coffee, then wiped his mouth with a paper napkin. "I don't think so, not yet. I've got myself only one uncorroborated witness, and the way he talks about Gray—if it really *was* Gray—he wouldn't stand up against a good defense lawyer for five minutes. Just keep your eyes open, if you don't mind, and find out what you can about the Grays. I'll come down myself later today and see if I can't get to talk to them."

"Whatever you say, my friend. But have a care in the snow, okay?"

"All the best, George. And thanks." ·

Jack put down the phone. Norman brushed sugar off his shirt and said, "You've found him? Just like that?"

"Just like that. His name's Maurice Gray, and he lives right outside Darien. Rich and eccentric, from what George says."

"You're not going down to Darien today?" Norman asked.

"I think I have to. Supposing there *is* a connection with the Nepaug Reservoir death. Suppose Gray was trying the same kind of assault on our friend downstairs. If he's done it twice, maybe he attempted it a third time. If so, he could easily do it again."

Norman wrote down the name "Maurice Gray." Then he said, "You want me to run this through the FBI?"

"No harm. And put it through Interpol, too. Maurice Gray's been living in France or Belgium for most of his life, maybe for *all* of his life. The Grays left Connecticut fifty or sixty years ago according to George, and this is the first time they've been back."

"Any indication of why they should come back now?"

"George said something about European taxes being too high. But who knows? The only way I'm going to find out for sure is by asking them."

Norman turned toward the window. "It's snowing real bad out there, Sheriff."

"I'll take the Cherokee. And if I get myself stuck, I'll call in."

"Okay," Norman said. Jack knew that Norman's real concern was over being left in charge of the office in the middle of a blizzard, with cars and trucks sliding everywhere and motorists trapped in snowdrifts, pipes freezing, and families imprisoned in their houses. It was the nightmare season in Connecticut if you were a policeman, in the same way midsummer was the nightmare season for police forces in Phoenix and Dallas and downtown Los Angeles.

Jack said, "Listen. I won't be long. All I have to do is talk to Gray, size him up and find out what the hell is going on."

"Sure," Norman said and picked up the remaining half of Jack's doughnut, chewing noisily but without relish.

Jack sat back in his chair, wishing just as much as Norman that he didn't have to drive down to Darien; but a homicide was a homicide, and he began to believe he might have almost solved it.

Thirteen

New Milford, December 18

It had been snowing so thickly that Dr. Serling had to leave his car at the intersection with the New Milford road, where the snowplow had already been through, and walk the rest of the way to the Miller house. It was four o'clock, already twilight, but the snow lent a strange luminosity to everything around him.

He reached the Miller house and rapped on the door. Mrs. Miller opened up almost immediately and fussily hurried him in. "I was worried you wouldn't come," she told him, brushing the snowflakes off his lapels. "I was afraid the snow was too bad. But you're here, God bless you. Would you like a cup of coffee? Or some soup?"

"I'm fine for now, thank you," Dr. Serling said and handed her his coat. He was a large, slow-moving, big-nosed man with a reassuring weatherbeaten face that had made him one of Litchfield's most popular doctors. He rubbed his hands briskly to stimulate the circulation, then picked up his bag and said, "How's that son of yours today? Any better?"

"He still talks, still rambles. He hasn't said one word of sense since the last time you were here."

Mrs. Miller led the way into Ben's room. The television was on, tuned to *Love, American Style*, but Ben wasn't watching it. He was lying back in bed, shrunken and pallid. He kept muttering and twitching and feinting at imaginary assailants, and even when Dr. Serling leaned over him, grasped his shoulder and shook him, he paid no attention.

"He doesn't talk to me anymore," Mrs. Miller said. "He

mumbles and mutters and waves his fists around, but that's all. I feel like I've lost him."

Dr. Serling sat down on the edge of the bed. He leaned forward and lifted one of Ben's eyelids. Then he reached into his vest pocket for his pencil flashlight and shone it directly into Ben's eye. "Hm, pupils not dilated. How's his appetite?"

"He's been off his food, at least since the last time you came. I can't barely get him to eat nothing more than a bit of warm cereal."

"Any vomiting? Diarrhea?"

"Well, his bowels have been a little loose, but nothing too serious."

Dr. Serling let Ben rest back on his pillow and sat up straight. "I'm going to have to take some blood and urine samples to check, but my first guess is that he's started to suffer from uremia. That means a failure of his kidneys to get rid of everything they ought to, a condition that unfortunately isn't uncommon among paraplegics. Has his urine been dark? Darker than usual?"

Mrs. Miller shook her head. "It's been just regular. It seems to me like he's more frightened than sick."

"Well, uremia frequently brings on convulsions and fits and all the hallucinations that go with them. I think I'm probably going to have to take Ben into the hospital for a day or two for observation. The trouble is, May, that a really severe attack may cripple him more severely, or even kill him."

Mrs. Miller looked down at her son as he lay softly gibbering on the bed. Dr. Serling, his hand resting on Ben Miller's wrist, said nothing. He had already recognized that fleeting glimmer in Mrs. Miller's eye, a glimmer he was quite used to. It was the tiny, guilty light of private hope. *Perhaps after all these years of bad temper, incontinence and mutual suffering, the Lord at last will take him away. Oh, please, dear Lord, take him away.*

Dr. Serling opened his black executive-style medical case. It was his only concession to the twentieth century. His daughter had given it to him for his last birthday to replace his old Victorian bag. He took out a syringe, a bottle of sedative, and a bottle of alcohol to clean Ben's arm with.

"I'll put on the coffee," Mrs. Miller said. "I never could abide the sight of blood."

"This is only a sedative," Dr. Serling told her. "I want him to sleep and get some real rest; then we'll see what he's like in the morning."

Mrs. Miller was just opening the bedroom door when Ben suddenly shrieked out, "*Back!* They're back! Oh, God, don't let them get me! Oh, God, *don't let them get me!*"

He violently jerked and heaved beneath the blankets. Dr. Serling's executive case tilted and then went crashing to the floor—syringes, bottles, tongue depressors, scissors, pills. Dr. Serling made a grab for Ben's waist to hold him still, but Ben twisted around and threw himself off the opposite side of the bed, hitting the floor with a jarring thump.

"*Ben!*" Dr. Serling shouted.

But Ben seemed to be deaf to everything except what was happening inside his head. The dreams, the nightmares, the shapes that came in the darkness. He screamed, babbled and threw himself wildly around the floor, knocking his face against the legs of the bed, colliding his shoulder against the edge of his closet, scratching and scuffling at the floor until his fingernails bled. Dr. Serling was forced to struggle into a kneeling position beside him and pin his wrists, but somehow Ben still managed to twist and writhe from side to side as if someone were torturing him.

"Ben, listen to me!" Dr. Serling commanded. "Ben, this is Dr. Serling! Listen to me! You've got to pull yourself out of this! Do you hear me? You've got to pull yourself out of this. Right now, Ben, right this minute!"

Ben let loose a hideous, ullulating scream and stared up at the doctor with eyes crimson with broken capillaries. Between his screams and his garbled rushes of unintelligible speech, he took in deep, painful breaths of air, breaths that made his whole crippled body shudder.

"Listen, Ben, you have to calm yourself," Dr. Serling told him. "If you don't settle down, I'm going to have to have you restrained and taken away, and you know that would break your mother's heart. Now, please, try to get a grip on yourself."

"They're close," Ben moaned in desperation. "Please don't let them get me. You won't, will you? Please don't let them. Promise me, won't you? Please!"

"Ben, listen to me. *Who's* back?"

Ben stopped twitching and suddenly stared directly into Dr. Serling's face, his expression fierce and agonized, frightened beyond anything Dr. Serling could imagine. "*Who*?" he demanded. "You keep insisting they're back, but you haven't told me *who's* back."

"They're just the same," Ben murmured. His eyelids drooped, although his pupils began to dart rapidly from side to side. "They're just the same as they were before. And you know what they're going to do, don't you? They have to! They can't live without it! Oh, God, don't let them!"

Ben fell into another convulsive sleep. Dr. Serling raised him and then, with Mrs. Miller's help, lifted him back on the bed and tucked him in. There was a long and difficult silence between them as they looked down at him, the mother and the doctor, mainly because the doctor knew what he was going to have to say and the mother knew she didn't want to hear it.

"I'm sorry, May."

"You're going to have to take him in, aren't you?"

"I can't see what else I can do. This could be chronic uremia; it could be something else, worse. Some kind of pressure on the brain. But either way, he needs to be someplace safe, under constant supervision."

"What about the cost?"

"Well, it depends. But we'll try to keep it down."

Mrs. Miller hesitated. On the bed, his shrunken legs drawn up under him, Ben Miller was muttering and worrying, shaking his head from time to time as if he were arguing with someone. He had told his mother after the accident that he was only half a man, and it was true, partly because he had allowed himself to be. He had become corrosively testy, critical and vexatious, and he rarely gave his mother a word of thanks or a single compliment, nor even told her once that he loved her.

What price could Mrs. Miller put on a life like that? She thought of her meager savings in the New Milford Savings Bank. It had taken her eleven years to save that money, mainly out of her wages from cleaning the Pearson house. Now was Ben going to take that away from her, too?

She turned away. Dr. Serling watched her, saying nothing. In the end, under her breath, she said, "You'd better do what's best, Doctor. I can't say any more than that."

Dr. Serling cleared his throat as if he were about to say

something very personal, but then he changed his mind and shrugged. "I'd better call the ambulance. I don't really see any alternative."

He straightened Ben's blankets and waited for a moment to give Mrs. Miller a last opportunity to change her mind, but she said, "It's all for the best, I know. It's the Lord's choice, not mine."

But Ben suddenly hissed, "Don't you come anywhere near!"

"What?" Dr. Serling asked.

"Don't you come anywhere near!" Ben repeated. "Don't you touch me. Don't touch my skin."

"Ben?" Dr. Serling murmured softly.

Ben gargled and made a choking sound; then he stared at Dr. Serling and whispered. "Don't you dare touch my skin. I've seen you looking at me. I know what you want. You just take your eyes off me. I know what you're going to do! God Almighty, I know what you're going to do!"

Dr. Serling sat down on the edge of the bed and gently but firmly pried Ben's fingers from the bed rail. Ben kept throwing him odd sideways looks like a beaten dog, as if he were frightened of him but angry with him, too. "Don't you dare touch my skin," he breathed, harshly. "Don't you dare."

At length Ben dropped into a shallow sleep; Dr. Serling straightened his bedcovers again and stood up wearily. "He's hallucinating badly," he told Mrs. Miller. "I don't know why. Maybe it's a side effect from all that albumin in his system. That's what happens with renal failure. The body backs up like a blocked drain, and the blockage can affect the mind."

"He seems so *frightened*," Mrs. Miller said, distracted.

Dr. Serling picked up the last of his scattered bottles and closed his medical case. "I've seen worse. Do you remember old man Burack, who used to live across at Boardman's Bridge? He was convinced that FBI men kept coming into his bedroom at night and beating him with rubber hoses. And I mean he *believed* it, to the point where he started coming up in bruises. That was renal failure, too."

"What did Ben mean about not touching his skin?"

"I don't know. When the human mind hallucinates, it doesn't usually follow a logical pattern. It just erupts like a volcano, and all the things that have been scaring and worrying it the most just come bursting out.''

"He never said anything like that before," Mrs. Miller said, almost in tears.

Dr. Serling laid a comforting hand on her shoulder. "How about a good hot cup of coffee? I'm still only half thawed out."

She looked back at her son. "Do you think it's all right to leave him? Supposing he wakes up again and has another of those fits?''

"We'll leave the door open," Dr. Serling suggested.

They left the bedroom as Ben slept on in a disturbed and murmuring sleep. Mrs. Miller went through to the kitchen to put on the percolator, while Dr. Serling, with the familiarity of one who knew the house well, went into the parlor, took out his glasses and picked up the telephone.

Mrs. Miller came back into the parlor just as he got through to the Litchfield County Hospital. She stood in the doorway, her hands clasped over her flowered apron, watching him with sadness and resignation. He was saying, "That's right. Good. Well—the sooner you can get him into dialysis, the better."

"Coffee won't be long," Mrs. Miller said.

It was only five minutes later, while they talked in the kitchen and the percolator popped and bubbled, that Ben suddenly opened his eyes. He lay back on his pillow for a while, his lips silently shaping unfamiliar words, listening to the clinking of cups as his mother set out the coffee tray, the banging of the kitchen cupboard doors, the murmur of conversation.

Mrs. Miller was saying, " . . . ever since that time he nearly died . . . the nightmares he's had . . . but not like this. . . ."

With a shuddering grunt of effort, Ben raised his head and looked across at his bedside table. The digital clock flickered to 4:33, and the surface of his glass of water gleamed, an ellipse of silver as bright as mercury.

"Not *my* skin," he whispered hoarsely. And he reached over to the table, groping around with a half-paralyzed hand until he managed to grasp the water glass tightly and bring it back toward him so it rested on his chest.

With a convulsive tremble, he emptied the water all over his blankets and then raised the glass to his face.

"Not *my* skin," he repeated. "You're not going to touch *my* skin."

He gripped the rim of the glass between his teeth, clenched his jaws for a moment and then bit the glass so hard that it broke with a sharp snap. A curved crescent of glass glittered in his mouth, like fangs.

Carefully he picked the crescent out from between his teeth and let the rest of the glass roll onto the floor. "Skin," he murmured, and there was a curious sensuality in his voice.

Holding the piece of glass between index finger and thumb, he slowly but unhesitatingly drew a deep cut on his right cheek, close to his nose. A line of dark red blood ran immediately down to his chin and slithered down his neck, forming a pool at the base of his throat. Ben held the curve of glass up to the light. Its tip was tinged with red and he murmured to himself, "Stained glass. Like a church. That's the secret. That's the secret. Holy, holy glass."

He sliced at his face again, lifting a large, bloody flap of skin and flesh from his cheekbone. He felt the edge of the glass run coldly against the bone itself, and it made him quake. But then he cut again, across the same cheek, in a criss-cross; the diagonal wound became two pale triangles.

Systematically, with his hand as bloody as a slit throat, he cut up his forehead, his chin and both cheeks. One slice went halfway through his left ear, across his cheek, and penetrated through to the inside of his mouth, so that he cut his tongue as well.

It was only then that he let out a screech of agony, hurled aside the broken glass and dug his fingers deep into the terrible cuts in his cheeks as if he wanted to wrench his entire face away from its roots so that he was no longer human.

Dr. Serling came bursting into the bedroom violently. Mrs. Miller was right behind him, but he took one look at Ben and immediately swung around, forcing her back out of the room and across the hallway, knocking two pictures awry.

"I saw blood!" Mrs. Miller screamed. "What's happened? God in Heaven, what's happened?"

Dr. Serling held her wrist tightly. His face was wild. "Mrs. Miller, May, listen to me. The ambulance is already on its way. There's been an accident, I don't know what. But stay away, please. Stay out; let me deal with it."

"Accident?" Mrs. Miller asked, near hysteria. "Accident?"

Dr. Serling refused to let go of her wrist. "Go back into the parlor," he told her. "Stay there, keep calm, and call me when the ambulance arrives. Now, please. I beg you. Let me deal with Ben. It's probably far less serious than it looks."

Ben roared out again, a terrible bubbling roar as though he were choking on his own blood. "*Please,*" Dr. Serling insisted; and at last, quivering, Mrs. Miller returned to the parlor, pausing for a moment halfway to stare at Dr. Serling with an expression he hoped he would never have to see again.

It was the most frightening experience he could imagine: witnessing total fear on somebody else's face.

Dr. Serling pressed his hand against his mouth for a moment, summoning up strength and courage, trying to suppress his wildly racing heartbeat. He took a long, steadying breath, and then he stepped back into Ben's bedroom.

God Almighty, blood everywhere.

"Ben," he said softly. He stared at Ben Miller in complete horror, and Ben Miller stared back at him like a creature from the bottom of the ocean, a bloody squid, hooked and dying.

"Ben, for God's sake," Dr. Serling whispered.

Ben said nothing while Dr. Serling tore up the sheets from the bed and used them to staunch the flow of blood that poured out of the torn face. It was a miracle that Ben hadn't severed any arteries, but Dr. Serling had never before seen anyone who had mutilated himself as severely as this, not even in Litchfield, where bored and isolated wives were occasionally moved to burn the backs of their hands with lighted cigarettes, or stick barbecue skewers into themselves.

"Ben," Dr. Serling said thickly. "Ben, what happened?"

Ben turned his bandaged head and slowly nodded. The torn-up sheets were already dark with blood, and Ben's face was so ghastly that Dr. Serling could scarcely bear to look at it. And as Ben panted for breath, a stream of bloody saliva and bubbles ran down his neck.

"*Why*, Ben?" Dr. Serling asked, although he didn't really expect an answer.

Ben nodded, and to Dr. Serling's horror, almost managed to smile. "Won't want me now," he gurgled. "Won't want me now, not like this. I'm safe."

"*Who* won't want you? What are you talking about?"

"All twelve," Ben choked. "All twelve. Won't want me now."

Ben's eyes rolled upward, and he suddenly lapsed into shock. Dr. Serling shook him and called his name again and again, but couldn't rouse him. Almost immediately he heard the wailing of the ambulance's siren and the barking of Mr. Dunfey's dog, and red lights flashed against the bedroom windows.

Mrs. Miller had already opened the door for the ambulance medics when Dr. Serling came out to greet them. They stamped the snow from their boots and clapped their hands together like performing seals. One was Irish, ginger-haired and freckle-faced; the other was black, an Eddie Murphy look-alike. Randy and Wellington, Dr. Serling knew them both well.

"What's up, Doc?" Randy asked, his familiar greeting.

Without speaking, Dr. Serling beckoned him across the hallway; at the same time, he nodded to Wellington to take care of Mrs. Miller.

"It's Ben Miller," he said in a low voice. "He's cut himself up pretty bad."

"Attempted suicide?"

"Worse than that."

"*Worse*?" Randy asked, raising his gingery eyebrows.

"Go in and see for yourself. But make sure Mrs. Miller doesn't get even a glimpse. There are some sights no mother should ever have to see."

Randy stared at Dr. Serling for a moment, then said, "I'm beginning to think I shouldn't have bolted that hot dog."

While Randy and Wellington brought in their gurney and their first-aid packs and dealt with Ben, Dr. Serling took Mrs. Miller back into the parlor. She wouldn't sit down, but stood under the cheap brass-and-teak light fixture, looking old and defeated, a woman condemned by the world to suffer.

"Will he die?" she asked.

"He's badly hurt. But he's in good hands."

"I saw blood."

Dr. Serling nodded. "For some reason, Ben cut himself. I'm not sure why. He broke his water glass and cut his face."

"It's the nightmares," she said, as if that explained everything.

They heard Randy and Wellington roll the gurney across the hallway, but neither of them went out to take a look. A sharp, wintry draft blew into the house; the medics had left the door open behind them. Mrs. Miller's gray hair rose up as if by some strange electromagnetic force.

Randy came in and said, "We're off now, Doc. Will we see you later?"

"Give me a couple of hours."

"Sure thing," Randy said, and then, "Good night, ma'am. Don't worry. They're really going to take good care of your boy."

Dr. Serling listened to the four-wheel-drive ambulance whoop its way back toward the main highway, then took Mrs. Miller's hand.

"My boy," said Mrs. Miller, and in those words there was everything Ben had ever meant to her: a newborn baby, a carefree grade-school child, in summers and winters, in laughter and Christmases and sunny afternoons gone by; until that last afternoon, when he had dived as if in a dream into solid concrete . . . and ended Mrs. Miller's happiness forever.

"I'm sorry, May," Dr. Serling said. "I'm sorrier than I can tell you."

Fourteen

New Milford, December 18

Aaron had said, "You have to come up. I'm sorry. You have to."

Vincent had retorted, "Aaron, I'm coming up for Christmas in any case. Margot's bringing Thomas over, and Charlotte's probably coming up, too. So what's the panic? You only have five days to wait."

"Vincent," Aaron had told him, "I hardly ever ask you a favor. When was the last time I asked you a favor?"

"You asked me to bring back fifty-six pounds of Italian plaster from Milan. That was a favor, believe me."

"This is serious, Vincent. Something's happened to Van Gogh."

Vincent had been right on the edge of making a sharp witticism about Aaron and his overindulged cat when he suddenly thought of Danny Monblat's cat, bloody and dead in its bottle.

"Aaron," he had asked cautiously, "you don't mean something bad? Like an accident?"

"I can't describe it," Aaron had told him, and there had been a sudden surge of grief in his voice. "Vincent, will you please come up here?"

Vincent had been obliged to break another date with Meggsy, although this time he had gone around to her office on 47th Street, where she was sitting in her tight white angora sweater and her tight black mini-skirt in a fluorescently lit, partitioned office, with plastic cacti and acrylic paperclips in the shape of copulating couples, under a calendar depicting

Michelangelo's "David." Vincent had given her a sword plant in a pot, a half-bottle of Moët champagne and a kiss.

"I'm sorry," he had told her. "But Aaron's really upset. I'll make it up to you."

Meggsy had taken off her tinted glasses and looked up at him with that myopic, blue-eyed stare that always aroused him, especially when her huge, warm, angora-coddled breasts were pressed against his chest.

"If I didn't *revere* you so much," she had whispered, "I would hate you to death."

He had kissed her, tasted Givenchy perfume and smiled the smile of a man fully aware that when girls start to revere him, he is growing a little too old.

Now he was driving back to New Milford to have the house opened up so that after he visited Aaron, he could spend the night in his own bed. It had stopped snowing, thank God, although some of the narrower roads were still icy and gleamed in his headlights like the spines of petrified whales. He had been playing Vivaldi on the stereo, but as the roads grew skiddier, he switched it off so he could concentrate on driving. The tires made a hollow, crunching sound as they crushed lumps of ice and slush scattered across the highway.

When he reached Mrs. Miller's house shortly after six, he parked outside and tiptoed his way inelegantly through the drifts toward the front door, wishing he had been blessed with the presence of mind to bring his rubbers with him. Strangely, the Miller house was in darkness. He rang the doorbell, then banged on the door with his fist and called out.

It began to snow again, very lightly, no more than a dusting. It wetly prickled his face.

"Mrs. Miller!" he called. "Mrs. Miller, it's Mr. Pearson!"

He walked around to the side of the house, the seams of his Bally shoes already letting in chilly water. Mr. Dunfey's dog started to yap at him, tugging at the chain that held it close to its kennel; and then Mr. Dunfey himself appeared, thin, weasel-eyed and wearing a brown zip-up cardigan over OshKosh overalls.

"Yell as loud as you like," he said, leaning laconically against the rail that ran down the side of his steps. Vincent saw the scarlet glow of his cigarette.

"Isn't she in?"

"Went out just about 'n hour ago. Ambulance came and took poor Ben; then Mrs. Miller follered."

"What happened to Ben?"

"Didn't see; the medics had him covered up. Dead, I thought, to begin with, but Dr. Serling said it was just routine. One of them fits of his, more than likely."

"Do you know which hospital?"

"Litchfield County, that's my guess."

"Well, thanks," Vincent said.

"Don't mention it," Mr. Dunfey said, leaning on his stair rail as if he intended to stay there all night.

Vincent walked back to his car. Mr. Dunfey called, "Wouldn't go that way, it's all snowed up. Go back the way you come, then make a detour through South Kent. Would if I was you."

"Thanks," Vincent said. It was very dark now, and bitterly cold. The wind-chill factor was at least fifteen. He climbed into his car, started up the engine and perversely drove by the shortest route, in the opposite direction to that suggested by Mr. Dunfey, following the tracks left in the hardened snow by the ambulance. Mr. Dunfey watched him go and spat his cigarette butt into the darkness. "Can't tell the bastards nothing."

The drive was jolting and uncomfortable, but after ten minutes, Vincent was out on clear highway again, heading northeast. He decided to drive straight to Bantam to see Aaron. If the snow grew any heavier, he could always ask Aaron for the use of one of his dilapidated sofas to spend the night on. He switched on Vivaldi once more and began to hum along. Then, after a minute or two, he switched it off to think of what might have happened to Ben Miller.

It seemed like there was so much fear in the air. Ben had talked about somebody or something coming back; Laura Monblat had disappeared; Edward had died in a mass of maggots. Now Aaron had called for help. Vincent glanced at his reflection in the rearview mirror and wondered if he were some kind of plague-carrier, some kind of albatross who brought bad fortune and alarm.

He reached Bantam, parked in the shadow of Aaron's giant oak and stiffly climbed out of the car. Nobody came out to greet him. He stood on the porch chafing his hands and waiting for someone to answer the bell. At last Marcia appeared, looking pale. She said, "Oh, Vincent. I'm so glad you could make it! Come on in."

The house was unusually quiet and cold. "Can I take your coat?" she asked. Vincent smiled as cheerfully as he could and said, "Sure. Thank you. Is Aaron around?"

"In the studio," Marcia said, helping him out of his coat. "He's very upset, Vincent. He loved that cat. Whenever he was working, Van Gogh was always sitting there right beside him. Not only that, it happened so suddenly. And the *way* it happened—"

"The *way* it happened?" Vincent frowned. "What do you mean?"

"I'm sorry. You'll have to go see for yourself."

"Marcia—" Vincent began but she took his hand and squeezed it; there were tears glistening in the corners of her eyes, which meant *I'm hurt, we're all hurt, and we're frightened, so please treat us gently.*

"Okay," Vincent said, taking a breath.

He went through to the studio. Only a single electric bulb was lit, way down at the far end, and at first Vincent didn't think Aaron was anywhere around. The light cast huge shadows, transforming canvases and easels into hunchbacks and trolls and prong-horned devils, changing Aaron's half-squeezed tubes of paint into mountains of wriggling metal maggots. Vincent slowly walked the length of the worktable until he found Aaron sitting on a small painter's stool, a half-empty bottle of *Bantam Beaujolais* beside him, his ginger-bearded head resting in his hands.

"Well," Vincent said, "you called me, Maestro, and here I am."

Aaron didn't look up, but poured himself another glass of wine.

Vincent waited for a long time, his hands in his pockets, trying to be restrained, trying to be patient, but when Aaron still refused to acknowledge him, he said, "I'm here, Aaron. But unless you say hello, I don't think I'm going to be here for much longer."

Aaron glanced up, then glanced away. "I'm sorry, I guess I'm shocked, that's all."

"Are you going to tell me what happened?"

Aaron made a face, then nodded. "I don't have to tell you. I can show you."

"All right. *Show* me what happened."

"You're going to have to forgive me, Vincent. I can't look at it myself. And when I first saw it, I blamed you. You and your family, anyway. You and your grandfather and that goddamn . . . good-luck painting."

"The Waldegrave?"

"See for yourself." With a dismissive and vague wave, Aaron directed Vincent toward the easel at the far end of the studio, still draped in a bedspread.

Vincent took two or three steps toward it and then hesitated. "What is it?" he asked, feeling suddenly unsettled. "It hasn't—*changed* has it?"

"See for yourself."

Vincent took hold of the bedspread and gradually drew it away from the dark-painted canvas. He was secretly prepared for some kind of gruesome shock, but on first glance, the painting appeared the same as usual. The same group of white-faced people clothed in black. The same red room. The same sense of arrested decay. A fashionable leper colony in a long-forgotten drawing room, doomed by Walter Waldegrave's talents to slowly rot forever.

Vincent turned around and said, as brusquely as he could, "There's no difference, Aaron. It's old, yes, I'll grant you that; and it hasn't been very well preserved, but there's nothing else."

Aaron fixed him with a long-sighted look of annoyance. "You saw this painting time and time again when you were a boy?"

"Yes. What of it?"

"Don't turn around, but tell me what the woman seated third from the left is holding on her lap."

Vincent stared at him.

"Tell me," Aaron demanded, gently but insistently.

"We never knew what it was," Vincent said in a rasping voice.

"All right, you didn't know what it was," Aaron agreed. "But *describe* it."

"It was a—well, what could you call it? A fuzz of black fur. A monkey, a cat, a spider. I don't know."

"Look at it now."

Vincent slowly turned and looked, and he was amazed that he hadn't noticed it before. Yet there it was, its paws tucked in, its eyes closed, sitting contentedly on the lap of the faceless woman in black while her hand hovered just an inch above its head, about to stroke it. A marmalade cat, exactly like Van Gogh. In fact, so much like Van Gogh that it could only *be* Van Gogh.

Vincent tentatively touched the portrait of the cat with his fingertips; they came away sticky with treacle-colored paint.

"I'm sorry," he said. "I didn't realize it was still wet. I've smudged it."

"It doesn't matter," Aaron said, easing himself off his painter's stool. "I didn't paint it."

"That new assistant of yours? The girl from Gaylordsville?"

Aaron shook his head.

"Then what you're trying to tell me is that somebody broke in here and painted Van Gogh on one of your canvases? Just for a joke?" Vincent leaned forward, screwed up his eyes and re-examined the canvas. "A reasonably competent painter, too. Quite like Waldegrave himself."

"Nobody broke in here, and nobody was playing jokes," Aaron said. He lost his balance a little as he came around the end of the worktable. "What you see there, Vincent my friend, is reality. That—that smudge you have just smudged even more—that smudge *is* Van Gogh. That's all that's left of him, anyway."

"Aaron," Vincent said, trying to be conciliatory. "Aaron, that's just a painting. That isn't Van Gogh."

"That's Van Gogh himself," Aaron insisted, his voice slurring from the effect of two bottles of homemade red wine on an empty stomach.

"Aaron, what the hell are you talking about?" Vincent demanded. Then he said, "You're drunk, for Christ's sake."

"Yes," Aaron said, "I'm drunk. But not for Christ's sake. I'm drunk because my cat has been killed and now he's turned up in that goddamn painting of yours, alive, as if nothing had happened, except that he's only paint now, and not flesh, not fur."

Vincent licked his lips; they felt dry. Then he took out his embroidered Irish-linen handkerchief and wiped his mouth. In

Aaron's presence, he felt incongruously citified and over-dressed. "I don't understand," he said. He didn't. He couldn't decide whether Aaron was playing some kind of an elaborate joke on him or whether too much of the *Bantam Beaujolais* had finally sent him over the edge.

Yet Danny Monblat's cat had died an agonizing death in a bottle trying to escape a nemesis too frightening to even think about; and here was Van Gogh, captured in paint on a canvas characterized only by its decay and its deep sense of mid-Victorian doom.

"Well, you don't understand and neither do I," Aaron said. He looked away for a moment, trying to collect himself, trying not to weep. "I don't understand it one goddamn bit. But there it is."

Vincent took hold of Aaron's arm, looked at him closely and anxiously and said, "Aaron, this is only a painting."

Aaron drew his arm away. "My dear friend, this is not 'only a painting.' I wish it were."

"But it's not as if Van Gogh has been *hurt* simply by having his portrait painted. That doesn't prove anything. He probably got lost in the snow, that's all, and someone's keeping ahold of him until the weather clears up."

Aaron stared at Vincent for a moment, watery-eyed. "I found Van Gogh," he said. "That's the trouble. I *found* him."

"Was he hurt?"

"I'll show you. You want to see? I'll show you."

Aaron walked along to the far end of the studio and took down a large flashlight from a peg on a rafter. "Come on," he said. "I'll show you."

Hesitantly Vincent followed him out the studio door and into the snowy night. A bitter northwest wind was slicing across from Mount Prospect, which towered almost fifteen hundred feet into the wintry darkness, separating the village of Bantam from Nepaug Reservoir. "Should I get my coat?" he asked. "It's as cold as a polar bear's lunch out here."

"This won't take long," Aaron said. Vincent had never known him to be so evasive, so mysterious and so unfriendly. He stalked ahead through the garden, the beam of his light freckled with sudden whirls of dry snow. Vincent followed, his shoes soaked, his collar turned up against the wind, his hands thrust into his pockets.

They reached the base of the giant oak. In the beam of the flashlight, the trunk looked even more deeply furrowed and gnarled than usual, like some hideous creation by Arthur Rackham. Aaron stood beside it, his eyes rimmed with scarlet, his beard sparkling with snow, and pointed the beam upward so it illuminated the lower branches.

"What am I supposed to be looking at?" Vincent asked, shuddering with the cold.

"Follow the light," Aaron said flatly. "Follow the light and tell me what you see."

Vincent squinted upward, his eyes tearing in the wind. At last he could make something out, something that dangled from one of the limbs close to the roof. It was red, and ragged, and very long, like a twisted scarf. It spun around and around slowly in the freezing wind, and then spun back in the other direction.

Vincent took out his handkerchief, wiped his eyes and then peered at the scarf again. This time he could see that it wasn't a scarf at all; it was the skinned body of an animal, strung up by the neck with wire.

Vincent stared at it for one chilled and disbelieving second before turning back to Aaron.

"That's Van Gogh?" he asked, horror-struck.

Aaron nodded and switched off the beam.

"But how do you know?"

Aaron fumbled around in his jacket pocket and at last produced a small red cat collar. "I found this on the ground, just over there."

"I can't imagine anyone would want to *do* such a thing."

"Well, me neither, but someone did."

"Did you call the police?"

"I called Sheriff Smith. They said he was down in Darien today and the rest of the officers were all tied up with traffic problems on account of the snow. But they can send somebody 'round in the morning; that's why I have to leave him strung up like that. They didn't want the scene of the crime disturbed."

"We're not treading on any valuable footprints, are we?" asked Vincent, looking around.

Aaron shook his head. "Whoever killed him must have done it before the fresh snow started. When I came out here looking for him, there wasn't a footprint anywhere."

Vincent glanced up into the darkness of the tree once more and then followed Aaron back into the studio. Briskly rubbing his hands, he approached the Waldegrave portrait again and examined it closely. It still gave off that pungent odor of decay; it was still as gloomy and scaly as ever. Yet here in the front was Van Gogh, the marmalade cat, painted fresh and bright and in scrupulously accurate style.

"This just doesn't make any sense."

"It doesn't make the kind of sense we usually like to think of as sense," Aaron remarked. "But the facts speak for themselves. Van Gogh disappeared, was skinned and then showed up in the portrait."

"I have to ask myself whether you might have painted him into the portrait yourself," Vincent said gently.

"Vincent, I've asked myself the very same question. Whether I might have done it while I was drunk; or whether I found Van Gogh's body hanging up in the tree and did it kind of automatically, or hysterically out of shock. But look at it. It's beautifully painted. It's painted in Waldegrave's idiom, in Waldegrave's color range, and it's incredibly detailed. I couldn't have painted anything like that in a week, let alone in a couple of hours. And that's quite apart from the fact that up until now, I haven't been able to get any fresh paint to adhere to this goddamn portrait."

He paused, one fist clenched and trembling, and then said quietly, "I didn't do it, Vincent. I swear to God. It simply appeared."

"Are you going to mention it to Sheriff Smith? The painting, I mean?"

"I don't know yet. I haven't been able to think straight. He'll probably tell me I'm out of my head."

Vincent drew up a chair splattered with hundreds of hues of dried paint and sat down so he could study the Waldegrave portrait at close range. "Something is happening," he said.

"Well, you *bet* something is happening," Aaron expostulated. "Goddamn bloody cat murder."

Vincent shook his head. "No, no, it's like . . . I don't know . . . it's like a party. You know when you go to a party and everybody's laughing and chattering and having a good time, and then suddenly somebody walks in and that one person has such an atmosphere about him that the whole place falls silent and nobody feels comfortable anymore? Well, that's the same feeling I get. It's like somebody's walked into our lives and made us all feel awkward and tense and uncomfortable.''

Aaron said, "Who? *Who's* walked into our lives and made us feel awkward and uncomfortable?"

"I don't know. But things have been happening that don't seem at all connected, and yet they may be in some strange way."

Aaron tugged morosely at his beard. "Have some wine," he said. "I don't think I understand you any more than I can understand what's happened to Van Gogh."

"Listen . . . first of all, Edward died . . . in an incredibly terrible way. Then Mrs. Miller's son Ben had some kind of psychic fit. From what I hear they've taken him into the hospital. Then Edward's previous girlfriend disappeared . . . and her cat jammed itself into a bottle and ripped itself to pieces. Now Van Gogh has been skinned."

"I don't see any connection at all."

"The connection, Aaron, is *me*. All these incidents have happened to people *I* know."

"You can't blame yourself. That isn't any kind of connection."

"I don't know. What you said earlier . . . about this portrait . . . well, that may have something to do with it. My grandfather wasn't just protective about this portrait; he was almost obsessive about it. There were whole clauses in his will about it; how my father had to keep it safe; how it was never supposed to be sold; how it should never be lent to any outside gallery, or sent abroad, or put on public display. And here it is, right in the center of everything that's been going on. It's falling to pieces, sure. It's almost beyond restoration. And yet I can't help having the feeling that it has some kind of life of its own. In fact, I have the feeling that it has *more* life now that it did when I was a boy. As if it's woken up somehow."

Aaron poured himself a large goblet of wine and drank half of it straight off. "I have to tell you, Vincent, I don't understand what the hell you're trying to say. But you're right. That portrait has a life of its own, including the life of my cat."

"I'll take it off your hands. Don't worry. I'll take it home with me tonight."

"Well, I wish you would. I can't stand the sight of it and I can't stand the *smell* of it. I don't ever want to hear the name of Walter Waldegrave again as long as I live."

"If you do decide to tell Sheriff Smith about it, refer him to me."

"I don't think I will tell him." Aaron finished his wine and wiped his mouth with the back of his hand. "He'd probably lock me up. And you, too, unless you're careful."

They had little else to say to each other. Each had been deeply disturbed by what had happened to Van Gogh and by the thought that the portrait somehow contained a key to the horrifying events of the past few days. Aaron wrapped the painting in sheets of packing paper, more carefully than was necessary, and Vincent carried it on his shoulder out to his car and locked it in the trunk. They stood together in the light of Aaron's porch, their breath smoking in the wind.

"I'll tell you what the sheriff says once he's visited," Aaron said, clasping Vincent's hand.

"Thanks. And believe me, I'm sorry about the picture."

"Well, we're probably letting our imagination run away with us. It'll all seem ridiculous in the morning."

"Sure."

Aaron hesitated for a moment, then put a hand on Vincent's shoulder. "Take care, won't you? I mean, you never know." He inclined his head toward the trunk of the car.

Vincent drove back to Candlemas feeling unhappy and unsettled. The house was in darkness when he arrived, and fresh snow was beginning to spiral out of the sky. He drove the Bentley around to the side of the house, where the garages and the stables were, and left the engine running while he climbed out and opened the old-fashioned, green-painted garage doors. He parked the car inside, killed the headlights and switched off the engine. As he did so, he was sure he heard a screeching noise.

He sat listening for a while. There were no sounds now but the ticking of cooling metal and the gurgling of the air-conditioning system. Perhaps the screech had been nothing more than a slipping fan belt. He shrugged to himself, removed the keys and climbed out of the car.

It was then that he heard it again, high and shrill. He stood where he was, but it had faded, and there was no indication where it might have come from or what it might have been. A dog maybe, or a child playing games. A cat in pain.

He lifted the Waldegrave portrait from the trunk and carried it around to the front of the house. He unlocked the door and stepped inside, groping for the light switch. The hallway was chilly and musty, and smelled of dead log fires and neglect. He propped the portrait against the wall and went through to the kitchen to turn off the burglar alarm and to switch on more lights.

It took him an hour to stoke up the boiler in the cellar and then light log fires in three of the downstairs rooms as well as in his bedroom. But soon the house began to feel warm and cheerful, and he rewarded himself by pouring a large glass of Irish whiskey and searching out a sirloin steak from the freezer, thinking to microwave himself a decent supper.

He was selecting a record to play—Beethoven's "Pastorale?" Or Tchaikovsky's "Serenade for Strings in C Major?"—when the telephone rang. He reached over, picked it up and said, "Pearson."

"Oh, it's you, Vincent," said a dry, elderly voice. "This is Gary Spellecy, from across the way. I saw your house lights on and I wanted to make sure it wasn't an intruder."

"Thanks, Gary. I came up unexpectedly. I did go 'round to Mrs. Miller's to see if she could open up the house, but she wasn't home."

"Well, she won't be for a while. She's gone to stay with the Guthries."

"I heard that Ben has been taken to the hospital. Is it anything serious?"

"Not sure it's my place to say," Gary Spellecy said.

"Gary, what's happened?" Vincent wanted to know. The logs in the fireplace popped noisily and a sudden downdraft blew smoke into the room.

"Well, Ben disfigured himself; that was the word I heard."

"*Disfigured* himself? How?"

"Cut his face to pieces with a broken drinking glass. Worst case of self-mutilation he'd ever seen, that's what Dr. Serling said."

Vincent felt as if his brain were suddenly swelling and

threatening to burst his skull. His forehead pounded and he had an aching sensation around his lower jaw that penetrated clear to the roots of his wisdom teeth. It was the effect of cold, tension and sudden shock.

"You okay?" Gary Spellecy asked.

"Yes, sure, I'm fine."

"You don't *sound* okay."

"I'm tired, that's all. Listen, do you have the Guthrie number? I think I ought to give Mrs. Miller a call."

"She was back down at the hospital last I heard."

Vincent put down the phone. He stared at his glass of whiskey as if it were a fatal draft of hemlock, but then he swallowed it in three larynx-bobbing gulps. It burned his tongue and stung the corners of his mouth.

He knew his intuition was right. Something, or somebody, had arrived in his life and was affecting everything around him. It might not be anyone he knew. The only clue he had so far was the vague description, given to him by the old woman at the Wentworth Apartments, of a black-dressed, white-faced woman in her mid-thirties.

Vincent went into the hallway and stood looking at the wrapped-up Waldegrave. He was still not completely sure Aaron hadn't been suffering under the influence of too much homemade wine. Aaron was the most skillful inpainter Vincent knew, and if anyone could have created that portrait of Van Gogh, it was Aaron. It seemed incredible that the cat had appeared on the canvas as if by some sinister magical force, as if it had been painted there by the spirit of Walter Waldegrave himself.

The most rational explanation was that Aaron had painted it himself, perhaps in remorse for having killed Van Gogh in a burst of drunken temper. But then, Vincent had never known Aaron to lose his temper, at least not violently, not even when he was pickled beyond redemption.

There was no doubt that something was seriously wrong. The cold winds of Christmas were bringing terrible events, and no matter how logically he tried to think about them, Vincent was growing increasingly convinced that he himself was at the center of the vortex.

Fifteen

Darien, December 18

They had locked her in a small upstairs bedroom, the windows bolted and shuttered so that even when the sun burned brightly for a few minutes just before twilight, all she could see were narrow cracks of orange light as fine as overheated wires. She cupped her hand up to the shutter, catching the sunlight in her palm like a glowing lifeline, whispering to herself, "Please, God, don't let them kill me."

The room was woolly with dust. The walls must have once been eggshell blue, but now they were faded gray and blotched with dampness. There was a single iron bed with a sagging horsehair mattress, but no sheets or blankets. The only other furniture was a wooden chair with a broken back and a small Victorian bureau, its chipped walnut veneer scabrous.

In spite of her discomfort, Laura had slept for two or three hours during the morning, and when she awakened, she found that a tray had been left for her on top of the bureau. Under a tarnished silver lid she discovered a salad of smoked chicken, coleslaw and pickled beetroot. A freshly baked muffin rested on a napkin. There was also a glass of white wine, tasting sharp and vinegary, as if it had aged past its prime.

Laura hadn't wanted to touch the food at first, but during the afternoon she had grown hungry and tasted a few mouthfuls. It reminded her for some reason of the food her grandmother used to prepare.

Now it was dark, and she sat forlornly on the edge of the bed waiting, listening, wondering if her captors had forgotten her.

A clock in the hallway downstairs chimed eight times.

Laura had never before in her life been frightened, or

threatened, or locked up. Her parents had always taken care of her; Edward had always taken care of her; and Danny had treated her as though she were actually fragile. It wouldn't occur to her to shout out and bang on the door and demand that Cordelia Gray set her free. All she could think of to do was to sit and wait for something to happen, for someone to come tell her that her imprisonment was at an end. Or that they were going to kill her.

At half-past eight, she heard footsteps on the uncarpeted stairs, and voices. Two people were arguing on the landing outside; they sounded like Maurice and Cordelia Gray. Maurice kept saying something about "selfishness, selfishness" and Cordelia was snapping, "You're always so judgmental. How can *you* decide what's best?"

"Because I have had the experience," Maurice said. He was standing almost directly outside Laura's door now; she could hear him distinctly. "Besides, Father always left such decisions to me, and if you're challenging me, well, you're challenging Father, too."

"Father is not the Lord Almighty, Maurice. He never has been and he never will be. The only reason he left *you* to decide who should benefit and who should not is because he could never bear to make such decisions himself; and you are the oldest surviving male. His weakness and Albert's accident aren't exactly what I call credentials for family authority."

"Nevertheless," Maurice insisted, "you will not have the girl."

"Which is more important?" Cordelia demanded. "*My* appearance, or Mother's? It's been seven years since Mother was fit to come out in public. What difference will another year make? Or even another two? Look at my face. Look at it! You can see for yourself what's happening to me. How can I get ahold of the picture unless I can go wherever I please—unless I'm charming? Unless I'm *more* than charming?"

"God, you're so vain. That's all that really matters to you, isn't it? The admiring looks of handsome young men. I can't think of a better name for you to have taken than that of Sybil Vane."

"You never knew Sybil," Cordelia replied, and there was a haughty kind of pain in her voice. "I loved Sybil, dearly."

"It was certainly a very dear love as far as *she* was

concerned," Maurice retorted. "In fact, the most expensive love she was ever to have."

"Don't speak of her," Cordelia said.

There was a pause, and then Cordelia said something indistinct. After a while, Maurice said, "I will wait until Christmas, but that is all I am prepared to do. It is only fair that Mother have her. You haven't even been up to *see* Mother since we returned; you don't know how ill she is. All that traveling, and now to come back to Wilderlings. She had her greatest triumphs here, and her greatest tragedies. It's been a terrible strain on her. She wouldn't have come, you know, if you hadn't persuaded her you could find the picture."

"Well, I've found it, haven't I?"

"Yes, and I congratulate you on your persistence. Unfortunately, we don't yet *have* it."

"We'll get it, don't worry. It was far too risky yesterday. There are still people in Litchfield County who would kill us all if they knew we were back."

"You're talking like Mother now. Nobody remembers."

Cordelia said nothing for a moment or two and then remarked, "We have to get the picture without anyone's knowing where it has gone, or why. That was Father's fatal mistake the last time, letting those people know."

There was more muttered conversation Laura was unable to hear, but then Maurice said, ". . . that cat."

"Well, what of it? It was so like Firework. And have *you* ever thought about Firework, or doing for Firework what the rest of us have been so assiduously doing for ourselves?"

"Firework is dead, Cordelia. There was no earthly point in Henry's taking all of that risk. Once one of us is gone, there is no restitution; you know that for yourself. That is why you must think of Mother."

Maurice walked a little way down the corridor and then added, "Besides, Henry is so clumsy. Henry is a pork butcher."

"I was thinking of giving the girl to Henry," Cordelia said calmly.

"Not to—?"

Cordelia laughed, a high, glassy laugh. "Of course not. Do you think I'd let him ruin her?"

"She's not for you, Cordelia. I hope I've made myself clear."

"Well, we can wait until Christmas Day, can't we, before we make up our minds about that? Perhaps Mother and I should play rummy for her; don't you think that's a good idea?"

"You curdle my blood sometimes, Cordelia."

"But you don't mind if Henry has the girl for now?"

"Is it so important to you?"

Cordelia said archly, "I enjoy it, when Henry has his girls. I think it arouses a certain sort of *fin-de-siècle* corruptness in me. He does it with such panache. It brings back those days in Berlin. Do you remember the Dodo Club?"

"I remember your getting drunk on crème-de-menthe and dizzy with cocaine, both at the same time."

"You're the stuffiest brother anyone could have, Maurice."

"And *you*, Cordelia, are the most relentless of sisters."

Without warning, Cordelia turned the key in the lock of Laura's door and opened it. Laura stepped back, alarmed that they might realize she had been listening, but Cordelia stalked into the tiny bedroom with glacial elegance and smiled at Laura indulgently, as if Laura were a scullery maid who happened to have polished the firedogs rather well. Laura couldn't help but feel there was something oddly old-fashioned about the Grays, a traditionalism deeper than the usual WASPish conservatism of Darien, Westport and all parts east.

Cordelia wore a black off-the-shoulder evening dress, replete with sparkling black sequins. There were diamond combs in her hair and a diamond choker around her neck. Her makeup was deathly white, and although she was still beautiful, she looked as if she had been completely drained of blood. Even her lips were white.

She glanced at the lunch tray and smiled. "I'm pleased that you've eaten," she said. "Sophonisba hasn't used the kitchen for years and years, but she'll improve." She paused and then added, "We were so spoiled in Europe, you know."

Laura said tightly, "I want to call my husband."

"You shall, my dear. Shan't she, Maurice?"

Maurice appeared in the doorway, immaculate in a black tuxedo with a high collar, and nodded in a vague, unhelpful, James Masonish kind of way. "Of course she shall; all in good time."

Laura said, "Are you going to kill me?"

"Kill you?" Cordelia asked, pressing her hand incredulous-ly against her white bosom. "What on earth has given you that idea?"

"You keep saying you're going to *give* me . . . either to your mother, or to Henry, or . . ." Laura's voice trailed off.

"Well, you mustn't get the wrong idea," Cordelia said, linking her arm through Laura's. "Come, you must come downstairs with us and meet some of the rest of the family. Then I'm sure you and Henry should get better acquainted."

"Please . . ." Laura protested. "Please, all I want to do is go home."

Yet although she knew urgently and strongly that she *did* want to go home, somehow she couldn't bring herself to speak with real conviction. It was more like the urgency she might have felt in a dream, slow and glutinous and complicated. She began to feel that if she did what she was told, and smiled and behaved herself, everything was going to be all right. She looked into Cordelia's mirrorlike eyes and she saw for certain that everything was going to be all right.

"I mustn't stay too long, though," she said, allowing Cordelia to lead her through the door and along the landing. From somewhere downstairs she could hear piano music, an odd melody that almost sounded as if someone were playing it backward.

"Of course not," Cordelia reassured her. Maurice, a little way behind them, grunted in what might have been approba-tion.

They descended the stairs to the hallway. On their left, the double mahogany doors to the music room were open, and without hesitation, Cordelia led Laura by the arm straight into the room. There, for the first time, Laura saw the Gray family.

There were eight more of them at least. They were gathered around the huge grand piano, which was draped in a brown shawllike piano cover, and they were in evening dress. Three men, including Henry, with stiff, upright collars, and five women, variously dressed in green and black and crimson gowns that seemed to have borrowed their styles from every period from late Victorian to the heyday of Princess Grace.

Henry was seated at the piano; he stopped playing and rose to bow to Laura as Cordelia brought her in. "I have been waiting to see you again, with the same anticipation of the Lappish people when they look forward to the coming of spring," he said.

"Henry can be obscure," Cordelia remarked from the side of her mouth as Henry took Laura's hand and kissed it.

"This is my Uncle John," Cordelia said as a tall, white-haired man came forward, inclining his head in welcome. Uncle John looked as pale and dry-skinned as the rest of the Grays, and there was a noticeable *collapsed* appearance to his face, like the hull of a boat beginning to rot. He mouthed the word "Charmed" and retreated.

In turn, Cordelia took Laura around to her Uncle Belvedere, her mother's brother, a slight, small man with the constant nodding of Parkinson's disease; her Aunt Willa, a stout woman in a green silk dress far too tight under the arms; her cousins Emily, Ermintrude and Nora, three prim, lisping little girls with ringlets whom Laura found it difficult to tell apart; and, in the background, Cordelia's sister Alicia, who looked younger than Cordelia but far more withered; and, lastly, her second cousin Netty, who was paralyzed and sat in an incongruously modern wheelchair, her knees covered with a pink blanket.

"We were singing," Henry said. "At least I was playing and we were about to sing."

"Aunt Alicia says we have nothing to sing about," Ermintrude said, giggling. "Aunt Alicia says that life is a tragedy."

"Well, then," Henry said, "we shall sing that life is a tragedy."

He began to play the same backward-sounding music, the rings on his fingers glittering as his hands wandered over the keyboard. Laura stood where she was, in dread of this extraordinary company, yet hypnotized by the melody and by a feeling that if she tried to leave now, she would be missing the most important event of her life. Something was going to happen to her. She couldn't think what, and it didn't occur to her to ask. But she knew it was important.

> *The kiss of death is on our lips,*
> *The day of mourning dawns.*
> *The marble angels cast their shade*
> *Across the frosty lawns.*

Henry sang with robustness, as if it were a marching song, and then immediately broke into "The Boers Have Got My Daddy."

> *The Boers have got my Daddy,*
> *My soldier Dad.*
> *I don't like to hear my Mammy sigh,*
> *I don't like to hear my Mammy cry. . . .*

At this, Uncle Belvedere banged the flat of his hand on top of the piano and Henry fell silent. Everyone looked around in embarrassment. Cordelia moved behind Henry and said, "That wasn't quite the thing, was it, Henry?"

Henry stood up. He pressed one key, middle C, waited until the tone had died away and then closed the piano lid.

"My apologies, Uncle," he said. "I would have thought that all happened rather a long time ago."

"To *you*, perhaps," Belvedere replied. His voice was reedy and hoarse. "But there are some of us who will remember to the very end of time."

"You already have my apology," Henry repeated and walked quickly out of the room into the hallway, where he stood with his hands on his hips, his head raised in temper. Cordelia followed him, beckoning Laura to join her. Laura was rather relieved to be excused from the midst of the Gray family and came after her at once.

"How long before we can get hold of the painting?" Henry was asking testily. "Uncle Belvedere grows more irritating with every day that passes."

"We're going to try again on Sunday," Cordelia reassured him. "If we're lucky, Mr. Halperin will be out for brunch."

"You're absolutely sure he has it?"

"No question at all. Mr. Astengo said he had seen it in Halperin's studio himself."

Henry took hold of Cordelia's shoulder. "Well," he said, "I have to admire your intelligence. I don't think *I* would have thought of tracking down all the picture restorers in the northeastern United States, let alone phoning them all."

Cordelia smiled. "Meanwhile, Maurice is quite agreeable to your having this young lady to amuse you, at least until we decide what to do with her."

"Well, well, that's excellent," Henry said. He turned to Laura and looked her up and down with undisguised pleasure. "And when will you decide? You and the estimable Maurice?"

"Christmas," Cordelia said. "So you have a few days."

"Thank you," Henry told her.

"Only one thing to remember," warned Cordelia.

Henry made a smirking face. "Very well, I'll try. *That* would rather ruin things for you and Aunt Isobel, wouldn't it? You wouldn't have very much left to fight over. Still, she's quite pretty. I hope I'm not tempted."

Laura kept on thinking: *I must call Danny, I must get away.* But the more she repeated the words, the less meaning they seemed to have, and as she stood next to Cordelia and Henry Gray in the hallway of Wilderlings, she felt no real urge to escape. She was caught by the aura of the Gray family as helplessly as if she were an insect in a web.

"Come," Henry said, beckoning Laura across the hallway to the staircase. She followed him obediently. The patterns on the floor appeared to lean away from her at all the wrong angles. As she started up the stairs, the steps seemed to slope. She told herself, *I must tell Danny where I am,* but then she couldn't even think who Danny was.

Henry led her the length of the landing to a large bedroom with double doors, which he opened with a flourish. Nodding, he indicated that she was to step inside. Laura hesitated for a second, trying to see by his eyes what he was thinking, what he was feeling, what he was going to do with her; but his eye sockets might just as well have contained polished ball bearings for all the expression she could see in them.

Inside the bedroom there was a wide bed with an elaborately carved headboard of dark and dusty oak. The drapes were half drawn, but Laura could make out the pale radiance of snow outside the window. There was an uncomfortable-looking ottoman, a heavy wardrobe and a rococo bureau in the French style.

Henry closed the doors and turned the key. "You must forgive my family sometimes," he said. "Over the years, they have become obsessed by their memories."

"Why was your uncle so upset by that song?"

"Well," Henry smiled, casually taking off his tuxedo and draping it over the ottoman, "it always reminds him of Albert."

"Albert?"

"My cousin. He was killed, you know."

"But not in the Boer War."

Henry was unlinking his cuffs. He looked at Laura in surprise and then laughed. "Please," he said, "you must make yourself comfortable."

"I don't understand."

Henry came over and took hold of her shoulders. He stared into her eyes for a long time. She couldn't imagine how long it actually was, although she thought she heard the clock chiming again. All she could remember afterward was watching Henry's beautifully curved lips as they softly told her what she had to do.

"You are mine now. Do you understand that? You belong to me. You are my servant, and you will do everything I ask of you, without question. Your will is completely subjugated to mine. There is nothing you will not do for me."

Laura stood quietly and bowed her head.

Henry told her with even greater gentleness, "I will be kind to you, you can be sure of that, unless you try to disobey me, in which case I shall have to punish you severely. You will always ask for your punishment when you have distressed me. Punishments will not be given unless requested; but by the same token, you will not be absolved from your guilt unless you have been punished."

At last he turned away, and walked across the bedroom and into a dressing room at the side. He returned with a Hasselblad camera, rather an old one, and a tripod, which he set at the foot of the bed. Laura watched him dully. She felt as if she lacked energy to either move or speak.

"You can undress now," Henry said. "I want you completely naked."

He went back to the dressing room and returned with a floodlight on a stand and a silver photographer's umbrella. He set these up on either side of the bed and plugged the lamp in, switching it on momentarily to test that it was working.

"But you're not undressed," he said. "Let me help you."

Laura could see a bright green afterimage of the floodlight's element dancing in front of her eyes. Behind it, Henry appeared and stood close to her; with cool hands and an expressionless face, he began to unbutton her blouse. "I am the most fortunate and at the same time the most unfortunate of men," he said. "I have met some of the most entrancing women in the world, from child-women to those in the full sensual flare of their maturity. I have photographed hundreds of them. But that is all I can do. I cannot take them. I am prevented by the unnatural strictures of my existence from ever satisfying my desires. Thus I have to satisfy myself with film, with negatives and transparencies. How right those words are! Negatives and transparencies. And those are all that I am able to love. A company of ghosts."

Laura hardly heard him. Her eyes were half-closed now, and she felt as if she were falling into a kind of waking sleep. She felt Henry's fingers unbutton her cuffs and then draw her blouse off her shoulders. She felt his cold breath on her neck as he leaned forward and reached around to unclasp her bra. She smelled his cologne. Then he bared her breasts, and with the lightest of touches, his fingertips traced around the curves of each of them, cupping their heaviness for a moment, caressing each nipple until it crinkled and stiffened.

Now his hands ran down her sides, making her shudder. He unfastened her skirt and let it fall to the floor. Without apparent effort, he lifted her in his arms and carried her over to the bed.

She opened her eyes and stared up at him. In the lamp light, he was remarkably handsome. She could have believed she was in a Regency romance, being carried to bed by a good-looking swain. Yet there was something infinitely corrupt and cold about Henry, some crucial lack of humanity that was both erotic and frightening. She feared him, but she also desired him. There was no whisper of Danny in her mind; no whisper of home, or safety, or getting away.

Henry laid her on the bed. Then he knelt beside her, leaned over and kissed her on the mouth; a strange, chaste kiss with his lips closed.

"You don't know how much I long for you," he said.

He bent his head and kissed each of her breasts, his lips brushing her nipples and arousing them again. His cool fingers traced their way down her stomach, and around her thighs. His knuckles trailed between her legs.

"*Henry*," she said in a voice that didn't sound like her own.

He didn't reply. He gently tugged down her white-cotton panties and drew them off. For a fleeting second, his middle finger ran down the neatly closed line of her vulva; but even as she shuddered again, he stood up, smiled at her and turned away.

"You tempt me as much as the very best of them," he said. His hand was clasped over his mouth; she could scarcely hear what he was saying.

"What do you *want*?" she asked.

He went across to the floodlight and switched it on, drowning the bed in dazzling white light.

"I want to take pictures of you," he said. "I want to add you to my collection."

He bent over his Hasselblad and adjusted it. "I don't want you to pose. All I want you to do is to listen to what I say and try to conjure up a picture in your mind. You are mine, remember. You have no soul of your own. Whatever I want you to be, you will be, without question. You are a servant; as such, you must fear your master."

Laura lay back naked on the bed, staring up at the ceiling. The bright light made her feel somehow as if scores of people were watching her out of the darkness. Defensively she crossed her hands over her breasts and strained her eyes to see beyond the circle of light. All she could distinguish was Henry's hunchbacked silhouette as he bent over the camera, and the reflected glint of its lens.

"You are a Swedish girl, blonde and blue-eyed, who has been abducted while on vacation in Egypt by an Arabian slavetrader, a *caboceer*. You have been chained by the ankles and led far across the desert in a coffle of black slavegirls, your white skin protected from the sun by a white, flowing burnous. At last you arrive at an oasis, far out in the desert, and here you are to be sold."

Laura closed her eyes. She hardly heard the discreet, chirring sound of Henry's camera. But she could hear the soft and abrasive whisper of sand blowing across the dunes; she could hear the snorting of camels and the billowing of tent flaps; she could almost see the setting sun's red reflection in the oasis.

She was led into the tent. There was a red woven carpet spread on the ground; smoky torches burned all around her. By the flickering light of the torches she could make out a circle of Arabian faces, hook-nosed men in black robes; Nubians in pale *djellabas*; Tuaregs with faces wrapped to the eyes, displaying curved daggers in jeweled sheaths. There was a smell of charcoal and lamb fat and spices, mingled with the sharper odor of human sweat. When somebody clapped, a springy-sounding drum started up and a few of the men began to clap and tap their feet in time to its complicated rhythm.

"She will dance for you!" a voice declared, close to her. And with a single tug, her white robes were pulled away and she stood suddenly nude in front of the lascivious faces of her would-be owners.

As the drum beat on, Laura began to dance, elegantly and slowly at first, running her fingers through her hair, swaying her hips. When the beat grew faster, she ran her hands up and down her body and caressed her breasts. The Arabs shouted out to her and cheered her, and one of them let loose a white cockatoo that fluttered in panic around the tent.

Laura twisted and turned as provocatively as she could, sometimes approaching the men so closely she could smell the lamb and licorice on their breath. Her body was glossy with sweat, and she shone in the torch light, her hair clinging damply to her head. At the very back of the tent, a stark-naked boy of no more than fourteen watched her with calm and sensuous eyes, his penis half-erect.

Now she knelt, arching her body backward, opening her thighs. The drumming rose to a fierce and rousing patter. The Arabs shouted, clapped and grew restless, never once taking their ogling eyes from her body. She reached down between her legs with both hands and opened herself out for them, glistening pink, wider and wider, giving them everything they wanted—her privacy, her pride, her sexuality, her very soul.

She could feel a climax rising up within her, tightening the muscles of her pelvis, and she ground her teeth and shook her head from side to side. But when she was on the very brink, the bright light suddenly died, the tent collapsed, the desert blew away, the oasis dried up . . . and she was lying naked on a strange, dusty bed in a gloomy room, panting, perspiring and shocked.

The drumming resolved itself into a persistent knocking at the door. Henry went to answer it, while Laura lay back on the bed, stunned, unable to understand where she was or what had happened.

Henry opened the door. "What is it, Maurice?" he asked irritably. "You must have known that I was busy."

Maurice said, "I simply wish to advise you, dear boy, to remain as quiet as possible. The police are here."

Henry said, "Very well," and returned to the bed. He held out a hand to Laura and smiled. "You did very well, my love. You have far more imagination than I would have expected."

Laura, unable to find words to respond with, took his hand and shakily stood up.

"You may dress now," Henry said. "If you look in the wardrobe, on the left-hand side, you will find a number of dresses. They are all black, but then you are a servant and must wear black anyway. There are some shoes there, too. You will wear no underwear. I forbid it."

Laura nodded. Henry took her arm and kissed her on the forehead. "We have until Christmas," he said. "Four days! That will be plenty of time for some of my finest adventures. Have you ever been to Berlin, to the Salambo Club, where men can dance with naked women? Have you ever been to Thailand, to the brothels?"

"No," Laura whispered.

"You shall go," Henry promised, kissing her again.

Sixteen

Darien, December 18

George Kelly showed his badge and asked, "Are you Maurice Gray?"

Uncle John smiled thinly. "I'm sorry," he replied. "I regret not."

"Is Maurice Gray here?"

"Not that I am aware of."

Jack, who was standing next to George with the collar of his sheepskin coat turned up, pointed around to the side of the house. "That Cadillac parked there. Does that belong to Maurice Gray?"

Uncle John shook his head. Although the snow was beginning to fall heavily now, and George and Jack were shuffling their feet on the doorstep to keep themselves warm, he showed no inclination to invite them inside.

"If it doesn't belong to Maurice Gray, who does it belong to?" asked Jack.

"I'm afraid I really don't know."

George sniffed and patiently massaged his leather-gloved hands. "We want to talk to Maurice Gray in connection with a homicide inquiry. It's important, you understand; several people have been killed. It's important we talk to him so we can eliminate him from our investigation."

"I see," Uncle John nodded.

Jack said, "If he's not here now, can you tell us when you're expecting him?"

"I'm not expecting him."

"Then do you happen to know where we could find him?"

"I'm sorry, I regret not."

At that moment Cordelia appeared, gliding across the hallway in her black evening gown. "John," she said, "do you have to leave the door open? Netty's complaining of the draft."

She looked at George and Jack and smiled vaguely, her eyes already moving on to something else.

Jack stared at her in fascination. He tried to look away from her, but found that he couldn't. He tried to think conventional thoughts about her: procedural, sherifflike thoughts, but found that he couldn't do that, either. She was so glacially self-assured; so haughtily erotic; so contemptuous. She stood with her head tilted slightly upward, her eyes narrowed as if she found it difficult to focus on tradesmen and uninvited callers; one hand perched in a mannered fashion on her left hip.

And yet, if Elmer Tweed's story had any truth in it, and George's suspicions were correct, this woman was closely related to a psychopathic killer. It was possible that she was implicated in the homicides herself.

Jack usually found people who killed other people to be boring and clumsy. They were never startling, like Cordelia Gray. They never made him feel socially inferior, the way that she did. Nor did they ever make him feel like prey.

"I'm Cordelia Gray; Maurice Gray's sister. Who are you?"

Jack tried to introduce himself as clearly and as confidently as possible. "My name's Jack Smith, ma'am. Sheriff Jack Smith, from Litchfield County. This is George Kelly, from the Darien Police Department."

Cordelia's eyes returned to them briefly. "What are you looking for?" she asked.

"We're looking for somebody called Maurice Gray."

"Has he done anything wrong?"

"We don't know that yet, ma'am. But it's vital that we talk to him."

Cordelia thought for a moment and then said, "You can't."

"Any good reason?" Jack asked. He was beginning to find these people baffling and frustrating. What was more, his toes had already disappeared, and he was sure the rest of his feet were soon going to follow. The temperature was eight below, and still dropping.

Cordelia said, "My dear man, you can have any reason you want. He isn't here; rather, he *is* here, but he isn't well enough to talk to strangers; he won't talk to anybody from the police without his lawyer being present; he died last year; he didn't die, but he feels as if he might."

George gave a vigorous sniff. "If you'll pardon me, ma'am, none of this is very constructive. We're only trying to carry out our duty to the community."

"Do you have a warrant for Maurice Gray's detention?"

"No, ma'am, we don't."

"Do you have a subpoena for him to appear before a judge or a jury?"

"No, ma'am, that neither."

"What about a search warrant?"

George shook his head.

"In that case," Cordelia told him, "you may go. Come back only if you have the necessary papers. We have been in Europe for a long time, but now that we have returned to the States, we expect to enjoy our Constitutional guarantees."

Jack was about to say something, but George firmly squeezed his elbow and said, "Come on, Jack. This lady's quite right. We shouldn't go making a nuisance of ourselves, not without warrants."

Jack glanced at him, but George remained affable and avuncular. "Here, ma'am," he said, slipping a card out of his coat pocket and handing it to Cordelia. "That's my number down at headquarters. If Maurice Gray decides he might like to have a chat with us purely out of public service, we'll be glad to hear from him. Meanwhile, we'll see what we can do to roust out some warrants."

Cordelia refused to take the card, keeping her hands by her sides. But George was unfazed. He tucked the card back in his pocket, beamed and said, "You can find me in the phone book, under Cops."

There was an instant when Jack found himself locked with Cordelia in an exchange of stares as complicated and hostile as barbed wire. Usually, Jack found it easy to read other people's eyes. The kind of people who found their way into police cells never found it necessary to conceal their feelings. If they hated your guts, it showed. But Cordelia's eyes transmitted an evil of peculiar complexity; an evil that might have been no more than arrogance and vanity, but which could encompass sadistic acts of unimaginable terror.

"Let's go, Jack," said George, and for the first time Jack

understood that for all of his offhandedness, George was also wary of Cordelia. "Let's go find some coffee, before our butts fall off."

Jack and George walked away from the house and back down the snowy drive. Jack turned round as the front door slammed shut behind them, but George grabbed his arm again, and pulled him along.

"Now that is a woman who could make a man's toes curl," Jack remarked. George raised a finger to his lips, indicating that they wait until they got to the car before they discussed it.

When they reached George's Chevy Silverado, the windshield was already covered with freshly fallen snow.

"I'll bet you two months' salary that was Maurice Gray's Cadillac parked outside there and another two months' salary that Maurice Gray was home," Jack said as George started up the wagon's engine, switched on the wipers and pulled away from Wilderlings in a tight, crunching circle.

"Sure it was, and sure he is. You don't have to bet me money."

"Then why did we beat the retreat so easily?"

George said, "Hand me those cigarettes, will you?" He shook one out of the pack with his right hand and propped it between his thick, comfortable lips. "We beat the retreat because those people are very wealthy and because they're not stupid, and also because we won't get a search warrant, not for all the snow on Stratford Street."

"We have Elmer Tweed's testimony."

"That won't count for chickenshit, not when we're trying to get a warrant against the Gray family."

George lit his cigarette, jostling it from one side of his mouth to the other. "The Grays may have been living in Europe for seventy-odd years, but they still have plenty of influence here. They own a lot of land and a lot of property, and there are quite a few families around Darien who still count them as friends."

"Did you find out *why* they went to live in Europe?"

"Nobody knows for sure. I looked it up in the newspaper morgue, but there wasn't even a mention that they'd left. One week the Grays were being regularly reported as a leading local family; the next thing, they were gone."

"Does anybody remember them personally? Any old-timers?"

"I managed to find one, Mrs. Elizabeth Cartwright. She lives in Stamford now, but in the old days she and her family used to live next door to Wilderlings, in a house they called The Juggs. She played in the Grays' orchard when she was a girl, and she says she remembers some of the ladies of the family promenading under the apple trees in August, beautiful women they were, that's what Mrs. Cartwright says. Beautiful women. And she remembers the father of the family, Algernon Gray, and his wife Isobel. She remembers some cousins, too. She played with them once, with hoops, even though they didn't visit Wilderlings often. A girl called Ermintrude; she doesn't recall the rest of the names. But anyway, she went to play there one day and all the trunks were packed and waiting outside in the drive and the whole family just took off, cousins and all, and she never saw them again. She remembers the family seemed very upset, though. Isobel Gray was wearing a black veil over her hat, and she was crying."

Jack sat back in his seat and blew out his cheeks in frustration. "How about immigration? Did you have any luck with them?"

"Not a thing. The Gray family flew into Boston on November eighteenth on a Sabena flight direct from Brussels. Their passports and customs documents were in perfect order. None of them have any criminal records in Europe, none of them belong to the Communist Party, none of them are known to be affiliated with any subversive or illegal groups. They weren't carrying dope, guns, knives or pornography."

"Maybe I'm just kidding myself. Maybe Maurice Gray doesn't have anything to do with these skinning murders at all."

"Maybe he doesn't. But I don't think we should let it go until we find out a little bit more about the Gray family."

"George, this isn't your problem."

"I know it isn't my problem, but I'm curious. Those people looked interesting to me; didn't they look interesting to you? You don't see people like that every day, even in Darien. Very chic, did you notice? Evening dress, expensive perfume, yet the house is still looking pretty run-down. Do you know what they remind me of? 'The Addams Family.' I wouldn't be surprised if they had a butler called Lurch."

"You're up to something," Jack said.

"I'm just satisfying my natural and commendable interest in local affairs," George told him. "I'm supposed to police this district, right? In that case, I need to know everything that's going on. Who lives here, what kind of people they are."

"So what are you proposing?"

They could see a gas station up ahead, its pale light blurry in the evening snow. "You want a coffee?" George asked, and Jack said, "Sure."

They pulled up outside the small diner attached to the gas station and climbed down from the wagon. As they walked across the untrodden snow to the doorway, George laid his arm around Jack's shoulder and said, "Listen, go back to Litchfield for a couple of days, at least until Christmas is over. I need a little more time, that's all, to see if I can't pull together enough evidence for you to go for a warrant."

"How are you going to do that?"

"I'm going to make believe that the Judge of Natural Justice has just issued me a valid permit to search Wilderlings from attic to basement and all stops in between."

"What happens if somebody finds out what you're up to?"

"They won't. I wasn't trained in midtown Manhattan for nothing."

"Well, I'm not sure I like the idea of your taking the risk. Besides which, any evidence you find will be inadmissible. Illegal search."

"There are ways of making it admissible, believe me."

Jack half-opened the diner door and somebody inside called out, "Are you coming in, asshole, or are you going out?"

Jack said, "Let's get that coffee. But two words of warning. One, don't do it. Two, don't get *caught* doing it."

George grinned and winked. "You're talking to a pro here, Jack my boy. Believe me. We'll get our own back on those haughty-talking Grays, fair and square. Well, square, if not fair."

They said little on the way back to George's headquarters. They shook hands and wished each other a happy Christmas; then Jack collected his wagon from the parking lot and headed to Torrington. The snow had died away, and he found he could drive quite fast; he was alone on the highway, a single car in a world of deathly white.

He knew he should have insisted that George stay away from Wilderlings. He almost felt like calling him up when he got back to Torrington and demand that he drop his plans. His worst fear was that George would find clear-cut evidence linking Maurice Gray with the skinning murders and that it would be thrown out of court because he had obtained it by subterfuge, violating Maurice Gray's legal and Constitutional rights. On the other hand, he knew that Elmer Tweed was an unreliable witness with a shaky past and that no judge would grant them a warrant of any kind on the basis of Tweed's half-hysterical ramblings about hypodermic needles, roaring noises and inconclusive conversations about the beauty of skin. They needed more, much more, and he simply prayed that George would be able to dig it up.

It was ten past eleven when he arrived back at headquarters. He eased himself stiffly out of the wagon and walked with a weary limp into the reception area. Norman Goldberg was sitting behind the desk talking to somebody on the telephone, but he raised a hand as Jack came in to indicate that he wanted to talk to him.

"Yes, ma'am," Norman was saying. "Well, I'm sorry, ma'am. No, it's not, I'm afraid. No. You'll have to take it up with your husband. Well, yes, you could wake him up now, but why don't you wait until morning?"

Jack leaned on the desk and dry-washed his face with his hands.

"What's cooking?" he asked.

"That lady wanted to know if we could arrest her husband."

"What for?"

"He came home from an Elks meeting, skidded on his front driveway and rear-ended her brand-new Topaz."

Jack grunted in amusement. "I wonder whether that comes under Domestic Disturbance or Traffic Accident. Anything else?"

"Yes. You had a call from Dr. Serling out at New Milford. He says he wants to talk to you about some kind of medical incident that happened this afternoon."

"Is it urgent?"

"He said soonest, if you could spare the time. He's at Litchfield County, extension four twenty-two."

Jack yawned. "Okay, then. Can you put me through?"

Norman punched out the number. While he waited to be connected, he said, "How did it go with Maurice Gray?"

"It didn't. We went to the house but his family said he wasn't home, and that even if he were, he wasn't going to talk to us."

"Well, you guessed they might be awkward, didn't you?"

Jack took out his chewing gum and unwrapped a stick. "I guess so. It was the way they did it, though, that rubbed my fur the wrong way. George and I might just as well have been a couple of Fuller Brush salesmen for all the respect they showed us."

"Crime is a buyer's market these days, Sheriff."

Norman got through to the hospital, and after a short delay, he was transferred to Dr. Serling. He handed the phone to Jack, then sat back with his hands clasped over his pot belly.

"Dr. Serling? Sheriff Jack Smith, from Torrington."

"Ah, thank you for calling, Sheriff. We've met a few times, you and I. Remember the Cancer Research cookout at Kent Furnace? We had quite a talk there about postmortems."

"Yes, Doctor. I remember. What seems to be the problem?"

"Well," Dr. Serling said, "I've had to deal with a serious case of self-mutilation here today. A young paraplegic patient of mine, Ben Miller. He was paralyzed from the waist down a few years back when he fell off a roof, and ever since then, he's been depressed, and occasionally hysterical—understandably, of course, since his whole future was taken from him."

"So what's happened?" Jack asked impatiently.

"What's happened is that he's cut up his face, so seriously the surgeons thought earlier this evening that he might not live. He's lost a lot of blood, his nervous system is traumatized and he's still in a state of psychological and physiological crisis."

Jack rubbed his forehead. He could feel the deep-seated beginnings of a bad headache. "I'm sorry to hear that, Doctor. I'm not quite sure what I can do about it."

"Well—I hope this doesn't sound ridiculous—"

"No, no, Doctor, believe me—"

"I heard, you see, that you were involved in trying to solve these terrible murders in which people were skinned alive—"

"That's correct."

"Well, Ben Miller, before he committed this act of self-mutilation, had been growing increasingly anxious for several days; first of all that somebody or something had come back, somebody or something threatening to him; and then this afternoon he panicked thinking they wanted his skin; he decided that whatever happened, they weren't going to get it."

Jack slowly stood up straight. Norman sensed he was suddenly interested in what Dr. Serling was saying, and he straightened up, too.

"What did he say, precisely?" Jack asked.

"He said, 'Don't you come anywhere near!' He said, 'Whatever you do, don't touch *my* skin!'"

Jack was silent for a moment, then said, "Was Miller physically or mentally ill in any way before he mutilated himself?"

"I thought he might be. It was my suspicion that he was suffering from the side effects of a renal breakdown. But when they operated on him this evening, the surgeons discovered that his kidneys were functioning extremely well, given his paralyzed condition."

"Was he very suggestible?"

"He wasn't particularly stable, if that's what you mean. He could occasionally fly off into terrible tempers; but then, many chair-bound people do."

Jack tried to make himself clearer. "What I'm actually suggesting is that he might have heard about the skinning murders in the news and taken it into his head that the killer was after him, too. That happens pretty often, even among completely rational people."

Dr. Sterling said stiffly, "Ben Miller isn't insane, Sheriff."

"I'm sorry," Jack replied. "I didn't mean to say he is. I'm simply saying that when a series of murders is highly publicized, it isn't uncommon for certain susceptible people to have—what shall we call it?— ∟xaggerated fear of being next on the list."

"You're quite a psychiatrist, Sheriff."

"I have to be," Jack retorted. He was too tired for sarcasm.

Dr. Serling said, "All right. I accept your point. And, after all, what I'm trying to suggest isn't particularly logical. I accept that, too. But Ben Miller, after the accident in which he broke his spine, was very close to death. Clinically, for a short period of time, he actually was dead."

"I'm not sure I'm following you."

"Well, it isn't easy to explain. But accident victims who have technically died almost always emerge from their experience with a sharply heightened sensitivity to death and danger. There are many recorded instances of it. Only last year in Seattle a woman who'd nearly died in an accident when she was a teenager managed to save her child by pulling him away from a construction site just seconds before the scaffolding collapsed. She claimed afterward that she had actually *seen* the disaster before it even started to happen."

"Doctor, this is very interesting stuff, but—"

"Listen to me, please," Dr. Serling interrupted. "I'm as skeptical as you are; probably more so. But I've been talking to Ben Miller's mother all evening while the surgeons have been operating on Ben, and I believe that Ben's case is at least worth a look. Ben may have sensed something or worked something out in his mind that you, with your usual police procedures, may have missed."

"Doctor," Jack said, "I'll tell you what I'll do. I'll come around to the hospital tomorrow morning, say at eleven o'clock, and talk with you some more. Maybe I can get to see Ben Miller, too. Don't think I don't appreciate your call. I do. I'm a little pooped, that's all. I'm always interested in theories that come off the wall. I'm even a little bit interested in the occult myself. My wife has a friend who tells a mean fortune. Tea leaves, cards, even the way the hairs grow out of your nose."

"Very well," Dr. Serling said. "Make it ten-thirty and I can be there. Room Four fifty-four at Litchfield County."

When Jack put down the phone, Norman asked, "What was that all about?"

"I don't know exactly. Dr. Serling thinks one of his patients may be psychic or something and that he might have picked up some kind of—what do you call it?—*aura*."

"Aura?"

"Oh, search me. I think I'm going to go home to bed."

"There was one more thing," Norman said, leafing through the pad of telephone messages.

Jack waited, halfway across the reception area, his car keys jingling in his hand.

"Here it is. Two telephone calls from Aaron Halperin—you know him, that picture-restorer guy out at Bantam, the one we keep pulling in for drunk driving—the first to say that somebody had stolen his cat, the second to say that he had found the cat in his garden."

Jack could hardly believe what he was hearing. "You're preventing me from going home to my wife because a drunken picture restorer lost his cat and then found it?"

"Uh-uh," Norman said, shaking his head. "He found it hanging in a tree. It was skinned."

Jack stopped jingling his keys.

"Something's going down here," he said. "Something very, very unpleasant is going down here. Get me some coffee. Black, no sugar. I'm going to call home to tell Nancy I'm okay. Then I'm going to drive over to Litchfield County."

"You're going now? Tonight?"

"Do you think I'll be able to sleep if I don't?"

Seventeen

Litchfield, December 18

Dr. Serling was hurrying out of the hospital as Jack arrived. He was crossing the brightly lit reception area, shucking on his brown tweed coat and jamming his crumpled brown fisherman's hat on his head. They almost collided in the swinging doors, and Dr. Serling's medical case caught Jack a sharp knock on the knee.

"Sheriff Smith!" Dr. Serling exclaimed. Then he frowned and peered at Jack narrowly. "It *is* Sheriff Smith, isn't it?"

Jack rubbed his knee. "Yes. I'm glad I caught you."

"I didn't expect you until morning," Dr. Serling said, extending his hand. "You've changed, haven't you, since the last time we met? Didn't you used to sport a mustache?"

"I've lost about twenty pounds," Jack said. "I gave up beer, and maple syrup, and corn chips, and I started coaching a kids' football team. Would you believe it, the Harwinton Hackers?"

"Tonight I think I'm pretty much ready to believe anything," Dr. Serling said. He checked his watch. "Look, it's late. If you want to see Ben Miller tonight, you'd better come up and meet Dr. Schuhmacher right away. He's the surgeon who did the operation. He was washing up to go home last I saw him."

Dr. Serling ushered Jack over to the shiny glass-fronted elevators and pushed the button for "Up." Jack looked around while they waited. Litchfield County was one of the most modern medical facilities in New England, with gleaming, white-tiled floors and a huge abstract statue of twisted bronze, entitled "Healing" in the center of the reception area. Dr.

Serling thought it looked like a bay horse with a chronic case of the staggers, but he had never said so.

There was a strong aroma of synthetic apple blossoms around, and a constant *acappella* chorus of dissonant squeaks from the nurses' vinyl-soled shoes.

"This case has upset me," Dr. Serling told Jack, leaning against the wall of the elevator as they rose up to the fourth floor.

"Believe me, this case has upset me, too," Jack responded, unwrapping another stick of gum.

Dr. Serling nodded and kept on nodding, as if to say he knew, he knew. "I never believed much in psychic phenomena," he remarked. "You know, levitation, ectoplasm, that kind of thing. What I really believe in is the human spirit. I believe that our minds and our bodies have extraordinary powers that in everyday life are only half understood. When you run a country practice like mine, you come across all kinds of wild and wonderful things, and most of the time you can only guess at how they might have occurred. Do you know something? Last year, out in South Kent, an elderly female patient of mine claimed to have dug a tumor out of her stomach with nothing more than a wooden spoon. She showed me the spoon, and she showed me the tumor in a pickle jar, and she showed me her stomach, too, with a small red scar that was perfectly healed."

The elevator reached the fourth floor and they stepped out. It was quieter up here, although the smell of synthetic apple blossoms was just as distinctive. When Jack sniffed, Dr. Serling said, "The hospital administrators believe people would rather suffer in an orchard than in a public toilet."

He walked in front, swinging his medical case. "I was always aware that Ben Miller had been mentally affected by what he had experienced that time he almost died. And there are dozens of recorded cases where people who have been brought back from the very brink of clinical death claim to have acquired what you might describe as 'second sight.' But I never would have believed any of it, not for certain—not unless I had talked to Ben this afternoon, and not unless I had heard what his mother had to say."

"And what *did* his mother have to say?" Jack asked.

Dr. Serling stopped, halfway along the corridor, and looked at Jack with a face as grave as a country mortician's. "She told me that ever since his accident, Ben had been able to forecast storms, and to tell her in advance whenever one of her friends was going to get sick or die, and that he had predicted auto wrecks out on the highway, and fires, and all kinds of disasters.''

"And you believed her?"

"Not at first. I asked her why she had never told me about it before, and she said she had always been afraid to in case I might think Ben was crazy and have him committed."

"I suppose that's a plausible explanation. But it's still no reason to believe it was true."

Dr. Serling said in a quiet and measured voice, "Mrs. Miller also told me that Ben had felt sorry for me the day my daughter died."

"Your daughter isn't dead, though, is she? Didn't I read something about her just last week in the Litchfield *Sentinel*? She was organizing some fair or something, wasn't she, for cancer research?"

Dr. Serling nodded. "That's the daughter everybody knows. But years ago, when I was still at medical school, I conceived another daughter. I never saw her, scarcely ever heard from her. Her name was Fay, and she lived in Gainesville, Florida. She died about a year ago from multiple sclerosis."

"Is there any way Ben Miller could have found that out?"

Dr. Serling shook his head. "No one knew, except for Fay, her mother and myself. Now you know, too, but you're the only other person who does."

"So you genuinely believe that Ben Miller may be psychic and that he's been picking up threatening feelings from this killer?"

"I don't know," Dr. Serling answered. "I may be making a fool of myself. I may be acting overemotionally about Fay. I didn't really allow myself to grieve for her, after all, and believing in Ben Miller's psychic abilities may be a way of expressing my grief."

Jack pushed a wad of gum from one side of his mouth to the other. "Physician, stop trying to heal thyself," he said. "If Ben Miller knew something about you that it was impossible for him to know, then what you're suggesting about his psychic abilities may not be as wacky as you think."

"Do you suppose he might be able to help you catch the killer?" Dr. Serling asked.

Jack shrugged. "Right now, I'm just about ready to try anything."

"Come along and take a look at him, then. Dr. Schuhmacher has him in intensive care."

They walked side by side down to the end of the corridor to a waiting area with potted yuccas, a coffee table, leather-covered sofas and an original print on the wall of Geoffrey Callender's "Sunflowers and Cats." The two cats in the print were marmalade cats, with intense green eyes. Mrs. Miller was sitting beneath the picture looking white and distraught; a gray-haired woman in a plaid overcoat and glasses sat close beside her, holding her hands to comfort her.

"This is Mrs. Miller," Dr. Serling said. "I've allowed her to stay for a while, at least until Dr. Kellstrom comes on duty."

"Mrs. Miller," Jack said, nodding sympathetically. "I'm Sheriff Jack Smith. I'm real sorry to hear what happened to your son. It must have been a bad shock."

Mrs. Miller looked up at him vaguely but didn't reply. The woman next to her said, "She's been sedated, Sheriff. I'll be taking her home in just a moment, as soon as Dr. Schuhmacher has made his last examination."

"This is Mrs. Guthrie," Dr. Serling said. "She and her husband will be taking care of Mrs. Miller while Ben's in the hospital."

Just then Dr. Schuhmacher appeared, a small, black-bearded man with glasses as strong as magnifying lenses. His hair was neatly and systematically combed over a widening bald patch.

"Dr. Serling," he said in surprise. "I thought you'd gone."

"I was about to, but then I met my friend the sheriff here. He decided he'd very much like to take a look at Ben Miller tonight, if that's agreeable."

Dr. Schuhmacher glanced toward Mrs. Miller and said, "I don't see why not. Listen, first let me talk to the mother, give her some reassurance and get her off home. Then I'll take you in."

Whatever Dr. Schuhmacher said to Mrs. Miller, she and Mrs. Guthrie soon left, and he came back to Jack and Dr. Serling, busily cleaning his glasses with his white doctor's coat.

"She needs to rest," he said. "She's had a really traumatic day. In fact, I'm almost more worried about her than I am about her son."

He led the way farther along the corridor and then smartly turned right through a pair of swinging doors marked "Intensive Care." Jack asked, "How's the son shaping up?"

Dr. Schuhmacher said, "Badly. He was making progress for a while, but in the past hour or so, he's started to show signs of serious deterioration. Dr. Ahuja's with him now, as well as the cardiac-crisis team, but to be honest, I don't think his system is going to be able to stand the shock. He's a paraplegic, remember, and his heart and kidneys are already in a bad way. Now he's suffering from every kind of physiological emergency you can think of. His lungs collapsed twice during the operation, and that almost finished him."

"What do you give him?" Jack asked.

Dr. Schuhmacher stared nearsightedly at Jack through his fish-bowl glasses. "It isn't up to me to *give* him anything," he replied. "It's all up to good medical care and his own degree of survivability."

Jack was unfazed by Dr. Schuhmacher's attitude. He had never yet come across a surgeon who liked policemen. "Give me an educated guess," he said.

Dr. Schuhmacher glanced at Dr. Serling, obviously displeased, but Dr. Serling gave him an encouraging nod.

"Very well then," he said. "Six or seven hours, at the outside."

"Is he conscious?"

Dr. Schuhmacher shook his head.

"Is he likely to regain consciousness?"

"I don't think so. And even if he did, he wouldn't be able to talk to you. His mouth was very severely cut up, and at the moment, he's unable to move his lips."

Wearily Jack massaged the back of his neck. The Cherokee's passenger window didn't fit properly, and a cold draft had been blowing down his back all the way from Darien. "All right," he said. "Let's take a look at him."

Dr. Schuhmacher led the way through to the observation room, next to the intensive-care unit where Ben Miller was now struggling to stay alive. Jack walked up to the window and stared at Ben Miller in silence. The patient was surrounded by doctors, nurses and blue-coated medics from Litchfield County's cardiovascular crisis team. All that Jack could see of him behind the gleaming complexities of equipment was a head bandaged up like the Invisible Man, with two dark and impenetrable eyeholes.

"He *felt* something," Jack said, more to himself than to Dr. Serling. "He *felt* something, the same way I felt something."

"You felt something, too?" Dr. Serling asked.

"About a couple of days ago, after I had my fortune read. The cards were full of bad luck, you know? Beware of strangers and stuff like that. Then I cut my hand on one of the cards and practically bled to death all over my wife's new rug. And I just had this *feeling*, you know—"

Dr. Serling raised an eyebrow and turned to Dr. Schuhmacher, but Dr. Schuhmacher merely said, "Excuse me, I have to get home now. I have a mastectomy at nine in the morning."

When he had gone, leaving the door swinging behind him, Jack said to Dr. Serling, "I have an idea. If you're really serious about Ben Miller—if you really believe he has some supernatural sense—then I want you to back me up."

"I'll go along with anything, within reason."

Jack inclined his head toward Ben Miller. "He's only got six or seven hours left, right? And if you ask me, Dr. Schuhmacher was being optimistic. Ben's not going to regain consciousness, so we won't be able to ask him exactly what he felt, or what he saw, or what it is that made him so scared."

"Go on," Dr. Serling said.

"All I'm thinking is this—that if his psychic senses are as strong as you seem to believe they could be, we might be able to talk to him while he's still out for the count."

"I'm not sure I understand."

Jack said, "I'm a well-balanced, well-trained, non-superstitious, normality-oriented person. I don't believe in magic and I don't believe in ghosts. But I'm beginning to convince myself that there *are* powers and there *are* auras and there *are* weird kinds of influences that make themselves felt from beyond our normal experience. And why not, you know? They may be around us all the time, and most of us would never notice. You ought to try interviewing seven different witnesses to the same auto accident. You wouldn't even think the accident happened to the same cars on the same day on the same goddam street."

"Well, I'm inclined to agree with you," Dr. Serling said. "But the point is, how do we communicate with Ben Miller while he's still completely unconscious?"

Jack thrust his hands into his back pants pockets. Then, as diffidently as if he were suggesting they go across the street for a late-night cup of coffee, he said, "We call my wife's friend Pat down here, the one who does the tea leaves and everything, and we hold a what-do-you-call-it. A séance."

"A séance? In Litchfield County Hospital? Are you kidding me? Dr. Schuhmacher would hemorrhage!"

"Does Dr. Schuhmacher have to know?"

"I don't see how we could possibly arrange it *without* his knowing."

"Could he be convinced?"

Dr. Serling pressed his hand against his forehead, thought for a moment and then said decisively, "No. There isn't a chance. He has his professional reputation to think of, not to mention the reputation of Litchfield County."

"You have a professional reputation, too; so do I."

"Yes, but we're the kind of men to whom practical results are more important than reputations. That's not to say that Jerry Schuhmacher isn't a very fine surgeon; he is. But the kind of clients he has to deal with wouldn't take particularly kindly to the idea that he believed in black magic."

"Nobody said this was black magic."

"Nobody said it wasn't."

"Listen," Jack said, "I was reading about this just last week. Police forces all over the world have been using psychics to track down criminals and turn up missing children, and who knows what else. They even had a seminar on it last year in Phoenix."

"Well, I really don't know," Dr. Serling said. "I mean— quite apart from the ethics of it—do you think it could *work*?"

"We don't have any other way of talking to Ben, do we? Maybe it won't work. But I know that Pat's pretty good at it. There isn't any harm in trying."

They were about to leave the observation room and go back to the waiting area when there was a quick knock at the door and Vincent Pearson appeared, his expensive black overcoat sparkling with melted snowflakes.

"Ah, Dr. Serling. The surgical nurse said you might be here."

"How are you, Mr. Pearson?" Dr. Serling asked and shook his hand. "This is Sheriff Jack Smith."

"I believe we've met, briefly," Vincent said and nodded to Jack.

Jack acknowledged Vincent's nod but didn't particularly care for the lord-of-the-manor way in which Vincent had walked into the observation room and taken over the situation as if he had some kind of royal authority.

"I guess you came to visit Ben," Dr. Serling asked Vincent. "There—you can see for yourself. Dr. Schuhmacher thinks he might not last the night."

"Have you seen Mrs. Miller?" Vincent asked, tugging off his gloves.

"She's still in shock, but Martha Guthrie's taken her home."

Vincent peered through the glass at Ben Miller, at the tangle of life-support machinery and at the doctors and nurses clustered around the bed. He remained silent for a long time, then he turned away.

Dr. Serling said, "Ben's already had his entire blood supply replaced three times."

Vincent unbuttoned his overcoat and looked at Dr. Serling with a serious face. "They don't hold out much hope, then?"

"Six or seven hours," Jack told him. "We're a little pushed here, if you really don't mind."

Vincent nodded, not understanding that he was being asked to leave. Jack was anxious to call Pat, and to get her down to the hospital to start a séance; but he wasn't at all sure what Vincent's reaction would be, if he were to find out what they wanted to do; and apart from that he wasn't at all sure that he wanted Vincent to become involved. To Jack, Vincent represented New York, and money; and all the people whose wealth Jack was paid to protect, even though they visited Connecticut rarely, and made about as much contribution to the life of the community as the Pope did to little-league baseball.

"You know, it probably sounds absurd," said Vincent. "But I feel partly responsible for what's happened to Ben."

"How could *you* be responsible?" Jack asked, impatiently.

"Well, it doesn't have very much to do with logic, or scientific reasoning, or police procedure for that matter. But— over the past week or so—well, I find it very difficult to explain it—but all kinds of very unpleasant and tragic things have been happening, to me and people I know, not only here in Connecticut but in New York, too."

He paused, and then he said expressively, "I feel as if I'm at the eye of a storm; as if I'm surrounded by a great speeding whirl of unnaturally bad fortune. Almost as if I've attracted it."

"Bad fortune?" asked Jack. The question wasn't meant as cynically as it sounded. Bad fortune was exactly how *he* would have described the feeling that was rising in the air. Vincent, however, interpreted the query as the natural skepticism of a small-town law-enforcement officer.

"Perhaps I'm imagining it," he said. "But—when you look at what's happened to Ben here . . ."

"What exactly do you define as bad fortune?" Jack asked him.

"Well," said Vincent carefully, smoothing the palms of his hands together. "My assistant in New York died last weekend. He was quite young, in his twenties. No history of illness. But, when I went to call on him on Monday morning, he was dead. Not only that, but . . . well, he had badly decomposed."

Jack raised an eyebrow. Vincent, remembering Edward's body with a slow spasm of greasy internal disgust, said, in a low and hurried voice, "He was almost completely devoured by maggots."

"After being dead for how long?" asked Jack.

"No more than thirty-six hours. Probably less."

"So what did the New York police have to say about it?"

Vincent ran his hand through his hair. "I think they wanted to believe that I killed him myself, several days before. Unfortunately for them, too many people had seen him alive, right up until the afternoon before I found him."

Jack said, "Any clues? Any witnesses? Anything at all?" He was trying to assert himself over Vincent's suaveness by being abrasive and professional.

"A woman was seen leaving Edward's apartment. A very beautiful woman, apparently, dressed in black, very pale in the face. But that was all."

"You said there were other incidents," Jack reminded him.

Vincent said, hoarsely, "Yes," and told Jack and Dr. Serling about Van Gogh, the cat; and about the Waldegrave portrait. "The cat was dangling in the tree, it had been hideously mutilated."

"How mutilated?"

"Well, somebody had—skinned it."

Jack watched Vincent intently. He was looking for any flicker of insincerity; any hint at all that Vincent might be lying, or joking, or center-staging. But Vincent's fear of what was happening was genuine, and just as strong as Jack's, although he was expressing it in a different way. Unlike Jack, he felt himself to be responsible for it; and perhaps he was. But Jack could spot a liar; and he could spot a fraud; and he could spot a florid eccentric, too, and Vincent Pearson was none of these.

He said, in a level tone, "If it's any consolation, Mr. Pearson, I believe you."

Vincent looked up. "You believe everything? Even the way that Edward died?"

"Why should you lie?" Jack asked him.

"To conceal the fact that I killed Edward myself," Vincent suggested.

Jack shook his head. For a long while, he stood with his arms folded and looked at Vincent and said nothing. Then he said, "Tell me something—that woman who was seen leaving Edward Merriam's apartment—in her mid-thirties, is that right? Dressed in black? Very pale complexion but outstanding in appearance?"

"That was the first description I was given, although the witness denied everything later. I guess she just didn't want trouble."

Jack said, "I think I've seen her."

"You think you've *seen* her?" Vincent repeated. "Where, for goodness' sake?"

"Today. Well, yesterday now. I drove down to Darien to interview a man named Maurice Gray in connection with these skinning murders we've been having around here. I didn't get to see Maurice Gray himself, but I did get to see the lady of the house, Ms. Cordelia Gray, and she answers that description pretty well exactly."

Thoughtfully, Vincent said, "There's a connection here, isn't there? I mean, sure, it takes quite a sideways leap of the imagination. But when you add them all up—all these individual incidents—they seem like they're part of the same jigsaw."

Jack remarked, "I'm interested in what you said about Ben Miller shouting 'They're back.' The Gray family has only just returned from seventy years in Europe."

"He said more," Dr. Serling added. "He said, 'Don't touch my skin!' He was frantic about it. 'Don't touch my skin.' Then—when I asked him who he was frightened of—he said, 'All twelve.'"

"All twelve?" Jack frowned. "What do you think he meant by that?"

Vincent felt another piece of the jigsaw slot silently into place. "There are twelve people in the Waldegrave portrait," he said.

"The Grays," Dr. Serling said, although he needn't have voiced it.

"I'd like to take a look at that portrait," Jack told Vincent. "Maybe I can call by your house sometime during the morning. Meanwhile—"

Vincent said, "That sounds like you're trying to get rid of me, that 'Meanwhile'—"

"Well, no, but—"

"Tell him, Sheriff," Dr. Serling put in. "From what he's said to us here tonight, I think he's more likely to help us than stand in our way."

Jack hesitated. He felt rural and unsophisticated in front of Vincent, and he would rather have kept the idea of holding a séance to himself. Vincent looked like the kind of man who might have friends in influential places, the kind of man who probably played golf with the mayor and went to cocktail parties with district attorneys. Still, what the hell. If the séance didn't work, nobody would be any the wiser; and if it did, the ends could well justify the means.

"We've been thinking of holding an impromptu séance," he said, trying to sound as level and matter-of-fact as possible. "Well, not exactly a séance but kind of a telepathy session, to see if we can communicate with Ben before he dies. Ben knows something for sure, and if there's any chance we can tap into his mind, find out what it is. . . ."

Vincent stared at Jack in silence.

"Well, the point is," Jack went on, embarrassed, "whatever we find out—that's if we *do* find out anything—won't be usable as evidence in a court of law. I mean, can you imagine presenting a judge with a transcript of a séance? But it may give us a lead. It may give us enough to turn up some concrete evidence; once we've got that, we're on our way."

Vincent said, "Forgive me for being obtuse, but how are you planning to hold a séance in a hospital? Especially when the person you're trying to contact isn't even dead yet and happens to be surrounded by medical staff."

"It's a shot in the dark," Jack told him. "Maybe it won't work, maybe it will. But police forces all over the world use psychics to help them out."

"Well," Vincent said, "I don't think it's up to me to be skeptical."

They returned to the waiting area. Jack went off to call Pat while Vincent and Dr. Serling found a drinks machine outside on the staircase and bought themselves each a root beer, which was all the machine had to offer.

"Do you know, I always hated root beer," Dr. Serling remarked. Vincent couldn't keep his eyes off the two marmalade cats in the print on the wall. He knew it was just a coincidence, but they made him feel uneasy. It was as if the world he lived in were suddenly revealing itself to be crowded with secret and threatening signs that he had never noticed before. He could understand how people became paranoid, how they could interpret everyday events and objects as warnings that something disastrous was about to happen.

Jack came back from the pay phone. He was red in the face from the embarrassing and difficult task of having persuaded Pat to leave her bed in the middle of a freezing-cold December night and drive over to Litchfield County Hospital.

"Believe me, Pat honey, if this wasn't a matter of life and death, I wouldn't ask you."

"Believe me, Jack honey, if this turns out to be a wild-turkey shoot, you're going to regret that you asked me for the rest of your natural life."

Jack went to buy himself a root beer while they waited. It

was a little after two; outside the windows of Litchfield County Hospital, the snow was tumbling thickly and silently onto a sleeping world.

"Do you really think a séance is a good idea?" Vincent asked Jack. He remembered his grandmother with her Ouija board and her Tarot cards, and the way she whispered to herself when she was telling her own fortune.

Jack stuck his hands in his back pants pockets and looked at Vincent belligerently. "Sure it's a good idea. Do you have a better one?"

He paused, and said, "Besides, I've seen Pat work. I've seen her talk to people's dead relatives. If anyone can get Ben Miller to talk to us, she can."

Vincent said, "Very well. As long as you think that we can bear to hear what he's got to say."

Eighteen

Darien, December 19

George Kelly arrived outside the gates of Wilderlings at a little after three o'clock in the morning and killed the engine of his Silverado wagon with a twist of his wrist.

He had picked his time carefully. At three o'clock in the morning, even insomniacs start to nod off. It was the deadest and coldest hour of the night, eleven hours since darkness had fallen, and still another four and a half hours to go before it grew light. He eased himself out of the driver's seat and stepped down into the snow. He was equipped with a flashlight, a small black-leather case of lock-picking instruments and a ten-inch screwdriver. Wedged between his back and his broad leather belt, he carried a hefty .357 Python revolver, its muzzle nestling in the cleavage of his considerable buttocks. He felt calm, peaceful and confident. He liked it when he was challenged. He knew he was professional enough to be able to get his own back and still come up smelling like lavender. Even after that shooting in New York, when he had gunned down the Loretta brothers, all four of them, for no particular reason other than to save himself the nuisance of having to arrest them the next time they held up a grocery store, nobody had been able to establish anything for certain. George had been too circumspect.

Because of the snow, the Grays had left their wrought-iron gates open, the curlicues of elaborately decorated metal stood out in semicircular crusts of ice. George walked between the gates and up the driveway, keeping himself close to the shadowy cypress trees that bordered it just in case someone happened to be looking out a front window. His breath smoked in the darkness and his boots made a felty, squeaking noise on the snow.

As he approached the front of the house, he left the driveway and crossed the lawn on the left-hand side, passing a wide flight of stone steps and a pair of carved stone urns heaped with snow. Soon he was skirting around the back, crouching behind the low brick wall that bordered the patio. Not far away, in the center of the lawn, there was a circular ornamental pond, its surface frozen as blind as a leper's eye. There were no lights in the house; every window was black. Leafless creeper trailed down the southern wall like a tangle of witch's hair. He coughed once, a high dry bark, and then suppressed another.

It took him only a few moments to find what he was looking for: a stone staircase leading down behind the kitchen to the cellar door. He stopped and listened for a moment, but the silence of the night was complete.

Propping his flashlight between the stair railings opposite so its beam shone directly on the corroded bronze doorplate, George took out his lock picks and set to work. He smiled as he did so; the lock was Victorian and very simple, although it was stiff from years of disuse. It took him three minutes of concentrated picking before the levers at last relented. He coughed, turned the handle and the door swung open.

Taking down his flashlight, he advanced cautiously into the first room of the cellar, closing the door behind him. The circular beam illuminated whitewashed walls, cobwebs as thick as ladies' summer scarves and an old-fashioned sink with a wooden drain board on which, inexplicably, a saddle rested, its leather cracked and dry. George crossed the room and came to a second door, which was unlocked. He opened it, pausing for a moment or two when its hinges grated, listening; but there was no sound from the house above him, no footsteps, no shuffling, no squeaking of stairs. He opened the door wider and shone his flashlight ahead of him, down a long, whitewashed corridor.

George walked as quietly and as gracefully as his bulk allowed. On either side of the corridor there were separate storerooms, with iron-barred doors, in which he could make out stacks of packing cases and tangles of old dining-room chairs and thick bundles of folded-up curtains. There was dust everywhere: it clung like a gray and unshakable memory of times gone by. There was a smell, too: a strange, suffocating smell like dying summer flowers, or potpourri.

In one of the storerooms there were racks and racks of wine bottles, most of them with crusted corks, and labels illegible from years of damp and dust. He picked up one bottle and wiped the dust off. The label read "Chateau Duhart-Milon, 1905." George put the bottle back. He didn't know much about wine, but he did know that anything over eighty years old was probably undrinkable. He rubbed two or three more labels clean, but he was unable to find a single bottle later than 1909.

George continued his search, poking and probing, opening up old linen chests and trunks, moving from storeroom to storeroom until he came to the end of the corridor, where there was yet another door, locked this time, and sheeted in lead, presumably to keep out the damp.

It took him a difficult ten minutes to open the lock, but when he did, the door opened easily, as if the hinges had been recently oiled. He stepped into the next storeroom, which was as large as all the others put together, and quickly shone the beam around.

It was drier in here, although spiders had taken advantage of the dryness to spin webs and nests so thick it was almost impossible to make out what was stacked beneath them. It was only after he had twisted a rope of spiderweb around the blade of his screwdriver and dragged it away sticky that he saw the dull gleaming of gilt and realized this was where the Gray family stored its pictures.

He cleared cobwebs from two or three of them. The first showed a bacchanalian scene in the style of Rubens, crowded with fat, pink nudes and welterweight cherubs. The second showed a severe forest, dark and uncompromising, on the side of a looming mountain. The third depicted a dead child lying in its cradle while its distraught mother buried her face in her hands. Behind the mother, his skeletal face barely visible inside his shadowy hood, stood the Grim Reaper, his scythe over his shoulder.

George looked all around the storeroom, but there was nothing incriminating here, only scores of scores of Victorian paintings. He had never seen so many paintings in his life. He clenched his flashlight between his thighs and took out his handkerchief to wipe the sweat and dust from his face. He coughed again and then blew his nose. It was time to search the upstairs, and he didn't want to be coughing and sneezing while he was going through the bedrooms.

It took him quite a while to find the staircase that led up to the first floor. It was concealed behind a plain wooden door that looked the same as every other plain wooden door in the cellar. But he mounted the stairs at last and made his way up to the door at the top, which was of carved oak and presumably led out to the hallway. Taking a deep breath, he grasped the door handle and turned it. To his relief, the door was unlocked.

No goddam security, he thought to himself. If I were a professional yegg, I could empty this whole goddam house before breakfast and these people would never even know it.

The door from the cellar opened out beneath the main staircase. George eased his way through it, closing it behind him but making sure he could open it again if he had to. Then he padded softly across the hallway to the double doors of the music room.

He had just taken hold of the handles when he thought he heard the faintest of sounds. He froze, holding his breath, his ears aching to pick up any further noises. But almost half a minute went by and he heard nothing else. Wilderlings was the most silent of houses; nothing stirred, nothing moved. The place was like a mausoleum sealed away from the outside world, dreaming its own impenetrable dreams of times past.

George maintained his sweaty grasp on the door handles, but some extraordinary reluctance prevented him from opening the doors. He had never felt like this before, and he couldn't wholly understand what the feeling was. He was cold, but there were rivulets of sweat under his armpits; and the handle of his revolver was beginning to dig into the flesh of his back. He began to think for the first time that here was a challenge he would have been wiser not to accept. In fact, without knowing it, he was frightened.

He hesitated for a second longer, but then he said under his breath, "Ah, bullshit," and swung open both of the music room doors.

Simultaneously, with a plangent and echoing chord, the grand piano struck up the first few bars of Beethoven's Symphony No. 2, in D. George stood where he was, speechless, his mouth wide open, unable to move, while gradually the music room's electric chandeliers brightened from dull orange to glittering white, tier upon tier of sparkling crystal shining on mirrors and pictures and ornaments.

At the piano sat a middle-aged man in evening dress. Beside him stood a younger man, also in evening dress, with one hand in his trousers pocket, the other raised lightly to his chin. Next to the younger man, a little way behind him, was a young woman, quite pretty but oddly expressionless, wearing a white-lace maid's cap and what—as far down as the waist— was a black, long-sleeved dress of impeccable modesty. Below the waist, however, the front of the dress had been drawn up and tucked into her thin, black-leather belt, baring, for anyone to see, her ivory-white thighs in black silk stockings and garters, and the dark, furry triangle of her pubic hair.

Neither of the two men in evening dress appeared to think there was anything startling or unusual about the way in which the young woman was dressed. In fact, both of them ignored her. Their attention was undividedly fastened on George.

"Good evening," said the middle-aged man, rising from the piano stool. "Or should I say good morning?"

George could think of nothing to say. For a taut split second, he wondered if he ought to make a run for it, back down to the cellar, or even through the front door. But if he tried to escape through the cellar, they would be able to catch him easily, and he didn't know whether the front door was locked or not. Besides, to run would be a *prima facie* admission of guilt. He was a police officer. He was searching the house of a suspected murderer. He might not be doing it by the book, but at least he had good reason for being here.

The middle-aged man walked slowly toward him, his hands clasped behind his back. "My name is Maurice Gray," he said courteously. "You must be one of the officers seeking to talk to me yesterday afternoon."

"That's correct, sir," George stumbled, although he could have bitten off his tongue for calling a homicide suspect "sir."

Maurice Gray smiled in a tight, thoughtful, displeased kind of way and walked around George, inspecting him as if he were an unsatisfactory used car.

"You won't, of course, need this," he said and abruptly lifted George's windbreaker to tug out his revolver.

George was scratched on the small of the back by the Python's forward sights. He whipped around in pain and irritation and snapped, "Give me that gun back! That's police property! You hear me? Give me that gun!"

Maurice turned the revolver this way and that, peering at it closely. "I really don't think I should. It strikes me as a dangerous weapon, to say the least. It also gives you an unfair advantage."

"I'm a police officer," George blustered. "If you don't return that weapon to me right now, I'm going to have to arrest you."

Maurice handed the Python to Henry. "You may be a police officer when you are patrolling the streets. You may be a police officer when you are searching the houses of suspected criminals, armed with an appropriate warrant. But this morning, my dear fellow, you are nothing more than an armed intruder; and as such, you have very few rights. You depend more on my personal mercy now than you do the law. I hope you realize that."

George said, "I'm leaving. I'm going to turn around and I'm going to walk straight out that door. I'll be back for the gun, with all the warrants you like."

He turned his back on Maurice and walked smartly across the hallway until he reached the front door. Maurice and Henry remained where they were, watching him with restrained amusement as he tried to open the bolts and locks. Laura came forward and touched Henry's arm, and Henry took hold of her hand and kissed it with ice-cold lips.

After a minute of sweating and struggling, George knew he wasn't going to get out. He walked back across the hallway and stood in front of Maurice Gray, his fists on his hips.

"All right," he said, "I admit I was wrong to intrude. But there isn't any future in keeping me here, is there?"

Maurice inclined his head benignly. "Not for you, I have to admit. Well, not for *all* of you, let me put it that way. A part of you will find its way into the scheme of immortality."

"What are you, crazy?" George demanded. Then he looked at Laura. "And what's this? This girl walking around showing off everything she's got. Some kind of perversion or something?"

"Perversion is only in the mind of the perverse," Henry

remarked. He deliberately let his hand stray down between Laura's thighs, continuing to smile at George. Laura registered nothing on her face; it was as if she were asleep with her eyes open.

"She will permit you to do the same," Henry said. "Whatever you ask of her, provided I approve, she will do. Would you like her to bend over a chair so you can have sex with her?" He paused and then said, "I don't really think that 'making love' is an appropriate term for anyone dressed in a dirty windbreaker and size forty-two denims, do you?"

George said, "You people are out of your minds. Now, you let me out of here. My wagon's outside. If it's still there by daylight, people are going to start wondering; then they're going to come right up here, asking where I am."

Maurice laid an arm around George's shoulders. "The thing is, old fellow, we've already taken care of your wagon. While you were down in the cellars, we drove it around back and put it under shelter. Nobody will ever find it, you know. By tomorrow evening, it will be completely dismantled."

George wrenched himself away from Maurice's embrace. He was panicky now, and crimson-faced. "You listen to me!" he shouted. "That vehicle is police property! You lay one finger on that vehicle and that's an offense! The same goes for the weapon, and the same goes for me! I'm an officer of the law, and I'm warning you! I'm warning you here and now!"

Maurice looked almost embarrassed by George's outburst, but when George had finished, he said, "We are quite aware of all that, my dear chap, but we really can't let you go. Apart from the fact that you have been intruding without a warrant, we need you. You are a godsend as well as a nuisance. You see, you're not what we call *quality*, but there is so much of you."

"What the fuck are you talking about?" George demanded, frightened and defensive. "You're nuts, both of you."

Maurice turned his back on George and looked at Henry, his forehead creased in sophisticated indecision. "I don't really want to puncture the back in any way," he told Henry. "So what do you think?"

Henry made the slightest of resigned shrugs. "The eyes, I suppose. Not very satisfactory, but there you are."

"I want to know what's going on here," George butted in. "You—Gray—what in hell goes on here?"

He reached out and grasped Maurice's shoulder, trying to pull him around. Maurice was only too delighted to oblige. Spinning deftly on the ball of his left foot, in a remarkable Fred Astaire-like movement, he turned and faced George with his right hand upraised. George snarled, "Now, you hear this—" and in his pugnacity, he didn't even see what Maurice was holding.

With malicious accuracy, Maurice jabbed George's left eye with the sharp point of his silver pipe cleaner. George's hands rose to his face protectively, but Maurice was too practised and too quick for him; the second jab penetrated the optic nerve of his right eye.

George roared out in agony and collapsed to the floor on his knees, clutching his hands over his eyes. Maurice stepped back and shook out his handkerchief to wipe his pipe cleaner. Henry clapped his hands and said, "*Toro! Toro!* You would have made a first-rate matador, Maurice!"

"I'm blind! Oh, Jesus Christ, I'm blind!" George screamed. "You've blinded me, you bastard! Oh, God!"

He lost his balance and toppled on his back on to the floor, where he twisted and writhed, not only in pain, but in abject fear. Maurice watched him for a while dispassionately and then said to Henry, "We'd better have him taken upstairs, hadn't we?"

Henry said to Laura, "Will you go to the room at the far end of the landing, my dear? Here's the key. On the second shelf down you will find a clear glass bottle labeled 'Chloroform.' Bring me that bottle, please, and some clean cotton."

While Laura went to fetch the chloroform, Maurice returned to the piano and began to play, accurately but rather heartlessly, a selection of Chopin's "Polonaises." During this time, George stumbled and groped around the hallway, crouching and whimpering to himself. Henry stood with his hand resting on the back of a chair, his ankles carelessly crossed, watching George with a smile.

Eventually Laura returned, her white thighs shining, her black stockings perfectly seamed. Henry took the bottle from her and kissed her on the cheek. "You are an angel," he told her. "If only I could keep you forever."

Maurice and Henry now cornered the weeping George. "I'm here," Maurice told him in a tone of voice that was almost kind. "I'm holding out my hands for you. Take them, and I shall guide you."

George blubbered, "I'm blind, I'm totally blind." But Maurice said, "Don't worry, old man, there are far worse things than being blind," and gave him his hands. George grasped them eagerly and tried to pull Maurice toward him as if to embrace him but now Henry stepped forward from behind and pressed a large pad of chloroform-soaked cotton over George's nose and mouth.

George struggled, but Maurice kept a tight grip on his hands; the more desperately George fought, the more stertoriously he breathed in the chloroform. It was only a matter of seconds before he staggered, dropped to one knee and then fell face down on the floor. Maurice said, "How *are* the mighty fallen," and then fastidiously inspected his wrist to make sure George hadn't scratched him in the struggle.

Between them, Maurice and Henry carried George upstairs. They took him along the landing to Maurice's operating room, which was bare, high-ceilinged and decorated in two drab shades of green, like an Edwardian hospital. In the center of the room, underneath a large metal-shaded lamp, there was a marble-topped table, with grooves around it into which the blood and fluids could flow. Against the side wall there was a high, veneered sideboard on which a copper sterilizing kettle was already simmering beside the laid-out surgical instruments Maurice would require.

There was a steamy odor in the room from the sterilizer, and a smell of carbolic. But underlying them both, there was that persistent and cloying odor of opened human flesh. Maurice was accustomed to it; in fact, he found it quite exhilarating, in the same way that soldiers who fought in Normandy after D-Day found, in later years, the smell of apples exhilarating. It reminded them forever of blood, and fear, and orchards.

George was laid out on the marble table, on his back. Henry undressed him, struggling with his heavy-duty jeans. Underneath, George wore large boxer shorts sporting pictures of palm trees and deck chairs. Henry removed these, too.

Naked, George was white and hairy and huge, a human walrus. Maurice examined him with distaste. All that could be said for him was that his skin was in good condition, supple and fine, and that there was plenty of it. Maurice took off his evening coat, unfastened his cuff links and rolled up his shirt sleeves. Henry said, "Shall Laura get you a drink?"

"Later, thank you," Maurice replied. "I think I'm going to require a very steady hand for this one."

The operation started at four-thirty and continued for nearly six hours. Outside, the ink-black sky faded into light snowy gray, and Henry could see the leafless trees down at the far end of the paddock, or what had once been the paddock when Wilderlings had been crowded with laughter and parties and the Gray's had kept a full complement of horses. Henry had rather hoped when he returned to Wilderlings that just a little of that gaiety would still be here; but the world was no longer effervescent, not in the way it had been then. Where were the Goulds and the Vanderbilts and the Zimmermanns? Where were the parasols, and the boating parties, and the pink champagne? Where were the Gibson girls? In those days, seduction had been flavorful, and corruption had been a dizzying cup drunk deep. But now what was left? A life of averages, without extremes; a life in which the wealthy were shy of flaunting their wealth, and forbidden love affairs were internationally publicized and uniformly tiresome.

Henry had once ridden in a dog cart drawn by six naked girls, all of them society belles, and he had whipped them mercilessly until they had taken him all the way around the grounds of Wilderlings and back. After that, he had taken all six of them to his bed.

As he stared out the window now and peeled back the pages of his memories, so Maurice conscientiously peeled away George Kelly's skin. Even as he separated the layers on George's back, Maurice knew that this was one of his most accomplished operations.

Henry said, "A hundred dollars says you'll lose him before you're through."

"No, no," Maurice replied. "He'll rally at the last, you'll see."

And Maurice's prediction was correct, for George suddenly quaked and cried out, "Mother of God! Mother of God! Mother of God!"

When the operation was over they wrapped the bulk of

George's body in a green vinyl bag and carried it downstairs. They walked across the snowy yard with it and lifted it into the trunk of Maurice's Cadillac. After that, they stood in the cold for a while, rubbing their hands together, enjoying the freshness of the winter morning.

"Uncle Algernon will be reasonably satisfied with that night's work, don't you think?" Henry asked.

Maurice looked tired. "I hope so. It's the best I can do. I just wish to God that Cordelia would hurry up and get hold of the portrait. We can't go on at this rate for much longer."

Henry said, "I'll get rid of him, if you like." He nodded toward the open trunk of the Cadillac.

But Maurice shook his head. "I feel like a drive. The house is becoming rather oppressive. I have nothing against your father, but there's Belvedere, and those sickly girls of his. Besides, Father and Mother aren't exactly easy."

Henry said, "Will you buy some oysters while you're out? I have a craving for oysters."

They were about to walk back to the house when they heard the faintest mewling sound. Maurice said, "That sounds like a cat," and almost as he said it, a marmalade tom jumped down from the snowy roof of the garages and curled itself affectionately around his leg. Maurice lifted the cat and peered at it with fascination. Its eyes were not green, but as dark as mirrors.

"Do you know something, Henry?" he said. "This is Firework. I can't believe it after all these years. This is actually Firework."

"What did I tell you?" Henry smiled. "It seems as if the day of true revival is at hand."

Nineteen

Litchfield, December 19

Pat was not particularly amused when she reached the hospital and heard what Jack had to say.

"A séance?" she said. Her eyes were still puffy with sleep, and her lime-green plastic curlers were only half-concealed by a pink nylon scarf.

"It's the last possible chance we have of learning what Ben was actually frightened of," Jack told her. "He's not going to make the morning, Pat. The doctor said he was going pretty fast."

Pat said, "I don't believe what I'm hearing. It's three o'clock in the morning, and I've just driven fifteen miles in the snow because my friend's husband wants me to hold a séance."

"I thought *I* was your friend, too."

"You were, Jack—until tonight."

Jack rubbed the back of his neck. "Listen, Pat, you know I'll make it up to you. But as of now, I don't see any alternative."

"He doesn't see any alternative," Pat informed the ceiling. "He's the sheriff of Litchfield County, the man on whom one hundred fifty-five thousand people depend for their safety and their security, and he doesn't see any alternative. Jack—what happened to good old-fashioned detection? Don't they do that anymore?"

Jack glanced across to the waiting area where Vincent and Dr. Serling were holding a subdued conversation while they waited for him to persuade Pat that a séance in Litchfield County Hospital at three o'clock in the morning was a red-hot, first-rate idea. "Pat," Jack said, "this isn't quite your normal kind of case. It has some very bizarre aspects to it."

"Do you want to tell me about it?" Pat demanded. "As long as I'm here, I might as well know why."

"You can go back home if you want to. I'll pay for your gas."

"No, I want to hear what's going on. I want to hear what it is that makes a shrewd and sensible police officer ask for the help of a tea-leaf reader."

Haltingly, trying to make it all sound believable, Jack told her what had happened to Ben Miller, and about Aaron Halperin's cat, and Edward, about his abortive attempt to talk to Maurice Gray, about Laura Monblat, and about his belief that all these incidents were somehow connected with the flaying murders.

When he had finished, Pat opened her pocketbook and took out a cigarette. Vincent came over, lit it for her and asked Jack, "Any luck?"

"This is out of my league," Pat told him.

"Out of your league?"

"It may be a whole lot of baloney, but if it isn't, I don't want to get involved."

"But why?" Vincent asked. "All we're asking you to do is to get in touch with a perfectly ordinary young man."

"Oh, yes?" Pat challenged him. "He's so ordinary he's cut his face off. What do you think it's like inside his mind? Anybody who could cut his face off must be crazy, half-crazy or scared to death. And what you're asking me to do is to get right inside of that craziness, right inside of that fear, no matter what caused it. That's what happens in a séance, my friend. The medium, who in this instance happens to be *me*, has to experience firsthand the feelings inside the person she's trying to get in touch with. Now, I've contacted with dead people, and that isn't too bad because you kind of experience it faintly, like feeling something through the wrong end of a telescope. But even so, you can get upset sometimes, particularly if the person's angry, or frightened, or hurt. Here, though—*here* you want me to feel exactly what that guy's feeling—firsthand, while he's still alive. I can't take it. I'm sorry. I don't need it."

Jack was silent for a moment; then he raised a hand in resignation. "Okay, Pat. I should have thought about it more carefully. It was just an idea, and I guess it was a pretty rotten one. You go on home. I can have someone drive you if you're too tired."

Pat said, "You really have nothing else to go on?"

Jack counted off on his fingers. "I have a hitchhiker from Moultrie, Georgia, with a farfetched story and a criminal record. I have two skinned humans and one skinned cat. I have a hundred-year-old painting that's falling to pieces. Then I have a dead art dealer who decomposed even before he was buried, and a missing wife, and a white-faced woman in a black dress who might be one of the Gray family but who, in fact, could be anyone at all."

Pat said, "I see your problem. But what can I say?"

"Well, don't worry about it," Jack said. "I'll manage. There has to be an answer somewhere. It's just a question of finding it."

At that moment, sensing that Jack was having difficulty, Dr. Serling came up. "Have you decided how you're going to arrange it?" he asked Pat paternally.

"Arrange what?"

"Well, the séance. We *are* going to have a séance, aren't we?"

Pat hesitated for a moment, looking at Jack in helpless sympathy. With all the expertise of someone who knew from years of professional experience how to make other people feel guilty, Jack shook his head as if to tell Pat she shouldn't do it, not unless she really wanted to, not unless she wanted to help out a friend who needed her badly and didn't know who else to turn to.

Pat said cagily, "I don't see what *good* it would do, holding a séance. All you're going to get from the guy is pain and fear."

"It's all right," Jack said, laying a hand on her shoulder. "Just go home, Pat, and get back to bed."

She shook her head and turned from Jack to Dr. Serling and back again. "Okay," she said, "you win. We'll do it. But I want one thing clearly understood—if it gets too upsetting, if it gets too heavy, then it's finished straightaway. No arguments."

"You're sure this is what you want?" Jack asked. "I mean, I don't want you to think I'm blackmailing you into it."

"What I think is my business," Pat said.

"Do we have to hold the séance in Ben Miller's room?" Dr. Serling asked.

Pat said, "No. Anyplace close will do. All this mumbo-jumbo about holding hands and sitting in circles isn't necessary. Spirits are everywhere and nowhere, both at once."

Dr. Serling looked at Jack and said, "Well, Sheriff, shall we begin now?"

Jack nodded. There was nothing more to be said. He felt desperately awkward and unsure of what he was doing, and if he tried to justify it, he would probably talk himself out of it. He knew it was unusual but acceptable police procedure to enlist the help of psychics and that he would probably be able to convince the county authorities that holding a séance had been worth attempting. What really concerned him, though, was that the idea had come to him so readily and had seemed at the time so logical. He had discovered, to his surprise, that he believed in the supernatural.

Vincent didn't need convincing that there were influences in the world apart from those of flesh and blood. His grandfather had always sworn that he believed in ghosts and that Candlemas was haunted by the spirit of a young Puritan woman who had been strangled on her wedding night. Quite apart from that, any natural skepticism that he might have had had been completely overwhelmed in the past week by the horrors of Edward's death and by the skinning of Aaron's cat. He had seen for himself the painting of Van Gogh on the Waldegrave portrait; that was evidence enough.

He felt reassured by Sheriff Smith's response to everything he had told him, particularly after the suspicious cynicism of Detective Green in New York; and he was gratified that an officer of the law should accept the presence of occult forces without, apparently, turning a hair.

Dr. Serling stepped forward now. "Are we ready?" he asked. There were plum-colored circles under his eyes, and he looked very weary.

Vincent said, "Is there a room we can use? Somewhere quiet, where we won't be disturbed?"

Dr. Serling said, "There's an office upstairs for the use of outside doctors. Nobody's likely to interrupt us there, particularly at this time of the morning."

They went upstairs in the elevator. They hardly spoke to

each other, out of tiredness and tension and apprehensiveness. Jack pulled out his gum, which his colleagues at headquarters always took as a sign that he was getting serious.

The doctor's office was wood-paneled and had a low sofa, three large armchairs, and a glass-topped coffee table on which there was an arrangement of dried flowers and a stack of recent issues of *World Medicine*. Dr. Serling closed the door behind them and Pat said, "Will everybody sit down, please? It doesn't matter where."

Jack asked, "Would you like the table cleared?" and Pat nodded yes, she would.

"How about the lights?" Dr. Serling asked.

Pat said, "You can leave the lights. None of the spirits I've been in contact with have worried much about lights."

Vincent asked, "This won't be dangerous, will it?"

"I don't know," Pat told him. "I've never tried to get in touch with a living person before. It may not work at all." She gave a sardonic laugh. "Who knows, it might even kill me."

"That's not a joke, Pat," Jack said.

She took the center armchair, between Vincent and Dr. Serling. "You're telling me?"

She sat up straight, clasped her hands together and closed her eyes. "I want you to think about Ben Miller," she said matter-of-factly. "If Ben Miller's spirit is able to get in touch with us, then the more deeply we think about him, the sooner he's likely to come. It's like fishing in a pool of spirits. He's out there somewhere, just like we all are, floating."

Vincent glanced at Jack, then closed his eyes and thought of Ben. He tried to picture Ben's face; he tried to remember the day Ben had gone berserk. He also tried to think of Ben before he had fallen from the roof; Ben as a teenager, coming around to Candlemas in his white Ford pickup to collect his mother from work.

"Concentrate," Pat urged. "Try to imagine that Ben is in the room with us, sitting close. Try to believe that he's here, that he's actually here, because we can really bring him here if we try hard enough."

With his eyes shut tight, Vincent did his best to imagine that Ben was sitting on the sofa opposite him.

Pat whispered, "Ben Miller, Ben Miller, I know you're

near. Ben Miller, I'm calling you, Ben. I want you to come to me, Ben, and talk to me."

Vincent opened his eyes for a moment and saw that Jack was staring at Pat with deep uncertainty. Jack saw that he was looking and quickly closed his eyes.

"Ben Miller," Pat murmured, "where are you, Ben Miller? I want to talk to you, that's all. I don't want to hurt you. I don't want to frighten you. I just want to talk."

"Do you think this is really going to work?" Dr. Serling asked impatiently. "I can't feel anything at all."

"Quiet," Pat told him. "All you have to do is concentrate, think of Ben."

They sat in silence for over a minute. The office was well-insulated from the corridor outside; they could hear only their own steady breathing and the distant ringing of a telephone.

"Ben Miller, I know you're there," Pat repeated, but this time her voice sounded peculiarly blurry, as if she were speaking through muslin. "Ben Miller, come close; we want to talk to you, Ben. We're friends."

Vincent was suddenly aware of a soft, crackling sound, as if something was alight. He opened his eyes to find the room in total darkness.

"The lights have gone out," he said, and his voice sounded strange and slurred to himself.

"The lights are still on," Pat replied. "What has happened is that the darkness inside our minds has filled the room. Now, quiet. I think Ben is quite close. I think I can feel him coming nearer."

"I can't see," Jack protested.

"You haven't lost your sight," Pat reassured him. "Your perception has turned inward, that's all. What you see in front of your eyes now is the inside of your own mind."

Dr. Serling said, "This is quite amazing. I've never experienced anything like it."

Pat shushed him. "Ben Miller," she called, softly and encouragingly. "Ben Miller, are you there, Ben Miller?"

Vincent strained his eyes; the darkness was seamless, and the harder he stared, the more impenetrable it seemed to become. He felt as if time had somehow wound down, as if they were traveling through each second of each minute with infinite slowness, a caravan of imperceptibly moving figures making their way through the endless desert of the days. He wasn't afraid. He felt a sense of calmness, almost as if he had been drugged. He could feel the others close to him, too, their personalities as real to him as their physical presence, their minds as tangible as their bodies.

The crackling noise altered and became a low fizzing sound, like static electricity. Vincent suddenly became aware that someone else was in the room; someone different. He could hear Pat calling, but her voice was so slow and muffled it was impossible to make out what she was saying.

Then he heard a man's voice mumbling, "*. . . leave me alone . . . leave me alone. . . .*"

Pat's words became more distinct, although they continued to rise and fall as if she were speaking on a short-wave radio.

"Ben Miller . . . is that you, Ben Miller?"

"*Leave me alone,*" the man replied. Vincent couldn't be sure it was Ben.

"Are you Ben Miller?" Pat persisted.

"*Leave me alone; they'll find me if you don't leave me alone.*"

"Tell me who you are," Pat demanded. "Tell me what your name is."

There was a long pause and then Vincent heard the words, "*Bennnn . . . Millerrr. . . .*"

"Ben," Pat said, "I want you to show yourself. I want to see you, Ben, so I know it's really you."

"*. . . leave . . . alone. . . .*"

"Ben, listen to me. We're your friends here, people who know you, people who care about you. You can help us protect you. You can help us stop those other people from coming after you. Please, Ben, this is your only chance."

There was another long pause. Vincent thought he saw a flickering of light in the darkness, but it must have been his imagination, or something floating across the surface of his eye. Pat called again. There was still no sign of Ben Miller, nothing but the blackness, crowded with thoughts and hopes and strange terrors.

"Ben, if you don't show yourself, we're going to leave you," Pat said. "Do you want us to leave you so *they* can get you? Do you want us to do that? Listen to me, Ben. This is your last hope."

Almost immediately the static sound grew more intense and the darkness appeared to clot itself together, like blood. Then, silently, a shower of brilliant white specks slid through the air, a meteorite display in slow motion, and assembled itself over the center of the glass-topped table into a negative image of Ben Miller. The image wavered and broke up from time to time, like the picture on a black-and-white television tube, but it was clearly Ben, his eyes gleaming white from a face as black as graphite.

"Ben," Pat coaxed, "you have to help us. We have to know who you're frightened of."

At once, Ben's image opened its mouth wide and let out a sharp, chilling howl of anguish. Vincent wasn't sure he had heard the sound aloud. It seemed to have been transmitted through the bones of his face rather than through his ears. It was a hideous, horrifying howl, a howl of panic and pain and utter desperation. It was a howl of a man being crushed to death by his own overwhelming fear.

Pat screamed, too, just as piercingly. Vincent couldn't see her, but he could sense that she had doubled up and that she was clenching her fists in anguish. He heard Dr. Serling say, "Let go! Pat, if it's hurting you, *let go!*"

But Pat either couldn't or wouldn't let go. Ben screeched and roared, and Pat screeched with him, the two of them intertangled in terror and pain.

"Pat!" Jack shouted, and Vincent could feel that he was trying to get up off the sofa but somehow finding it impossible. The darkness they perceived before them was the darkness of their mental landscape, their souls externalized, and as long as they were collectively joined in it, they were physically unable to move. It was as if they had been turned inside out so that their minds surrounded them and the material world had been shrunk within their heads.

But the screaming went on and on, and none of them could do anything but sit where they were and pray it would stop.

Vincent began to feel a sharp pain in the sides of his jaws, just below his ears. He winced and bent his head forward in an effort to relieve it. Pat was still screaming, but as the pain in his jaw grew more unbearable, he found he could no longer hear her because he was shouting himself.

The negative image of Ben Miller became insanely distorted; his face stretched diagonally and his body was drawn out across the room. He began to flicker and fade, and Vincent realized, not without relief, that they were probably going to lose him.

"He's going!" Jack shouted. He, too, sounded as if he were in pain. "Pat! Pat! For Christ's sake stop him! Stop him, Pat! He's going!"

Pat suddenly screamed, "Don't you realize why? He's *dying!* I can't stop him! He's dying!"

"Pat! I have to know who it is! I have to know who's been after him!"

"No, Jack. Let him go. If you don't let him go, he'll suffer terrible pain. His spirit may not even survive."

Vincent could feel Jack thrashing around on the sofa, trying to get up and seize Ben Miller's image before it finally died away.

"God damn you, Ben Miller!" Jack yelled. "God damn you to hell, Ben Miller! Who were you frightened of? Who was it scared you? Do you hear me, Ben Miller? Who was it scared you so much? Who was it wanted your skin?"

". . . can't say . . ." Ben murmured. "*They'll kill me . . . if I tell . . . even after I'm dead. . . .*"

"Ben!" Jack roared, "Ben, risk it! We'll get them for you, I promise! Ben, for God's sake, tell us who it is!"

There was some indistinct muttering, but then Vincent clearly heard the words "*Litchfield Cemetery . . . Johnson . . . next to the oak. . . .*"

There was a sound then like no sound Vincent had ever heard before, a kind of warping, twisting, tearing sound. Ben Miller's image shrank and shriveled, and for a fraction of a second, Vincent saw something that looked like a human embryo, only strangely slippery and transparent. Then the lights abruptly reappeared and the doctor's office came into view; they were sitting there staring at each other in stunned disbelief.

Pat was trembling. Jack came across, bent over her and asked, "Are you okay?"

She nodded. "I could use a glass of water."

Dr. Serling went through to the small kitchen that adjoined the office and brought her a glass of water and a mild sedative.

"If I were you, I'd have one of Sheriff Smith's people take you home. You're not in any condition to drive."

"I'm all right," Pat said. "The pain's gone now."

"All the same," Dr. Serling insisted.

Vincent asked, "Is Ben really dead? What we saw just now—was that Ben dying?"

Pat unsteadily drank some water and then said, "I've never seen that before, but I could feel it. He wanted to go. He was desperate to go. He wanted to go so much that I was almost tempted to go with him. Can you understand that? He was *aching* for it."

Jack turned to Dr. Serling. "Do you want to call down to intensive care to see what's happened?"

Dr. Serling picked up the phone and asked the switchboard operator to put him through to Dr. Kellstrom.

While they waited, Jack unwrapped his last stick of chewing gum and pushed it into his mouth in three measured bites. "Seems as if I made a fool of myself, doesn't it?" he remarked.

"I wouldn't say that," Vincent reassured him. "It was worth taking a shot at."

"We've almost certainly killed Ben Miller before he was due to go," Pat said.

"He only had a couple of hours, if that."

Pat finished her water. "We still killed him. He was in a coma, and that coma was protecting his mind from whatever it was that frightened him. The coma was giving his nervous system a chance to recover. What we did was to dive deep down underneath that coma and drag him out of it. He wasn't ready for it. His system couldn't stand the stress."

Dr. Serling had been talking to Dr. Kellstrom. Eventually he put down the phone, turned around and said, "He's dead, all right. Shock, loss of blood, renal failure. You name it, he had it."

"And we're still none the wiser about what frightened him," Jack said.

"I'd lay money that what scared him was those twelve people in the Waldegrave portrait," Vincent commented.

"Well—you could be right," Jack told him. "But 'all twelve' could have meant anything at all. Ben was pretty religious, especially after his accident. Maybe he was talking about the twelve disciples. Maybe he was talking about twelve-card poker. Maybe he didn't say 'all twelve' at all but something that sounded like that.''

Pat put in, "Stop inventing complications, Jack." She turned to Vincent and explained, "He's always creating complications. If the snow started to melt tomorrow, Jack would give you a dozen reasons why it shouldn't."

"What did he mean about Litchfield Cemetery?" Vincent asked.

"He was rambling," Jack replied. "He was frightened out of his mind."

"But he mentioned a name, Johnson. And a place, too— 'next to the oak.'"

"I must confess I didn't hear that," Dr. Serling said. He wiped his glasses and then very loudly blew his nose. "I think I'm allergic to the supernatural."

"I heard it," Pat said.

"Maybe that's where he wants to be buried," Jack suggested.

Vincent said, "I think we should go take a look."

"It's still dark," Jack pointed out.

"You have a flashlight, don't you?" Vincent asked him.

"Sure, but what are we supposed to be looking for?"

"I don't know. But you specifically asked him what he was frightened of, and he said he couldn't tell you because they'd kill him, whoever they are, even after he was dead."

"That doesn't sound very logical," Dr. Serling remarked.

"It does to me," Pat said.

"How come?" Jack asked her. He felt irritable, not only because the séance had been so inconclusive, but because he knew it had been rash of him to urge Ben Miller to stay longer when Pat had been suffering such agony. Neither Vincent nor Dr. Serling had criticized him openly for it, but all of them were conscious that his action could have cost her her sanity, even her life.

As a sheriff who had been elected for his traditional down-home views on law enforcement, it had been risky and unorthodox for him to decide on holding a séance. He had been convinced that it would be a success; and to the extent that Pat had managed to raise Ben Miller's spirit, it had been. But Jack needed more. He needed evidence, and his failure to get it made him feel sharply diminished.

Vincent said encouragingly to Pat, "You sound as if you've come across this kind of thing before."

"I have. Some of the spirits I've been in touch with, even though they're dead, say they're still frightened of dying."

"Well, what could that mean?" Dr. Serling asked.

"I'm never quite sure. At first I thought they said it because they didn't realize they were actually dead. Then I thought, well, if I'm talking to them, if they're talking to me, if we're having constructive conversations, they *can't* be dead. So maybe people live much longer than we think but in different forms, like butterflies. Maybe we go through five or six stages before we finally cease to exist. Maybe *this* part of our lives, the flesh-and-blood part, is like stage two or three in the whole process. Maybe there are ghostlike people living around us who are terrified of 'dying' and turning into solid creatures like us. Like—they believe *we're* the ghosts and *they're* alive."

Vincent said, "That's an interesting theory. I don't know how you could ever prove it."

"But you saw Ben Miller for yourself," she said. "When he died, he turned into something like an embryo. A baby spirit, if you want to call it that, just about to be born again."

"None of this makes any sense of what Ben said about the cemetery," Jack put in.

"Well, maybe it does," Vincent told him thoughtfully. "If Pat's right and we *do* live four or five lives, then Ben's fear of being killed could have been genuine. In which case, what he told us could have been some kind of clue—you know, like a crossword-puzzle clue. He wanted to tell us who was after him; he wanted to tell us who was frightening him so much, but he didn't dare say it straight out."

"I think we ought to try the cemetery," Dr. Serling said.

Jack checked his watch. "It's five after four," he said, trying to sound brisk. "I vote we leave it until it gets light. I could do with a wash and a cup of coffee."

"I think we all could," Dr. Serling agreed. "It's been a strain, this séance, and I don't mind admitting it."

They went to Bonnie's All-Nite Drugstore on the other side of the snow-covered green and huddled in their overcoats and wearily drank coffee. They were too tense to eat, although Jack bought himself two more packs of gum and a chocolate bar. They talked for a while about the séance and what had happened, although as dawn gradually broke over Litchfield County Hospital, they found it increasingly difficult to believe that any of it had been real.

Snow clouds were hanging over the town like gray chiffon veils by the time they drove out to the cemetery in Jack's Cherokee wagon. The houses and stores along the way lay closed and silent, as if a plague had silently swept through Litchfield during the night and left its population dead in their beds. Vincent, in the back seat, yawned and covered his mouth with his hand. In spite of the coffee, he was beginning to feel jaded and to wonder what on earth he was doing driving out to Litchfield Cemetery at first light after a night without sleep and in the highly assorted company of the county sheriff, a country doctor and a lady spiritualist in plastic hair curlers.

They reached the cemetery shortly after seven. The wide iron gates were open; Jack drove straight in and parked next to the House of Remembrance—a scaled-down version of the Charles Clapp dwelling in Portland, Maine, all Ionic columns, pilasters and oval windows. Smoke was blowing out of the building's chimney, evidence that the cemetery caretaker had already arrived.

They walked through the chilly marble hall. Jack knocked on the caretaker's door and then opened it. The caretaker was a severe, dry-voiced, haughty man with a pinched mouth, pale, disapproving eyes and shiny black hair that looked as if it had been varnished to his narrow skull.

"We're looking for the Johnson tomb," Jack said without any introductions. He had attended dozens of funerals here— friends, relatives, homicide victims, suicides, sudden deaths— and he and the caretaker knew each other well. They didn't like each other. The caretaker believed that once the dead were buried here, they were his, and he resented further investigation into the causes of death. He particularly objected to exhumations, which disturbed the peace of his sleeping charges and ruined the lawns.

"There are three Johnson tombs," he said coldly. "Which is the one you want?"

"Is there one close to an oak tree? Jack asked.

The caretaker regarded him suspiciously. "The Frederick E.

Johnson tomb. Frederick E. Johnson, Mrs. Philomena Johnson and their two children, Charles F. Johnson, aged eight years, and Henrietta Johnson, spinster, aged seventy-nine years."

Dr. Serling said, "Strange, isn't it, what death does to people? A sister of seventy-nine and a brother of eight."

The caretaker peered at Dr. Serling over his glasses. "They grow not old, Doctor, as we who are left grow old."

He gave Jack a Xeroxed copy of the cemetery map, and Jack led the way between the rows of graves under a lemon-yellow sun. Marble angels with snow on their wings regarded these trespassers with expressionless eyes. Flowers sprawled dead in frozen vases. The gravel paths had been salted to clear them of snow, but the gravel itself was crunchy with ice, and as the four progressed up the hill, their footsteps echoed across the cemetery, the living walking among the dead.

The oak tree stood close to the edge of the cemetery, amid the older graves. It was only ten or eleven years old, so it was little more than a sapling; but the plan had been to plant scores of shade trees between the graves, with the hope that eventually the cemetery would take on the appearance of a garden. The Johnson tomb, nearby, was a dark, Barre-granite catafalque with the names of the Johnson family deeply engraved on it. There was white gravel around the foot of the catafalque, surrounded by a low granite wall, heavy with moss.

Dr. Serling pointed to another grave a short distance away. "You can see why Ben Miller knew this place. Look." The grave's headstone read, "Zachariah Miller, 1862–1903." "Must have been his great-grandfather."

Vincent clapped his hands to warm himself. "I don't understand this at all. There's nothing here."

Jack sniffed. "I told you. Ben was frightened out of his mind. What he said simply didn't make any sense. Come on— he just happened to think about dying, and for some reason, he remembered this tomb."

Pat said, "There has to be more to it than that. I know he was frightened, I know he was hurting, but I really got the impression that he was trying to tell me something."

Jack shook his head. "I'm sorry. The whole ridiculous thing

went wrong. It was my fault. I never should have tried it, and I never should have exposed you to any of that pain."

"Jack—he was desperately trying to communicate with us. Why do you think he appeared at all? Spirits manifest themselves only when they want to, not because we call them."

"Well, maybe you're right," Jack told her, "but he didn't manage it, did he? All I've got now is egg on my face."

Vincent meanwhile was frowning at the Johnson tomb. If Ben really *had* been trying to tell them something, why had he picked this particular grave? Why hadn't he picked his great-grandfather's grave, or any of the other graves in the cemetery? There was nothing out of the ordinary about the Johnson tomb. There was no special epitaph carved on it; there was no decoration, except for the hammered granite; and there was no statue. Vincent even tried to work out anagrams and acrostics from the Johnson family's names, but that produced only nonsense.

"I'm for calling it a day," Dr. Serling said. "Let's all go home and have a long think about it; then maybe we can come up with an answer when our brains are refreshed."

Jack said, "It looks like snow. I'd better get myself back to headquarters."

They left the cemetery in silence. The caretaker stood in the doorway of the House of Remembrance and smiled at them tartly, enjoying their obvious dejection.

"Everything was satisfactory, I hope?" he asked Jack.

"Fine," Jack told him. "You've got yourself a very fine body of people here."

Jack drove them back to the hospital, where they collected their cars. "If anyone comes up with even half an idea, let me know," he said.

They promised they would. He hesitated for a moment and then said, "I'm not at all sure that séance was a good idea. I don't think I handled it very well, either. If I caused you any grief, well, I just want to say I'm sorry. You especially, Pat. I feel like I used you."

Pat took his hand and kissed him on the cheek. "Don't start feeling bad about it. I did it of my own free will. Maybe I learned something, too."

Vincent gave Jack a wave and walked across the parking lot with Dr. Serling.

"An interesting man, our sheriff," he remarked.

"He took a chance, I'll give you that," Dr. Serling replied. "It's a pity he didn't have more courage in his convictions. That could be dangerous one day; if not for him, for somebody else."

Vincent cleared his throat. "Did you ever go to a séance before?"

"One."

"Was it successful?"

"Do you think I would have gone along with last night's performance if it hadn't been?"

"Then you're a believer, too."

Dr. Serling smiled. "I suppose I am, although I don't quite know what it is I believe in."

Vincent said, "About Ben—"

Dr. Serling had reached his car, and now he was digging in his coat pocket for his keys. He looked at Vincent keenly. "What you're going to ask me about Ben is whether we killed him by holding that séance. Well, the answer is probably yes— a few hours earlier than he was expected to die in any event. And if your next unspoken question is whether I feel guilty about it, especially since I happen to be his doctor and morally charged with doing everything I can to prolong his life, well, the answer to that is also yes."

Vincent didn't know how to answer that, but after a moment or two, Dr. Serling said, "They give you the power of life and death when they make you a doctor. There are no two ways about it. I have to exercise that power day in and day out, and last night wasn't any different. I can accept the guilt. If I couldn't, I'd hang up my stethoscope and retire to Florida. I'll be judged when the time comes for judgment, and if I've done wrong, I'll be punished for it. That's all."

It was snowing yet again as Vincent drove back to Candlemas, but the snow was dry and flaky and didn't settle. He kept on thinking about what Dr. Serling had said, and about the séance, and about the Johnson tomb underneath the oak up on the hill.

Ben Miller must have had a reason for mentioning that particular tomb, but why *that* tomb instead of any of the others? The only distinctive feature it possessed, the only thing that made it at all different from any of the other tombs, was the low granite wall that ran around it.

Vincent was usually excellent when it came to solving puzzles. His mind was both educated and quirky. He could see the Johnson tomb as an intellectual problem, and yet his brain just didn't know where to begin.

Perhaps he was trying to be too complicated about it. Ben Miller, after all, had been a pretty simpleminded young man, with little more than a grade-school education. If a simpleminded person were setting a problem, how would he go about it? Not with words perhaps; certainly not with academic references; probably not with numbers. No—the puzzle would more likely be very direct and very *visual*. Ben Miller had been a television watcher, one of Marshall McLuhan's audio-visual generation, and if someone like that had thought about the Johnson tomb, he would have seen a mental image of a—

Vincent said, "God *damn* it," out loud.

The Johnson tomb was a grave with a wall. The *only* grave with a wall. The walled grave. And that was what Ben had been so frightened of.

The Waldegrave.

Twenty

New Milford, December 19

When Vincent arrived back at Candlemas, he saw Charlotte's bright red Datsun sports car parked outside and the lights shining in the living room. Charlotte came to open the door for him, wearing the maroon wool dressing gown he had bought at Harrod's in London.

"I've been waiting for you all night," she said, kissing him. "Where on earth have you been?"

He took off his overcoat and hung it up. "If I told you, I don't think you'd believe me. But I'm all right. In fact, I'm a little *better* than all right. I think I'm beginning to understand what's going on. Or half-understand it, anyway."

"For goodness' sake, come and have some hot coffee. You look absolutely beat."

"I'm okay," Vincent insisted. "What time did you get here?"

Charlotte led the way into the living room. She had already raked out the fire and stacked it with fresh logs; it was starting to crackle merrily. "I got here just after midnight. I guess I missed you, that's all."

Vincent stripped off his tie and sport coat. "That doesn't sound like the whole story."

"Well, it isn't," she said. "I went out to dinner with Dick, and we had a fight."

"Do I know Dick?"

"Dick Cortabitarte. He works for Artprint."

"Oh, *that* Dick. Well, it doesn't surprise me. Dick Cortabitarte has a very obnoxious personality indeed, as far as I remember. In fact, I seem to remember that even his *hair* is obnoxious."

"That's the man. Dick, with the obnoxious hair."

Charlotte made coffee while Vincent went upstairs. As he sat on the end of the bed, stripping off his necktie and unbuttoning his shirt, he lifted the receiver off his bedroom telephone and punched out Jack Smith's number. After a long pause, one of Jack's deputies answered. "He's not here right now. Can I take a message?"

"Yes, please. Tell him that the Johnson tomb was a walled grave, like a grave with a wall. Then spell out the name W - a - l - d - e - g - r - a - v - e for him."

"Will he understand what you mean?"

"About as much and about as little as I do."

"Okay, sir. I'll see that he gets the message."

Vincent took a shower and changed. When he came downstairs, dressed in a black wool suit and a cream-colored silk shirt, she said, "You're going out again? I was going to fix you some lunch."

"I have to go out. You can come with me if you like."

"Where are you going?"

"Only over to Litchfield. I have to look up some papers."

"Vincent," Charlotte protested, "something's going on here, and I think I'd like to know what it is."

Vincent went out into the hallway and came back with the Waldegrave portrait. He took the paper wrapping off it and propped it up on a chair. Charlotte examined it closely and then turned to him with her nose wrinkled up.

"It's awful," she said. "It *smells*. It smells like rotting meat."

Vincent said, "My grandfather said this picture was the Pearson family's good-luck charm. He thought it so important that we keep it that he even had a special clause written in his will about it."

"And your father? He thought that, too?"

"My father was more ambivalent about it. But he did what my grandfather had told him and kept it safe, the same way I did. Not because we understood *why*, but simply because we were told to. And the Pearson family has always been very obedient to its elders. My father told me not to buy any painting I didn't understand, and I never did; that's why the Pearson gallery has always flourished."

Charlotte said tartly, "Apart from acquiring a peerless reputation for stuffiness."

"Is that what you think of me?" Vincent asked.

"You've never tried to seduce me. What else should I think?"

Vincent gave her a long, considered look. "Is this a backlash from Dick Cortabitarte?"

Charlotte slowly and deliberately shook her head from side to side. "No," she said.

Vincent finished his coffee and put down the cup. "I hope you realize that this is going to spoil everything."

"Why should it?"

"I don't know. But I don't want to lose you. I don't want to lose your friendship. And the very first thing that gets laid on the line when people decide to be lovers is friendship. If we love and then fall out of love, bang goes everything. The walks, the talks, the theater, the meals, the weekends up here in Connecticut."

Charlotte reached across and took his hand. "Sometimes you have to take risks. You can't go through your entire lifetime not taking risks. I'm in love with you and you're in love with me, so why are we wearing these invisible chastity belts just in case we happen to lose our friendship? One second of true love is worth five years of friendship."

"Not always."

Charlotte knelt forward and kissed his cheek, then his lips. The kiss began innocently, lips closed, but then she probed into his mouth with the tip of her tongue, and after a moment, they were kissing passionately and deeply; Vincent at last felt all of his long-stored affection for Charlotte welling up inside him, irresistibly; each of them knew before the hour was out that they would become lovers.

It happened with dignity and grace: up in the master bedroom, among the grainy violet shadows, on the bed that had witnessed the intimate history of the Pearson family for the past hundred years. Naked, Charlotte lay between the sheets, and as Vincent climbed into bed with her, she reached up, touched his cheek and kissed him. His fingers traced her nerve endings in tingling and anticipatory whorls: from her neck to her shoulders, to the curve of her breasts so that her nipples rose like the tight buds of Mme. Grégoire roses.

She grasped his hardened penis in her hand and guided it between her parted thighs. He slid quickly inside her, as deep as he could, and she shuddered with the pleasure of it, and with the emotional release of having at last consummated their relationship. They held each other tight as the rhythm of their thrusting steadily increased. Vincent said, "You're murdering me," and laughed; and then Charlotte felt the overwhelming spasms of an oncoming orgasm, and there was nothing she could do to hold it back any longer. She quaked and cried out, and the rippling of her vagina brought Vincent to his climax, too; and as she clung to him, he flooded her with warmth. . . .

They made love once more before they left the bed, more slowly this time, savoring the feel of their bodies together, their fingers lingering between their legs, tracing, with wonder and satisfaction, their physical joining together.

Vincent said, "If this never happens again, believe me, it will have been worth it."

Charlotte propped herself on an elbow and looked at him with mischievous eyes. "We should have done this years ago."

"No, I don't think so. This is the right time for it. I never like to make love to a stranger."

"What about Meggsy?"

"That was lust, not love."

"*Was?*"

Vincent reached across to the bedside table and checked his watch. "You don't think I'd two-time a nice sweet girl like that?"

"What about a nice sweet girl like me?"

"I wouldn't two-time you, either."

They dressed and had a drink together beside the fire; then Vincent said, "We have to go. I promised Mr. Morris I would be down at his office before lunch. He closes on Saturday afternoons."

"Mr. Morris?"

"The family lawyer."

They drove over to Litchfield under a sun that was no longer yellow, but deathly white. The countryside around them was like a silvery dream: misty hills and pearl-gray distances. Charlotte sat close to Vincent, one hand resting on his thigh, not possessively but with the reassurance of shared experience. Warm friendship had bloomed into love; riskier perhaps, but so very much sweeter.

"Do you have to go back to MOMA before Christmas?" Vincent asked.

"I was supposed to call in on Monday."

"That sounds like you've changed your mind."

"It depends. Are *you* going back to the city?"

"I don't think so."

"Well then, I'll stay with you."

Vincent glanced at her and smiled. Charlotte kissed the tips of her fingers and pressed them against his lips.

The offices of Morris, McClure & Winterman were situated just outside Litchfield in a large eighteenth-century building that had once been a farmhouse. The roof was covered in thick white snow beneath which the dark weatherboarded walls appeared even darker and the small leaded windows even smaller. It was the kind of house in which Vincent could easily have believed witches had once lived: one of those suffocating colonial mansions riddled with narrow corridors, musty cupboards and crazily angled staircases. Mr. Morris occupied an aerie in the eaves, an untidy nest lined with legal documents and sprawling files. He was white-haired and big-nosed, with horn-rimmed glasses heavily obscured with thumbprints, and when he sat down and crossed his knees, the leg of his long johns was exposed above his sock. He was always glad to see Vincent. He shook his hand, beamed and offered Vincent and Charlotte a glass of his English-bottled sherry.

Charlotte sat down in an old leather-covered chair as deep as a bathtub.

"Your great-grandfather was a copious diary-keeper," Mr. Morris said, untying the ribbons that had for more than seventy years held together a box file marked "Pearson, 1891–1913."

"He was not a communicative man, not to speak to; but he wrote everything down: from the sale of the smallest and most insignificant painting, to whom it was sold and why, and whether he believed the new owner was worthy of it, to his own marital affairs and the arguments he had with your great-grandmother, and . . . er . . . some of his more personal adventures."

"It's the Grays I'm interested in," Vincent said.

"Well, indeed, as you said on the telephone. I've heard the name, of course. They were a mainstay of Connecticut society from the eighteen seventies until the nineteen hundreds, when they suddenly decamped and left for Europe. The departure of the Grays caused a tremendous stir at the time and left local society bereft. Just imagine what would have happened to Newport if the Vanderbilts had suddenly disappeared. There are many older people in Darien today who believe that Darien could have been the jewel of American society if the Grays hadn't left. In their day, they were as wealthy and as popular as any Astor or Frick or Havemeyer."

"The Grays are mentioned in my great-grandfather's papers?" Vincent asked.

Mr. Morris nodded. "Several times. I did as you asked and tried to find as many references to them as possible. Unfortunately, I've been rather pressed this morning; I've been dealing with the Hartley case, for all of my sins; and so I've managed to get only halfway through. If you'd like to examine the papers for yourself, of course. . . ."

"I'd be delighted," Vincent told him. "Is there an office we can use?"

"Use this one. I have to be in court in twenty minutes. You won't disturb me, except if you drink too much of my sherry. My cousin brings it over, you know. Don't you think it's rather fine?"

Vincent sipped a little more and lifted the glass. "Very fine indeed," he said.

Vincent and Charlotte took the bulky box file and crowded together at a small side desk while the lawyer shuffled papers, repeatedly cleared his throat and picked up his telephone from time to time to speak in baffling terms to his secretary.

The Pearson file contained page after page of faint-ruled quarto paper, softened and yellowed with age and filled on both sides with tiny handwriting in purple ink. It began in the summer of 1891, when Vincent's great-grandfather was twenty-seven and his grandfather was five. There were pages about

Candlemas, describing how it was being redecorated and altered, and telling how the family had spent the summer riding, boating and going on picnics. Mr. Morris had left strips of torn blotting-paper as markers in between the pages on which the Grays were mentioned. Vincent's great-grandfather had obviously met the Grays some years before, because the first reference, on August 12, 1891, read, "Algernon Gray came up this weekend from Darien, bringing his wife Isobel and his daughter Cordelia. He seemed as sprightly as ever; in fact, he has scarcely changed since I was first introduced to him at the age of nineteen at the Darien Independence Day Ball, and Cordelia appeared as youthful and as blooming as she was on that day, although she must have attained her twenty-fifth year by now. Mr. Gray was much interested in some paintings of the Rouen Cathedral that Jean Laplage recently sent me from Paris, and I agreed to consider a purchase price of $150 each for two of the best of them, although I have never thought the Grays were the kind of family to whom sensitive paintings should be sold. There is something altogether too *feral* about them, as if they are meat-eaters with a vengeance."

The next mention of the Grays was in 1893, when Vincent's great-grandfather met Belvedere and Willa Gray at the theater in New York. "They were not their usual selves, although they looked well enough. They spoke a great deal of Oscar Wilde and what a great playwright he is, and of Tree's production of *A Woman of No Importance*, which has just opened in London. I am growing curious about the Gray family; whenever I see them, they seem to be possessed of such unnatural joyfulness, and they have confidence in the future far outweighing the normal optimism with which one usually regards one's remaining years. Belvedere spoke of the turn of the twentieth century and how different it would be from the turn of the nineteenth century, almost as if he expected he would be there to witness it. Most odd!"

There were further mentions of social meetings with the Gray family, extending all the way through to 1905. In February, 1905, Vincent's great-grandfather wrote, "I am almost persuaded that the Gray family must have formed some pact with the Devil himself. They remain, all of them, as youthful as they were more than fifteen years ago. Cordelia cannot be younger than thirty-six now, yet she happily remains unmarried and looks no older than twenty. The last time I spoke to her, at the Newport regatta, she said she was thinking of marrying 'soon' but she wanted to be sure her husband-to-be was suitable. 'There is, after all, no hurry.' For a woman of thirty-six to say there is no hurry when she is considering the question of marriage is quite startling; but no less startling is Cordelia herself, whose neck remains smooth, whose complexion remains unwrinkled, whose hair remains as glossy and as lustrous as ever. And what can I say of Algernon and Isobel, whose freshness is remarkable? I myself grow older and grayer by the month; yet Algernon, who is some years older than I, remains as well-preserved as if he were in amber.''

There were two or three gaps in the diary until 1911; and it was then that Vincent's great-grandfather became completely convinced that the Grays were no ordinary family, and he set out to find out how they were different, and why. In June, 1911, he dressed himself "in a nondescript linen suit" and traveled to Darien to talk to some of the Grays' neighbors and "those of the townsfolk of Darien who had their wits about them, which were not as many as I would have liked."

Suddenly, Vincent pointed to a lengthy paragraph, denser than the rest, as if it had been copied out from notes. "*This* is what we've been looking for!" he told Charlotte. "This is the proof. The family in the Waldegrave portrait *are* the Grays; without a shadow of a doubt."

The paragraph was a deposition that Vincent's great-grandfather had taken from a woman called Nora Cartwright, who used to run the domestic staff at Wilderlings. Apparently she had found it almost impossible to find regular employment after she had left the Grays; even in those days, they already had a "sinister" reputation; and she had gladly spoken to Vincent's great-grandfather in exchange for a boiled ham and $10.

"In December of 1882, after a tour of America that included San Francisco, Leadville, Denver and Savannah, the celebrated Irish aesthete, Oscar Wilde, visited Newport, R.I., and there became acquainted with Algernon and Isobel Gray at a supper party given by the Goelets. Algernon and Isobel Gray were both enthusiastic collectors of modern art and were

delighted when Wilde introduced them some days later to
Walter Waldegrave, a fashionable British painter who had
accompanied Mrs. Lily Langtry to the United States when she
visited New York just after Christmas, 1882. Waldegrave was a
realist of the pre-Raphaelite school, and Algernon was very
keen for him to paint a family portrait of the Grays at their
home in Darien. Unfortunately, Waldegrave contracted pneu-
monia during his visit to New York and returned to England
prematurely in February, 1883, still too weak to undertake any
commissions. The Grays, however, traveled to London during
the summer of 1883, specifically to visit Walter Waldegrave at
his house in Norbury, in South London, and to have their
family portrait painted. They returned to Darien in October,
but their behavior was 'much changed.' They began to treat
their staff very cruelly, and both Maurice and Henry Gray were
guilty of taking improper advantage of the family's maids, so
much so that local families refused to let their daughters work
at Wilderlings. There were stories of riotous parties, of
narcotics and of unusual sexual practices, particularly whipping and bondage, and although many of these were undoubt-
edly exaggerated by fear and superstition, there was no doubt
that some strange influence had taken possession of the Grays
and that they seemed to believe they were beyond the law, both
the law of man, and the law of heaven. They did not lose their
position in society, for in the company of their friends, they
always behaved impeccably. But the young children of Darien
were warned by their parents not to venture too close to
Wilderlings for fear of being consumed alive, and whenever
the Grays walked abroad, they were always given the widest of
berths.''

Just as Vincent and Charlotte finished reading this entry, Mr.
Morris rose from his desk, took Vincent by the hand and said,
"I wish I could stay and take you to lunch. But you know how
it is. *Hartley versus Hartley.* The most complicated custody
case in Connecticut's legal history. Except *O'Connell versus
O'Connell*, but that, of course, was an epic, my God! An epic, my God!
And the best legal fees since the *Matter of Vanderbilt.*"

Vincent said, "You've been a great help. You don't mind if
we stay here for a while and finish reading these papers?"

"Well, help yourself," Mr. Morris said, trying to wink.

"I'm not really supposed to let you do it under the terms of the will, but since you're the only surviving member of the family, I can't see that we're at very much risk legally, can you?"

He uttered the oddest of laughs, as if someone had suddenly seized hold of his throat and waggled his head from side to side, choking him.

They sat in the claustrophobic silence of Mr. Morris's room in that house built for witches, and they read through the rest of the file, far beyond the pages the lawyer had marked, carefully running their fingers down the columns for any sign of the family Gray, or any mention of Waldegrave, Darien or Oscar Wilde.

The purple ink ran out; abruptly, in 1910, they were reading pages written in black India ink on a different quality of paper, in far more energetic writing. Writing with loops under the "y's" and squiggles under the "g's" and thunderbolts under the "q's," with brisk crosses on every "t" and diamond-shaped dots on every "i." This was the diary of Vincent's grandfather, who had taken over the pursuit of the Grays and seemed determined to hunt them down to prove their venality beyond doubt.

"I have talked now to scores of servants, friends and acquaintances, and I have become convinced *in spite of the apparent absurdity of it* that the Grays underwent some extraordinary transmogrification when they visited England in 1883. The writings of Mr. Oscar Wilde appear to bear me out; and although he has been dead these past ten years, I have been fortunate in being able to interview several of those who met him when he visited New England in 1882; the consensus seems to be that the Grays were much taken with Wilde, and also with Walter Waldegrave, and that during the Christmas of 1882, they could speak of nothing else. In fact, the entire Gray family seems to have been on tenterhooks until word arrived from England in the summer of 1883 that Mr. Waldegrave was now quite well and willing to paint their family portrait."

There was a long gap in the diary and then a heavily underlined entry for May, 1911. "My correspondent in England, Mr. Frederick Rickwood, has now informed me that Walter Waldegrave, before his suicide in 1885, was under suspicion for blasphemy and witchcraft and that he was a member of that infamous coven known as the Norbury Nine, many of whom were prosecuted in 1884 for unnatural acts and for the pagan sacrificing of sheep. Waldegrave had apparently discovered the formula by which those who promised to live a life of corruption and devilry could survive forever without growing old. Mr. Rickwood says that a competent artist had only to paint the supplicants' portrait and that the words of the Exorcism had only to be said over them backwards, and immortality would be assured. Their portrait would age as they might have done, but they themselves would remain young."

Vincent's grandfather quoted the Exorcism, in reverse, *"Nos audi, rogamus te, digneris humiliare Ecclesiae sanctae inimicos ut; nos audi, rogamus te, seruire libertate facias tibi secura tuam Ecclesiam ut; Domine nos libera, diabolii insidiis ab."*

The diary went on: "I talked about the Grays with Father Summers, from the College of Jesuits, and during July, he agreed at last to travel to Darien with me and to pay them an uninvited visit. Both of us, I think, were apprehensive."

Charlotte said hesitantly, "You don't think that Maurice Gray—I mean the Maurice Gray your Sheriff Smith was talking about—you don't think he's the *same* Maurice Gray, do you? I mean, this Maurice Gray was alive in eighteen eighty-two. He couldn't have—"

Vincent leafed through the pages again. " 'Waldegrave had apparently discovered the formula by which those who promised to live a life of corruption and devilry could survive forever,' " he read aloud.

"But you don't believe that? If you *believed* that, Maurice Gray would be more than a hundred and thirty years old!"

"Yesterday morning I would have said it wasn't possible."

"But the séance changed your mind, is that it?"

Vincent raised his hands to show that he understood just as little as she did. "I saw the spirit of a dying man floating in the air; I heard voices when there was nobody talking. Right at this moment I think I could well believe anything—even a hundred-and-thirty-year-old art connoisseur."

"You were tired. What did you really see?"

He looked at her narrowly. "You don't believe me? I saw Ben Miller, the same way everybody else at that séance saw Ben Miller. He was there, for real. There's no denying it."

Charlotte touched the back of his hand. "These Gray people—if this is true—"

"You mean they frighten you?"

"Yes, of course they do."

"Well, if it's any consolation, they frighten me, too."

Vincent went back to the diary and read out the next entry, slowly and doggedly, as if it was the operating instructions for a Whirlpool dishwasher.

"'Father Summers and I went to Wilderlings and found the Gray family outside in the garden, taking tea. It was a lovely afternoon. The Grays were the picture of elegant courtesy. They seemed to be oblivious to the fact that this was now nineteen eleven, almost thirty years after their portrait had been painted by Walter Waldegrave, and that none of them had aged even one whit since that time. Algernon Gray should have been sixty-three by now, and yet he looked like a young man of thirty. His wife Isobel looked almost as young as her own daughter, Cordelia, who should now have reached her fortieth year and yet was as fresh and pale as a twenty-year-old. They had the same cat I remembered as a child, a marmalade cat with a kink in his ear, called Firework. Yet this cat should have been dead by now, three times over. Father Summers and I said nothing to the Grays, not directly; but on the way out, while we waited for our hats, I showed Father Summers the Waldegrave portrait in the hall, and it was plain what had happened. The portrait showed the Gray family as we might have expected to see them—Algernon white-haired and aged, Isobel wrinkled, and Cordelia looking like a middle-aged matron. The cat Firework was gone and in its place was nothing more than a furry black shadow. Maurice was gray-haired, still stylish, but showing his years; and Henry was lined with worry. It seemed to us then that the people sitting out in the garden were like the characters out of a dream and that this portrait showed their waking selves, showed them as they really were. Father Summers crossed himself and said a prayer, but he was interrupted by the sudden appearance of Maurice Gray, who courteously but firmly escorted us away from the house and down to the driveway, where our motor vehicle was waiting. Maurice Gray said very little, but he made it clear to us that the Gray family would not welcome any further unsolicited visits and that we should stay away from Wilderlings in the future.'"

During the summer of 1911, Vincent's grandfather recorded the deaths of seven young women in the Darien area, all of them unexplained, and he became increasingly convinced they were the work of the Gray family, particularly since most of the bodies showed signs of having been whipped and tied up and he had heard reports that Henry Gray had talked to his friends incessantly of the pleasures of bondage and of how much he appreciated the "less acceptable" work of Swinburne. When Henry Gray was charged with culpable homicide in September, 1911, but quickly released because of "insufficient evidence," Vincent's grandfather decided it was time for him to act. He engaged a professional thief to enter Wilderlings at night and steal the Waldegrave portrait. Then he wrote to Algernon Gray, inviting him to meet him at Candlemas "if he should wish to know where the Waldegrave portrait might have been spirited away."

The meeting apparently was acrimonious. Algernon Gray accused Vincent's grandfather of theft and conspiracy and said he would have him hung. But Vincent's grandfather quite calmly explained that he intended to hold on to the Waldegrave portrait and that he would keep it safe provided the Grays left Connecticut immediately and never came back. If they returned, he said, or if they attempted to retrieve the portrait, he would burn it.

It was a dangerous gamble, of course, for Vincent's grandfather had no way of knowing for sure whether the stories about Walter Waldegrave had any foundation in fact. It was conceivable that the Grays had remained so youthful-looking because of their excellent health. But when Algernon Gray grudgingly agreed to leave the country with the guarantee that the Waldegrave portrait would not be harmed, Vincent's grandfather knew then that everything he had heard about the Grays was true.

"The very life essence of the Gray family was contained within the painting, and whatever marks the years made upon the family members, the painting reflected each and every one, although the faces of the Grays themselves remained smooth. Every debauch, every drug-riddled party, every perversion, each appeared on the portrait as if by some magical hand, a hand that kept count of every second, a hand that recorded every corrupt and self-indulgent pleasure. For time and corruption must always make their marks somewhere, just as surely as a man must make his mark when he walks across the snow.''

There were few entries in the journal at the time the Grays actually packed up and left Connecticut, although one line read, "Algernon has tried again to bribe me; when that failed, he threatened me!" Vincent's grandfather must have been bullied and cajoled by the Grays far more than he admitted. After all, the painting was not just a painting. It was not just a family heirloom. The painting was *them*, the Grays themselves, their living identities. The moment it ceased to exist, so would they. Their fear when they left Connecticut must have been enormous, and they must have continued to live in fear for every second of every day ever since. It would have taken nothing more than a fire, a flood or an over-enthusiastic vandal, and "all twelve" would instantly have perished.

Now the Grays were back in Connecticut, roosted again at Wilderlings, and they were looking for their portrait. Vincent thought to himself, *that's why Edward died*. The woman in black hadn't wanted his body; she probably hadn't even wanted to kill him. She had wanted his keys, nothing more, so she could search the gallery. And what had she taken? Nothing, because the Waldegrave portrait hadn't been there. In fact, it was the only painting an outsider might reasonably have expected to be there that wasn't, and that was only because Aaron Halperin had been trying to restore it, up in Bantam, Connecticut.

She had left Edward with a corrupt and terrible gift: the maggots out of the grave, the maggots that should have devoured *her* more than sixty years ago.

Charlotte said in an awed whisper, "Vincent—does this mean what I think it means?"

He nodded. "The Grays found a way of living forever, or at least what they believed would be living forever. The only trouble was, they took advantage of their immortality and started to live completely debauched lives, without caring who they hurt, or even who they killed."

"And your grandfather found out—and stopped them."

Vincent breathed, "If only he'd told us why we had to take care of that picture."

"Do you think any of you would have believed him if he had?"

"I don't know. I don't think my father would have."

"Well, then," Charlotte said, "perhaps it was better that he kept silent."

"These skinning murders . . . Sheriff Smith seems to think they might be connected with the Grays, that maybe they're part and parcel of the same thing."

"What do you mean?"

"Well, the portrait is decaying because of Walter Waldegrave's poor technique. Perhaps as the portrait falls apart, the Grays are falling apart, too. You see what it says here in my grandfather's diary: 'The very life essence of the Gray family was contained within the painting.' If the painting is flaking, then the Grays' life essence must be falling to pieces, too. I mean—perhaps I'm being unjust. The only evidence Sheriff Smith has so far that connects the Grays to the skinning murders is the uncorroborated testimony of a notoriously unreliable hitchhiker. But it all seems to fit together, doesn't it? The Grays have a reason for wanting fresh skin. Because if you go back and smell that picture, what you're smelling isn't egg tempera, or damp canvas, or decomposing varnish. That's the smell of real people, rotting. That's human gangrene. And if they're rotting, what do the Grays need more than anything else so they can keep up a respectable front?"

Charlotte said, "*Skin*," and stared at Vincent in horror.

"Don't look so shocked. I think you're right. They want fresh, unspoiled skin to cover themselves with. They want human masks so the rest of us can't see what's been happening to them. They've been rotting alive, but they've been keeping up a reasonable day-to-day appearance by stealing the skin of other people and wearing it as naturally as if it were part of themselves, the same way a clown puts on his slapstick. It's the Grays, all right. They've been murdering people for nothing except their skin, and as that painting decomposes more and more—well, what do you think?"

"They'll want more skin?"

Vincent said, "God, it seems like it, doesn't it? God. It's disgusting."

"And they want the picture, too, just as badly?"

"At least I've left the house locked tight," said Vincent. "The Lord only knows what they could be capable of doing if they ever manage to lay their hands on that picture."

"Can't you just go arrest them?" Charlotte demanded. "If they're all that evil, if they're really murderers, why doesn't Sheriff Smith drive straight down to Darien and collar them before they kill someone else?"

"You can't arrest anybody without evidence, my love." Vincent was acutely conscious of the fresh connotations that this morning's events gave the words "my love." "And—no matter what we might *believe*—all the evidence we have so far is the unsubstantiated story of a hitchhiker, which any half-decent defense attorney could have thrown out of court before the judge's bottom hit the chair."

"But your great-grandfather's diaries. Your *grandfather's* diaries."

"They don't prove anything except that my great-grandfather and my grandfather had a bit of trouble around the turn of the century with some people called the Grays, all of whom should now be long dead. Come on, Charlotte, are you seriously asking this court to believe that Maurice Gray, who stands accused here today of homicide in the first degree, is the *same* Maurice Gray with whom my great-grandfather was acquainted in eighteen ninety-one? The very idea is preposterous. Immediate acquittal, and costs against the county."

"Then what can we do?"

Vincent finished his glass of sherry and said, "We could destroy the portrait. Then the Grays would be destroyed, too—according to what my grandfather says, at least."

"You really think you could deliberately kill twelve people?" Charlotte asked. Her eyes in the mid-morning sunlight were as green as onyxes and twice as bright.

"It wouldn't be the same as shooting them, would it? It would be execution, by remote control. I wouldn't even have to go anywhere near them. I could torch the painting and read in the Darien newspapers the next day that the Grays were dead."

"I'm not talking about the *method*," Charlotte said. "I'm talking about the morality."

"Well, let's put it this way. There's nothing intrinsically immoral about destroying a rotten old Victorian painting that long ago lost any artistic or financial value, is there? And if the Grays *do* happen to die at the same time I burn the painting, then all I can say is that what my grandfather said about them was true and that it was time they were dead anyway. But if they *don't* die, then no harm has been done to anyone."

"I'm not sure about the logic of that," Charlotte said doubtfully.

"I'm not sure about the logic of *any* of this," Vincent told her. He stood up and closed his grandfather's file. "But let's go back to Candlemas and burn that painting."

They left the offices of Morris, McClure & Winterman and trudged across the snowy parking lot. Charlotte asked, "Why didn't your grandfather destroy the painting if he believed the Grays were so evil?"

Vincent shrugged. "The one thing you can say about my grandfather is that he was always a man of honor, a man who kept his word, no matter what. If he had promised Algernon Gray to keep the painting safe, he would have kept it safe."

"And you're prepared to break his word of honor?"

Vincent unlocked the car door. "I don't think my grandfather had any inkling that the Grays would take to skinning people alive."

They drove back to Candlemas in silence, Charlotte huddling close to him. When Vincent opened the front door of the house, his telephone-answering machine was blinking, which indicated that somebody had called him, but he ignored it for the moment and walked through to the living room, where he had left the Waldegrave portrait. The fire in the living-room grate had sunk low and the wind was blowing softly down the chimney, scattering ashes across the rug, although the room was still warm. He lifted the portrait and said to Charlotte as she came through the door, "Are you going to watch?"

She stared at him. "It's changed," she said, her voice as dry as cardboard.

Vincent frowned and turned the portrait around to see it more clearly. "Changed? How?"

"There," Charlotte said. "She wasn't there before, surely?"

And it was true; she hadn't been there before. In the very front row of the portrait, where the ladies of the family were posed, sat a girl in a maid's black dress, severe and prim except that the hem had been drawn up high to reveal her thighs, and even a smudgy suggestion of pubic hair. The girl's expression was calm and blank, unlike everyone else's in the portrait, all of whom had been smiling before the rot set in. She looked quite modern, too; her hair style was 1980s, as was her makeup.

"Laura Monblat!" Vincent gasped. He touched the image with a fingertip, but if any fresh paint had been applied to the canvas, it was dry by now.

"Laura Monblat? You mean Edward's ex-girlfriend?"

Vincent sat down, propping the painting across his knees. "That's Laura, all right. Edward brought her into the gallery once, the second or third day he worked for me. Now the whole damned thing is beginning to make sense."

"*Sense*? It's sense that Edward's ex-girlfriend mysteriously turns up in the middle of a Victorian painting? She wasn't there before, was she—before we went out? So someone must have broken into the house and painted her there, in two hours, in oil paint, and the paint's perfectly dry?"

"I don't think anyone broke in," Vincent said. "I think Laura has appeared on the portrait because she's actually there, down at Wilderlings with the Grays. In some strange way, they've made her part of the family, the same way that Aaron's cat has appeared in place of the Grays' original ginger cat, Firework."

"So they kidnapped her? Is that what you're saying?"

"That's the assumption I'm making, admittedly with not much in the way of evidence."

"I can't believe this!" Charlotte cried. "The very first day we decide to be lovers instead of friends, and it's crazy and weird from start to finish."

Vincent said, "They may have done it on purpose."

"Done *what* on purpose?"

"They may have included Laura in the painting so I wouldn't be able to burn it."

"I just don't understand you."

"It's dreadfully simple. I wish it weren't. But anyone who appears in this portrait has his life essence inextricably caught up in it. The painting grows old while *he*—or *she*—stays young. So from the very second anyone first appears in it, his survival depends on the survival of the painting."

Charlotte stared at the portrait without speaking. Finally she breathed, "That poor girl."

"Yes, that poor girl. If I burn the picture, the chances are I will burn her, too."

Twenty-One

Housatonic Meadows, December 20

"They found him by chance," Norman Goldberg said, the collar of his sheepskin coat turned up against the driving snow. "They were looking for their hunting dog—still ain't whistled it up yet—but there he was, facedown. They thought he was a hog at first, or a dead moose. But, well, when they looked closer. . . ."

Jack could see the obscenity that was George Kelly's body, even from twenty yards away through wind and snow. George was lying half-submerged in a frozen puddle, crusts of ice between his skinned fingers. Wallace Greenstreet, wearing a wide-brimmed hat, was crouching over him, and fastidiously lifting up layers of skin and muscle with a scalpel.

"Any tire tracks?" Jack asked. "They couldn't have carried him here on foot."

"No tire tracks worth casting," Norman replied.

"How about footprints?"

"It's snowed and frozen over since they left him here."

Jack thrust his hands into his windbreaker pockets, chewed warm gum for a while and then said, "Shit."

Norman said, "You think it's those Grays, don't you?"

Jack nodded emphatically. "Of course I think it's those Grays. Elmer Tweed put the finger on Maurice Gray, and George was trying to prove it." He walked forward until he was standing only a dozen yards from the body. "Wallace?"

Without turning around, Wallace said, "I hear you, Jack."

"How long do you think he's been here, Wallace? Looks to me like he's frozen pretty solid."

Wallace adjusted his hat and laid his hands on his thighs,

contemplating George Kelly's body with professional glumness. "You'd need a chain saw to cut him up."

"Do your best, anyway," Jack told him. "Look for drugs in the bloodstream, especially. Elmer Tweed said Gray had tried to inject him with a hypodermic."

"I'll call you," Wallace assured him.

As Jack walked back to the Cherokee, Norman Goldberg caught up with him. "What are you going to do?" he asked.

"I'm going to go talk to Vincent Pearson, that's what I'm going to do. Then I'm going to drive down to Darien and get myself a warrant to search the Gray house; then I'm going to bust the whole damned family on suspicion of kidnap, attempted kidnap and as many counts of first-degree homicide as I think I can prove."

"Maybe you should wait a while," Norman suggested. "You know, gather a little more evidence."

Jack retorted, "George Kelly was murdered trying to gather evidence. I'm not risking any more lives, especially my own. With any luck, the Grays will resist arrest and I'll be able to shoot them all. They're vermin, Norman. They're totally corrupt. People like the Grays, you don't give them second chances. You shoot them first and worry about the consequences afterward."

Norman looked unhappy. He clung to the Cherokee's door, snow blowing in his face, and said, "You're the best sheriff Litchfield County has had in a long time, you know that? I wouldn't like to see any drastic changes, not just yet."

Jack said, "You want to stand here and have a long debate about a sheriff's duty to protect the public? I didn't put myself up for this job because I thought it was safe, Norman. I put myself up for this job because I care about people's security, and their right to stay alive. I put myself up for this job because there are so many people who don't think personal safety matters a damn so long as everybody enjoys their rights under the Constitution. Well—as far as I'm concerned—blacks have rights, and women have rights, and gays have rights, and even goddam Bay Staters have rights. But homicidal lunatics like the Gray family *don't* have rights, and all I'm going to do is point that out to them, in person."

"Jack—" Norman warned him, "don't get too mad."

"Just watch me," Jack said and drove the Cherokee off

through the snow, bumping over tussocks and ditches and rutted tracks, his teeth clenched with anger and grief. God knew what George must have suffered before he died. And only God knew who else was going to have to suffer before the Grays were finally caught.

He drove directly down to New Milford and over to Candlemas. Vincent and Charlotte were just finishing a late lunch of microwaved pizza and lightly chilled Corvo. Log fires were crackling in the fireplaces and the house was comfortable and warm. After Charlotte took his coat and poured him a crystal glass of wine, he sat down in the big brocaded armchair next to the hearth and began to feel human again.

Vincent said, "I've been trying to get in touch with you since yesterday. I called your office about a hundred times."

Jack told him, "I've been out. I just came back from Housatonic Meadows. You remember my friend George Kelly down in Darien—the one who was trying to roust out a little more solid evidence about the Grays? Well, two duck hunters found him this morning dead, not too far from Cornwall Bridge. At first they thought he was a slaughtered deer someone had shot and skinned and left to rot."

"You mean they skinned him, too?" Vincent asked, shocked.

"That's about it." Jack didn't want to say more in case he would sound hysterical or vengeful. "They killed him, and they skinned him. Not necessarily in that order."

Charlotte came over, sat down beside him and put her hand on his. "I don't know what to say. I'm so sorry."

Jack swallowed hard, and looked away.

Vincent sipped his wine, then said, "We've found out more."

"About the Grays, you mean?"

Vincent nodded. "It isn't evidence, not in the sense you could present it to a judge and jury and hope to get a conviction. But it may help us combat the Grays on their own terms."

Vincent explained about his and Charlotte's visit to his family's lawyer in Litchfield, and about Walter Waldegrave and his unnatural portrait. He also explained about Laura; as he did so, he lifted the portrait from behind the sofa, took off the wrapping and presented it to Jack for closer inspection.

Jack studied it in silence. Then he looked at Vincent soberly. "This is for real, isn't it? I mean, this isn't a dream or any kind of collective hallucination? This is for real?"

Vincent said quietly, "Yes. I believe it is."

"Then I'm driving down to Darien right now, and I'm going to arrest the Grays on suspicion of kidnap and homicide in the first degree. Either that or I'm going to blow them away."

"You think your friend George Kelly would have approved of that?"

"George would have relished it. George was always in favor of blowing criminals away. And who are you to criticize? You were just about to set fire to the whole damned painting, and the Gray family with it. And you *would* have, too, if it hadn't have been for Mrs. Monblat being there."

"If you kill the Grays," Vincent said, "the chances are that we may never get Mrs. Monblat back. Not as her normal self, anyway."

"What do you mean?"

"I mean that Laura Monblat has turned up in this painting for a very good reason. The Grays have somehow gotten her in there to protect themselves. Like, 'You can't destroy this painting, because if you do, you'll destroy Mrs. Monblat, too.' Besides, the Grays are the only people who know how to get her off the canvas and back into real life. Back into normal, mortal life—the kind of life that ends when it's supposed to end. Well, I'm *hoping* they know, anyway, because if they don't, she's going to be trapped in that picture forever."

Jack didn't know what to say to that. Vincent was very persuasive, very sophisticated, and yet Jack wasn't entirely sure he ought to believe him.

"Do you think Mrs. Monblat is in any immediate danger?" he asked.

Vincent lit a cigarette and puffed at it without inhaling, the last self-indulgence of a reformed smoker. "I think we have to assume she is—although it's quite unusual, isn't it, for any of the Grays' victims to have been kept alive for so long? The young man you found in the Nepaug Reservoir had been killed and skinned almost straightaway; so had that other body you discovered down at West Haven; so was George Kelly. I can't do anything except guess, but it seems to me that Laura Monblat may have been taken into the family as some kind of maid or servant. Take a look at that dress. I know it's been pulled up to expose her, but it's a maid's uniform, isn't it? It reminds me of those bondage drawings of Sweet Gwendoline, and we know from my grandfather's papers that Henry Gray was very interested in bondage.''

Jack said, "You don't think Laura Monblat is dead already? Maybe they put her·into the portrait just to confuse us?''

"I don't think so," Vincent told him. "It seems to me that the picture and the people in it are inextricably tied up together. It's just as if the picture is some kind of life-support machine, keeping the Grays alive long past the time they were supposed to be dead. I considered the thought that Laura Monblat might have been killed, but then I looked at the cat. You see that cat? My great-grandfather knew that cat; when it was still alive, he mentioned it in his diary, and it appeared in the portrait when it was first painted. But when I was a boy, the cat was gone. There was only a black fuzz, nothing more than a shadow, like an empty hole in the canvas.''

"I don't follow," Jack said.

"Well, look at it this way. When the Grays reached the age when they should have died, when they all reached the end of their normal and natural lifespan, the picture slowly began to decompose, and I think they did, too. Maybe Waldegrave's technique wasn't sufficiently polished. Maybe his magic wasn't up to it, if it really was magic. But the portrait and the family began gradually and simultaneously to fall to pieces, that's my opinion. That's why the Grays keep on murdering people and taking their skins. They have to keep themselves looking young; they have to keep themselves together or they'll die.''

"And the cat?" Jack asked.

."They were probably so worried about themselves it didn't occur to them to think about the cat. The cat died, leaving nothing on the canvas but a black, empty outline where once it had sat; and it was only this week, when one of the Grays killed Aaron Halperin's cat and skinned it, that Firework reappeared. Miraculously, as if it had been reborn.''

Jack said nothing. Vincent's interpretation of what was happening was bizarre to say the least, but it did have some peculiar kind of logic. The trouble was, Jack had never handled a case even remotely similar; for all he knew, he was being taken for a sucker. What if Vincent were in collusion with the Grays, for example? What if the Grays had paid off Pat? What if Nancy knew something about it and wasn't telling? And how come Dr. Serling had been so ready to join a séance—him, the down-to-earth country doctor?

Jack had accepted the séance and the appearance of Ben Miller's spirit because it had been his own idea—at least he *thought* it had been his own. But supposing Dr. Serling had set up some kind of projector in the doctor's office and faked the séance? And supposing this story about Laura Monblat were nothing at all but nonsense? After all, he had never seen the Waldegrave portrait *before* Laura Monblat appeared in it. How was he to know now that the portrait was genuine?

Vincent was watching Jack closely. He sold paintings, he was a good judge of doubt. "You're having second thoughts, aren't you?" he asked. Jack shot him a quick, defensive look and then turned away.

"Don't think *I* don't have doubts," Vincent said. "I change my opinion about what's going on here from one minute to the next. But—no matter which way I twist and turn it—the matter has only one basic explanation, which is that the Waldegrave portrait has in some way been keeping the Gray family alive. Don't ask me scientifically how, because I couldn't tell you, and besides, I don't think it's scientifically possible. After that, everything is guesswork, everything is supposition. But what I've been trying to do is to rationalize everything as much as I can, based on what we know—right from the diaries my great-grandfather kept back in the eighteen nineties up to Elmer Tweed's evidence of last week."

Jack finished his Corvo but kept his hand over the glass when Charlotte tried to pour him another. "What do you think we ought to do now?" he asked.

Vincent said, "I've been thinking about it. The key to the whole situation, as far as I can make out, is this Waldegrave portrait. So—what we have to do is to find out more about Walter Waldegrave. If we can get even half an inkling of how this was achieved—how the portrait grows old while the Grays stay young—then maybe we stand a chance of fighting and defeating the Grays on their own territory."

"You said something about reciting the Exorcism backward."

"Well, that's what my grandfather said. But I'm not sure that a couple of lines of Latin in reverse is really the answer, are you? Not in this day and age."

Jack shrugged and unwrapped a fresh pack of gum.

"What we have to find out," Vincent told him, "is how Waldegrave painted this portrait so that the people on the canvas grew old while the real people stayed just as they were. And—most important of all—how is it being done today? How could Laura Monblat have appeared on that canvas, painted in the same style as Walter Waldegrave's, without anybody having touched the portrait? I mean, how the hell is that *done*?"

"More to the point, how the hell is it *un*done?" Jack added philosophically.

Charlotte, quite suddenly, said, "I have an idea."

Jack made a face and told Vincent, "The lady has an idea. That's exactly one more idea than I have, I promise you."

Charlotte said, "Listen, do you remember that special exhibition we held at MOMA about eighteen months ago?"

"Not the Kandinsky," Vincent said, baffled.

"No, no, no. The one we held in the fall. 'Modern Allegorical Art.'"

"Yes, I remember," Vincent told her. "I hated it."

"I know you did. But the man who organized it knew just about everything anyone could ever want to know about art and magic. What was his name? Mac something. McKinley, I think it was. Do you mind if I call up David Smedley and find out where we could get in touch with McKinley?"

Vincent picked up the phone and handed it to her. "Be my guest, if you think it will help."

While Charlotte called her executive director, Vincent and Jack stood and examined the Waldegrave painting. Vincent looked more closely at the portrait of Laura. There was something impassive yet infinitely sad about her; something that reminded him of J.M. Barrie's Wendy, flying half-asleep through a fairy-tale sky, calling as she flew, "Poor Wendy, poor Wendy." Jack remarked, "The last time I saw anyone who looked like that, they were high on scopolamine."

Vincent carefully touched the portrait's face. He brought his fingers away; one of them was wet. He frowned at it. Jack asked, "Is the paint still tacky?"

Vincent tentatively licked his finger. "It's salt," he said. "Like tears."

"Now you're letting your imagination run away with you."

"Maybe."

Vincent regarded the faces of the twelve Grays: Algernon and Isobel standing at the back; Belvedere and Willa close beside them on the left; John and Henry on their right; Maurice standing jealously close to Algernon, almost as if he were supporting him from behind. And in the front, seated on chairs, the ladies: Emily, Ermintrude and Nora; Cordelia, Alicia and the crippled Netty. On Netty's lap sat Firework. And beside her, just below Henry, sat Laura Monblat.

Twelve blurred and decomposing faces—faces that looked as if they had been photographed far away and long ago with a hand-held camera that had been jogged at the crucial moment so they were all out of focus. Only Laura's face was clear, but then, Laura had not yet reached the age when she should have been dead.

Charlotte came away from the phone. "We're in luck," she said. "The man who organized the exhibition of modern allegorical art is Percy McKinnon. He lives in Seekonk, Massachusetts. Here's his telephone number."

"Go ahead, call him," Vincent said.

Charlotte punched out the number and waited. After a long while, she said, "Hello? Is this Mr. Percy McKinnon?"

"This is Doctor Percy McKinnon," replied a sharp, professorial voice, so loud that Vincent could hear it on the other side of the room.

Charlotte explained who she was and what she wanted. There was a short, asthmatic pause; then Dr. McKinnon said, "You'd better come and see me. This is not really the kind of question one can discuss over the telephone. I need to see you face-to-face. To be quite frank, I need to know if you're serious."

Charlotte put her hand over the telephone and said to Jack, "Can we get up to Seekonk?"

"I guess so," he replied. "I could drive you over in the Cherokee. Norman Goldberg can take care of the store for me."

Vincent checked his watch. "We'd be running pretty late if we tried to go today. How about tomorrow, around noon?"

Charlotte suggested the time to Dr. McKinnon. Then she said, "He can only make Monday."

"That loses us the whole weekend," Jack said. "The Grays could have skinned somebody else by then."

"Dr. McKinnon has a sick sister; he has to visit her. I'm sorry—he won't change his mind."

"Okay then, Monday," Jack agreed. "In the meantime, perhaps we can dig up something in the way of solid evidence."

While Charlotte confirmed the time and place with Dr. McKinnon, Vincent suggested to Jack, "Maybe you could go home and get yourself some rest. Your wife must think you're a stranger these days."

Jack bit off some gum and pushed it into the side of his cheek. "Yes, you're probably right. I can't remember the last time I slept at home. As a matter of fact, I can't remember the last time I slept."

Charlotte hung up the phone and found his coat; Vincent escorted him to the door. Outside, the snow was falling thickly; the draft that blew in through the open door was as sharp as the edge of a freshly opened tin can.

Jack tugged on his cap and wriggled his fingers into his gloves. "Listen," he said without looking directly at Vincent, "this whole case is wacky beyond normal belief. So don't get upset if sometimes I find it difficult to credit what you're trying to suggest, like I did just now. For some reason I guess I always believed in whatever you want to call it—the supernatural—except that until now there wasn't any need to. Now there *is* a need to, but that's not making it any easier. Just understand that we're both on the same side and that we're going to nail those Grays one way or another, no matter what we have to believe in."

Vincent grasped his elbow. "You bet," he said. "Now go home, before your wife decides that you're more turned on by police work than you are by her."

Vincent closed the door and came back into the living room, chafing his hands to warm them. "It looks like it's working itself up to a blizzard out there. I just hope it eases off before Monday."

Charlotte said, "Do you want me to open another bottle of wine?"

"Why not?" Vincent asked, kissing her hair. "And let's take it to bed."

"Don't tell me you're tired already," she teased him.

They were just about to go upstairs, carrying the bottle of wine, two large crystal goblets and a bowl of pretzels, when they heard a car drawing up outside. Vincent went across to the living-room window, held aside the curtains and peered out into the snow. "Damn it," he said. "It's Margot."

"But she's two days early," Charlotte complained.

"Margot is a law unto Margot and unto nobody else," Vincent replied irritably.

He opened the front door again. Margot had parked her red Mercedes at the usual awkward angle across the driveway; how many times had he told her that when she parked it like that, it made turning around almost impossible and nobody else could get into the drive? She was struggling with armfuls of parcels, while Thomas stood beside her with his suitcase and a new pair of snowshoes. Vincent was silently furious. A new pair of snowshoes was already waiting for Thomas up in his bedroom as a Christmas surprise. Vincent had walked all the way over to the sporting-goods store on 58th Street on a freezing afternoon to buy them, and he had *told* Margot all about them.

"You're a little previous," he said caustically, taking some of the parcels and closing the trunk lid. "I thought we said Sunday." He smiled at Thomas, gave him a squeeze around the shoulders with his one free hand and said, "Hi, Terror."

Margot adjusted her red woolly hat. "He doesn't like to be called Terror anymore. He says it's childish, and I agree with him. He asked me to speak to you about it."

Through the falling snowflakes, Vincent looked at his son and said, "That true?"

Thomas shrugged, embarrassed, unwilling to be used by one parent against the other. Vincent knew he loved his mother, and that he loved his father equally. Neither of them should force any choices on him, one way or another, but of course they always did. "Let's get inside," Vincent said. "The fire's burning up real well. We could toast some marshmallows."

"I'm glad to hear that your Boy Scout days are not yet over," Margot remarked. Then she caught sight of Charlotte standing in the doorway in her blue and white silk robe. "Oh," she said. "Perhaps they are."

Margot bustled her way into the house and through to the kitchen as if the place still belonged to her. She deposited her parcels on the kitchen counter and then took off her hat and shook the melting snow off it. "The forecast predicted blizzards for tomorrow. Bruce said that if I couldn't get Thomas up here today, I probably wouldn't be able to manage it at all, not before Christmas."

Margot was physically and temperamentally the exact opposite of Charlotte. She was just over five feet two, with short, dark, curly hair and a heart-shaped face Vincent had once described to his mother as "almost unbearably sweet." She wore "directional clothing" these days, baggy khaki culotte suits with huge, aggressive shoulders, the uniform of women who want to show everyone they meet that they no longer depend on men. Vincent thought she looked like a preshrunk General Patton, but he had always been polite enough not to tell her so. Her perfume and her shoes were expensive, a sure sign she didn't have as much money as she thought she ought to.

She was as untidy as ever, too. Her parcels were sprawled everywhere. Her hat lay on the counter. She took off her shoes and left them kicked across the floor.

"It *is* Charlotte, isn't it?" she asked. "Yes, I thought it was Charlotte. Is Charlotte cooking the Christmas dinner, Vincent?"

"No. We're going over to the Housatonic Hotel."

"How awful for you. Doesn't Charlotte cook?"

"Why don't you ask her yourself, dear? She speaks English."

Margot rustled through her parcels. "Don't you cook, Charlotte? Thomas does enjoy his traditional holiday food, don't you, Thomas?"

Thomas said nothing, but stood there in his windbreaker, his snowshoes under his arm, looking exactly like his father: serious-faced, curly-haired, good-looking, broad-shouldered . . . and waiting for his mother to leave.

Charlotte said, "I shall be cooking on Christmas Eve. Carp, goose, sweet potatoes. Very traditional. Thomas won't go hungry."

"Well, all your Christmas gifts are here," Margot said. "I'm sorry I didn't bring anything for Charlotte, but, well, I wasn't aware she was going to be ensconced. Besides, what *does* one buy for the girl who has everything?"

Vincent said, "I wouldn't stay, Margot, if I were you. The snow's thickening up, and it's going to be dark soon. You wouldn't want to be stranded here for Christmas, would you?"

"No," she answered. "I certainly wouldn't. Now—would you please make sure that Mrs. Charlesworth gets this present? It doesn't have her name on it, but you can remember it by the paper. And this one's for Jennie. And that's for the Ullmans. All the rest are marked."

"Would you care for some coffee before you go?" Charlotte asked.

Margot gave her an unexpectedly warm smile and tossed her curls. "Thank you all the same. Bruce will be wondering what's happened to me if I'm late."

"Sure he will," Vincent said, putting his arm around her—after she had struggled back into her shoes—and guiding her gently toward the door.

Once they were there, he handed over her woolly hat. "You used to put it on for me," she pouted.

"That was before."

"Before, and never again?" she asked.

He kissed her cheek. Her skin was as soft as ever, but now it felt unfamiliar. "Merry Christmas," he told her. It was only their second Christmas apart.

"Merry Christmas," she replied quietly. Then she kissed and hugged Thomas and walked out into the snow. Vincent saw her to her car and guided her when she turned it around in the driveway. Backward and forward, backward and forward, eleven times. When they were married, he would have climbed into the driver's seat and turned the Mercedes for her, but not now. Eventually, however, she managed to maneuver herself around and disappeared down the sloping driveway with a cheerful toot of the horn.

Vincent came back inside and closed the door. "You *really* don't want me to call you Terror?" he asked Thomas.

Thomas gave him a lopsided, embarrassed smile.

"I know, I know," Vincent said. "How about a glass of wine, to celebrate Christmas?"

"Yes, please," Thomas said. His voice seemed to be deeper now than it had been only three months ago. He was almost as

tall as Vincent, and Vincent realized it wouldn't be long before
his son was looking down on him. The thought suddenly made
him feel very old. The thought suddenly made him wonder:
*What if the Grays can live forever? And what if I can find out
how they do it? Presented with the choice of dying at the age of
seventy or thereabouts—in less than twenty-five years—and
living practically forever, what would I do?*

Thomas said, "Mom bought me these snowshoes. Maybe
we could try them out tomorrow."

"Well, that's a very fine pair of snowshoes," Vincent told
him. He turned them over and inspected the webbing and the
straps. "They match your other pair."

"What other pair?"

"The pair *I* bought you for Christmas, dummy."

Thomas looked at him in dismay, but Vincent simply
laughed. "Don't worry about it. You're nothing but the poor
innocent victim of parental rivalry. As a matter of fact, now
that we have two pairs, you and I can go out together. How
about trekking over to Gaylordsville tomorrow, and maybe
calling on the Fosters, too? Susie Foster came home from
school last week."

Thomas didn't look too interested, but Vincent said, "You
haven't seen her. She's grown up. And when I say she's grown
up, I mean she's really grown up."

"I hope you're not putting unhealthy ideas in his head,"
Charlotte smiled.

"When he sees Susie Foster, he won't need *me* to put any
unhealthy ideas in his head."

They went through to the living room and sat down by the
fire. Vincent unhooked the toasting forks while Charlotte
searched for the marshmallows.

Outside, the snow fell soft and dense on rooftops and
chimneys, while the great silence of Christmas-about-to-be
descended across the valley of the Housatonic River, from the
Appalachian Trail to Painters Ridge.

At the foot of the driveway leading up to Candlemas, its tail
pipe issuing smoke and its windshield wipers intermittently
clearing away the fine wool of the snowfall, a black Cadillac
Fleetwood was parked. Inside it, wrapped in dark mink coats,
sat Maurice and Cordelia Gray. The heating was set to "High,"
and there was a stifling smell of fur and potpourri.

"You're quite sure now that the painting is here?" Maurice asked without attempting to conceal the sarcasm in his voice. They had suffered an embarrassing experience that afternoon at the Halperin house. While creeping around the outhouses, they had been surprised by the Halperins' gardener, who had been chopping wood just outside the studio. Aaron and the rest of the family had been out Christmas shopping, and Cordelia hadn't imagined there would be anyone at home. But—as it turned out—the gardener had been quite a help. Once Cordelia had reassured him that they were friends of the family, he had told them, along with sundry erratic gossip, that the Halperins were out looking for a new cat.

"After what happened to the last one, poor dumb critcher. Mr. Halperin said it was that painting he'd been working on. Bad luck, that painting, that's what he said. He gave it back to Mr. Pearson just as quick as he could. Wouldn't work on nothing that was bad luck; that's what he said. Don't say I blame him, neither. Mark you, he does like his sauce. A man who likes his sauce as much as that can' make some misjudgments."

So here they were at Candlemas—Maurice and Cordelia Gray, having at last tracked down the Gray family portrait.

"How much do you think Pearson knows about the painting?" Maurice asked. As he spoke, the windshield wipers cleared the snow with a rubbery shudder.

"I think we have to assume he knows at least as much as his grandfather did," Cordelia replied. "His *dear* grandfather."

Maurice rubbed his eyes. "Yes," he said, "I suppose you're right. We must be cautious. I'd hate for anything to go wrong now. After everything Father and Mother have suffered."

Cordelia glanced at her watch, although the time was displayed on the Cadillac's instrument panel. "It looks as though they've decided to stay in for the evening. Perhaps we ought to come back tomorrow."

"Indeed," Maurice agreed, "and there *is* something useful we can do now."

Cordelia turned to him, the reflected light from the snow making her skin look even whiter, her eyes as black as jets. "Ah," she said. "You're referring to Mr. Tweed."

Maurice released the parking brake, shifted the Fleetwood into gear and pulled out to the highway, heading toward

Torrington. As he drove, he hummed under his breath one of the old songs from days gone by, "Hello, Central, Give Me Heaven." Maurice had always considered himself "sentimental." There had once been a girl in his life, Pearl; he had loved her with excruciating passion. His father, however, had refused to have Pearl included in the family portrait, and the last time Maurice had seen Pearl, she had been gray-haired, married and looked old enough to have been his mother.

Cordelia asked, "What are you thinking about?"

Maurice smiled. "Nothing very much."

Cordelia touched his arm. "Don't think about the past," she said. "Think about the future. Very soon we will have the painting back, and then all our years of worry will be over."

Twenty-Two

Litchfield, December 21

The snow died down during the night; the following morning, Vincent and Thomas snowshoed through the woods to Gaylordsville. The sky was clear and pale; the trees were as dark as bears wrapped in cloaks of white. The snowshoes made a continuous shushing sound across the drifts, and their breath smoked.

Thomas was far fitter than Vincent, and he managed to keep ahead of his father for most of the time; but as they slid their way along the last mile, he slowed down and they walked side by side together.

"I've formed an arts club at school," Thomas said.

"Is that why you don't want me to call you Terror anymore?"

Thomas smiled and shook his head. "We have this really decadent password to get into meetings."

"Are you going to tell me what it is in case I'd want to come to a meeting?"

"Well, I hope I can pronounce it properly. It's '*Les sanglots longs des violons de l'automne.*'"

"Paul Verlaine," Vincent nodded. "'The long sobs of the violins of autumn.' You're right. It *is* decadent."

Thomas asked, "How long is Charlotte staying?"

Vincent looked at his son sideways. "She's staying until New Year's, I guess. That's when we both have to get back to the city. You don't mind, do you?"

"No, not at all. I like her. I think she's beautiful."

"Don't start getting ideas. You stick to Susie Foster."

They slid down a long white slope, marked only by the

arrowheads of birds' tracks, until they reached the darker crevice of the Gaylord Branch, half-frozen into knobs and columns and twisted curtains of ice but running still, so that its tributaries spread into a fingerlike pattern through the snow.

"When I was young, I used to call this the Amazon River," Vincent said. "Up there, right on top of that waterfall, that's where I used to fight crocodiles and undiscovered tribes of headhunters. You see that shelf of rock back there, with all the icicles on it? That used to be my lookout post. I used to lie up there for hours in the summer—or what seemed like hours. Sometimes I took off all my clothes and pretended I was the lost white chief of the Ugarugah tribe. I remember I was squatting up there stark naked when my cousin Tilda came looking for me. She was twelve and I was ten. Boy, was I embarrassed. I wouldn't come out of the woods until dark."

Thomas said, "Do you miss it?"

"What?" Vincent asked.

"Being young, being a boy. You sound like you miss it."

Vincent stood still in the snowy woods, looking around at the silent trees. "No," he said after a while. "I don't think I miss it. I sometimes wish I'd made more of it, but then I guess almost everybody does. You can't miss it. How can you? No matter what happens, there's always going to be a boy in these woods playing the lost white chief of the Ugarugahs, even if that boy is only a memory."

He laid his arm around Thomas's shoulders, realizing this was one of the last times he would be able to do it. "You have to grow up, and you have to grow old. Nothing can ever prevent that. Not all the wishing in the whole damned world."

They snowshoed their way up the opposite bank of the Gaylord Branch until they reached the road. As she had promised, Charlotte was waiting for them there in Vincent's Bentley so they could drive over to visit the Fosters; but Jack Smith's Cherokee was waiting there, too. As they crossed the hard-packed snow on the highway, Jack came over, accompanied by Charlotte, and said, "Good morning, Mr. Pearson; how was your walk?"

Vincent kissed Charlotte, partly because he felt like it and partly to show Sheriff Smith that he had intruded on his private family morning. "I think my calf muscles have started protesting already," he said. "Is there anything I can do?"

Jack looked at Thomas and said, "How're you doing?" and then turned back to Vincent. "Can we talk alone?"

"Surely," Vincent said. He followed the sheriff to the side of his wagon and said, "Well? What seems to be the problem?"

Jack cleared his throat and sniffed. "Elmer Tweed was found dead in his cell, about five o'clock this morning."

"You're joking."

"I wish I were."

"But Elmer Tweed was your only witness. Elmer Tweed was the only person who could have connected the skinning murders with Maurice Gray."

"How right you are; but he's dead."

Vincent took off his gloves and wiped the frost from his mouth. "How did he die? Is there any indication?"

"Apparently a man and a woman came to visit him at about eleven o'clock last night. They claimed they were Mr. and Mrs. Lyndon H. Tweed and that Elmer Tweed was their son. Norman Goldberg says they spoke in a distinctive Southern accent and because of that, he believed them."

"Jesus," breathed Vincent.

Jack said, "They were given five minutes to converse with Elmer Tweed. Tweed himself didn't say anything when they were brought into the interview room; I can only presume he wanted to wait and see who they were. Maybe they came from one of those do-gooding groups that specialize in springing waifs and strays out of jail. Quite often they gain admission to the suspect by masquerading as parents or relatives."

"Then what happened?"

"They talked for three or four minutes. The woman kissed Tweed, right on the mouth, more like she was his lover than his mother. Then they left, saying they would call again soon to see Elmer."

"And?"

Jack unfastened the pocket of his windbreaker and took out three color Polaroids. He passed them to Vincent without comment.

Vincent had only to glance at one of them to know what had happened to Elmer Tweed. The photographs showed a police-station bunk bed, a collapsed body and a torrential mass of off-white maggots.

"The Grays," he said. He took a deep breath, just to feel the clean, frosty Connecticut air drop far into his lungs, and then he handed the Polaroids back to Jack without bothering to look at the rest of them.

"It sure looks like it," Jack said.

"So where do we stand now, legally?"

"Flat on our *tochis*. We could pull Maurice and Cordelia Gray in for questioning, but all we have to go on is circumstantial evidence, identification by police witnesses, and the weirdest, most preposterous story anybody ever heard of in their whole life."

"Quite apart from which I'm sure the Grays have an immaculate alibi."

"Don't doubt it."

Vincent stood and thought for a moment. Then he said, "How about this for a suggestion? How about we ask your friend Pat to hold another séance for us, only this time we use the Waldegrave portrait as our central focus instead of poor Ben Miller? Perhaps we can rouse the spirits of the Grays, get them to tell us something that might incriminate them."

Jack didn't look pleased with the idea. "Pat's husband was furious when he found out what she'd been doing the last time."

"She wasn't hurt, was she? We could pay her this time."

"The Litchfield sheriff's department doesn't have a budget that runs to séances."

"I don't mind paying. Say, two hundred fifty dollars?"

Jack took out his handkerchief and busily blew his nose. "I guess she might consider it, under those circumstances."

"Say, four o'clock this afternoon then, round at Candlemas?"

"I'll try. Maybe Nancy can persuade her."

Before he went, Vincent said, "Let me take another look at those Polaroids."

This time his stomach was sufficiently settled to examine all three pictures carefully. "There isn't any question about it. This is the same thing that happened to Edward. As far as I'm concerned, this absolutely implicates the Grays in Edward's death."

Jack stared at him narrowly, chewing gum. "You'll be wanting your share of revenge, then, the same way I do."

"I don't know," Vincent said. "I'm not altogether sure revenge is the right word."

Jack drove off to see if he could organize another séance; Vincent, Charlotte and Thomas drove in the opposite direction to pay a Christmas call on the Foster family. The Fosters lived in a striking A-frame just north of Gaylordsville, down a narrow side turning, and had been friends with Vincent for nearly ten years. They had supported him during his divorce from Margot with patience, equanimity and plenty of good whiskey. Today they had their huge log fire crackling and plenty of hot cheese pastries and mulled punch. Everybody sat on large red and yellow Indian blankets amid heaps of cushions, laughing and talking of Christmas.

Thomas immediately took to Susie Foster, who had grown up spectacularly from a plain-looking thirteen-year-old bean pole into a curvaceous young woman. Thomas and Susie had a drink with their parents and then went out with their snowshoes. Vincent stood by the French windows watching them scuffle and play in the sloping, snowy yard; Jan Foster came up, stood beside him and said, "You must be proud of him, Vince. He's looking just like you."

Vincent put his arm around her. "They seem to be hitting it off, don't they? That's some pretty young lady you've raised there, Jan. If I were ten years younger. . . ."

Charlotte called from her cushion beside the fireplace, "You mean if you were *thirty* years younger. Don't take any notice of him, Jan. He's going through male menopause. Not only that, he's having his second childhood at the same time."

"What do you mean?" Vincent demanded. "I haven't even been bar-mitzvahed yet."

Doug Foster roared with laughter. "Vincent believes that he's still twelve years old because he hasn't been bar-mitzvahed. His parents forgot to tell him he wasn't Jewish and that he never would be. Oh, Vincent, you're crazy sometimes."

"Yes," Vincent said quietly, watching Thomas and Susie, but thinking about the Grays.

Jan noticed his sudden change of mood and asked, "Is anything wrong?"

He shook his head.

"Come on, Vincent," she said. "We've been through a lot together, you and I."

Vincent kissed her. "Sure we have. But this is something that goes way back, long before you and me."

"I don't know what you mean."

"I'll tell you all about it when I've sorted it out. It has to do with heritage. *Delicta maiorum immeritus lues*. Even though you are guiltless, you must expiate the sins of your fathers. And your grandfathers. And your great-grandfathers."

"You've got me foxed," Jan said, cheerful but plainly concerned about him.

"I'm okay," Vincent told her. "How about some more of this hot Kool-Aid?"

Doug Foster laughed again. "Jan spends two hours making Old Connecticut Spiced Punch and he calls it hot Kool-Aid. Vincent, you kill me."

Thomas was invited to lunch at the Fosters and begged to stay, which suited Vincent very well. As they drove back to Candlemas along snowy, deserted highways, he told Charlotte what had happened to Elmer Tweed, and also that he planned to hold a séance.

Charlotte asked, "Is it really necessary? It frightens me. I mean, what frightens me about it is that you're so serious."

"We have to find out more about the Grays somehow."

"We're going to Seekonk tomorrow to talk to Dr. McKinnon. He'll tell us everything we need to know."

"That's what we're hoping. But he may tell us nothing at all."

"Couldn't we wait, at least until we've seen him?"

Vincent shrugged. "We *could*. But those Grays are homicidal savages as far as I'm concerned, and right at the moment, they're holding Laura Monblat. If they haven't killed and skinned her already, they could well be thinking of doing it soon."

Charlotte watched the white-faced world turning past her window. "Have you called her husband?"

"Danny Monblat? No, not yet."

"Don't you think he has a right to know where his wife might be?"

"Not just yet."

"But surely the police can go right in there and arrest the Grays if they're holding her against her will."

Vincent shook his head. "You heard what happened to Sheriff Smith's best buddy. And look what's happened to his best and only witness. Sheriff Smith would like nothing better than to burst in on the Grays and round them all up, but this isn't any ordinary police investigation and the Grays aren't any ordinary suspects. They've managed to survive for decades after they were supposed to be dead. Anybody who's done what they did to cling on to life, well, you don't think they're going to give up easily, do you?"

Charlotte reached across and touched his shoulder. "They've made it the worst winter ever, haven't they, those Grays? Your grandfather should have burned the portrait long ago."

They reached Candlemas and pulled into the driveway. Vincent wearily climbed out of the car and hobbled around it with aching leg muscles to open the door for Charlotte.

"You look like Quasimodo," she smiled. "Go take a hot shower; then I'll give you a massage."

"The local residents aren't too keen about massage parlors. They've only just accepted the idea of self-service gas stations."

They spent a quiet and thoughtful afternoon. They spoke little, drank wine and let the strains of Mozart ease their minds. Outside, although it was only mid-afternoon, darkness began to encroach on the woods and gardens surrounding Candlemas, and sudden gusts of sub-zero wind made snow devils dance on the pallid lawns like omens.

Jack didn't telephone. He drove up a few minutes after four o'clock in a squad car, with Pat sitting beside him. Vincent opened the front door, and they came into the large hallway stamping snow from their feet. Jack looked at Vincent behind Pat's back and made a face that meant, "Don't argue about it, here she is."

Pat took off her gloves and unwound her scarf. "I didn't come for the money, I'd like you to know," she told Vincent.

"I didn't think you had," he said.

She stared at him sharply. "How did you know?"

"Because you struck me back at the hospital as the kind of lady who cares about other people. You have a very special gift and you know it, but you also know that having a very special gift like that gives you certain responsibilities to the people around you, whether you like it or not." Vincent paused and then added, "You wouldn't have agreed to hold that séance at the hospital otherwise. You didn't take very much convincing."

Pat looked at Jack, her lips pursed. "He's better than my analyst," she told him. "Motivation, sense of responsibility, he knows it all."

They went through to the living room. Vincent had set the Waldegrave portrait on an easel at the end of the room. He hadn't yet drawn the drapes, but apart from the firelight that skipped across the hearthrug, the room was almost in darkness.

Pat approached the portrait slowly. After a while, she reached toward it with her hand.

"*That's evil*," she whispered.

"Evil?" Jack asked. "What do you mean, evil?"

Pat slowly shook her head. "This picture has such an *atmosphere* about it."

"It smells of decay," Vincent said.

"I'm not talking about just physical things; I'm talking about psychic things. There is a spiritual atmosphere around this picture that's absolutely terrifying. I've never come up against anything like it."

She reached closer. Her hand, as it neared the surface of the painting, began to tremble. "This is just awful," she said. "It feels so cold. It's like sliding your hand into icy slush. You know, it has a sort of a lumpy feeling about it, apart from being so cold."

Vincent and Jack came closer; Charlotte stayed away, by the fire. Pat reached out her other hand toward the painting and closed her eyes.

"What can you feel?" Jack asked, chewing gum with rhythmic rapidity. "Can you feel anything?"

Pat was silent at first, her eyes still shut, her hands gradually feeling their way around the portrait as if she were a blind person exploring the face of someone she had just met in order to familiarize herself with every feature.

After a while, she said, "These spirits are dead, or *should* be dead."

Vincent asked, "How do you know that, Pat?"

"I can feel their bodies," she replied in a horrified murmur. "I can actually feel their dead bodies. They're very cold, as if they're in ice, but it's like the ice has half-melted and they're kind of floating around, rotting. Soft, cold, slimy flesh."

There was another long silence. Pat remained where she was, but now she began to breathe deeply and regularly, as if she were falling asleep. Charlotte asked, "Do you think she's all right?" but Vincent waved her to stay as quiet as she could.

For an instant Vincent thought he saw something clinging around the portrait, like a glowing, transparent veil of whitish gas, but then Pat immediately withdrew her hands and opened her eyes, and it vanished.

"What was that?" Vincent asked.

"You actually saw it?"

"I'm not sure. Just for a blink of the eye. It was like a cloud."

Pat nodded. "What you saw was the soul of one of these people in the picture."

"A soul that should be dead, but isn't?" Jack asked.

"A soul that should have passed on to the next part of its existence," Pat corrected him.

"Then why hasn't it?" Vincent wanted to know.

"I'm not sure. It's a very vain soul, a very proud soul. It thinks of nothing but how great its own physical beauty was when it was properly alive. It has very little kindness or understanding, although I think it might have had once, when it was young."

"You can tell all that just from reaching out toward the picture?"

"There's a whole lot more," Pat said, not taking her eyes from the portrait. "There seem to be hundreds of souls in there. There are twelve dominant spirits, but there are crowds and crowds of others, most of them mutilated and hurt."

"Victims," Jack commented. "The people they've murdered."

"Probably so," Pat said.

"You mean that the spirits of their victims don't pass on to the next life, either? They stay trapped in here, inside the portrait?"

Pat lifted her hand again. She closed her eyes. "The victims of violent or painful death often find it difficult to pass on to the next life—especially if they don't have the prayers and good thoughts of the people they left behind to carry them through. It's just like they're unborn babies, conceived in a moment of terrible trauma and then undernourished and ignored.''

"But why *didn't* anyone pray for them?" Charlotte asked. "Surely their relatives, or their friends. . . .''

Pat answered, "When somebody goes missing, the only thing friends or relatives pray for is that he or she is alive. They *will* that person to be alive. But what they don't understand is that if the missing person is already dead, if that person has been murdered, then that very act of willing him to be alive can prevent his spirit from passing through. People don't have any idea of the effect they have on each other; not just physically, but spiritually. You can knock somebody down with your fist. But you can totally wipe somebody out with your spirit.''

Jack glanced at Vincent as though seeking his support to believe in what Pat was saying. Vincent deliberately avoided his gaze. He didn't want in any way to be held responsible for anyone else's belief or disbelief.

The log fire flickered low and made an odd, guttering sound. Pat raised her hands toward the Waldegrave portrait once more and whispered, "Come out. I command you. Come out.''

For a long time nothing happened. But—whether it was a draft or not, blowing in from under the front door—Vincent felt a distinct chill. He shivered; Charlotte took his hand and shivered, too. Jack shuffled his feet, sniffed and chewed gum, trying to show that he was broadminded about the occult, but at the same time, pragmatic about its potential usefulness; a believer, yes, but a *practical* kind of believer.

"I command you, come out," Pat repeated. Her voice sounded harsh now, and imperative. "Come out or suffer whatever punishment I choose to give you.''

"You can punish a spirit?" Jack asked.

Pat opened her eyes for a moment and looked at him. "The human spirit's most burning desire is to continue on its journey from the previous life to this life, from this life to the next. Someone like me, a spiritual sensitive, has the power to delay someone else from passing through, and believe me, spirits will do absolutely anything to pass through. If you want it in adult terms, it's like stopping somebody from having a sexual climax right at the very last moment."

Vincent said, "Let her get on, Sheriff, please."

Pat closed her eyes and began to recite, "Spirit, I command you to come out. I command you to make yourself known to me. You have no choice, for otherwise I will imprison you in limbo forever and ever, while other souls come and go."

The white gaseous cloud seemed to return, twisting and writhing around the portrait like gauze blown in the wind. The temperature in the room dropped again, and again, until Vincent felt a cold ache in his back and his temples, and he was sure his breath was beginning to smoke. He began to *hear* something, too, like a deep organ note, *basso profundo*, so low it was scarcely audible. The china ornaments on the mantel began to rattle and buzz until one of Vincent's favorite pieces, an eighteenth-century Staffordshire shepherdess, abruptly exploded in a shower of white porcelain.

Pat took two or three slow, calculated steps back. She raised her hands upward and cried out loudly, "Come out! I command you! Come out!"

Gradually the twisting white cloud began to funnel downward toward the floor. Then, in utter silence, it twisted up into a column again, a wavering column of boiling fumes. A girl appeared, naked, her hands manacled behind her back, her ankles fastened with shackles. Her head was lowered, out of shame or exhaustion, and even when Pat commanded her to speak, she said nothing.

"It's Laura," Vincent said. He took a step toward her. "Laura! Can you hear me? It's Vincent Pearson! Edward used to work at my gallery. Laura! Just lift your head and speak to me!"

Laura slowly lifted her head. Her image was transparent, as if she were nothing more than a hologram, but the way in which she looked at Vincent made him believe that part of her, if not most of her, was actually present. She opened her mouth and said something, but it was too slow and indistinct for Vincent to make it out.

"Laura!" he shouted; but Pat, her eyes still closed, swung out her left arm and grasped his sleeve to prevent him from nearing the portrait.

"But, damn it, that's Laura Monblat," Vincent protested.

Pat shook her head dismissively. "That's not Laura Monblat; that's an illusion. They're testing us. The twelve spirits in the picture are testing us. They want to see how much we care about Laura Monblat; because if we don't care at all, she won't be very much use to them as a hostage."

"You mean they'll kill her straightaway?"

"How do I know, for God's sake? Jack—I'm cold! Jack! If you want to ask her any questions, ask them now! I can't hold on to this much longer!"

Jack approached the image of Laura Monblat. She was even more transparent now, as if she were composed of nothing more than the glassy heat waves that rise in the winter from an outdoor brazier and ripple across the snow.

"Laura," he said as decisively as he could. "Laura, do you want to tell us where you are? We could come and get you, Laura. Help you get free. Just tell us where you are, is all; and tell us if you're still alive. You know, seeing like you're a ghost, it's pretty hard for a guy like me to know for sure."

Laura turned toward Jack with large, liquid eyes. Then she began to dance to some unheard music. Jack could scarcely see her now; she flickered in and out of his vision, her hands snaking down the sides of her hips, circling around her breasts.

Just before she vanished, she suddenly opened her eyes wide and held out her hands, just as Pat had held out hers toward the portrait, and mouthed almost inaudibly the two terrible words, "*Save me.*"

The gaseous white robe around the portrait turned in on itself and began to disappear. The fire in the hearth burned brighter. Vincent turned away from the portrait, took out his neatly folded handkerchief and dabbed at the chilly sweat around his forehead.

Jack said, "That performance was controlled by the Grays from start to finish. They're keeping her hostage, no doubt about that. And they're making her do just what they want her to do. Even that phony 'Save me'! What's that supposed to do? Send us rushing around there like half-assed heroes, with no warrant and no shred of reasonable suspicion? That would blow our arrest from moment one."

Just then, however, when they thought everything was over,

they heard Pat cry, "Don't!" She was still standing in front of the portrait, her head down, her fists clenched, shaking.

Charlotte said, "Pat—are you all right? Pat?"

Pat said, "Don't—come—closer—don't—"

"Pat, what the hell's the matter?" Jack asked and took hold of her arm.

She jerked her head around and stared at him with bulging eyes, her teeth clamped so tight that blood ran from the corner of her mouth. "They—won't let go. They—"

"Vincent," Jack said urgently. "Come over here. We've got trouble."

They took hold of Pat but she continued to shudder and twitch, and her arms were as rigid as if she were being electrocuted.

"Jack," Pat appealed, her head dropping against her shoulder. The seizure was so intense now that she could scarcely speak. Vincent could feel an extraordinary galvanic tingling running through his nerves and his muscles; even the front of his head began to feel numb. He was conscious that he was shouting at Jack at the top of his voice, but for some reason, he didn't seem to be able to make himself heard.

"Back—take her back—away from the—"

He could see through jolted, unfocused eyes that Jack had understood him, that Jack too was trying to drag Pat away from the malevolent influence of the Waldegrave portrait. Vincent's first analogy had been remarkably accurate. Pat was quaking because of the power emanating from the portrait, quaking in much the same way electrocution victims quake until someone manages to pull them from the source of the voltage.

Jack was screaming, "Don't let her go! Vincent, do you hear me? Don't let her go! She's going! For Christ's sake, she's—"

There was a huge echoing shout, like a subway train suddenly hurtling into a tunnel. Pat shuddered and shook between the two men, but they were powerless to move. The whitish gas began to blossom out of the portrait, only it wasn't gas; it was a miasma of twisted, evanescent faces and grasping, clawlike hands; it was a hideous tangle of arms, legs and viscera. And then suddenly there was something sharp, like a huge butcher's knife, and it flashed upward into Pat's stomach so that Vincent could see the point of it momentarily glinting next to her spine. Pat collapsed and sprawled facedown on the floor, while the gaseous apparition suddenly shrank away and fled. At last the living room was still.

"Call the medics," Vincent told Jack.

But Pat, her face against the rug, said, "It's okay. Please. It's over now. It was only an illusion. Illusions can't hurt you."

Charlotte knelt beside her. "That knife—"

"Just another illusion. They're warning me off."

"Well, you're sure you're okay?"

Pat sat up, took out her handkerchief and pressed it against her face. "I'm okay. Don't fuss."

Vincent hunkered down beside her and put his arm around her shoulders. "That didn't hurt you? I thought you were dead."

Pat smiled wanly. "I could use a drink. Brandy, maybe? My circulation feels like death, even if I am still alive."

While Charlotte unstoppered the brandy decanter, Vincent said to Pat, "You knew how dangerous this was the moment you held your hand out in front of that painting. You knew what would happen, didn't you?"

Pat didn't answer but accepted a large glass of Courvoisier from Charlotte with a nod and a slightly twisted smile.

Jack said, "Jesus. I thought for a second I was dealing with another homicide there."

Pat didn't look as if she were arguing. She drained the glass of brandy in one gulp and held it out for a refill. Charlotte took it from her without a word.

"That was a warning?" Jack asked.

Pat nodded.

"God. If that's what they do for a warning, you can imagine what they're like when they're really upset."

Pat said, "That was only their psyche, reacting against intrusion."

"What does that mean?" Vincent asked.

"It means that the flesh-and-blood Grays who are alive and well and living in Darien may not even know that we've been sticking our noses in here. This wasn't their doing. Well, let's put it this way—it was nothing to do with the physical people you want to arrest. This was their spirits, the spirits that occupy their painting."

"I don't think I get the difference," Jack said, not altogether patiently.

"Usually there *isn't* a difference," Pat told him. "Usually a person is a person and a portrait is a portrait. The soul stays with the person, not with the portrait, even when that person is dead. How many stories have you heard about a haunted portrait?"

Jack, who rarely had a chance to read, or to watch television, or to do anything else but run after one scofflaw after another, gave an indifferent shrug.

Pat said, "That portrait, believe me, is possessed."

"Ah," Jack murmured.

"That portrait," Pat went on, stepping away from it as she spoke, "that portrait is possessed. Believe me."

"So what can we do about it?" Jack asked impatiently.

"You can burn it, you can smash it with a hammer, you can take it out to Fire Island and commit it to the waves, or Vincent can sell it to anybody who might be freaky enough to buy it. But you really ought to get rid of it. And I mean *permanently*. I don't know what's happened here. I don't know why this portrait should feel so evil. But it does, and it's dangerous, and I beg you to get rid of it."

Vincent said, "The girl Laura, the one who appeared in front of you—"

"She's alive."

"You mean that?" Vincent asked. "I mean, alive in the sense that—?"

Pat said, "Alive in the sense that they haven't killed her yet, that's all."

Vincent looked toward Jack, who was regarding the portrait with serious eyes. Then he turned back to Pat and gave her his hand to help her to her feet. Charlotte stoked the fire, then suddenly went across and draped the Waldegrave in its bedspread.

Vincent said to Pat, "What I mean is, if Laura's still alive, and if we destroy the portrait—"

Pat said, "It depends on what you want. As it is, the Grays own her completely, body and soul. They will kill her eventually, but the question you have to ask yourself is when."

"You really believe that they'll kill her?"

"There isn't any doubt. You didn't feel the portrait the way I did."

Vincent said, "If we burn the portrait, Laura will burn, too. Is that it?"

Pat tried to smile. "I'm not an expert, Mr. Pearson. I never said I was."

"But that's what you believe?"

Pat nodded and turned away. Vincent had the impression that the séance had disturbed her more than she was willing to admit.

"Are you feeling okay?" Jack asked her. "Maybe you should sit down. Miss Clarke, do you have any tea? Or coffee maybe?"

"Pat?" Charlotte asked. "What would you like?"

Pat perched on the edge of one of the sofas by the fire. She stared at the Waldegrave portrait under its bedspread and continually rubbed her arm, the way a nervous child does. "That painting is *so* evil," she said. "It's like a psychic morgue in there."

"I'm sorry," Vincent told her. "When I suggested you come take a look at it, I didn't think that—"

"You must get rid of it," she interrupted. "You don't have any choice."

"But what about Laura Monblat?"

Pat shivered and rubbed her arm even more nervously. "Do you seriously think you can save her? Did you see what they made her do? They won't let her live. They won't let anybody live, anybody who threatens them, or anybody they can make use of. They're determined to go on living, Mr. Pearson, and they don't care what they do, or how they do it, or how many people they kill."

She hesitated for a moment, then she suddenly frowned and clasped her stomach with both hands. "I think they've hurt me," she said, swallowing a bubbling mouthful of saliva.

Vincent sat down beside her and gently turned her face around so he could look into her eyes. "She's going into shock," he told Jack. "You'd better call those medics, and call them quick. Try Dr. Serling, too."

Jack went immediately across to the telephone and punched out the emergency number for the Litchfield paramedics.

Charlotte helped Vincent lay Pat on the sofa and then she went to the bureau in the hallway to fetch a warm blanket. Pat's face had turned white, and she was shuddering almost as badly as she had when the ectoplasm from the painting had reached out toward her.

"It's all right," Charlotte reassured her, wrapping the blanket around her. "It's only shock. You're going to be fine."

Jack finished talking to Dr. Serling, then came over and knelt down beside the sofa. Pat was perspiring copiously now; sweat was running down the sides of her neck, and she was twisting, turning and clawing at the blanket.

"Standard symptoms of shock," Jack said. "Charlotte, would you fetch me some water, please."

"Don't—touch me—" Pat whispered. "Whatever you do—don't—"

She coughed, bringing up saliva streaked with blood. Charlotte said, "My God, Vincent, she really *is* hurt!"

"The medics are on their way," Jack told her. "Vincent, would you help me keep her still. Charlotte, please, that water."

Charlotte brought the water and Pat managed to sip a little. She was still sweating and shaking, but the water and the warmth of the blanket seemed to have calmed her down. "I'm all right, really," she whispered to Jack. "Please, it's nothing to worry about."

"Are you kidding?" Jack smiled, using his handkerchief to mop the shining perspiration from her forehead. "I'd worry about you if you so much as hiccuped."

"You have to—destroy the picture," she insisted.

"We've got it in mind," Jack said, stroking her cheek. "Don't you worry about it. Those Grays aren't going to get away with anything."

Pat suddenly clutched Jack's arm and shut her eyes tight. "Oh, God!" she cried. "Oh, God, it hurts!"

"Where does it hurt?" Jack asked. "Pat, please, tell me. *Where* does it hurt?"

She pushed him away and sat up, one hand against her throat, the other against her stomach. "I'm going to be sick," she said in the quietest of voices. "It must be that water—I—"

Without any further warning, she vomited bright red blood.

It ran down the leg of Jack's trousers. She stared at him in horror and fright.

"Jack!" she gagged. "Jack! Save me!"

Jack yelled at Vincent, "Call those goddam paramedics again! Ask them what in hell is keeping them!"

Vincent stood up, but as he did, Pat let out a gargling scream and brought up more blood. It splashed over the rug, over the walls, into the hearth. She sat where she was, shaking, staring with glassy and disbelieving eyes at the mess around her feet and in her lap, knowing she had no chance of survival. No one could speak; the horror of what had happened had been too abrupt. No one could do anything but watch Pat slowly twist around and collapse sideways, falling face down on the floor.

Vincent said, "I—Charlotte, I—" but then he couldn't carry on and he turned away, standing with his hands clutching his head, trying to keep himself under control, trying to stop his mind from exploding. He could hear Charlotte sobbing, and that was what managed to bring him together, although for one brief moment of psychic vertigo, he had felt he could have gone mad.

It was then that he felt Jack's hand on his sleeve. "Vincent. Vincent, look!"

Vincent turned around, keeping his eyes on Jack but then slowly allowing his gaze to fall toward the floor where Pat was lying. Charlotte, on the other side of the living room, was already staring at Pat in horror and fascination.

For the splattered blood was gradually fading away, as if it had never existed. Within four or five minutes—while they stood and watched, disbelieving—all trace of Pat's terrible sickness had completely vanished.

Jack whispered, "We're imagining this."

"Either that or somebody's *making* us imagine it," Vincent hazarded.

"The Grays?"

"More than likely," Vincent said unsteadily. "Just remember that they've had over a hundred years to perfect their psychic abilities, which is well over three times what anybody else is ever allowed, forgive me, God."

Pat lay unmoving, white-faced. Charlotte knelt down beside her and checked her pulse. "I can scarcely feel it," she said, "but it's very fast."

"That's consistent with shock," Jack told her. "Fast, faint pulse, shallow breathing. Let's get her back on the sofa and keep her warm."

They lifted her gently onto the cushions and covered her. "Charlotte, would you call her husband?" Jack asked. "Jerome Lerner; you can find his number in the book."

Pat opened her eyes. Her pupils were widely dilated, and her voice was hoarse. "I thought I was dying," she whispered.

"You're all right," Vincent said. "It was just the Grays, fighting back."

"I feel terrible," Pat told him, although she attempted a smile.

They heard the warbling of a siren outside, and then the ambulance scrunched to a stop out front. "You're in luck," Jack said, leaning over the sofa and kissing her on the forehead. "They didn't take the scenic route today."

Only a few minutes after the medics had carried Pat out across the snow and the ambulance had whooped off, its red lights flashing pink against the white-blanketed woods, Dr. Serling arrived. Jack had interrupted Dr. Serling's attendance at a Sunday tea party for some of his wife's cousins, for which interruption the doctor was grateful, despite the cause.

"I'll follow the ambulance," he said out of his car window. "No need for you three to stand out here and freeze your butts off."

"I want you to come inside for a moment," Jack told him.

Dr. Serling frowned and switched off the engine. He climbed out of the car like an artist's easel being folded up to shove through an attic door, and then he unfolded himself in front of Jack until he was standing a good two inches taller than the sheriff.

"What's wrong? I thought you said Mrs. Lerner had fainted."

"She didn't faint," Vincent said and took hold of his arm. "Come on in. We'll tell you what happened."

As they walked side by side into the house, Vincent tried as graphically as he could to explain about the second séance, about the intense feelings of evil that had emanated from the Waldegrave portrait, about the horrifying sensation Pat had described, like plunging her hand into a pool of chilly, floating corpses, half-preserved in the quintessential liquors of their own gradual decay.

He told Dr. Serling about the imaginary knife that had flashed into Pat's abdomen, and about the way in which she had vomited blood.

Dr. Serling carefully filled his pipe and lit it. He inspected the rug Pat had covered with hallucinatory blood, and then he checked the sofa.

"You saw this, too?" he asked Charlotte.

She nodded.

Dr. Serling puffed on his pipe for a while. "This isn't for me," he told them finally. "This is for somebody who knows what he's doing. A qualified medium, with powers to fight back."

Jack said, "That doesn't sound like somebody who's going to be easy to locate."

Dr. Serling made a face that meant it shouldn't be a problem. "You could always treat this as a police matter, of course, and nothing else. You don't *have* to fight fire with fire. After all, even though the Grays seem to be more adept at psychic jiggery-pokery than any of us, Mrs. Lerner obviously wasn't hurt today, not seriously, which leads me to suspect that the Grays can't hurt anybody by spiritual powers alone. Maybe they could if they were *completely* dead, if they were nothing *but* spirits. But they appear to be divided. Their spirits are here, their bodies are there. If they want to do anybody any real mischief, they seem to have to do it with their own hands."

Vincent was fixing drinks for everyone. He looked up and said, "You sound as if you've dealt with troublesome spirits before, Doctor."

Dr. Serling tried to be gruff. "The first visible evidence of the human spirit I ever saw was at Ben Miller's séance."

"But you're a doctor. A country doctor at that. Don't tell me you haven't come across possessions before, or imaginary possessions, or ghosts."

Dr. Serling accepted his glass of whiskey. "I'm trying to make educated guesses, that's all."

Jack walked across to the Waldegrave portrait and lifted the bedspread so he could look again at the decomposing faces of the Gray family. "Would you believe it?" he said. "The worst case I ever had, and all the suspects are dead before I've even started."

Vincent came and stood beside him. "Not dead enough, that's the trouble. Dead, but not dead enough."

Twenty-Three

Seekonk, December 23

Dr. Percy McKinnon was a short, heavily built man with one of those potentially explosive faces that reminded Vincent of Teddy Roosevelt; he favored overly tight three-piece suits of ginger tweed.

He had lectured for twenty-three years at Brown University on the history of art. Now he was retired and lived on County Street in one of those white-painted houses favored by genteel ladies with reminiscent names, and on Sundays he could be seen, stiff-backed, walking his white bull mastiff in Slater Memorial Park.

He had made coffee for his visitors, which he carried in a copper coffeepot through to his relentlessly old-fashioned library and put down next to bone-china cups on a lace tablecloth. Charlotte asked and received permission to pour. Then Dr. McKinnon settled himself by his black pot-bellied stove, crossed his hamlike thighs and challenged them to tell him what they wanted.

Vincent said, "My family happens to own a portrait by Walter Waldegrave."

"Unhappily for them, then," Dr. McKinnon put in.

"What makes you say that?"

"How many reasons do you want?" Dr. McKinnon countered. He took off his steel-rimmed glasses and addressed himself to Vincent with pale-blue, bulging eyes.

"As many as you can think of."

"Very well," Dr. McKinnon said. "Walter Waldegrave was mentally immature, intellectually obscure, easily compromised

305

both in morals and artistic integrity, a poor strategist, a worse colorist, and far too readily swayed by fads and fashions."

"I don't think my family acquired the painting for its artistic merit," said Vincent.

"Well, that's one consolation, I suppose," Dr. McKinnon said, sipping his coffee. "The only thing that concerns me, however, is that if your family didn't acquire it for its artistic merit, why *did* they acquire it? I can think of only one possible reason, and believe me, I don't care for it at all. No, sir."

"We don't have to beat around the bush," Vincent said. "My grandfather took the picture away from its owners because he feared that they were abusing it. He feared, in fact, that Walter Waldegrave had somehow arranged it so the portrait grew old while the family who sat for it remained young."

Vincent couldn't have put it more directly. Charlotte squeezed his hand. If Dr. McKinnon was one of those academics who would have no truck with the supernatural, at least they would know it from the beginning.

Dr. McKinnon, however, replaced his glasses, swung slowly around on his chair, the kind of revolving wooden chair featured in Hollywood interpretations of the *Tombstone Epitaph*, and peered up at his shelves for one of his leather-backed books.

"Let me tell you," he said, trying to locate the volume he had in mind, "Walter Waldegrave was mischief, with a capital M. He was a weak, surly, half-talented young man, and he would have remained completely unknown to the world of art if he hadn't happened quite by accident to catch the eye of Oscar Wilde and Frank Miles."

Jack, who was sitting in the corner with his legs crossed, trying to appear officially authoritative, said, "We know that Walter Waldegrave was involved with black magic, Dr. McKinnon. We wouldn't have come here otherwise."

Dr. McKinnon found the book he was looking for and opened it; then he peered at Jack over his spectacles and said, "You're a sheriff, aren't you? Don't tell me *sheriffs* believe in black magic."

"I've kept an open mind about it all my life, sir," Jack said. "Now, for better or for worse, I've had it proven to me."

Dr. McKinnon suddenly turned to Vincent and said, "The

Gray portrait! That's it! You have the Gray portrait. Am I correct?"

Vincent nodded. "My grandfather acquired it in nineteen eleven. There was a series of murders in that year, and my grandfather believed they were committed by the Grays; and so, not to put too fine a point on it, he stole the portrait and told them that if they didn't leave the country, he would burn it."

Dr. McKinnon said emphatically, "Ah . . . so *that's* what happened! I had always suspected something of the sort. But I hadn't realized it was Pearson who got hold of it. This is quite a revelation! This almost deserves a brandy. A brandy with your coffee. Would that go down well?"

"I wouldn't say no," Jack put in. It had been a long and difficult journey from Litchfield, with tricky detours around Willimantic and Norwich.

Vincent said, "Thank you. We'd all appreciate it."

"Do you know something?" Dr. McKinnon said after he had given them each a less-then-generous glass of brandy. "I always believed that the Waldegrave portrait would turn up someday. Your family were very secretive about it, weren't they? They never displayed it or wrote about it; nothing. The Pearsons! I should have guessed, I suppose, that it was you! Your grandfather was quite religious, wasn't he? He wrote a monograph in nineteen twenty—something on 'inspirational' art. Well, of course the moral laxity the Grays had always exhibited must have been anathema to him. But you still have it! It still exists! Waldegrave's portrait of the Grays!"

Vincent said, "I was hoping you could tell me how it was done."

"I'm sorry," blinked Dr. McKinnon. "How *what* was done?"

"How the portrait was made to grow old while the people in it stayed young."

"Do you have the portrait here?" Dr. McKinnon asked with sudden anxiety.

"No. It's back in New Milford. Back at my house."

"Well, that's a pity. I would very much like to see it for myself. Can you arrange that, do you think?"

"Of course."

"The secret is this," Dr. McKinnon said, holding up his book. "*Any* effigy of *any* living person, *any* representation of *any* living person, can *always* be used to affect the course of that person's life. You've heard of voodoo dolls, of course. Primitive figures into which pins are stuck to discomfort, or even kill, somebody the witch doctor's supplicant happens to dislike. Well, you may smile about those dolls, but I have documentary evidence here that voodoo dolls were used to very excellent effect during the coming-to-power of Jean-Claude Duvalier in Haiti; and I have even more startling evidence that certain parties considered the use of magical effigies during the closing stages of the Watergate fiasco. The history of magical effigies is fascinating. Fascinating! But it probably reached its peak during the late Victorian era, when photography became sufficiently widespread for images to be taken of almost anybody the necromancer chose so he could inflict whatever punishment he desired, sometimes with remarkable accuracy. It is said, for instance, that Ulysses S. Grant was given throat cancer by a political rival, but there you are. We have no way of proving such suggestions for certain."

Dr. McKinnon swallowed brandy, folded up his glasses and leaned toward Vincent conspiratorially. "As far as art is concerned, the use of images and effigies came into flower with the pre-Raphaelites: Rossetti and Holman Hunt and all their followers and imitators. Their technique was so meticulous, their detail so perfect, their likenesses so accurate, that their portraits could be used in the same way voodoo effigies had once been used, given that whoever owned the portrait happened to know the right incantations."

He leaned even closer and, in a hoarse whisper, said, "I heard it claimed that Millais' portrait of Lady Penelope Cleaver was used by her husband to destroy her looks, from face cancer, when she was having an affair with one of his associates."

Vincent said, "Tell me something about Walter Waldegrave."

"*Well*," Dr. McKinnon expostulated, "the whole point about Walter Waldegrave is that he wasn't just a painter whose portraits were used by other people to inflict pain on their enemies or adversaries. Walter Waldegrave was interested in black magic and the power of symbols and effigies himself, even before he first put brush to canvas. So when he painted, he painted with the specific intention of having his paintings used for occult purposes. If you like, he was the chief religious artist for the anti-Christian movement of the nineteenth century; that was one of the reasons Oscar Wilde liked him so much. Oscar Wilde absolutely adored beautiful-looking men, and Walter Waldegrave certainly qualified, although you wouldn't say so now, not from his photographs; and Wilde absolutely adored irreligious young men."

"So," Vincent put in, "when Walter Waldegrave came to the United States with Lily Langtry, and Oscar Wilde introduced him to the Grays—"

"The fusion of interests was both natural and historical," Dr. McKinnon said, snapping his short, squat thumbs. "The Grays were wealthy, charming and impossibly vain. They felt they had reached their social apogee, and they wanted to stay there. So when Walter Waldegrave suggested that he should paint their family portrait and that *certain rituals* should accompany the signing of the painting when it was finished— well, how could they deny his offer? There was a chance they would live forever. There was a chance they would be able to mix in wealthy society for season after season: Palm Beach in the winter, Bar Harbor in the summer, London and Paris whenever the mood took them. Not just for this season, not just for next season, but *forever*. Can you imagine that? To know with complete certainty, with complete confidence, that you will still be alive in a hundred years' time. And not just alive, but *young*?"

Vincent said nothing as he looked across at Jack. Although they were learning more and more about the Grays, still they had no ideas about how they could destroy them; either straightforwardly by arresting them for homicide and kidnap, or psychically by breaking their link with the Waldegrave portrait.

Vincent said, "My grandfather mentioned something about reciting the Exorcism backwards."

Dr. McKinnon leafed through his book. "That's partly it," he said, raising his hand. "You have to have your portrait painted with great attention to detail by a competent artist. If possible, a magnificent artist. It has to be a full-length portrait, otherwise your legs will age long before the rest of you, and you will become a cripple, a young man with very old legs."

He found the page he was looking for. "This is the ritual. It is partly based on the Exorcism, yes; because it seeks to separate your spirit and your fleshly body without actually killing you. In other words, your spirit becomes entrapped in the painting, embedded in the molecules of paint assembled to look like you, while your body and your intellect walk free. If anybody had ever *done* this, of course, he would have been completely joyless and heartless, because he would have been surviving on this earth without a soul, which, as everybody knows, includes the conscience, the sense of communal responsibility, kindness, pity, and even a sense of humor. A very serious matter—not to have a sense of humor.''

Dr. McKinnon sniffed, coughed and swallowed brandy. "If you're after the Grays, my friends, all I can say is, good luck, because you're going to need it. You say they've committed homicides; three, if not more. Well that, for the moment, is a comparatively modest score. They will go on killing people for as long as they want to, for as long as they need to, without any qualms or compunction. They have no souls, Mr. Pearson, not in the way you and I have a soul. You can sink down inside yourself and feel your personality swimming around like a trained dolphin. They can feel none of that. They're empty. And that's how they survive. They're immortal, but they're completely superficial. They're stuffed animals. They have skin, which is immaculate on the outside, but what that skin is covering, God alone can imagine.''

Vincent swirled the last of his coffee around the bottom of his cup. "They keep trying to find out where the portrait is,'' he said. "They even attempted a burglary 'round at my restorer's house, in Bantam.''

"Well, of course they did!'' Dr. McKinnon exclaimed. "They want the portrait for themselves; they want to feel they're secure and that their existence, such as it is, will not suddenly fall into the hands of irresponsible or antipathetic people.''

"Is that all it amounts to?'' Charlotte asked. She had a headache and she felt like she needed a cigarette.

Dr. McKinnon frowned at her. "Young lady, this is elementary social psychology, book one, page one; not some lurid paperback about psychic manifestations.''

Jack said, "They've already shown us they can use the portrait against us, even when we've got it safe. Is there anything more they could do if they were actually to lay their hands on it?"

Dr. McKinnon made a face. "I don't think they would *need* to do anything to you if they ever laid hands on the portrait, although they might be malevolent enough to want revenge against you because of what your grandfather did to them. No—the real danger would be that they would restore the painting to its original condition and continue to survive as youthful-looking as ever for generation after generation. Remember, they have no conscience, no pity. Your grandfather first acted against them when they began to murder people, and I am sure they were guilty of many other debased and profane acts, which for their victims were almost as damaging as murder. If they ever manage to get their portrait back, they would be virtually untouchable. There are an influential family in their local area, remember. They have old money, and plenty of it; and I suspect their capacity for bribery and blackmail rivals that of the Mafia. They weren't always alone when they held their debauches in the eighteen nineties, and how many upper-class Connecticut families would like it to be known that their grandfathers took drugs, for instance, or fornicated with sheep and underage girls, or bred children out of wedlock?"

Dr. McKinnon refilled his brandy glass but didn't offer any around. "Not only would they be immortal and untouchable," he added, "they would *always* have a means of escape, no matter what."

"Means of escape? What are you talking about?" Jack asked.

"The *portrait*, my dear sir. The *portrait*!" Dr. McKinnon responded. "Here—look in this book. Oh, well, it won't mean very much to you, it's all in Latin. But what it says here is that those who have gained immortality by means of representation in a portrait can always leave their physical bodies and retreat into the picture itself. In other words, they can conceal their physical bodies in places where nobody would normally think of looking for somebody who was hiding—buried in a coffin, even—and they can rejoin their souls inside the painting. Or, indeed—and this is where it all becomes most interesting— inside *any* painting."

Jack frowned. "I don't get this, I don't get this at all."

"Well, in police terms, let me put it this way," said Dr.

McKinnon. "If the Grays ever regain possession of their portrait, and let us all pray to whatever gods that guide us that they do not, they will be uncatchable. You may extradite a murderer from Indiana; but how do you extradite a murderer from an oil painting? You will have lost them for ever, my dear sir, and they will be able to continue their murders and their debauches whenever it so pleases them, for time everlasting, amen."

Twenty-Four

New Milford, December 23

Thomas arrived back at the house a little after two o'clock in the afternoon. His cheeks were rough and red, his toes were freezing, but he felt ineffably terrific. He and Susie had been playing and tumbling in the snow for most of the morning; and then Susie's mom had given them hamburgers for lunch; and Susie's dad had allowed him a glass of Miller, without even making a big issue out of it, and he had felt grownup and confident and more than a little infatuated with Susie.

Before he had left for home, he had said goodbye to her by the mailbox, and kissed her—warm wet lips and dry cold nose—and then he had slalomed his way through the woods toward Candlemas, whistling and singing to himself.

He reached Candlemas, and came up through the whitened garden, where the trees stood as frigidly as ghosts, and where the pathways of summer were buried like memories that would never return. There was no smoke blowing from the chimneys, which meant that the fires had gone out. He would have to stack them and light them before Dad got home, but in the mood he was in after visiting Susie, he didn't mind at all.

He found the front-door keys in his pocket, and walked around the side of the house, jingling them. And there they were, darkly dressed and silent, in black overcoats, and black gloves, standing beside their long black limousine, waiting for him with dispassion and with absolute patience.

"Master Pearson, I presume?" the man called out, in a dry, clear voice.

Thomas stayed where he was. His father had warned him against visitors. *If you happen to get back home before I do sit* tight, and don't let anyone in. Don't even answer the door. But what was he supposed to do when the visitors were actually barring the way to the door, so that he couldn't get inside, and lock himself safely behind it?

"I'm, uh, just delivering something," said Thomas. "Mr. Pearson left something around at my parents' house, and I'm . . . just delivering it."

"Come, come, Master Pearson." The man smiled, in chilled amusement. "We know your face quite well, my sister and I. We're friends of the family."

Thomas cautiously approached the front door. They looked civilized enough, these two, the man and the woman in their expensive black coats. Their Cadillac was rather too reminiscent of a hearse for Thomas's liking, but they must be rich to run a car like that, and whoever heard of rich burglars?

"My father won't be back until later. Maybe you should call tomorrow?"

The man sighed, and drew back his leather glove, so that he could inspect his wristwatch. "If only it were possible, my dear young friend. Unfortunately, we have to be back in Darien later this afternoon; and after that . . . well, who knows *where* we might have to be after that?"

"You're such a good-looking boy," said the woman, speaking for the first time. She came balancing through the snow on high heels, one ungloved hand clutching a black mink wrap against her bosom. Thomas glimpsed the sharp white glitter of a massive diamond brooch. "Isn't he just like Vincent? The very same eyes! And that sullen mouth!"

Thomas backed away a little as the woman approached, although it seemed rather ungracious to retreat from two people who obviously knew his father. The woman came close, and lifted the smoky black veil that covered her face, so that Thomas could see how beautiful she was. She was smiling. Her eyes were so black that the sockets could have been empty.

"Didn't your father tell you that we were coming?" she cooed in a peculiarly irritating voice, as if she were talking to a toddler?"

"He must have," the man asserted, grunting jovially. "We called Vincent from Darien, before we left."

"He's in Seekonk today," said Thomas.

"Seekonk, well, well," the man replied. "It's not like Vincent to forget his dear friends."

"Maybe I should go inside and call him," Thomas suggested. "He left a number, in case anything happened. Can you wait for a little while?"

"Well," smiled the woman, "we'd rather step inside, if you wouldn't mind awfully. It *is* rather cold out here."

Thomas hesitated for one last moment. There was something not quite real about this couple. They were too polite, too formal, and they never seemed to say anything straightforwardly. But his father would be furious if he turned away a couple of old friends; and equally angry if he were rude to them, and left them standing in the snow.

He knelt down on the porch and unfastened his snowshoes.

"Nice snowshoes," the man said, standing so close that all Thomas could see of him were the sharply creased legs of his pants, and his well-polished black Oxfords. "I could do with a pair of those myself."

Thomas unlocked the front door of the house. The man and the woman followed him into the hallway so closely that their eagerness appeared to Thomas almost to have a hint of indecency about it.

"I don't know your names," he said, unzipping his windbreaker.

"Basil Hallward," the man told him, taking off his hat and fastidiously brushing the snow from around the crown. "And my sister, Mrs. Vane."

"Is this the living room?" asked the woman.

"I'm afraid the fires went out," Thomas explained. "The kitchen should be warmer, if you don't mind waiting there."

"No, no, don't trouble," the woman replied. She appeared to have seen something in the living room which had caught her attention. "As long as I'm out of the wind."

Thomas followed them into the living room. The fire had only just died, and the ashes were measled wih orange sparks.

"This could well be revived," the man said, crouching down in front of it, and prodding it with the poker. "A few sticks of kindling, a log or two, and we could soon have a merry blaze."

The woman meanwhile had walked across to where the

Waldegrave portrait was standing, covered up, on its easel. Her arms were held rigidly down by her sides, but her fingers seemed to squirm with anticipation. Her chest rose and fell beneath her black mink wrap as if she were having difficulty in breathing.

Thomas picked up the telephone, listened for the dial tone, and then pressed out the number which his father had written on the pad for him. The man had continued to poke at the fire for a while, but now without saying a word he stood up, brushed down his coat, came over to Thomas's side, and placed his finger on the telephone cradle, cutting him off.

Thomas stared at him. The man said, "It really isn't necessary to bother your father. I think that we've found what we came for."

Thomas said, "You're thieves. That's it, isn't it? You're thieves! You don't know my father at all! Well, dammit, I'm going to call the police! And don't think I'm frightened!" His heart was pumping so madly that he found it difficult to speak.

The man laid a hand on his shoulder, and squeezed gently. "My dear chap, you've got us quite wrong. We're not thieves at all. We've come here simply to collect a single item of property which has always belonged to us; and which the Pearsons have been keeping for us—how shall I put it—on extended loan. Your father knows all about it. We're not going to pillage the house, or make off with the cutlery. All we're going to do is take this single insignificant item, and leave."

Thomas said hotly, "You can't take anything. You're not allowed to."

But he was silent then, for the woman had drawn off her fur wrap, laid it across the back of the sofa, and approached the shrouded portrait with the gliding step of an Egyptian hand-maiden approaching the effigy of Thoth. She took hold of the edge of the bedspread which covered the portrait, and waited for what seemed like minutes before summoning up the courage to drag it away.

At last she did so, and the portrait was revealed: decayed and glistening in the wintry afternoon light. The woman stared at it, aghast; and as she stared at it she slowly raised both of her hands until she was clutching tightly at her own hair.

With a high screech of anguish, she threw herself down on to her knees, and huddled on the floor, shuddering and trembling, and uttering extraordinary mewls and whimpers.

Even the man had turned white; and his pallor emphasized the plump-dark circles under his eyes.

"Look what they've done to us!" the woman cried. "Look what they've done to us! Oh God in heaven, Maurice, look what they've done!"

The man crossed the room, and laid his hands on the woman's shoulders, encouraging her to rise. She stood staring at the portrait, encradled by his arms, but feeling no comfort. For the first time in over seventy years, she had seen her face not as she had managed to preserve it, not masked by paints or powders or by the sacrificed skin of others, but as it really was.

Thomas took a cautious step toward the door. If he could escape from the house while the man and the woman were so preoccupied with the painting, then it would only need a fast run through the woods to reach the Waxman house, and then he could call the police. They were too old to run after him, these two; and they could never drive through the woods in their Cadillac.

On step, two, three. But then the edge of his jacket caught the small occasional table beside the door, and a glass ashtray nearly tumbled, and made a clonking noise against the wall. Thomas turned; the man turned. And with a voice like clashing cymbals, the man roared, "Stop!"

Thomas stopped. He didn't know why he stopped. He didn't know why he didn't run. But he stopped, and he waited in the doorway, stiff with fright, while the man walked firmly across to take hold of his arm.

"You mustn't go," the man said unctiously. "It's far too soon for you to go. And besides, we rather enjoy your company. You are what I like to think of as a pleasant boy; and believe me there are few enough of those. Boys are mostly scrofulous, and rude. You, on the other hand, are a pleasant boy."

The woman had at last turned away from the portrait. She looked shocked, and her cheeks were still shining with tears.

"You must try to think of the future now, my dear," the man told her. Thomas thought that he didn't sound very sympathetic; or even as if he were making any particular effort to be.

"Let us wrap the portrait, and take the boy, and then let us leave. His unfortunate father may be back before we know it."

The woman appeared still to be dazed, and she turned around hopelessly like someone who wishes they could faint, but can't.

Thomas said, in a small voice, "I don't want to go with you. Please. I won't tell anyone who you are. I promise I won't tell anyone."

"But we *like* you," said the man. "Come on, now, I won't hear of any argument. It's snowing, and we have quite a long way to go."

"Did you see what they have done to us?" the woman demanded, shrilly, all of a sudden.

The man laid his arm around Thomas's shoulders. "It's quite all right, my dear. You will soon have the opportunity to do very much worse to one of them."

Twenty-Five

Seekonk, December 23

Dr. McKinnon grew increasingly explosive the more he tried to explain. He kept appealing to Vincent, and to Charlotte, because he obviously felt that Jack was something of a half-wit. But the idea that a human being could actually enter their own portrait; that they could exist in three dimensions in a two-dimensional painting; that was more than any of them could accept.

"It's perfectly simple, once you grasp the idea in your imagination," Dr. McKinnon protested. "I'm not saying that it's easy to explain, either logically or scientifically, but it does have a logical and a scientific explanation."

"Even if there is an explanation," said Jack, "I'm not sure that I want to know it." He shook his watch, listened closely to it, and then asked, "What's the time?"

"Five after," said Vincent. "We ought to be getting back soon. But first, I really want to try and understand this whole business of living people getting inside paintings."

"I can only do my best," said Dr. McKinnon, in an offhand way which suggested that he was already tired of trying to lighten their darkness.

"Then, please, if you would," asked Charlotte.

"Well," sighed Dr. McKinnon, "there was a famous or rather notorious paper written by Professor Jerome Franck, in 1948, for the Institute of Dimensional Research at Berkeley. It was entitled something like 'Artistic Perspective and the Creation of Alternative Realities.' I have it here somewhere, it's really very interesting. But what Franck essentially said was that when an artist paints a picture, despite the fact that it

319

is two-dimensional—that is, flat—his creation of *visual* depth takes on a reality of its own.''

Vincent drained his already empty brandy glass with an ostentatious gesture. It was excellent brandy and he would have liked to have been offered a little more. But Dr. McKinnon kept his hand firmly around the neck of the brandy decanter as he went on.

''The theory is by no means a new one,'' he said. ''It has its roots in the psychic and psychological studies carried out in Vienna in the nineteen thirties. You may have heard of Meissner's theory of imaginative manifestation; or, even if you haven't, you've certainly heard of Jung and the collective unconscious. Meissner and Jung worked together for several years and corresponded a great deal; eventually, in nineteen thirty-three, they decided there was distinct if arguable evidence that people and places created in novels and paintings, *if readers or spectators believed in them with sufficient conviction*, could actually manifest themselves in the real world. They could take on physical form, though sometimes not very substantially, so they would appear as no more than ghosts—but at other times very solidly.''

He smiled to himself. ''It's rather like Peter Pan asking if enough children believed in fairies to keep Tinkerbell alive. Because after all, what are we made of, we human beings? We are nothing more than physical collections of electrically charged particles. And what is our imagination made of? *Abstract* collections of electrically charged particles. And, believe me, in terms of simple physics, there is but a hair's breadth between the hand you can imagine and the hand you can actually shake. Meissner became convinced that people out of books and paintings actually live among us: fiction and art made flesh. He was sure many houses and places described in books or created in imaginative paintings—once they had been mentally pictured within the collective unconscious of a sufficient number of people—actually came into being. Somewhere in the world, there *is* a Shangri-la.''

Vincent sat back. He was beginning to suspect that Dr. McKinnon was not going to give them much in the way of practical help. He had listened so far with as little skepticism as possible, trying to assure himself that Dr. McKinnon might know what he was talking about. But characters out of novels coming alive? Houses out of fictitious landscapes suddenly appearing in the countryside? Shangri-la?

But then Dr. McKinnon stood up, pushed the book back into its place on the upper shelf and said dryly, "Plenty of Meissner's colleagues thought he was mad. After a while even Jung disassociated himself from the work he had done with Meissner. Perhaps Meissner *was* mad. Certainly it is difficult to believe, for instance, that Castle Dracula is actually moldering away somewhere in Transylvania just because a great many people can imagine it."

"You're right," Jack said. "It *is* hard to believe."

"Ah," said Dr. McKinnon, "but you have already seen for yourself the power of that portrait; so you'll have to admit there must be some kind of unusual influence at work here. And I do believe this—paintings *do* constitute more than the sum of their colors and their pigments. An artist *does* create on his canvas some form of alternative reality; and it *is* possible for people like the Grays, who have entered into an extraordinary psychic and spiritual transaction in order to separate their bodies from their souls, to retreat completely into that alternative reality. To vanish, as it were, into their own paintings."

After a pause, Jack said, "All right. Let's just suppose for a moment that they can do that. Is there any way of pursuing them once they've disappeared?"

Dr. McKinnon pouted, deep in uncertainty. "Theoretically, I suppose, anyone who wanted to pursue them could have *his* portrait painted and then enter into the same psychic transaction."

"But that would mean *his* soul would be separated from *his* body, too," Charlotte said.

"Yes, indeed it would," Dr. McKinnon agreed. "Whoever decided to go after the Grays would have to make the same commitments the Grays did, to eternal life without the benefit of a soul."

"Couldn't we just destroy the portrait?" Jack asked.

"Well, naturally that is one alternative. But the Grays are not naive. They have been surviving for too long to allow themselves to be caught undefended. They have a hostage, in the shape of Mrs. Montag—"

"*Blat*," Vincent said. "Mrs. Monblat."

"Ah, yes, Mrs. Monblat," said Dr. McKinnon. "And already the Grays have put you into the position of having to decide if you are prepared to sacrifice her life as the price for getting rid of them. I assume that if Mrs. Monblat hadn't appeared in the picture, you would have burned it by now?"

"Yes," Vincent acknowledged. But then, frowning, he said, "No." He wasn't quite sure why, but something about the idea of destroying the Waldegrave portrait disturbed him. He began to wonder why his grandfather had never destroyed it, why his father had never destroyed it. He knew they were men of their word and that if one of them had promised the Grays the portrait would remain safe, they would have felt honor-bound to make sure it did. But it seemed strange that Vincent's grandfather hadn't destroyed the portrait as soon as he suspected the Grays were murdering people for the pleasure of it. And it also seemed strange that he himself should feel any qualms. He was prepared to wait until Laura Monblat was rescued from the Grays, but once that was accomplished and the Grays were alone in the portrait, why should he worry if they burned? They were utterly depraved: murderers, torturers and blasphemers. And yet—and yet—he didn't know. He couldn't understand his reluctance. He turned to look at Jack, but Jack hadn't noticed his musings and only raised his empty brandy glass and said, "Cheers."

Dr. McKinnon said, "The Grays, I imagine, if they were ever to take possession of that portrait, would disappear for several years, especially since they seem to have stirred up so much trouble and alarm. They could remain concealed in the portrait for as long as they wanted, until all of us were long dead. Then they could reemerge and reoccupy their bodies, or even presumably the bodies of others. I remember my father telling me that one should never sleep in a room in which a portrait hangs in case the spirit from the portrait emerges in the night, when you are deeply asleep, and takes over your body. You will then find that *you* are hanging on the wall, trapped in the portrait, while the spirit that was once inside the portrait occupies the person who was once you. Have you noticed that in the wards of Roman Catholic hospitals there are no portraits except of Christ and the Virgin Mary? Well, that is why. It dates from a Papal instruction of eighteen seventy-three, from

Pius the Ninth. '*Ab insidiis diaboli, libera nos Domine.*' Rescue us from insidious demons, O Lord."

Vincent asked, "Is there anything we can do to extricate Laura Monblat from the picture? The Grays put her in there; surely there must be some way of getting her out."

"Only by the method I described. By having your own portrait painted and pursuing them into their alternative reality."

Jack cleared his throat. "I think we may have to negotiate our way out of this one, Vincent. Maybe contact the Grays, call them up and ask them what it is they want. Treat it like a regular hostage situation. Unofficially, of course. I wouldn't be able to call up a SWAT squad—not on the evidence we have so far."

Vincent was thoughtful. "Supposing we tried to cut Laura Monblat out of the picture—I mean with scissors. What effect would that have?"

"It would kill her, I expect," Dr. McKinnon replied. "It may possibly kill the Grays, too, but there isn't any certainty of that. You see, the portrait's reality depends on its remaining whole, as the artist created it."

Vincent turned to Jack. "Here's a hard question, Jack. Supposing this *was* a hostage situation. Supposing the Grays were terrorists holed up in a house someplace, and you knew you couldn't get them out without risking the life of their hostage. You also knew that if they got away, they would almost certainly kill more people. What would you do?"

Jack lifted his hands. "The usual understanding is that every effort should be made to rescue the hostage without jeopardizing police lives unnecessarily, or endangering the civilian population."

"In other words?"

"In other words, although nobody ever admits it, the immediate apprehension of dangerous criminals is generally considered to be a marginally higher priority than the lives of any hostages they might be holding."

Jack hesitated for a moment, then added, "It depends, to a certain extent, on the hostage. The police public-relations department is usually called on to make an assessment of public reaction if a particular hostage were to die. Like, they wouldn't let Michael Jackson or Billy Graham go to the wall if they were being held hostage, but they wouldn't worry quite so much about Joe Blow or Jane Doe."

"My God, that sounds cynical," Charlotte said.

Jack shook his head. "It isn't as cynical as it sounds. Every reasonable effort is always made to save the life of every hostage. But there are times when you have to shut your eyes and go in shooting, and pray that nobody innocent gets hurt."

Charlotte said, "You're debating a woman's life here. You *can't* destroy that portrait, not if it means harming Laura Monblat."

"*We* know that," Vincent said, "but do the *Grays* know that? Remember, they have no conscience, no pity, no genuinely human feelings. They've been living without them for years now; do you think they can remember what it was like to feel a pang of concern for someone they hardly even knew?"

Dr. McKinnon said, "You're right. You may have a point. But if I were you, I'd keep a very close eye on your family, Mr. Pearson. If the Grays are uncertain about Mrs. Montag's value as a hostage, they may seek to take another hostage, one even closer to home."

Vincent suddenly thought of the Waldegrave portrait, standing in the living room on its easel. He suddenly thought of Thomas, walking home alone through the snowy woods after spending the morning with Susie Foster. He could hear his own words echoing in his ears, "If we're not home by the time you get back, just make yourself comfortable. There's *Star Wars* on the video and plenty of Coke and cookies in the kitchen. Stack up the fire. We won't be late."

He said to Dr. McKinnon, "Could I use your phone, please?"

Dr. McKinnon looked surprised but said, "Certainly. There's an extension in the hall."

Vincent went quickly out into the musty hall, stood in the multicolored light from the stained-glass window over the door and dialed Candlemas. The phone rang and rang but no one answered. He propped the receiver under his chin and leafed through his small black-leather address book until he found the Fosters' number. He dialed it and waited. After almost a minute, the Fosters' maid answered.

"Hallo? This is Vincent Pearson here. My son Thomas was spending the morning with Susie."

"That's right, Mr. Pearson, he was."

"Did he leave? Or is he still there?"

"Oh, he left, Mr. Pearson, 'round about an hour ago."

An hour, Vincent thought. Thomas had his snowshoes; maybe he could have taken a detour just to try them out. But an hour?

Damn it, he thought, stop worrying. Thomas is a big boy now. But he couldn't help thinking of yesterday's séance and all that bright, crimson blood.

He went back into Dr. McKinnon's library. "I'm sorry," he said. "I have to get back to New Milford. Dr. McKinnon— thank you for everything. Charlotte, Jack—I'm sorry to rush you."

"Is everything all right?" Charlotte asked.

They drove back across Connecticut in gathering darkness. When they reached Manchester, Jack had himself patched through on his radio to his headquarters; he told Norman Goldberg to send an officer around to Candlemas to check that everything was okay. "And no half-assed looks down the driveway, neither. He goes up to the house, he rings the bell, he speaks to the boy and makes sure he's hundred percent."

"Yes, sir, Sheriff."

They were almost out of Hartford when Norman called back.

"Is Mr. Pearson there with you, Sheriff?"

"Affirmative."

"Well, I don't want to cause him any unnecessary distress, but the house was found with the front door wide open, fires burning, but nobody around."

"Ask him about the portrait," Vincent demanded, feeling himself go cold. "*They may seek to take another hostage, Mr. Pearson, even closer to home.*"

"He says he doesn't know nothing about no portrait."

The snow flew at the Cherokee's windshield like white locusts. Vincent said, "Send him around there once more. Tell him he has to check."

Jack picked up the radio microphone again and said, "Send him back, Norman. We need to know if there's an oil painting there in the living room, draped in a bedspread."

There was a crackle, a pause, and then Norman came back. "He's here now. He says he saw the bedspread, it was lying on the floor. There was an easel on top of it, an artist's easel. That was all. No portrait."

Vincent took a deep breath and sat back. "Jack," he said, "drive me straight to Darien."

Jack looked at him intently. "Do you think that's the best idea?"

"Drive me to Darien, for Christ's sake! Those bastards have got hold of the picture, and they've taken my son, too!"

Twenty-Six

Darien, December 23

When they arrived outside the gates of Wilderlings, they found them closed, and shackled with a heavy-duty chain. It was snowing furiously and they could scarcely see what they were doing, but they climbed out of the Cherokee and made their way around to the side of the house, where the wall was lowest. They scrambled over it and struggled through a snowdrift three feet deep, Vincent in front, Jack close behind and Charlotte trying her best to keep up.

They reached the front door and Vincent pounded on the knocker. The echo barked out across the snowy garden, but there was no reply.

"Three alternatives," Jack said, lifting his fingers. His nose was red from the bitter cold. "Either they've left, they're not answering, or—"

Vincent finished the sentence for him. "Or Dr. McKinnon, for all his nuttiness, was right, and they've escaped into the portrait, with Thomas and Laura as hostages."

"It's so crazy!" Charlotte screamed. "You're acting like it's true! How can it possibly be true?"

"What else can I believe?" Vincent retorted. "You saw what happened to Pat; you saw what happened to Laura Monblat. They killed Edward to get that portrait. Do you think I'm going to stand around and let them kill Thomas the same way? God damn it, Charlotte, I know it's impossible, but what other explanation is there?"

Jack said, "I'm breaking in. There's a crowbar in the wagon. Keep on knocking just in case. . . ."

Jack waded back through the snowdrifts like an outgoing

surfer while Vincent and Charlotte waited outside the front
door. Vincent knocked again, half-heartedly, but he knew there
was no one there. The wind sighed briskly around the side of
the house; ice particles sizzled against the porch. The sky was
relentlessly dreary, the kind of sky that promises summer will
be late this year. If it comes at all. And Christmas only two
days away. And Thomas gone.

Jack came back and without a word began to lever open the
double doors. Oak splintered, hinges complained, and at last
the central lock sprang apart, the bolts burst, and the left-hand
door juddered open.

"It's a technique," he said tersely. "You have to pick the
correct point of leverage."

Vincent was the first to step into the darkened hallway. He
hesitated at the top of the marble steps and called, "Hello? Is
anybody here?" But the house was empty and silent and dusty;
a smug house, one that guarded its own secrets and would
continue to guard them, even when developers eventually
came and smashed down its brickwork.

Jack said, "Call them again, huh? We don't want to be guilty
of trespass."

Vincent called, but there was no reply. Jack looked around
and said, "I guess it's okay."

"You don't want to be here, do you?" Vincent chided him.

"I'm here. Isn't that enough?"

"Well, what the hell's wrong?" Vincent wanted to know.
"The Grays killed your friend George Kelly, you know that;
they killed Elmer Tweed, too, and they kidnapped Laura
Monblat. What more do you want before you bust them?"

"If you really want to know, I need evidence," Jack
retorted. "I need the kind of testimony that can stand up in
court. How do you think a judge is going to react if I bring a
man like Dr. McKinnon on the stand with all his theories about
characters from books and paintings coming to life? What do
you think a smart and expensive defense lawyer is going to
make of that? Think about Melvin Belli, my friend, because
that's about the league of lawyer the Grays can afford. 'Oh,
yes, Dr. McKinnon, characters out of books can come to life,
can they? So where are Raggedy Ann and Raggedy Andy
living right now? Palm Springs?'"

"For Christ's sake!" Vincent shouted at him. "Evidence, is

that all you care about? What about justice? These freaks took my son, what does that mean? You're the sheriff, aren't you? Elected and sworn to protect and to serve! Well, protect, damn it! And serve!''

At that moment Charlotte said, "Look!" and they turned their eyes across the hallway and saw it for the first time, standing on a gilded easel, swathed in purple drapes, the Waldegrave portrait.

Vincent walked over to it with mechanical steps and stood staring at it. "They did take it," he said. But he was incapable of saying out loud what he really meant and what he had immediately seen. Next to Nora, at the very edge of the picture, pale and staring, stood Thomas; his own son Thomas, in a black velvet Victorian suit with knickerbockers and a white lace collar, staring and submissive, painted in the immaculate style of Walter Waldegrave.

Charlotte came up beside him and took his hand. "Oh, God, Vincent," she said. "I'm so sorry."

"They're insane," he said. He felt as if someone had hit him in the face with a ten-pound hammer. *"They're insane!"*

He turned around to Jack and shouted, "There's your evidence, for God's sake! My son, in that painting! You want to show *that* to one of your judges? Is that proof enough? Why the hell didn't you kill the whole damned family while you had the chance?"

Jack came up and inspected the portrait carefully. He touched the painted image of Thomas; it was quite dry. "I don't know what to tell you," he said. "I'm sorry, believe me."

Vincent said, "I'm going to search the house. Maybe they've got him tied up somewhere." He strode across to the foot of the staircase and shouted out, "Thomas! Are you there, Thomas? Thomas!"

Charlotte suddenly said, "There's a note here, Vincent. Look."

Vincent turned around. On a small mahogany side table with twisted legs there was a plain cream-vellum envelope. He went across and picked it up. It was addressed in lilac-colored ink to "V. Pearson Esq."

"They planned this, God damn it," Vincent swore. He ripped open the envelope and shook out the letter.

It read:

Dear Mr. Pearson,   Wilderlings, December 23

As you will see, we have reclaimed at last the portrait
that was always rightfully ours. You will never understand the suffering your grandfather and succeeding
generations of Pearsons imposed on us; and it is only
because we are a sentimental family that we have not
taken revenge on you.

"Sentimental, for Christ's sake," Jack put in. He had been
reading the letter over Vincent's shoulder. "What do they mean
by sentimental?"
The letter went on:

We have taken your son with us as a precaution. He
will be kept quite safe, we assure you, just as your family
kept our portrait quite safe. You should understand,
however, if you do not understand it already, that any
attempt by you to damage or destroy the portrait will
result immediately in your son's death or serious injury.
You should resign yourself to the fact that you will never
see your son again and that we have gone quite beyond
your reach. You may search for us all over the world for
the rest of your life, but you will never find us.
    Leave the portrait where it is. If you try to take it away,
we shall punish your son severely. I think you know how
severe we can be when taxed. The portrait will be
collected by our agents after the Christmas vacation and
stored in proper conditions.
    We are satisfied now that justice has been done. We
wish you solace in your loss.

                                    Respectfully,
                                    Maurice Gray

Vincent read the letter again and then handed it to Jack so he
could examine it more closely. "What do you think?" he
asked, somewhat calmer now.
Jack said, "This line here about going beyond our reach. Do
you think they've actually managed to do what Dr. McKinnon

was talking about? Do you think they're actually *in* there, inside that portrait?"

"You're asking if I believe something that's absolutely impossible. The trouble is, it's the only reasonable explanation there is."

"They could simply have left and taken Thomas and Laura Monblat with them," Charlotte suggested. "I mean—perhaps they've gone to South America, or Mexico, or someplace like that."

Vincent turned around and looked at the dark and musty hallway with its breeze-blown draperies of cobwebs. "No," he said. "I think Dr. McKinnon was right. I think they're still here. I can feel them."

They made a search of the upper floors of the house, from the gloomy attics with their oval windows that overlooked the snowy and derelict gardens, to the dusty rococo bedrooms with their strange and claustrophobic perfumes, to the operating room with its marble-topped table and rows of immaculate surgical instruments. At last they arrived back in the hallway where the painting stood.

"That's it," Jack said. "If they're anywhere here at all, they're inside the painting."

"I think I'm going to have an hysterical screaming fit," Charlotte said. "I mean—I know it was my idea to go talk to Dr. McKinnon. But imaginative manifestations? People going in and out of paintings?"

"McKinnon mentioned something else, too," Jack said. "He said that when the people went inside the portrait, into that what-do-you-call-it—"

"Alternative reality," Vincent prompted.

"That's right. When they went into that alternative reality, they left their bodies behind and kind of stored them, like meat. So—if it's true, if any of this is true, and the Grays have disappeared inside the painting—their bodies must be somewhere in the house. Does that make sense?"

Vincent nodded grimly.

"Where would you think?" Jack asked. He unwrapped a piece of gum and began to masticate the sugar out of it. "The cellar maybe? We haven't looked there yet."

Charlotte took Vincent's arm again. "Please, Vincent, this is all getting out of control."

"No, no," Vincent said. He was beginning to feel more determined. After the initial shock of seeing Thomas in the portrait and knowing the Grays had kidnapped him, he was prepared to take some positive action now, no matter how bizarre it might be, to get his son back.

They found the cellar door under the stairs—the same cellar door through which George Kelly had emerged into the hands of Maurice and Henry Gray. Jack located the light switch, and one by one they cautiously crept down between the chilly plastered walls into the vaults beneath the house. "They don't make cellars like this anymore," Jack said, his breath smoking in the cold. "Look at those arches."

"Look at those cobwebs," Charlotte shuddered.

Their footsteps were grinding and noisy on the concrete floor. They passed one chamber after another, peering at wine and furniture and tea chests of china. Charlotte delved into one of the boxes and brought out an exquisite gold and blue plate. "Look at this. Royal Worcester, probably a hundred and fifty years old."

They found the storeroom filled with paintings. Vincent looked through five or six of them and said, "These are amazing. Bonnard, Vuillard, Denis. All first-class Nabis; worth anything up to a million and a half each. Look—there's a Moreau. He was a Symbolist. And that's a Signac."

"Some collection, huh?" Jack asked.

"That's the understatement of the eon. These paintings are probably worth more than two or three hundred million dollars, even if the rest of them are even half as good as these, which they probably are."

They found chamber after chamber, crowded with the relics of a family life that had outlived itself by seventy years. They found pots and jars and boxes and riding-tack and even parts of an early De Dion automobile engine. They found some leathery fabric carefully folded between sheets of yellowed tissue paper, and neither of them wanted to touch it in case it was human skin. But there was no sign of the Grays; and there was no sign of Thomas or Laura.

"Maybe we should try the stables," Jack suggested.

They went outside through the back door. The gardens were derelict and frozen. The sky was clamped over them like a pewter plate. Their feet squeaked in the snow; and Jack cleared his throat two or three times because the cold made his nose run.

The garages, the stables, and all of the outbuildings were deserted.

Jack stood in the snow with his hands in his pockets and his face contorted with frustration and cold.

"What did Dr. McKinnon say? They would probably hide their bodies in places where you wouldn't usually expect to find people."

"Do you think they buried themselves?" asked Vincent.

"They wouldn't have had time. And, in any case, as soon as the snow melts, somebody's bound to see where they did it. And, in any case, none of them are here, and if one of them had buried the others, which he would have had to, where is he? Or she, of course. I forgot. I mustn't discriminate."

Their breath smoked. They looked all around them, trying to think where fourteen people might quickly and easily conceal themselves. It was then that Vincent glimpsed a slight darkness in the snow in the center of the lawns.

"What's that over there?" he asked Jack, shielding his eyes.

"I don't know. Some kind of ornamental pond, looks like."

Vincent peered at the pond through the snowy twilight. "Where do criminals throw guns away when they don't want them any longer? Where do gangsters drop bodies? Where is the last place on earth that you'd think of looking for anybody who was hiding from you?"

They trudged quickly across the lawn until they reached the edge of the pond. Most of the surface was thickly frozen over, but the darker area which Vincent had noticed from the opposite side of the garden had recently been smashed. It was freezing solid again, and the water in it was an opaque porridge of slush; but in the past few hours somebody had obviously considered it worth their while to break though a crust of ice that was over four inches thick, in a perfect circle three feet in diameter; and then leave the hole to freeze over again.

In spite of the snow, Vincent got down on to his hands and knees, and strained his eyes to see what lay under the water.

"Give me your flashlight," he told Jack; and Jack obediently handed it over. Vincent shone the flashlight from side to side, illuminating ice, and goldfish, and trailing strands of weed.

He angled the light down, and it was then, with the greatest dread that he had ever experienced, that he saw the face. His son's face, as white as a fish's belly, staring up at him from four feet beneath the surface of the freezing pond. Next to Tom, holding him close in a cold and motherly embrace, lay Laura, and there was Belvedere, too, and Henry, and Netty the crippled girl. A tangle of arms and legs, chilled and white. They had obviously hoped that their bodies would be concealed during the winter by ice and snow; and during the summer by lily-pads and dancing reflections. This year, summer and winter would serve these aristocrats of death and immortality in the way that summer and winter had served them so far for three lifetimes, and always would.

Deep in the gelid water, with her face against a bank of weed, Vincent saw Cordelia; and there, lying close by, his face greenish and drawn, lay Maurice.

"I guess we should fish 'em out," said Jack, taking the light from Vincent and playing it from one side of the pond to the other. "This is a massacre."

"Not yet it isn't," Vincent told him. He stood up, and beckoned, and Jack reluctantly followed him. Vincent was shivering from cold, and from the shock of having seen Thomas under the surface of the pond. He kept telling himself that Thomas wasn't dead; that none of them were dead; that they had all escaped into the portrait. But there were moments where disbelief kept yawning beneath his feet; and he began to think that it would all end here, as a mass drowning in a squalid Connecticut pond, with bodies being brought up dripping by the coroner's department.

Charlotte came out of the house, looking for them. Jack beckoned her over. "They're all in the pond," he said, wiping his nose with the back of his hand.

"Not Thomas?" asked Charlotte, aghast.

Vincent nodded. "He's fourteen years old," he said with furious dullness. "That's all. Fourteen years old. Why the hell didn't I take him down to Seekonk with me?"

Confused, horrified, Charlotte said, "Are they—are they dead? Are they all drowned?"

Vincent turned away from the pond. "They're not dead," he said in a voice constricted with emotion and phlegm. "This is where they've chosen to conceal their bodies, that's all, while they escape. I guess they could have found somewhere more secure, but they probably didn't have very much time. What's more, they probably didn't realize that we knew what they could do."

"At least," he added, "what we *hope* that they can do, for Thomas's sake, and for Laura Monblat's."

"Do you really think that they've escaped into their picture?"

"God knows," said Vincent.

"But couldn't we just take out the Grays . . . drag them out of the pond . . . and shoot them or something?" Charlotte asked. She was as frantic as Vincent was despairing.

Vincent shook his head. "Maurice Gray said it all in his letter. The Grays have gone way beyond our reach. What you see here are simply their bodies. They themselves, their spirits, everything they really are; *they're* still free. They don't have to worry about being arrested, or growing old, or growing sick. They can do whatever they like, and whenever they like, to anybody they like."

They walked back toward the house. Vincent was tormented by the urge to run back to the pond and pull Thomas out of the freezing water. That's my son in there, my only son, lying cheek-by-jowl with half-decayed perverts and murderers.

But he knew that there was only one way in which Thomas could be saved. And Laura Monblat, too. And that was why he led Jack and Charlotte back into the house, feeling lightheaded and shocked and impossibly unreal, but still determined.

Back in the hallway, Jack said, "Okay—what are we going to do? Are we going to run with Dr. McKinnon's idea, or what?"

Vincent said, "We haven't any choice. If we don't pursue the Grays into their own painting, we're never going to get them back. You heard what Dr. McKinnon said: it's an escape route. They could stay hidden inside it for years and years, until we're all dead and forgotten. We daren't touch the painting because Thomas and Laura are in it, and we daren't touch any of those bodies because they'll punish Thomas and Laura in retaliation."

"So what do we do?" Jack repeated. "We go in after them, but how?"

"I'm going to call Aaron Halperin," Vincent said. "He's the

quickest and most competent professional artist I know. I'm going to ask him to come down here, right now, and paint my portrait. Charlotte, you call Dr. McKinnon again. Ask him to read you the whole Latin ritual that was used to separate a person's soul from his body. And, please, make sure you get it right. One mistake, and it may not work."

Jack said, "Listen, Vincent. I'm the investigating officer here. Don't you think *I* ought to be the one to get in there after the Grays?"

Vincent shook his head emphatically. "That's my son there, Jack. And besides, what is the Litchfield County Police Department going to do with a sheriff who lives forever? Not to mention his wife."

He took out his address book and called Aaron in Bantam. Aaron sounded slurry on the phone and Vincent found it hard to make himself understood.

"Vincent? Where are you calling from? I rang you at home. I was going to ask you over to try out my new plum brandy. I call it Slithervitz on account of it takes only two glasses and you're slithering all over the floor."

"Aaron, this is urgent. You remember the Waldegrave portrait?"

"My dear Vincent, how could I ever forget it?"

"Well, something's happened. Something serious. I want you to drive down to Darien, bring your paints, and paint a portrait of me, full length, right now."

There was a long pause, punctuated only by the suppressed thunder of Aaron's breathing. "A portrait? *Now*? You're out of your mind! It's Christmas Eve practically!"

"Aaron," Vincent said, "never in my whole life have I needed anybody as much as I need you now. Whatever you ask, I promise I'll pay it. I'll tell you what—you can have those pen-and-ink sketches by Charles Wilson Peale; and ten thousand dollars besides. But for God's sake, Aaron, I need you. It's life and death."

Aaron was silent for a long time. Then he said, "I'm drunk, you know."

"Well, call a taxi in that case. I'll pay the fare. But get on down here, please. I'm at a house called Wilderlings, just north of Darien on the New Canaan road. Will you please do it?"

"But *why,* Vincent? Why do you want your portrait painted

so urgently? You know, having your portrait painted, that's never anything *urgent*."

"Today, Aaron, it is. I promise you. You'll understand why when you get here."

Aaron hesitated for a moment, and then he said, "I've just talked to the family. The family consensus seems to be that I should stay here and that if you want a portrait of yourself so desperately, you should go to the photo booth in Woolworth's."

"Aaron," Vincent told him, "you remember Van Gogh?"

"Van Gogh? What about Van Gogh?"

"I'll tell you what about Van Gogh. Van Gogh is still in the Waldegrave portrait, but now Thomas is, too."

"*Thomas*? Oh, God, they didn't—"

"No, Aaron, they didn't hurt him. Not yet, as far as I can tell. But the chances are they will, and I want him out of there."

There was more hesitation, and then at last Aaron said, "I'm coming down there, Vincent. Give me a couple of hours. I have to get some paints and a canvas together first."

"Don't forget, take a taxi if you want to. I'll pay."

"I'm okay. Listen! I'm okay. A couple of hours, that's all, if you can wait that long."

"I'm counting on you, Aaron."

After Vincent finished talking to Aaron, Charlotte called Dr. McKinnon. He sounded offhanded and reticent at first. He was not a man accustomed to being walked out on abruptly, as Vincent and Charlotte and Jack had done, nor was he a man who suffered the psychospiritual quandaries of others, not happily anyway.

"I was left with the clear impression," he said, "that none of you quite believed what I was saying."

"Dr. McKinnon," Charlotte pleaded with him, "the Grays have abducted Mr. Pearson's son!"

"That is a matter for the police, I would have thought."

"Dr. McKinnon—they've taken him into the family portrait."

Prickly silence. Then, "Is this a practical joke, young lady? I began to suspect as much this morning."

"No joke, Dr. McKinnon, I promise you. But I need to know the ritual, the ritual for allowing a person to live forever while his portrait grows old."

"*Over the telephone*?" he remonstrated, obviously scandal-ized.

"Dr. McKinnon," Charlotte protested, "we really don't have any time. Believe me, if I could come over there myself, or send you a personal letter, I would. But all I need is the words. Please. And any special instructions."

"This isn't very regular, you know. The rituals are secret, and have been for five hundred years. To read them out to you over the telephone—"

"Dr. McKinnon," Charlotte snapped, "for God's sake, get off that old academic hobby horse of yours. This is the twentieth century, and people need help."

"Well, look here," Dr. McKinnon expostulated. "I don't have to put up with that kind of talk, I'll thank you."

All the same, he stayed on the line. Charlotte said, "I'm sorry, Dr. McKinnon, I'm panicking, that's all. Please. It's the very last hope we have left."

Dr. McKinnon was silent for so long that Charlotte had to say "hello?" to make sure that he was still listening. Vincent watched her closely, and raised one querying eyebrow, but Charlotte waved her hand to indicate that Dr. McKinnon was still there, and that he was apparently considering her request.

"You have an actual problem there?" Dr. McKinnon asked, at last.

"Yes, doctor. An actual problem."

"Well," said Dr. McKinnon, "I hope this isn't some terrible joke. Wait up; and I'll go find the book."

Charlotte covered the mouthpiece with her hand, and whispered to Vincent, "He's going to do it."

Vincent said, "Thank God."

Slowly and pedantically, Dr. McKinnon read out the words of the ritual; and Charlotte, who had once been an excellent secretary, wrote it all down in faultless shorthand. The Latin was difficult and archaic, but Dr. McKinnon read every word with explosive relish.

When he had finished, Charlotte said, "I don't know how to say thank you, doctor."

Dr. McKinnon half-snorted, half-coughed. "Use the ritual to good effect, that's all. And when you have rescued your people; well, let me know about it."

"Yes, sir. You're an angel."

Once Charlotte had written out the Latin words in longhand, Vincent scanned them, and said, "Okay. All we need now is the portrait; and then we can get after them."

Vincent and Charlotte stayed close while they waited for Aaron to arrive. Jack found the boiler and got it going again in case the temperature dropped severely during the afternoon. Wilderlings echoed with extraordinary creaks and shuffling noises while the pipes heated up. Jack at last appeared from the cellar, wiping his hands on a large swathe of cheesecloth. He didn't look at the Waldegrave portrait anymore; none of them did. The fear of what might happen if they failed was too great.

Jack was also conscious that he wasn't behaving at all like a sheriff. He should have called the Darien police long ago, had Wilderlings sealed off and thoroughly searched for drugs, bodies and concealed weapons. But he had already gone too far along the road as far as believing in the Grays was concerned; now there was no turning back. An official search would inevitably turn up the bodies in the pond, and if the coroner attempted an autopsy on them, the consequences would be bloody and disastrous.

Jack could just imagine it: Maurice Gray threatening to cut from Thomas each and every equivalent piece of flesh that the coroner removed from the Grays.

By the time Aaron arrived, it was dark. He came struggling through the snow with his box of oil paints under his arm and smiled at Vincent and Charlotte testily.

"I hope you realize I'm a saint."

"Do they canonize Jews?"

"St. Aaron of the Immutable Palette. Now, what's this all about?"

They showed him the Waldegrave portrait with its new additions, Laura and Thomas; then they took him out to the garden and showed him the bodies beneath the glistening ice.

"All right, already," he said at last, swallowing. "I understand."

"Then paint me," Vincent insisted.

"But do you know what this means, if I paint you and if you say that ritual? You're going to live forever, aren't you, like them? You're going to lose your soul, Vincent; and how are you going to get it back? Thomas, he's already lost his. What kind of a life is he going to live even if you rescue him? He's going to be a killer, skinning people to stay young? And are *you* going to be the same?''

"Aaron, for Christ's sake, just let me cross that bridge when I come to it. Right now my son's being held by a family of homicidal perverts in some imaginary place where I can't even reach him. Now, please, paint my portrait, and let me save him, at least.''

Aaron methodically opened his box of paints and laid out his brushes.

"Aaron, do you understand what I'm asking?" Vincent protested.

Aaron nodded and took out his palette and his sticks of willow charcoal. "I know what you want, Vincent, and I'll do it for you, for sure. Don't fret. I'm as scared as you are.''

Vincent sat in a large brown-velvet spoonback chair they had dragged in from the music room and crossed his legs so he was comfortable, and Aaron began to sketch. The outlines of Vincent's head and body began to appear on the canvas, then his legs. Quickly Aaron went over his charcoal outlines with a thin wash of crimson, painting deftly and accurately. After this, he rubbed in the background color, then the construction tones around the forehead, the sockets of the eyes, the cheek-bones and the side of the nose.

Painting with yellow ochre, viridian, light red, black and white, Aaron speedily produced a vivid portrait of Vincent's head: his dark, curly hair streaked with gray, his straight nose, his deep-set eyes, his strong jaw. When the clock struck nine, Aaron's brush was still flying, filling in tones and highlights and areas of unexpected shadow. By two o'clock in the morning, the portrait was almost completed; Aaron's hands were cold now, he was exhausted and it was taking him longer and longer to finish each detail.

At four, he suddenly flung down his sable brush and said, "That's all I can do. I'm sorry.''

Vincent rose stiffly out of the chair where he had been sitting for the past three hours bundled up in his overcoat. He examined the still-glistening portrait and then he laid a hand on Aaron's shoulder.

"Aaron, I always said you were a genius. This proves it. Whatever happens, forget restoration. Paint portraits. You'll be rich.''

"I think I need a drink," Aaron said, his voice hoarse. Standing up he stretched his shoulders and waggled his fingers.

"Now for the ritual," Vincent said.

Charlotte asked, "Now?"

"That's *Thomas* in there, Charlotte. That's my son."

"The painting is still wet."

"It doesn't matter. Let's do it."

"Where have I heard *that* phrase before?" Jack mused. "Oh, I know. Gary Gilmore."

"The ritual," Vincent repeated. He was too tired to argue.

Charlotte handed him the piece of paper on which she had written the same words that, ninety years ago, had given the Gray family the gift of immortality. Vincent's hands were shaking as he took it, and he had to breathe before he started to recite.

"*Sanctum suum Spiritum per concedat agere Dominus nobis quod. Superatis nequitiam multimodam eorum uobis in prius cum, imperabitis daemonibus aliis in recte etenim tunc.*"

Even in its shortened form, the ritual was long. It included not only the Exorcism in reverse, but a passage about the powers of time and the powers of creativity, noting that the forces of the world were pinioned in four quarters: Evil, Purity, Selflessness and Jealousy.

Jack and Charlotte watched Vincent closely while he recited these words; but at the end of them, he was still there, still tired, his head bowed, and the portrait remained on Aaron's portable easel, a slight run of viridian sliding down his left cheek. The early morning wind blew chilly and insistent through the broken front door; a pattern of snow had already crossed the threshold, like the spines of a catherine wheel. The huge house creaked, and outside, the world was white and hard and difficult to look at.

"It's not going to work," Jack said. He had known all along that it wasn't going to work. He had known all along that Dr. McKinnon had been too eccentric to be true, with all his talk about people and houses and landscapes coming alive. There were not many times in his life when Jack felt like poking the muzzle of his .38 into his mouth, up against his palate, although he supposed every policeman feels like doing it now and again; but tonight, for some reason, he could have done it. The cold, uncomfortable pressure of steel, and then oblivion.

Vincent kept his eyes closed. Nothing had happened; he hadn't been transported into another reality. But somehow the words had given him an extraordinary sensation that he knew was right. He turned around, his eyes still closed. Now he didn't know which way he was facing, but that wasn't important. The important thing was to *walk forward*, straight ahead, into the darkness that clustered behind his eyeballs.

Charlotte, Jack and Aaron saw him walk quite easily and methodically across the hallway, up the stairs, out the front door and into the early morning snow. Jack called, "Vincent! Are you okay?" but there was no answer. Charlotte hesitated for a moment, then ran to the door and looked out across the blindingly gray garden, and he was gone. His footprints continued for three or four paces beyond the porch and then vanished.

Jack came up behind her and laid a hand on her shoulder. "He's done it," he whispered. "He's gone. He's fucking immortal!"

Twenty-Seven

Darien, December 24

Maurice Gray was sitting in the crimson parlor smoking his pipe when Thomas came in, stood close to the fireplace and stared at him. Maurice was discomfited. He didn't like anybody staring at him when he read the newspaper, especially boys, and even more especially, unfamiliar boys. He tried to read a long paragraph about President Harrison's plans for the purchase of silver; but in the end, he had to shake his paper out and say, "Yes, young man? Is there something you want?"

"Please," Thomas said, "may I go home?"

Maurice sighed with melodramatic impatience. He laid his paper on the floor, the ultimate gesture a disturbed father uses to make his son feel guilty. *You have disturbed the Almighty Perusal of the News, my boy. But speak, and I shall suffer you.*

"I don't know where I am," Thomas said, his lower lip unsteady, but he refused to cry. "I don't know what's happening to me."

"Well," Maurice said, "I believe I can settle both of those uncertainties, although whether you find the answers satisfactory or not is up to you. You are at Wilderlings, in Darien, Connecticut. It is Christmas Eve. Tomorrow there will be presents, and goose, and plum puddings, and all the sweets that boys enjoy. And what is happening to you is that you have come to live here with us since you were recently made an orphan, and you are about to embark on a very satisfactory and rewarding life."

"An orphan?"

Maurice smiled and twiddled his fingers. "What else do you call a boy who has no living parents?"

"But my father's alive. My mother's alive."

Maurice shook his head. "Not a bit of it, Thomas. Neither your mother nor your father have yet been born. Look out the window, Thomas, and tell me what you see."

Thomas walked to the window and parted the heavy lace drapes, with their patterns of peacocks and flower baskets. Outside the window, he could see the snow and the drive and the gates of Wilderlings. But in the roadway beyond, he could see horse-drawn sleighs, ladies with sweeping coats and thick fur muffs, and gentlemen in tall hats.

Maurice stood up, approached the window and fastidiously cleaned his nails with the sharp point of a small silver penknife.

"This is the year the Waldegrave portrait was painted," he said. "We have returned there for the time being, because we are children of the picture. We are inside the picture, inside! And you, with the assistance of Uncle Belvedere's artistry, are inside it with us."

"I want to go home," Thomas insisted. He still couldn't be sure if this was a nightmare or not, but he was determined to get home, even if it meant nothing more complicated than waking up.

"No," Maurice said. "*This* is your home. *This*! You are part of our family now. In fact, I think you should meet them, so you know them better."

"I just want to go home," Thomas repeated.

But Maurice genially ignored him, took hold of his arm and led him through to the hallway, which was shining and bright and decorated with bronze Greek statues, muscular young men with perfectly formed bodies, preparing to throw the javelin or the discus, or to run the marathon. Maurice remarked, "Did you know that the word *gymnast* comes from the Greek word that means 'one who exercises naked'?"

Thomas was reluctant, but Maurice's grip on his arm was bitingly strong. He forced Thomas upstairs, along the landing, and up yet another flight of stairs, where dismal landscapes were hanging, views of Münster during a thunderstorm, and heavy seas off Helgoland. At last they arrived at a wide doorway with fruit carved on it; the fruit had once been painted but it was faded now, as if from listlessness. Maurice knocked and smiled at Thomas while they waited.

The doors were opened from the inside by a private nurse: a withered old woman in a white apron and a droopy white wing hat. She whispered, "He's sleeping. Please don't waken him."

Tiptoeing in darkness across a huge bedroom that smelled of disease and liniment, they arrived at the head of the bed where Algernon Gray, the father of the family, lay awkwardly propped up, asleep. He was snoring quietly, as if he were at peace with the world.

What horrified Thomas, however, was that his face was crawling with maggots. They wriggled in and out of his nose, poured into his mouth and made his sparse white hair ripple as if it were being blown by an unfelt wind.

"He's very sick, you see," Maurice remarked with apparent unconcern, "and Mother's the same. But now that we have the portrait back, we can have it restored, and *they* will be restored along with it. Father and Mother, God bless them."

Thomas couldn't think of anything to say. He felt frightened, nauseous and desperately lonely. *This must be a dream, mustn't it? Please, somebody, tell me for sure!*

"It was your family, you see, the Pearsons, who caused all the problems," Maurice said, leading Thomas out of the room. "They were friends of the Grays in the eighteen nineties. They were always going to parties together, they were always going boating together. Your father's great-grandfather was always visiting at Wilderlings."

"He had *maggots*!" Thomas whispered in terrible awe.

Maurice squeezed his hand. "Maggots, yes. Maggots! But none of us are quite what we were. It's sad, isn't it; rather melancholy, when you come to think of it. I've often thought of writing poems about it, about the sadness of dying. But here, of course, we don't die—although we do spend more time than we ought to in keeping ourselves in condition."

They descended the main staircase and walked along the downstairs corridor into the kitchens. There was no one there at the moment. Copper pans hung shining in order of size; silver spatulas gleamed like fresh sardines hung up to dry.

"We were always a close family, you know," Maurice told Thomas, his face half-concealed by the hanging pans. "If one of us caught the flu, well then, we *all* caught the flu. Some diseases became quite admirable family occasions, a cause to celebrate: 'You'll never guess! Hooray! I think I've caught the German measles! Break out a bottle of Gewurztraminer!' "

Maurice hesitated and then said, more seriously, "Nowadays it is becoming harder and harder for us to survive. We are outcasts; we know that, even if other people have managed to accept us. Without the portrait, we were lost; we had no control over our destiny, but we have it back now, and we can restore ourselves."

Thomas obviously didn't understand. Maurice offered him a high-backed stool and leaned himself against the kitchen range, his arms crossed, and said, "We wanted youth. What was so terrible about that? We wanted to stay as we were: young and bright and joyful. And we did. It was only when your great-grandfather intervened that we began to suffer. He stole the portrait and kept it under lock and key; and then he sent us to Europe as exiles. That was in nineteen eleven, a year that is yet to come in this portrait, and a year that never *will* come, because portraits stay as they were on the day they were painted. Young, vibrant and alive."

Maurice went through the cupboards and found a bottle of *kir*. He poured himself a small glass and knocked it back in one gulp.

"The portrait has to stay close to those who commissioned it, you see, because every now and then, to prevent ourselves from aging too drastically, we must return—*through the painting itself*—to the year in which it was painted. You might say it is like going to a health farm to be rejuvenated. As years go by, as we grow farther and farther away from the day when we *should* have died, our strength grows weaker and our youthful appearance begins to need some attention.

"Everything went well until your great-grandfather stole the portrait. Then we had to rely for our survival not on revisiting the portrait itself, as we had before, but on changing skin every two or three months to keep ourselves presentable to the outside world. Many innocent people died because of that need; we killed them; but I lay the blame for each of those deaths firmly at the Pearson family door. If the Pearsons hadn't meddled, the Grays might very well have hurt no one, offended no one, and remained *la crème de la crème* of Connecticut society."

Maurice rubbed his forehead with his fingertips in a gentle, circular motion as if he were beginning to feel the first pangs of a migraine. "The portrait is essential to our survival. To disappear inside it, each of has to physically touch his or her own image on it. And, amazing, here we are! Sitting in the kitchen, talking to each other, in eighteen eighty-three. But you're young. You must be getting bored. All this talk of rejuvenation, influenza and the sadness of lives that have long outlived their usefulness. No wonder God sends us down to earth for such a short time! Nobody is capable of making decent conversation."

Thomas said, "I want to go home."

"My dear fellow," Maurice told him, "from now on, this *is* home. At least for as long as I say so. You have no other way of getting back except through me, so you had better accept it and be nice. If you weren't here, your father would probably set fire to our portrait and burn us alive; but you are here, and so is Laura—and, well, we're quite reasonably protected, wouldn't you say? Hm?"

"I thought you had killed Laura," Thomas said.

"Killed her, my friend? Certainly not; although she does have certain drastic decisions to make about her life, as do the rest of us."

"Such as?"

Maurice smiled smugly. "She has to decide whether she wants to be Henry's servant for the rest of her life, which is almost immortal, or whether she wishes to sacrifice her skin to save my mother from losing her looks altogether."

"That's all she can choose? That's terrible! That's exploitation!"

"And this is eighteen eighty-three, my dear boy, before the word exploitation was in common currency, especially among boys your age. My God, you're a do-gooder, aren't you? Just like your father."

Maurice stroked Thomas's hair, but Thomas jerked his head away. "Let's go find Laura," Maurice suggested. "It might be amusing to see what Henry has in store for her today. Do you want to come? Or do you want to sit here all day and sulk?"

Maurice left the kitchen and walked through to the music room. Thomas felt he had no alternative but to follow. He was conscious that the air in the house was strangely hazy, as if everything were filtered through the finest of muslins. There was a music box playing somewhere, some long-forgotten tune; and he could hear a woman singing:

> *And should you gather lilies*
> *Beside the sliding stream;*
> *And should you breathe the perfume there*
> *In times that make you dream. . . .*

In the music room, Henry was sitting at the piano, his hair tousled, a black Russian *papirosi* cigarette dangling unlit between his lips. He was wearing full morning dress, complete with gray silk tie, although he had taken off his coat and hung it over the back of the chair. He wasn't playing the piano; he was only staring at the sheet music, a complicated piece by Chopin, a black forest of semiquavers.

Laura was sitting in a small upholstered armchair, her hands in her lap, rigid and silent. As Thomas came into the room, she turned to look at him with liquid eyes made misty by the hazy atmosphere, but she said nothing. She was wearing a severe black floor-length dress, fastened in the front with scores of tiny black buttons.

"Well, cousin," Henry said disconsolately, "what is the grand decision?"

Maurice systematically clicked his knuckles and looked around with that pained James Mason expression of his. "I don't think there has ever been any serious dispute about it, Henry. The girl must go to Mother."

"Tomorrow, I suppose?"

"Tomorrow is Christmas Day. I hardly wish to—"

Henry played a series of chords. "Of course not, Maurice. I know how delicate your stomach is. And since it would be better for Mother to have her sooner rather than later—"

"Yes, well, this afternoon would be suitable," Maurice said.

Henry spun around on the piano stool and said loudly to Laura, "Do you hear that, my angel? This afternoon you are to be skinned! All for the sake of Maurice's mother, who is not very well."

Thomas stared at Laura in horror, but she remained expressionless. Maurice laid his hand on Thomas's shoulder, patted it and said, "It is a wonderful thing, you know, regeneration. In addition to saving my mother's life, Laura will live again, in her. We are always very grateful."

Henry took out a box of matches and lit his cigarette. There was a sharp smell of burned sulphur and Balkan tobacco. "Maurice considers his gratitude to be reward enough for anything. You may die in agony, but as long as Maurice is grateful, what of it?"

"Come now," Maurice said to Thomas. "We have a fascinating library upstairs. Perhaps you would like to while away the afternoon by the fire and read some encyclopedias. Then we shall ask cook to bring us some crumpets, which we shall toast and eat with plenty of butter and jam."

There was nothing Thomas could say or do. Frightened and meek, he allowed Maurice to guide him out of the music room and up the stairs.

"You mustn't be concerned for your own safety," Maurice said as they walked along the landing. "Now that we have the portrait back, we need to restore ourselves only once. That means we need only one more gentleman for Father, and possibly one more young lady for my sister Cordelia. It isn't *really* necessary for Cordelia to have anybody else, but she is so vain about her appearance!"

Just as Thomas and Maurice went into the library and closed the door, the front door of the house opened cautiously and Vincent stepped in. It was warm in the hallway; the snowflakes on his shoulders died almost immediately. He hesitated and listened; he could tell by the crackling of the fires in every room, and by the aroma of tobacco and potpourri, that Dr. McKinnon's theory was correct and that he had actually managed to penetrate the creative existence of the Waldegrave portrait. There was an unusual quality to the air, and when he looked around the hallway, the furniture and the statues seemed distorted, as if he were seeing them through curved glass. The light was blurred, and the conversations he could hear sounded peculiarly flat. But apart from that, here was the house and here he was, and there was nothing to deny the "reality" of either of them.

There had been no sense of traveling in time or space when he had walked out the front door and into the garden. He had taken three or four paces, then turned around and walked back in.

Carefully he tiptoed his way across the hall until he reached the open doors of the music room. Henry was leaning against the keyboard of the piano, his back to Vincent, and Laura was standing by the window, staring out at the snow. Her hair had been brushed up Victorian style, and she was wearing tortoiseshell combs in it.

Vincent glanced behind him to make sure nobody else was around. He was breathing heavily with tension and determination. He loosened his necktie, then quietly tugged it off and wound the ends of it tightly around his hands, like a garrote.

Henry was saying, "Nobody knows what it was that Chopin saw in Konstancja Gladkowska. Why did he love her so much? Why didn't he marry her? And, of course, nobody can ask him now."

Vincent stepped boldly through the open doors of the music room, his necktie raised between his fists. At that moment Laura turned around from the window and saw him. She raised her hand to her mouth and stared at him in surprise.

"What's the matter with you?" Henry asked. "You look as if you've seen a ghost."

There was a moment when Vincent was sure Laura was about to point to him and give him away, and he was still too far from Henry to reach him before he could turn around to defend himself. But then Laura suddenly looked away and said, "It makes me sad, the story of Chopin."

"It makes you sad? What an extraordinary thing to say!" Henry exclaimed. He half-rose off the piano stool, but then he sat back down and that was when Vincent came up close behind him and whipped the necktie around his throat.

Henry lurched sideways. The piano stool crashed to the parquet floor. Henry twisted and struggled, and he was strong. Vincent could feel the muscles in Henry's shoulders straining against his thighs. But Vincent wrenched at the necktie with all the strength he could manage and kept his grip relentlessly tight, knowing that if he loosened it or let go, he was finished.

Henry roared and gargled, his neck bulging, his face crimson, his eyes protruding. He thrashed his legs, trying to lash out behind him so he could knock Vincent off his feet. His gray pumps scrabbled and clattered at the floor. But Vincent tugged tighter still, grunting with the effort of it, and pressed his knee forcibly into the middle of Henry's back to prevent him from rising.

Abruptly Henry began to cough up maggots. Small bursts of them at first, scattering across the floor, twisting and writhing. But then his whole body convulsed, and he collapsed, facedown, and Vincent prayed that he had finished him off. There seemed to be no substance to Henry now; his body was little more than a skeleton, flaccidly draped in fine, pale skin. The maggots began to crawl away from him, abandoning their host and home, presumably seeking someone else's body to occupy. Vincent brushed half a dozen of them off his hands and out of his sleeve; he had to shake his necktie two or three times to get the last of them off.

"Laura," he said, crossing the room and taking her hand. "Laura, it's Vincent Pearson. Don't you remember me? Vincent Pearson. I own the gallery where Edward used to work."

"Edward . . ." Laura murmured.

Vincent said urgently, "You have to get out of here, Laura. They intend to kill you. Laura, listen to me!"

"Is Edward here?" she asked vaguely. She frowned at him as if she found it difficult to focus on his face.

"Edward—Edward is outside," Vincent told her with sudden inspiration. "Come on, quickly, and I'll take you to him."

Doubtfully, dragging her silk-slippered feet, she allowed him to tug her out of the music room and into the hallway. He opened the front door for her and said, "There! Just outside! Hurry, or you might miss him!"

"But it's cold out there," Laura protested. "It's cold and it's snowing. And anyway, Henry said I wasn't to go anywhere. Henry said—"

Vincent took hold of her wrists and dragged her out onto the porch. "He's over there!" he screamed at her. "Go and find him!"

Confused, shivering, rubbing her wrists, Laura stepped out into the snow. At first Vincent was frightened that nothing would happen, that there was no way for them to escape from the painting. But as Laura walked out across the garden, her black dress began to fade to gray and then to look almost transparent. Within a matter of moments, she had vanished;

there was nothing to show she had been there except for the tracks of her slippers, suddenly disappearing into nothing.

Now Vincent had to look for Thomas. He went back into the house and began to open doors, one after the other, searching for his son. He looked into the music room again, but it was empty. Most of the maggots had crawled away and were teeming into the hems of the velvet drapes for warmth. He tried the kitchen, but that too was deserted. Then he suddenly burst into the morning room, where he came face-to-face with Willa and her daughters, and the crippled Netty.

Willa screamed, "Who are *you?* How dare you come trespassing into our house!"

Vincent hesitated. These were girls, after all; children; and one of them was crippled. But he knew what he was here for: to destroy the Grays, completely. The continuing lives of these girls had been bought with the flayed skins of other children, God only knew how many over the years. They had lived three times as long as they should have in any case, and at what cost to their victims. Hours of agony, days of fear, not even a consecrated grave. Their victims' spirits were still trapped at Wilderlings, waiting for release, and they would reach the next life only when the Grays themselves were dead.

Vincent went a little mad. It had to be done, but he could do it only in a fit of righteous hysteria, when his natural sense of justice and mercy was blotted out by fiery, red-eyed rage. He picked up the heavy brass-knobbed poker beside the fire, and with a single swing, he hit Willa in the side of the head, just above the ear where her lacy bonnet was tied. Then he hit her again as she fell, this time at the back of the neck; even if she wasn't dead, she would never walk again.

The girls screamed. Netty clutched at her mahogany wheelchair in terror, shaking her head from side to side. Emily and Ermintrude tried to hide behind the curtains, but Vincent struck at the folds again and again until Emily dropped into sight, concussed, and Ermintrude fell to her knees begging for mercy.

Somehow Vincent managed to kill them. Such an act of violence was completely out of character for him. But he was determined, and he knew there was nothing left to do. It was like clubbing seals. Ermintrude knelt in front of him, and he beat her twice so that her skull broke. Netty he dragged from the wheelchair and threw facedown on the floor, hitting her as hard as he could on the back of the head until she jerked and lay still. Blood and lace-trimmed Victorian dresses were strewn everywhere, like the casualty ward of a doll's hospital. Willa groaned and lifted one hand, embellished with diamond rings. Then the hand dropped limply.

Vincent stood in the doorway, his chest heaving. My God, he thought, I've killed them all. But just suppose this *isn't* some other reality; suppose I've gone crazy and just *think* it is. Suppose these were all ordinary, innocent girls, and I've cudgeled them all to death.

He didn't have long to wait, though, before the proof appeared that he was justified and that he was not deranged. The girls' skirts and pantaloons began to stir and ripple, as if the girls were waking up again. Their sleeves shifted; their petticoats rustled.

Vincent cautiously lifted Netty's body with the blackened tip of the poker, and there they were, in the thousands. The maggots that had infested the Gray family ever since the day the Grays should have died. Vincent retreated in disgust and closed the door behind him.

At the same moment, Cordelia appeared at the head of the staircase, in the act of powdering her face. She saw Vincent at once and snapped her compact shut.

"Maurice!" she called. She turned around and started to hurry along the landing. "Maurice! For God's sake, Maurice! Vincent Pearson is here! Maurice!"

Still brandishing the poker, Vincent ran across the hall and surged furiously up the stairs. As he reached the top, he was just in time to see the black hem of Cordelia's dress disappear into the library, like the fin of a vanishing shark. He jogged along the landing until he reached the library doors and then he stopped, listening. The last thing he wanted was to be caught by surprise, or to have Thomas hurt.

"Maurice Gray?" he called harshly.

There was no reply.

"Maurice Gray, this is Vincent Pearson. I want my son, Mr. Gray, and I want him now!"

He was just about to kick the library doors open when they were opened for him from inside, and Cordelia appeared. She stood white and silent, regarding him intently with eyes like mirrors.

"Where's my son?" Vincent demanded.

"Well, well," Cordelia said, stepping out onto the landing and circling around him. "So you're Vincent Pearson. So like your grandfather, you know. Both in looks and in moral recklessness. That is, you recklessly apply your morals to the lives of others, without a thought for the consequences."

Vincent raised the poker. "If you don't tell me where my son is, I'm going to kill you here and now."

Cordelia smiled with faultless frostiness. Then she opened the library doors a little wider. Vincent could see a fireplace, a hearthrug on which an encyclopedia lay, opened at a page about praying mantises, and a chair. Beyond the chair there was a paneled door, half ajar.

"Your son has gone on a journey with my brother Maurice. A fascinating journey to other lands! And I can promise you here and now, my dear, that you will never find him. You might as well resign yourself to returning to your own humdrum existence and to forgetting about the Grays forever."

Twenty-Eight

Darien, December 24

Vincent crossed the library and looked into the open door. Beyond it there was a narrow, spiral staircase.

"Where does this lead?"

"It leads to almost anywhere you wish," Cordelia said airily.

Without asking her anything else, Vincent went in through the door and rapidly began to descend the staircase. It was constructed of mahogany, beautifully carpentered, and it had obviously been intended to give the original master of the house a secret way out, perhaps from his creditors, or a secret way in, perhaps for his mistresses. It was dark and dry, and it smelled of furniture polish. Vincent remembered as he clattered down the stairs that this mid-Victorian house was only twenty or thirty years old in the alternative reality of the portrait.

There was a heavy door at the bottom of the staircase, and when he pushed it open, he found himself in the cellars. There were gas lamps burning, so Maurice Gray had obviously come down this way.

"Thomas!" Vincent called. "Thomas! Can you hear me, Thomas? It's Daddy! Thomas, shout if you can hear me!"

He waited and listened, but there was nothing. He walked swiftly along the central corridor that ran the length of the cellar, trying the doors, but all of them were locked. At last he reached the metal-clad door behind which the Grays' art collection was stored. It was open. Only a quarter of an inch, but it was open.

Vincent hefted the poker and warily stepped inside. It was

dark and cool and silent; all he could see was the faint gleaming of gilded frames.

"Thomas?" he whispered. "Thomas?"

At first there was no reply. But then he heard the smallest and faintest of voices; he knew at once that it was his son.

"Daddy. . . ." A voice so small it sounded as far away as the hum of the sea in a sea shell.

"Daddy . . . help me. . . ."

Vincent listened intently, but he couldn't tell where the calling came from. How could Thomas possibly sound so far away when the room was only thirty feet square? Unless— unless he wasn't in the room, not in the normal sense of the word. Because what had Cordelia said upstairs? "Your son has gone on a journey." And how could anybody go on a journey within the confines of this stone-built cellar unless he entered the paintings here, in the same way Vincent had entered *this* painting?

"Thomas!" Vincent shouted. "Thomas, can you hear me?"

"Faint . . ." came the reply.

Vincent searched furiously through stacks of canvases. "Thomas, give me a clue, for Christ's sake! Where are you? Thomas, where are you?"

"River . . ." Thomas called. "Reeds and grass and—"

It sounded as if Thomas had suddenly been cut short. Perhaps Maurice Gray had told him to stop shouting. River, thought Vincent desperately. River, reeds and grass. God Almighty, there were scores of landscapes here. He worked his way, sweating, through nearly twenty pictures, stacking them all to one side.

It was then that Thomas gave him a vital clue. In a voice so tiny it could have been nothing more than the settling of a fly on his shoulder, Vincent heard the words, "white . . . clock. . . ."

White clock. River, reeds and white clock. And there was only one painting that included all those characteristics as far as he could remember. "A View of Dennisburg," painted in 1854 by Charles K. Barraclough. It must have been sold by the Grays before they left Connecticut in 1911, because it was now on display at the Brightwell Gallery in Philadelphia. But this was 1883, and so the painting would still be here. Maybe

Maurice Gray had chosen to escape into it simply to confuse him.

Vincent found it easily. After all, Maurice Gray must have been in a hurry when he came down here. A large painting of the Heron River, bordered with reeds, and in the far distance, that distinctive white clock tower.

Vincent peered closely at the painting; there, on the bridge, hand in hand, he could make out the figures of a man and a boy, running.

Closing his eyes, he touched the surface of the painting with both hands. The paint was smooth and cool, still faintly aromatic. He didn't know whether it was necessary to recite the words of the Exorcism. If it was, he would have to go back into his own reality and get them. But he kept his eyes tightly shut and prayed to God that he could enter the painting; he thought of nothing else but saving Thomas. Surely that would be enough.

The painting began to feel rough, then dry, then stalky. Suddenly a wind was blowing, and there was the chafflike rustling of reeds. It was afternoon, in the springtime, and the sky was as clear as bright-blue glass. Vincent stood up, and he was knee-deep in grass by the eastern bank of the Heron River in Delaware, and there, not more than a quarter of a mile off, was the small shoreline town of Dennisburg, with its famous white clock tower and its clustered orange rooftops.

Seagulls wheeled and circled overhead, and there was a strong smell of salt in the air.

Vincent began to run. He was still clutching the brass-knobbed poker. His feet crackled through broken bracken, heaps of riverside shingle, and derelict herons' nests. It took him only five minutes to reach the white-painted wooden bridge, but by the time he got there, the man and the boy had gone. He crossed the river and walked along the boardwalk that lined the opposite bank. There were small, neat fishermen's cottages here, with yellow nasturtiums blowing in tubs, and nets hung up, and large zinc washbowls for cleaning fish.

An old woman in a white headscarf was leaning on her front fence. When she stared at Vincent openly, he realized he was something to be stared at, in his Bijan suit and his Turnbull & Asser shirt, carrying a long, brass poker.

"Did you see a man and a boy pass this way?" he asked the old woman.

"Where are *you* from?" she asked in return.

"New York. Did you see them?"

She pointed along the boardwalk. "Might have gone that way, if it's worth anything."

Vincent took out his wallet and gave her a dollar. He thought that five dollars might be rather too much in 1854. The old woman stared at the money, stared at him and then went back into her cottage so she could continue her staring through the window, from a safe distance.

Vincent continued along the boardwalk, which soon petered out into sand and grassy scrub. There was no sign of Thomas or Maurice Gray. But he kept on going until the ground began to rise into sand dunes and he could see the gray, glittering breast of the Atlantic Ocean off to his right. Near the horizon, a fishing smack leaned, its sails white and vibrant in the afternoon sunlight.

He topped one more sand dune and then he saw them, still hand in hand, hurrying along the shore. His heart expanded and adrenaline surged through his body. He recognized the color of Thomas's hair and that black-velvet Victorian suit the Grays had given him to wear.

Vincent was tempted to shout out, but he restrained himself. He jumped and bounded from one sand dune to the next, keeping low, ducking his head whenever he thought Maurice Gray might turn around. Soon he was almost abreast of them, leaping through the tufted seaside grass; and it was then that he broke cover and ran diagonally across the sand toward them, whirling the poker over his head so that it whistled, and at last screaming out, "Thomas! Thomas! It's Daddy!"

Thomas turned and immediately freed himself from Maurice Gray's grasp. He ran back toward his father, his arms and legs pumping, his face clenched in that furious sports-day expression of childish concentration.

Maurice Gray stood where he was, tall and dignified in morning dress, his spats stained dark with seawater, his gray hair lifted by the Atlantic wind.

"Well," he said, "my nemesis."

Vincent was too much out of breath to answer him, too furious, too crazy. Thomas stayed a little way behind him as he circled Maurice Gray, whirling the poker, listening to the way it whirred and whistled.

"Do you intend to strike me?" Maurice asked. He lifted his left wrist and carefully buttoned a gray-kid glove.

Vincent walked around Maurice, went behind his back. Maurice was just turning his head to see what he was doing when Vincent lashed him across the side of the neck, a blow so swift and furious it bent the shaft of the poker.

Maurice clapped his hand to his neck and murmured, "Good Lord," before falling to the sand, on his side. He lay there with his eyes open, not yet dead, while Vincent stood over him, still breathing hard.

"You'd better finish me off," Maurice said. "I can't stand to look at the sea from this point of view. It reminds me of how fragile we are."

Thomas looked away with his hands in his pockets, a gesture boys use to show their fathers they disapprove, and that they're frightened, and that they can't understand what's happening.

Vincent struck Maurice on the back of the head four times. It was probably three times more than necessary; but in Maurice's case, Vincent wanted to make absolutely sure his quarry was dead.

Maurice lay sprawled on the sand, his arms and legs twisted at ungainly angles. Blood seeped from his scalp and filled a small white cockleshell lying close beside him.

Vincent took hold of Thomas's hand and led him away quickly, along the shore. He didn't want Thomas to see the maggots that infested Maurice Gray's body come pouring out, although twenty yards along the beach, he glanced back himself to make sure they had. From this distance, they looked like nothing very much. Just as if somebody had spilled a sack of white rice across the sand.

Thomas said, "You killed him."

"Yes. I had to. He wasn't actually real. Not in the way we are."

"How do we get home?" Thomas asked.

Vincent squeezed his hand and smiled. "We keep our fingers crossed and say a prayer."

They walked back through the town, across the bridge and down through the reeds by the river. The old woman in the headscarf saw them pass her window, and out of curiosity, she followed them at a distance. She was standing on the bridge, shading her eyes against the sun, when they vanished from sight altogether, like ghosts. She had no way of telling that she herself existed only in a painting, which a hundred and thirty years later would hang on the wall of the Brightwell Gallery in Philadelphia.

Vincent and Thomas took one more step through the reeds, and the day began to fade, and grow darker; and, holding hands, they felt a strange sensation of sliding forward and down, as if they were descending a glacial escalator.

"We'll be safe now," Vincent told Thomas in a slow and fuzzy voice.

Quite suddenly, however, the day brightened again; and they found themselves walking along a brick-paved street. The houses were quite unfamiliar, with flat rendered facades and green-shuttered windows. There were church bells pealing somewhere, and dogs barking and, from somewhere close by, an extraordinary hollow clattering noise which sounded like hundreds of wooden spoons being rattled against the ground. Up above their heads, the clouds billowed as fulsomely as the sails of old-fashioned galleons, and the wind blew up dust and glittering specks of straw from the roadway.

"Where are we?" asked Thomas, frightened.

Vincent looked around. There was a butcher's shop across the street, with huge orange skinned ox carcasses hanging outside on hooks. The sign above the shop announced *Vleeswaren*, in faded gold letters. "That's Dutch," said Vincent. "We must have come the wrong way."

Thomas anxiously tugged his head. "Don't let's go on; let's go back."

"Thomas," Vincent told him, "I don't know how to go back. Don't you realize what this is? This is another painting."

"But if we walk back to where we came into it?"

"We walked back to where we came into the Dennisburg painting, didn't we? And all that did was to bring us here. Maybe if we can find out what picture this is, that might help."

Two nuns with white-winged wimples came bustling along the street toward them. As the nuns approached Vincent went up to them, and called, "Pardon me, sisters. Could you give me some directions, please?"

They stopped, and stared at him in perplexity. One of them

had the pale oval face of a saint, as pretty as a religious effigy. The other was blind in one eye, and had lips that were deformed into a permanent snarl.

"*Parlez-vous francais*?" asked Vincent.

"*Oui, monsieur*. Do you need assistance?"

"My son and I, we're lost. I wonder if you could tell us what town this is?"

"Leiden, monsieur. Is there anything else?"

"Yes. Do you know of any painters who live here, any artists?"

"*Non, monsieur*. Only the monks."

Vincent said, "You're very kind. Could you do one more thing for me?"

"Of course, *monsieur*."

"Could you please tell me what year this is?"

"*Quelle année*?" the snarling nun asked him, suspiciously. She was evidently beginning to believe that he was a lunatic, especially since he was dressed in such a peculiar way.

But the pretty nun said gently, "This is 1631, *monsieur*," and lowered her eyes bashfully, and hurried her sister away.

Vincent stood where he was, his hand pressed against the side of his neck as if he were trying to stem the flow of blood from an artery. Thomas stood watching him, biting his lips.

"My God," said Vincent at last. "Sixteen thirty-one. That means that Rembrandt is still alive; although I don't remember Rembrandt ever having painted anything like this. Besides, I don't think the Grays ever *owned* a Rembrandt."

"What are we going to do?" Thomas asked him miserably.

"I think the best thing we can do is take a look around. Now listen, don't panic. Don't get upset. We've got each other, haven't we? And we've beaten the Grays. All we have to do is work out a way to get back."

They turned the corner of the street; and they saw then what was causing the clattering noise. There was a market in the town's main square, with scores of stalls under flapping white awnings; and it was the wooden clogs of all the shoppers and the stallholders and the running children that was setting up the noise.

Cautiously, doing their best not to attract attention, Vincent and Thomas walked through the market. There were stalls heaped with shining yellow cheeses; fish stalls, with smoked herring and pickled elver; bread stalls, with coarse brown loaves as large as wheels. Most of the stallholders wore leather caps or headscarves, and long leather jerkins; but there were a few more elegantly dressed men around the square, with wide-brimmed hats, and cloaks, and calf-britches. Vincent was struck by the dullness of the women's dresses, in faded pinks and dusty browns, and remembered that the dyestuffs available to fabric-makers in 1631 were very limited.

The aroma of the cheeses and the smell of the fish blew through the marketplace on the afternoon wind. Vincent found it strange that nobody in the marketplace seemed to be talking, or crying out their wares, in spite of the fact that their clogs were making so much noise. It was almost as if they were miming the parts of the seventeenth-century Dutch townspeople, and Vincent found their silence extremely disquieting.

They had nearly reached the brick-fronted town hall when they were hailed by an ugly-looking man in a brown cape and lopsided leather cap. He walked directly up to them, and dragged off his cap, and bowed impudently low.

"What is it?" asked Vincent.

"Yoop thar," the man grinned at them.

"What?" asked Vincent. "*Parlez-vous francais?*"

"Nee, nee," the man replied, shaking his tangled curls. "Yoop thar." And he pointed to a second-story window, at the left of one of the houses that fronted the square. A yellow-washed house, with leaded lights, and numbers announcing that it had been built in 1611.

Vincent frowned at the house; and, as he did so, he saw a hand waving at the window.

"Yoop thar," the leather-capped man repeated, and beckoned Vincent with a hand that had lost two of its fingers. "Kom, kom, yoop thar."

"He means 'up there,'" Vincent told Thomas. "He wants us to go with him."

"Kom, kom," the fellow insisted.

But Vincent raised both hands. "We don't know anybody here. We're strangers. Do you understand that? We don't know that man, whoever he is. You're making a mistake."

"Winson?" the fellow demanded, pointing at Vincent. "You Winson?"

"That's right, I'm Vincent. But how on earth did you know that? And who's that, up there at the window?"

"Kom," the fellow repeated.

Vincent shrugged. "We don't seem to have any alternative. Let's go see who it is."

They followed the leather-capped man along by the town-hall steps, and across the side street that led to the yellow house. The fellow opened the front door for them, and ceremoniously waved them inside with his cap. Vincent kept his hand on Thomas's shoulder, and stepped carefully into the hallway.

The interior of the house was dark and musty. Through a side doorway, Vincent could see a young woman with an embroidered bonnet, sitting at a desk, sewing. A small songbird chirruped in a cage on the wall beside her. The scene reminded him strongly of an interior by Vermeer; but the nuns had told him that this was Leiden, not Delft, where Vermeer had lived; and again he doubted whether the Grays had been sufficiently wealthy to own any Vermeers.

They crossed the black-and-white tiled hallway, and the fellow in the leather cap hopped ahead of them upstairs. The staircase was solid oak, heavy, and carved with fruit. Their feet sounded flatly on the bare oak treads. At the top, there was an oval window, through which Vincent could see the branches of trees waving in the wind, like swimmers waving for help.

They were guided along the shadowy upstairs landing, until they reached a doorway at the very end of the house. The leather-capped man knocked on it loudly, and then opened it for them. "Kom," he nodded.

Vincent and Thomas entered the room. It was whitewashed, low-ceilinged, with diamond-leaded windows looking out over the wind-flapped awnings of the marketplace. The floor was polished oak. There was a desk, with an upright chair, and a silver inkwell with a plumed pen standing in it, as if somebody had recently been writing, although there was no paper there.

By the window, against the light, stood a tall figure in a hooded brown velvet robe. He was standing at a three-quarter angle away from them, so it was impossible for them to see who he was. He was very softly humming a tune, which Vincent did not recognize. It sounded repetitive, and medieval, one of those quaint songs about the harvest, or the fish, or the cow that never gave milk.

"You sent your man for us," said Vincent in a strained voice.

There was a moment's silence, and then the hooded figure nodded, and said, "Indeed I did." Its words were very indistinct, as if it were speaking with its mouth full.

"I don't think it's impertinent of me to ask who you are, and why you want to see us," said Vincent.

"Of course not," the figure replied. "But I would have thought that my identity was self-evident."

The figure turned, and drew off its hood. Thomas screamed in terror.

It was Maurice Gray, still alive, but with his gray scalp clustered with clots of drying blood, and with maggots teeming around the neck of his robe, and around his hairline, and dropping from the corners of his mouth. His eyes—which had always looked mirrorlike, and dark—now gleamed silver, as if they had been filled up to the brim with mercury.

Vincent seized Thomas's arm and made for the door; but the leather-capped man was waiting for them, grinning at them with a mouthful of rotting stumps, holding up a large bladed cleaver. He swung the cleaver around, from side to side, and cackled.

Maurice took two or three heavy-footed steps toward them. A maggot squeezed out from between his lips, and tumbled onto his cloak.

"I killed you," Vincent insisted. "I killed you on the beach at Dennisburg."

Maurice smiled, and said, almost indulgently, "Would that you had. But I am the inheritor of everything which the Grays have stood for, these past eighty years. The strength of the family is invested in me, Mr. Pearson, and I am a difficult man to dispose of."

He raised one hand. "Do you like this painting? I must say that I have always rather cared for it myself, despite the dullness of its subject matter. It was painted in 1631 by Gerard Dou, who was a pupil of Rembrandt. A most meticulous painter, something of a forerunner to Vermeer. The quality of the light is so interesting, don't you think?"

Vincent said, "All we want to do is get out of here."

Maurice stared at him with those blank silvery eyes. "The Pearsons have been the curse of my family ever since we met. You don't seriously believe that I am going to let you escape? You can stay here forever; that's probably the punishment most appropriate for a pretentious art dealer like you. Trapped in a seventeenth-century townscape of unsurpassed dullness."

He paused, and brushed maggots from his collar. "Better still, perhaps, I should have you hacked to death by my friend here, and fed to the dogs of Leiden."

Vincent took a step toward the man in the leather cap. He glanced at Maurice, and then he glanced toward Thomas.

"Thomas," he said, in a level voice. "Do you remember the old one-two?"

"What?" asked Thomas, petrified by Maurice's grisly appearance.

"The old one-two, Thomas. You remember. Back on the lawn at Candlemas."

Thomas turned and stared at him. Vincent wasn't at all sure that he understood.

"The boy is justifiably frightened," said Maurice smoothly. "Death, after all, is very greatly to be feared; wouldn't you say?"

But Vincent immediately swung backward catching the man in the leather cap by surprise. He seized the fellow's grimy wrist in both hands, banging his hand against the side of the door. The man dropped his cleaver. Vincent pushed him backward; and just as he did so, Thomas dived onto his knees, and crouched over, and the old one-two, and the man stumbled over him and fell flat on his back on the floor.

Vincent picked up the cleaver. He brandished it at Maurice Gray; and Maurice instinctively raised both arms above his head to protect himself.

"*Dad! No! Dad! You can't!*" Thomas shouted hysterically. But fiercely and blindly, Vincent chopped down at Maurice's arms, feeling the heavy metal blade strike soft decaying tissue, then bone. He struck again and again, until fragments of flesh and velvet began to fly around the room in a storm. There was scarcely any blood; only a kind of dark glutinous treacle, which stuck to the blade of the cleaver with every stroke.

Maurice soundlessly fell on to his knees. His mutilated arms dropped to his sides. Now Vincent chopped into the back of his skull, severing his ears, half-scalping him, leaving his head looking as if it had been flayed, and torn at by animals.

He would have hacked him into pieces, but Thomas held on to his arm, and shrieked at him, "*Stop! Stop! You've killed him! You've killed him! Dad! Stop. Dad, you've killed him!*"

Vincent at last threw down the cleaver, and stood staring at his son like the lunatic which the nuns had believed him to be. The man in the leather cap cowered in the far corner of the room, and when Vincent looked toward him, he tugged his cap right down over his forehead, and stammered, "Nee, nee, nee!"

The body of Maurice Gray collapsed sideways onto the floor; his silver eyes wide open. The shoulders of his gown began to stir, as the maggots poured out of him. Vincent held up his hands and stared at them. He had never hurt anybody before today. Now he was a wholesale killer.

"Dad, come on, let's go, Dad," Thomas begged him.

Vincent nodded, and followed his son into the corridor. He was so dazed by what he had done that he scarcely noticed the subtle transition from daytime to night; and that suddenly the corridor wasn't boarded beneath their feet, but carpeted, and that there were flickering blue-gray lights up ahead, and the booming of unfamiliar voices.

"Where are we?" Thomas asked him, and reached out to take hold of his hand.

Vincent stared into the darkness, willing his eyes to become accustomed to it. He could see a narrow entrance up ahead, partly draped by red curtains. He thought he could see somebody standing there, a woman perhaps, although she was wearing trousers. The lights kept shifting and flickering, and the booming voices continued. There was a strong smell of cigarette smoke in the air.

"This is a movie theater," Vincent told Thomas. "Maybe we're back in the present. Come on, let's take a look."

They walked the length of the corridor, until they reached the auditorium. It was a big shabby New York movie theater, with garish yellow walls and peach-colored lights. Under the lamps stood a blonde-haired usherette in a blue pants suit, studiously picking at the two-day-old nail-varnish on her fingers. She looked up at them as they came in, and said, "Tickets?"

Vincent pretended to search in his pockets, taking the opportunity to look around. He could see by the way that the audience was dressed that this wasn't the present day. The men wore coats with wide lapels, and the women mostly seemed to have dresses and jackets with shoulder pads. Nineteen-forties, maybe; or late 1930's. The movie that was flickering on the screen confirmed it. Robert Donat, in *Goodbye, Mr. Chips*. As far as Vincent could recall, that was 1939, the same year that *Gone With the Wind* had won the Oscar for best picture.

"Do you have a ticket or dontcha?" the usherette wanted to know.

"Well, I think I must have dropped it," said Vincent. He laid his hand on Thomas's shoulder. "I'll go back and see if I can find it."

They walked back along the corridor and up the stairs. Thomas asked fearfully, "Do you know where we are?"

"It looks very much like 'New York Movie.' That was a painting by Edward Hopper, 1939."

"But how do we get out of it?" Thomas begged.

"I don't know. But the Grays did it; and so there has to be a way."

They reached the theater lobby. It was night-time outside; and through the gleaming windows of the theater, Vincent could see a busy New York street crowded with Hudsons and Plymouths and Packards. The lobby was almost deserted, except for the girl in the box office, counting out the money she had taken, and two spotty young men smoking cigarettes and waiting for their dates to come out of the restrooms.

"What do we do now?" asked Thomas.

Vincent was about to suggest that they take a walk along the street outside when the red-painted door marked *Theater Manager* opened up, and a young man with a short haircut stepped out, and said, "Mr. Pearson?"

Vincent stopped, and squeezed Thomas's hand. "What is it?" he asked sharply. "How do you know who I am?"

"I wonder if you would step into the manager's office for a moment, sir?"

"I don't think that I care to, thank you."

The young man smiled. "The manager could assist you, I think. You *are* looking for a way out?"

Vincent hesitated. Then he said, carefully, "Yes."

"In that case, sir, please step this way."

Reluctantly, Vincent followed the young man into the manager's office. There was a wide veneered desk, and a row of pens, and an empty leather-backed chair. On the wall were twenty or thirty signed photographs of the stars.

"The manager will be right with you, sir, if you don't mind waiting."

The door closed behind them and Vincent and Thomas stood in the office in silence, feeling lost and desperate and tense.

"Do you really think that the manager might be able to help us?" asked Thomas.

Vincent shrugged. "I haven't any idea. I don't even see why he should be interested. A movie theater manager? But, well, I don't know—it seems like life inside these paintings has a different kind of logic from ordinary life. Did you notice how quiet all those people in that Dutch marketplace were? None of them spoke. Maybe it's something to do with the way the artist painted them."

They were still waiting when the lights in the office suddenly went out, and they were plunged into total darkness. Vincent groped behind him for the door handle, but when he jerked it down, he discovered that it was locked. Thomas said, "Dad— where are you? Dad!"

"Hold on," Vincent reassured him. "Let me just find the lightswitch."

He felt his way awkwardly along the wall, but he couldn't locate a lightswitch anywhere. He touched the manager's collection of framed photographs, and they clattered loudly in the darkness.

Thomas said worriedly, "Dad—are you okay?"

"I will be, as soon as I can find the lights."

They heard the key turn in the lock. Both of them froze, and held their breath. The door handle squeaked, and then the door swung open.

"Oh, my God," Vincent whispered.

Silhouetted in the doorway was a tall figure dressed in what looked like a tuxedo. Vincent could just make out the gleam of his shirt front. A smartly dressed movie-theater manager, in charge of a movie theater that existed only in a painting. He lifted his hands, and tugged his cuff.

"You're the manager?" Vincent asked him.

The figure stepped forward. "I am many things, my friend. I play many parts. Today, I am playing the role of the vengeful pursuer. An intriguing role, that of the vengeful pursuer, wouldn't you say?"

The lights abruptly blinked on; and Thomas gasped in shock. The movie theater manager was Maurice Gray. All that remained of his hair were a few bloody tufts. His hands, in spite of his immaculate cuffs, were chopped raw. And he crawled with maggots, everywhere. Even as Vincent stared at him in utter horror, they were devouring the scarlet scraps of flesh that still clung to Maurice's cheekbones.

Maurice Gray advanced toward them. His eyes were blank, as if he could no longer feel anything or think anything. "The vengeful pursuer," he said; he reached into his inside pocket, and with a theatrical gesture, produced a surgical scalpel. "Have you seen what one of these can do to human flesh? It can slice through to your liver without your feeling it. It can take off your face just like that, and leave it lying on the floor."

He took another step forward. Vincent, tugging Thomas's arm, retreated around the desk.

"You cannot escape me," Maurice whispered. "You cannot escape me, even in Hell."

Vincent seized the arms of the leather-backed chair, hefted it up over his head, and threw it as hard as he could, straight at Maurice's chest. Maurice staggered, and then stumbled. Vincent vaulted over the desk, and kicked out at him, sending him sprawling. Maurice flailed at him with the scalpel, cutting open the side of his shoe; but Vincent kicked him again, in the ribs. Maurice coughed maggots. Vincent picked up the fallen chair, held it up for a moment, and then slammed it down with a sickening crack on Maurice's head. Maurice's skull broke open like a china jug, and for one terrible moment the shattered pieces boiled with maggots.

Vincent stepped back, breathing harshly.

"Is he really dead now?" Thomas asked him.

Vincent desperately shook his head. "I hope so. God almighty, I hope so."

It was then, however, that he became aware of another figure standing in the doorway. She was slender, and elegant, and dressed in black. Her face was even more luminous than usual.

It was Cordelia Gray; and she stepped into the room with all the elegance of a Connecticut thoroughbred.

"You have destroyed my brother at last," she said in a sibilant whisper. "Perhaps you are feeling proud of your-selves."

She knelt down, and touched Maurice's shoulder. "He was a man of great breeding, you know. I don't think you really understand what you've done."

Vincent said, "This is the finish of it, Miss Gray. We want to get out of this picture, and back to reality."

"Reality? You deserve to stay here forever, for what you have done."

Vincent grasped her wrist, and wrenched it around. "You're going to show us how to get out of here, and that's all."

He had never felt a wrist so brittle, and so thin. He felt as if he could snap it, with one twist of his hand. But Cordelia Gray stared at him in absolute contempt.

"You may release me," she said.

Vincent shook his head. "Not until you take us back."

"I refuse to take you back."

"Do you want me to break your arm?"

"Will you let go of me? If you don't let go of me, I'll—" Cordelia shook herself loose, and stood up, and just when Vincent thought she was going to say something, she wrenched open the office door, and hurried away across the lobby.

"Quick!" Vincent urged Thomas.

Together, they ran across the lobby, and out through the shiny glass doors. They found themselves out on the street, on a warm evening in New York City, in early fall, with the cars honking and the sirens wailing and the sidewalks clamorous with shoppers and sightseers and home-going stenographers.

Vincent glimpsed a black figure, stalking toward Thirty-sixth and Fifth. "There!" he said, and began to jog after her. Side by side, he and Thomas ran across the Avenue of the Americas, rousing a battery of car horns; but they managed to keep Cordelia Gray in sight. They ran through the acrid smoke of bagel stands, jostled past shoppers, pushed aside beggars and street musicians and news hawkers. Up above them, the lighted mosaic of the Empire State Building shone through the clouds. But all the time, urgent as a sewing-machine bobbin, the black figure of Cordelia Gray pushed her way through the crowds.

On the corner of Thirty-eighth Street, Vincent was almost run over by a brand-new 1939 model DeSoto Custom S6. The driver wound down his window, and yelled at him, "What are you, dreaming?"

But as they approached Thirty-ninth Street, Vincent caught up with Cordelia, and seized hold of her arm.

"Let go of me!" she breathed furiously. "You've killed my brother, isn't that enough?"

"Take us back," Vincent demanded. "Take us back, before I twist your goddamned arm off."

"You haven't even worked it out yet, have you?" Cordelia mocked him. "You're like an infant. You can't even do it for yourself."

"Miss Gray, you're going to take us back," Vincent threatened her.

"My dear man, you can do it for yourself. This is your spirit, not your body. Instead of rushing from one painting to another, all you have to do is close your eyes and realize that you're back; and then you will be."

"I want you back with me."

"How can I guarantee that? And why should I guarantee anything?"

"Because I'm going to keep hold of your arm, and I'm not going to let you go."

"You're a swine, Mr. Pearson. A swine of the very first order."

Without any warning, the New York sidewalk vanished from under their feet and they were standing isolated in a hot and glaring desert, with strange constructions of wood leaning on the horizon.

Melting sluglike creatures slid all around them; and cannon barked and banged like dogs. Vincent recognized an allegorical painting by Salvador Dali; but, almost as soon as he did so, they were pitching on the deck of a sailing ship, in mid-Pacific, with the wind screaming through the rigging and the timbers growling beneath their feet.

"*Dad!*" shouted Thomas, clinging on to his arm.

Vincent knew then that Cordelia was playing with him; that she was showing him just how much of an innocent he was. He gripped Thomas's hand, and closed his eyes, and thought to himself, *This must stop. We're not really here at all. We're back in Connecticut, in our own time, in our own reality, and this is nothing more than sorcery.*

His face was lashed with freezing spray. The ship heeled and tossed; its decks running with foam, its halyards cracking, and then suddenly he was deluged with icy cold water. But it was stagnant water, cold and still; and when he opened his eyes and saw the murky gray outlines of bobbing bodies, he realized with a paralyzing shock that he was down at the bottom of the ornamental pond at Wilderlings, surrounded by the fleshly remains of all the Grays.

He broke the surface, rearing out of the slush like a sea lion, gasping for air; and right beside him, Thomas surfaced, too. Shouting, shivering, he waded over to Thomas with the bodies of the Grays bumping and nudging his legs. He seized his son in both arms, and lifted him out of the water, onto the snowy bank; and then heaved himself out.

The sky was dark now, and the first few whirls of another storm were beginning. They took three or four paces across the lawn, and then, shaking and trembling, scarcely able to articulate, Vincent said, "We're back, damn it! At least we *should* be back."

As if to reassure him, a 737 thundered overhead, its lights flashing, making its first approach to Bridgeport airfield. "We're back," said Vincent triumphantly. "Now, let's go on in, and burn that goddamned picture."

They waded through foot-deep snow, until they reached the house. Then they pushed open the back door, and walked through to the hall. Their shoes were filled with freezing water, and they squelched as they walked.

"We're here!" Vincent shouted. "We've done it! We've made it!"

They walked straight into the music room; but the *tableau vivant* that met their eyes had obviously been especially prepared for them only moments before. Charlotte and Aaron were there, one at each end of one of the Gray's old sofas. Laura Monblat was there, looking shocked and shaken, but alert. But none of them smiled when Vincent and Thomas came in through the door, nor raised their hands in welcome. Because Cordelia Gray was there, too, locked in what looked like an unholy embrace with Jack Smith, her black gown clinging wetly to her body, water running all around her high-heeled shoes; her hand holding a shining surgical scalpel up to Jack's throat.

Vincent quietly told Thomas, "Stay well back. Don't say anything." Then he stepped into the middle of the hallway and confronted Cordelia, his hands on his hips.

"It's all finished," he told Cordelia. "Thomas and Laura are back with us, here. You have no hostages. We can destroy the portrait, and you with it, any time we want to."

Cordelia visibly shuddered.

Vincent approached her and held out his hand. "Your family tried to do something humanly impossible, Miss Gray. I think you have to recognize that it's all over now. Would you please give me that knife?"

"And what do you intend to do with me?" she asked sharply. "Beat me to death, the way you beat all my poor young cousins to death? Strangle me, the way you did Henry?"

Vincent said, "I think you should remember what you and your family have been doing in order to stay alive for so long."

Jack said to Cordelia, "If you give evidence, you could wind up with twenty years inside, nothing more. With remission, that could be ten."

"Give me the knife," Vincent said.

Cordelia shook her head. "You have killed my brother, Mr. Pearson. You have murdered my cousins. A poor little crippled girl, her head crushed! I refuse to submit to your vigilante justice, any more than I intend to submit to your ridiculous twenty-year sentence! Should I *thank* you for that?"

Vincent walked across to the Waldegrave portrait. Cordelia watched him carefully, her scalpel still shimmering a quarter inch from Jack's Adam's apple. Jack said anxiously, "Vincent—will you please not do anything rash? I think this lady means what she says."

Vincent reached into his vest pocket and produced a small silver penknife, the one he used for probing into layers of canvas and paint. He opened out the blade and held its point a fraction of an inch from Cordelia's painted face.

"If you so much as scratch Sheriff Smith, Miss Gray, I will have no hesitation at all in sticking this knife into your portrait. And you know what *that* will do to you, don't you?"

Cordelia was silent for a second and then she laughed out loud: high and brittle, like breaking glass.

"Yes, I do, Mr. Pearson—but do you know what it will do to *you*?"

"She's bluffing," Charlotte said under her breath. "What does she mean?"

"I'm not so sure," Aaron said. "Hear her out."

With supreme satisfaction, Cordelia said, "You have probably asked yourself, Mr. Pearson, why your grandfather didn't destroy the Waldegrave portrait. After all, he may have been an honorable man, but he was also a moral man, a man of considerable social conscience, and you know what they say about promises made to murderers and thieves—one almost has a duty to break them. With one match, he could have obliterated all of us."

Vincent said nothing, but his hand began to waver over the portrait of Cordelia, and he glanced toward Charlotte anxiously.

"Similarly," Cordelia went on, "you have probably asked yourself why my father Algernon was prepared to leave the Waldegrave portrait in your grandfather's custody, knowing that the fate of himself, his wife and his family was in the hands of somebody else. Don't you think he should have fought your grandfather a little harder? Why did he agree to go into exile with such comparative meekness?"

"I think you'd better say what you have to say," Vincent told her.

"I intend to," Cordelia retorted. "You see, the Pearsons and the Grays were always very good friends. Sometimes they were *more* than good friends. Your great-grandfather, Mr. Pearson, used to come around calling almost every weekend."

"My great-grandfather said nothing about that in his diaries."

"He wouldn't have, Mr. Pearson, because the reason your great-grandfather came calling almost every weekend was me."

"What the hell are you talking about?" Vincent asked her fiercely.

"Let me make it plain," Cordelia smiled, and the hand that held the scalpel against Jack's throat remained as steady as if it were cast in alabaster. "Your great-grandfather and I were lovers, Mr. Pearson, in those days when I was still beautiful and still untouched by—what shall I call them?—our little white friends from the graveyard."

"You were lovers? You're out of your mind!"

"I have photographs to prove it, Mr. Pearson. Pictures of your great-grandfather and myself, yachting off Sherwood Island, letters, gifts, mementos signed with love. There was one long, wonderful summer, and by the end of that summer, I was pregnant. It was a scandal, I suppose, especially in those days; but the Grays were always considered to be rather a scandalous family, albeit *la crème de la crème*. I refused to go to a doctor because I loved your great-grandfather so much, and the following year I gave him a baby boy."

The silence in the hallway of Wilderlings was intense. Vincent could sense what was coming; he could feel it—that dark train rushing through the night—but he had to know for sure. "Go on," he said, his throat dry.

"I couldn't look after the child, of course. A single mother? In those days, the idea was ridiculous. I didn't want to look after it, either. There were parties to go to, as there will always be parties. But your great-grandfather didn't object, because his marriage had been childless. He and your dear dead great-grandmama took my son and reared him as their own. So you see, your grandfather was my son; your father was my grandson; and *you*, Mr. Pearson, God bless you, are my great-grandson.

"*That* is why your grandfather couldn't destroy the portrait. And *that* is why my father accepted your grandfather's assurances that the portrait would be kept safe. Of course none of us knew at the time how essential it would be for us to stay in communion with the portrait. As years went by and our condition grew increasingly desperate, we begged your grandfather and your father again and again to let us have the portrait back so we could restore ourselves; but they refused every time, and threatened to expose us for the murders we were supposed to have committed. There was nothing we could do but remain in exile, trying to survive the best way we could."

"So—if I stab the portrait now?" Vincent asked. "Then what happens?"

"If you stab the portrait now, you will destroy me. I will be grave dust and bones in front of your eyes. Yes, and maggots, too, because that is all I am. That is what your family has made me. But I have continued to exist through the courtesy of Walter Waldegrave. The way you see me now is the way I was, just before I met your great-grandfather. And if you destroy me now, the historical chain of impossibility will be broken; your grandfather will never have existed, nor your father, nor you."

Charlotte said, "*Vincent—*"

But Vincent, looking around at Thomas, suddenly understood what it would mean if he were to vanish as if he had never existed. Thomas would vanish, too. Lost in some unborn limbo, where souls wait hopelessly to be conceived and time and love have no meaning. Eternity, he thought, has no attractions.

He folded away his penknife. "All right," he said. "You can keep the portrait. And you're welcome to whatever punishments God gives you."

Cordelia smiled and took the scalpel from Jack's throat. "I suppose this has ended decently," she said.

Quickly Jack stepped away from Cordelia and turned to Vincent. "I don't know whether you saved my life there or not, pal. Pat predicted I was going to meet some beguiling lady and that I was going to have to watch out."

Vincent said quietly, "I think there was some mutual life-saving all around."

Charlotte held Vincent close, as if she never wanted to let him go but knew she had to. Vincent stroked her hair, although he had the strangest feeling that now she knew Cordelia Gray was his great-grandmother, he had somehow lost her. Their embrace was not the embrace of lovers anymore, but of friends, of friends who would gradually distance themselves. Maybe after Christmas he would call Meggsy.

Aaron said, "Don't forget your own portrait, Vincent. Those things are dynamite, as far as I can tell."

Vincent went over and picked up the portrait Aaron had painted. Because it was still tacky, he held it by one corner.

"You *were* devious, weren't you?" Cordelia asked with that chilly smile of hers. "I suppose it runs in the family." She touched her fingertips to her lips, and blew Vincent the coldest and most abstract of kisses.

They left Wilderlings and walked across the snowy garden. Vincent glanced only once toward the ornamental pond. The bodies of those Grays whose spirits he had killed would rot there now, among the weeds. Those who had survived his vengeance would one day rise out of the water again, but that was something he didn't want to think about. As he looked, a bedraggled creature came slinking across the snow toward him, crying pitifully because of the cold. It was Firework, the reincarnation of Van Gogh. Vincent held out his arms for the cat, and it jumped up, shivering, as if it already knew him. He stroked the cat's wet furry head.

The last Vincent saw of Cordelia, she was standing in the lighted doorway, one arm raised against the lintel, watching them. He supposed it was some sort of consolation that now the Grays had the portrait back, they would no longer need to kill anybody for skin. And the two most murderous and licentious members of the family, Maurice and Henry, were dead.

They drove back to New Milford, and on the way, Jack stopped the Cherokee by the side of the road where they all shook hands, kissed and congratulated themselves.

"What about that portrait of yours?" Jack asked as they drove on northward through the early hours. Subdued carols from *The Holly and the Ivy* were playing on the wagon's radio.

Vincent held it up and looked at it. "What about it?"

"Well, when you had the portrait painted, you made the same kind of pact the Grays did, didn't you? Now the portrait's going to grow old and you're going to stay young."

Vincent laughed. "Not me, my friend. Old age is going to overtake me gradually and naturally. I have seen immortality, and it doesn't work."

When they got back to Candlemas, Jack came in for a glass of Christmas Eve champagne, and then he went home to Nancy. Vincent, Charlotte and Thomas sat around the fire and talked about the Grays and all that had happened that day until the logs burned down and a chilly draft began to blow down the chimney stack. It was only two hours before Christmas Day. Since they had no presents to give each other, they went to bed and slept until it was time to go out to lunch.

After Christmas, Vincent went back to New York, Thomas went back to Margot and Charlotte went back to MOMA. Spring arrived, and the gardens of Candlemas were fragrant with blossom. Mrs. Miller came and cleaned the house, and Vincent spent Easter there with Thomas and Meggsy. Jack called in, and one evening they got drunk together and laughed a lot.

Summer drifted past, like a hot and golden wheel. Then fall, with its dying leaves and sad colors. Winter came again, and Vincent returned to Candlemas, alone this time because Meggsy had gone to Vancouver to live with a young Canadian architect called Zeke, and it was Margot's turn to have Thomas for Christmas.

Vincent sat in front of the fire drinking Irish whiskey and listening to Mozart. The portrait Aaron had painted for him had been framed now and hung over the mantelshelf. Vincent looked up at it, raised his glass and said, *"Prost!"*

He frowned then and looked at the portrait more carefully. He stood up, went close to the fireplace and stared at it for almost five minutes. On one side of the portrait's head, the left side, there was a streak of white hair, quite conspicuous. Yet— when he turned around to the mirror—there was no corresponding streak in his own hair.

"No!" he whispered.

He spent the whole night awake, staring at the portrait. In the morning, a few minutes after seven o'clock, he called the Grays' number in Darien and waited for an answer. He wasn't even sure of what he wanted. Reassurance? Comfort? But a monotonous recorded message told him, *"The number you have dialed . . . 203-555-9904 . . . is out of service. Please refer to your directory. The number you have dialed . . ."*

EPILOG

Tite Street
September 7, 1891

My dear Oscar,

I have just finished reading your draft story (at midnight, no less!), and I must confess that it is thrilling and alarming in the extreme, as well as being most exquisitely written.

However, my legal friends from New York (who were dining with me only yesterday) tell me that the Grays of Connecticut, apart from being *very* wealthy, are also *very* litiginous, and if you were to breathe even a whisper of *l'affaire Waldegrave*, they have no doubt at all but that the Grays would sue, and ruinously.

They suggest that if you *do* wish to make literary capital of this remarkable tale, you alter it sufficiently so the Gray family cannot find reasonable grounds for action. In other words, you could alter the family portrait to the portrait of a single individual, and alter the name somewhat.

Anyway, please consider it, because the notion is most original and eerie; and it will certainly leave me trembling in my bed for months to come.

Your devoted friend,
Charles Petrie

P.S. Enclosed, the manuscript of *The Picture of the Darien Grays*.

GRAHAM MASTERTON

☐	52195-1 CONDOR		$3.50
	52196-X	Canada	$3.95
☐	52191-9 IKON		$3.95
	52192-7	Canada	$4.50
☐	52193-5 THE PARIAH		$3.50
	52194-3	Canada	$3.95
☐	52189-7 SOLITAIRE		$3.95
	52190-0	Canada	$4.50
☐	48067-9 THE SPHINX		$2.95
☐	48061-X TENGU		$3.50
☐	48042-3 THE WELLS OF HELL		$2.95
☐	52199-4 PICTURE OF EVIL		$3.95
	52200-1	Canada	$4.95

Buy them at your local bookstore or use this handy coupon:
Clip and mail this page with your order

TOR BOOKS—Reader Service Dept.
P.O. Box 690, Rockville Centre, N.Y. 11571

Please send me the book(s) I have checked above. I am
enclosing $_____ (please add $1.00 to cover postage
and handling). Send check or money order only—no cash or
C.O.D.'s.

Mr./Mrs./Miss _____
Address _____
City _____ State/Zip _____
Please allow six weeks for delivery. Prices subject to change
without notice.

BESTSELLING BOOKS FROM TOR

MORE BESTSELLERS FROM TOR